Col

The journey to the altar was ~~too quick~~. The groom never turned his head to watch his bride walking toward him, her knees shaking but with her head held high. When Alyson and her lord reached the altar, she shot Darnley one desperate last look from beneath her veil, knowing there was no hope of mercy from that quarter. He didn't even glance her way as he placed her hand in the groom's and retreated.

Not for an eternity did Alyson look up, but when she did, what met her gaze was a darkly handsome countenance. In that instant, her new husband had bewitched her. Who *was* this man? And what had she just done? One slip, the slightest lapse in judgment, would mean her certain death. Alyson could not afford to be distracted from her goal . . .

The
Border
Bride

Elizabeth English

JOVE BOOKS, NEW YORK

THE BORDER BRIDE

A Jove Book / published by arrangement with
the author

PRINTING HISTORY
Jove edition / November 2001

Visit our website at
www.penguinputnam.com

ISBN: 0-515-13154-7

A JOVE BOOK®
Jove Books are published by The Berkley Publishing Group,
a division of Penguin Putnam Inc.,
375 Hudson Street, New York, New York 10014.
JOVE and the "J" design
are trademarks belonging to Penguin Putnam Inc.

PRINTED IN THE UNITED STATES OF AMERICA

10 9 8 7 6 5 4 3 2

To Gary
My parfit gentil knyght

Prologue

S tealing sheep was an honorable tradition on the border. For the poor it was a means to feed their families, for the rich, an exercise in power. To their sons it was a game, a test, a way to prove their manhood—a thing you had to do, whether you wanted to or not. And if you were a Darnley you crossed into Scotland and stole from the Kirallens, the same as they would steal from you, given half a chance. The only danger lay in getting back to England ahead of the pursuit.

Which was where Haddon Darnley had made his first mistake.

Now he stood bound and helpless on the raised dais in Kirallen's stronghold, a dagger pressed to the soft skin of his throat. He closed his eyes and tried to pray, but the familiar Latin words were all a jumble. So Haddon addressed his Lord directly, and what his prayer might lack in elegance, it made up for in sincerity.

"Please God, don't let Kirallen kill me," he pleaded

silently. "I don't know why he wouldn't, since my father killed his son, but please don't let him, anyway. Let my father give him what he wants. Anything. Just don't let me die today. Amen."

In center of the hall stood Kirallen's Laird himself, a dozen men-at-arms ranged protectively around him. But Kirallen wasn't looking at his prisoner. His eyes were fixed on Haddon's father, Lord Darnley, who had come under a flag of truce to bargain for his son's life.

"We'll have the Vale," Kirallen said. "And a hundred head of sheep."

"Very well," Darnley snapped after only the slightest hesitation.

Relief flooded Haddon, weakening his knees, but before he'd even finished his quick prayer of thanks, he'd begun to feel a bit insulted, too. A hundred head of sheep and a swampy bit of land! Is that all they judged him worth? The restraining hand released him and he staggered a little, then caught his balance and lifted his chin. He would show them that a Darnley had his pride if nothing else.

"And," Kirallen added casually, almost as an afterthought. "Your daughter."

Haddon stared about the crowded torchlit hall, seeing his own shock reflected on the faces of Kirallen's men. Behind him there was a harsh curse, and he was jerked half off his feet. This time when the blade touched his neck it drew a small trickle of blood, and the boy froze with a little cry of pain.

Darnley gave no sign of having heard his son. He threw back his russet head and did the last thing that Haddon expected. He laughed. Haddon didn't like that laugh; no, he didn't like it one bit. And neither did Kirallen's men.

"You're mad," Darnley spat contemptuously.

Kirallen stiffened. The Scotsman was fully as tall as Darnley, though much older, with white hair and deep-set eyes that burned with cold intensity as he confronted his ancient enemy.

What was Father doing? Haddon wondered with fresh terror. Had he himself gone mad, insulting the Laird in his own hall? Did he not see Kirallen's men on every side? They stood like statues, but their eyes were sharp upon the Englishman, waiting for him to make one move so they might kill him where he stood.

Kirallen spoke into the waiting silence.

"Our people have been at war since beyond living memory. Now my Ian lies in his grave, and I say it is *enough*," he cried, striking one palm upon the table. "I *will* see peace before I die, or by Christ's sweet wounds, I'll see my vengeance. Your daughter will wed my Jemmy—or this boy dies tonight."

Darnley stared at a point on the far wall, his thoughts concealed behind a mask of iron will. Haddon searched his father's face, desperate for a sign of hope, though he feared that there was no hope to be found. Faced with the choice of losing either son or daughter, surely Father would put Maude first. He always had before.

Slowly Darnley turned and fixed his son with an icy stare. A man can always get another heir, Haddon thought with chilling clarity. Nothing *I* have done has ever pleased him. A spasm of terror passed over his slight frame, and he bit his lip, trying desperately not to cry.

"So be it," Darnley said at last. "They will wed."

"We'll have your oath upon it."

Haddon could scarce believe what he was seeing as his father went down on his knees right there in the center of the hall, the crackling of the rushes very loud in the hush. Using his sword hilt as a cross, Darnley swore away his land, his sheep, and his daughter's hand, his voice tight with fury but very clear.

"The wedding will take place within the month," Kirallen said. He looked slowly about the hall, his eyes holding each of his men's in turn. At last he gave a short nod and swept from the room.

The dagger flashed before Haddon's eyes, but even as the boy recoiled, it moved downward and sliced the bonds around his wrists.

"Father—" Haddon began, scrambling down from the dais and holding out his hands.

"Not now," Darnley snapped, striding from the hall.

Haddon followed, his shoulders drooping. This was all his horse's fault. If the damned nag hadn't startled at a cony, he'd be safely home now and his father would be welcoming him with pride. As it was . . . He looked at his father's dark face and was afraid—and when he thought of what Maude would do he was more frightened still.

Facing his sister Maude in a temper was near as bad as anything that had happened to Haddon today. When she learned what had been agreed upon tonight, her rage would blister everyone in reach. He suspected that this thought had crossed his father's mind as well and was responsible for at least part of Lord Darnley's grimness as he walked briskly from the hall, Haddon following so closely he was in danger of treading on his father's booted heels. Even Uncle Robert, standing in the shadow of the doorway, looked serious as the clansmen parted to let them pass.

Haddon's horse had bolted when he was thrown, so he rode pillion behind his father. He was glad to lean against the broad, strong back and close his eyes, dizzy with both relief at what he had escaped and fear of what was to follow. But at last he plucked his courage up to ask, "Which one of them is Maude to marry? Is it the man who held me?"

He held his breath, waiting for the answer. He wouldn't wish even his sister such a fate. That one was no man; he was a fiend from Hell, and remembering the terrible things he'd threatened, Haddon shivered beneath his cloak.

"No," Darnley answered. "He wasn't there."

"Jemmy Kirallen," Uncle Robert said thoughtfully. "That's the second son, the one who went to sea. I heard a rumor once that he'd turned pirate, but that was years ago. I thought him dead long since."

"So did I," Darnley growled. "But no sooner had I rid myself of the eldest when Kirallen summoned the other back again. I have two men in Berwick watching for his ship, but now—God's teeth, if I'd had any idea what the old man was thinking, I'd have sent a dozen. God damn his soul to Hell—I'll kill him with my own hands before I let him lay one finger on my Maude. Now both of you shut up and let me think."

Dawn was streaking the sky by the time they reached Aylsford Manor. When they dismounted, two grooms who had been watching for their lord's return led the tired horses to the stables. As the hoofbeats faded into silence, Haddon tried and failed to meet his father's eyes.

"Get inside, lad," Darnley ordered. "I'll deal with you tomorrow."

Haddon walked slowly off, a small defeated figure in the gathering light, and Robert felt a moment's pity for the lad. He knew his nephew was a gentle boy at heart, far more interested in books than battle and had only undertaken the adventure to win his father's notice. Still, no matter what his motives were, the damage had been done.

"Christ's wounds, John, but this is a sorry pass!" he said with a mournful shake of his head, then staggered as Darnley gave him a hearty clout upon the shoulder.

"It'll be all right," Darnley said and, surprisingly, he grinned. "Come along, I'm famished."

The hall was dark, the varlets yawning as they swept the rushes from the floor and replaced the candles in their holders. By the time Robert reached the narrow, twisting stairway, Darnley was vanishing around the first corner.

"All *right?*" the knight demanded, his voice echoing

from cold stone. "How can you even say that? To send Maude there—to them—it is disgusting!"

Darnley glanced over one brawny shoulder, that strange smile still playing on his lips. "I promised him my daughter. But you'll ken I didn't say which one."

"You need to rest," the knight said gently, laying a comforting hand on the older man's forearm.

Darnley shook him off impatiently and climbed the stairs at a brisk trot. "I'm not daft, Robert—just think about it, man. My lady bore one daughter only, but I've sired several in my day."

They passed into Darnley's chamber, where his body squire blinked sleepily beside the fire. Darnley ordered bread and meat and cheese, then waved the boy away. He walked to the table and poured water from the ewer.

"I see," Robert said, sitting down before the fire. "Well, I don't suppose any of the Kirallens have seen Maude face to face. . . ."

Darnley shook his head, droplets flying from his russet hair. "Oh, they have spies here, just as I have there, but Maude's hardly been at home these past three years. I'll stake my life they know no more of her than her size and the color of her hair."

"Kirallen is no fool," Robert protested. "Some lass from the vill wouldn't deceive him for a moment. But even if she did, it couldn't last forever. He's bound to find out soon or late."

"I don't need much time. Just long enough to prepare for war. Good God, Robert, d'ye think I'd let this insult go unpunished? We have a month to start with, but it won't be enough. I'll go to Percy and ask for men—you'll have to help me think up some tale, for he's said already he's finished with the Kirallen business."

"No, Northumberland can't afford to be involved," Robert said, instantly diverted by the workings of royal policy. "Now that we're at peace with Scotland—and our lord is so thick with Lancaster—he doesn't dare to stir up trouble on the border over a family matter. But I can think of something . . ."

"Say another month—six weeks at most—and I'll have what I need. Nixon will help, I think. He and Kirallen have been at odds. I'll quarter the men there until I'm ready. And then . . ." Darnley grinned with a wolfish flash of teeth. "I'll fall on the Kirallens like the wrath of God when they're least expecting it."

"Six weeks?" Robert repeated doubtfully. "No common girl could possibly manage it."

"Mayhap not. But—d'ye remember that McLaran lass?" Darnley asked with a lift of one ruddy brow. "Ah, no, you wouldn't, would you? You were just a bairn."

"I remember all the trouble she caused."

"That one was no peasant," Darnley said. "And she bore a bonny daughter."

"You don't mean she's still *here?*"

"Nay, I gave her to Jacob Bowden when she quickened—I couldn't risk keeping her about. But she and Bowden are both dead now, and I've seen the lass about the kitchens. A little redheaded thing, just like Maude, and about the proper age. You can teach her what she needs to know."

"Perhaps," Robert said, his doubtful tone belied by the spark of interest in his eyes. Who would have thought John capable of such a plan? It was almost surely doomed to failure and yet . . . it had a certain subtle wit that appealed to Robert's instinct for intrigue. Could he actually take some common lass and in one month's time pass her off as a lady? It all depended on the girl, of course. She would need brains and courage . . . qualities not commonly found among the peasantry.

"Of course we needn't confine ourselves to the Bowden lass," he said. "Or any of your by-blows, for that matter. Any redheaded wench with a bit of wits would do."

"Christ forbid," Darnley said, signing himself hastily with the cross. "I said my *daughter* and gave my oath upon it. I'll not be forsworn."

The squire returned with food, which he set upon the table, and then retreated at an impatient command from his master. As they sat down before the window, Robert studied his half brother with amusement. What curious contradictions people were, just as his friend Chaucer often said! John wouldn't hesitate to send some poor wench in Maude's place, plotting treachery all the while, yet he balked at the breaking of his vow.

Though Robert had been planning to ride back to London within the week, his mind was changed in an instant. If they managed to carry this preposterous deception off, he would make a song of it, a story to match any that Chaucer could create. With any luck he'd sing it at Yule Court— perhaps for the Duke of Lancaster himself!

And if it went the other way—well, he rather imagined he'd be riding back to London before the battle was joined. John Darnley was only his half brother after all, and the tie between them was not so strong that Robert would risk his life for it.

"It may be we won't need her after all," Darnley said, breaking off a piece of warm bread and spreading it with honey. "If my men in Berwick do their work, all the better. There can be no wedding if the groom is rolling at the bottom of the sea with a dagger in his ribs," he finished with grim relish.

"True," Robert agreed, though he privately hoped Kirallen would escape the assassins. If he died now it would quite spoil all the fun.

"But either way, this time I'll finish them," Darnley said, fingers clenching on his knife. "The old man's gone soft—he must be mad in truth to think I'd ever give them Maude. Even if this other one, this Jemmy, does come back, I've naught to fear from him. I bested the elder brother, and by God, that one was a *man!* He rode where he pleased, took what he wanted—Christ, he was an arrogant bastard. But no match for my strength. With him gone there's no one who can stop me. They're dead men, every one of them, I swear it before God—d'ye hear me? *Do you?*" he cried, pounding his fist upon the table.

Robert shot him an uneasy glance. Darnley's lips were drawn back from his teeth, his eyes glittering with an eerie light just this side of madness. Lately Robert had begun to suspect his half brother *was* a little mad. Three months ago he'd slain the eldest Kirallen son in battle, a story Robert had heard a hundred times in the fortnight since he'd arrived. Yet the victory had done nothing to appease Darnley's anger against the clan—if anything, it had grown to an obsession.

"Aye," Robert said softly. "I hear you well and truly. God help Jemmy Kirallen and all his kin."

He raised his mug to drink, then set it down again untasted and stared out at the endless, empty moor. God's teeth, the borders were a desolate place, even in high spring. Had he really just agreed to prolong his visit by another two months?

But after a moment the merry light glinted once again in the knight's hazel eyes and he grinned, tapping his fingers on the tabletop as he composed the opening stanza of his ballad.

chapter 1

Jemmy Kirallen stood at the ship's prow and stared bleakly into falling rain. Of course it was raining. It always rained in Scotland. Until he went abroad he had never quite believed that there were places where fog and rain were not everyday occurrences, magical islands and white sand beaches where sunlight danced on water that was an ever-shifting patchwork of emerald and jade and teal.

Now he sighed and squinted into the gloom. Ahead he could just make out the docks of Berwick, a sullen collection of squat buildings and stark pilings crouched above a churning leaden sea. Tendrils of fog obscured the view for a moment, then the torchlit landing reappeared amid its swirling depths. The whole scene looked like something from a half-remembered dream. Or nightmare, Jemmy thought grimly.

Six weeks ago, word had reached him in Cadiz that his elder brother had been slain by Lord John Darnley. Jemmy had set off as soon as possible, settling what business he could and leaving the rest undone, knowing that his father would be expecting him to come at once. Ian was dead, his son a child, and the old man's health was failing. There was no question but that Jemmy must come back.

It all made perfect sense, and yet it made no sense at all. Scotland was not his home; it hadn't been for years. He belonged there even less now than he had twelve years ago.

Even as a child Jemmy had seen the futility of the age-old feud between his family and the Darnleys. It was a war with no end and no beginning, its only purpose to devour soldiers on both sides, shattering lives and hopes and dreams. Now he would be expected not only to fight, but to lead his clan in battle to avenge his brother's death.

Well, he thought, his expression growing even bleaker, he wouldn't do it. And once they realized he wasn't the leader they sought, their welcome would turn cold as ashes. They would name him a traitor and a coward, not fit to take Ian's place. As if he'd ever wanted to. It wouldn't be pleasant, but it would all be over quickly; he'd be back in Spain before autumn came. There was no reason to feel otherwise, no excuse for the nagging apprehension that gripped him, as though he walked into a trap. His visit would be a short one; his refusal to make war on Darnley would see to that. He didn't give a tinker's dam for what any of them thought about it, either.

Except his father.

The old man must be distraught. Ian had been the light of his life—as well as the darling of the clan. No doubt the lot of them were mad with grief and clamoring for vengeance. Did they really think that killing any number of Darnleys would make a difference? No matter what they did now, Ian would still be dead.

The ship docked and he went slowly down the plank, feeling as though he was walking back in time. Here, just here, he had taken his first berth. Now he was back again, exactly where he'd started, as though the past twelve years had never been.

A group of Spaniards stood bewildered in the falling rain, their tentative inquiries brushed aside by the hurrying sailors. As Jemmy passed by, one man touched his arm.

"Con permiso, señor," he said in the fluid accents of Castile. "Please, if you could direct me to the nearest inn, I would be grateful."

Jemmy answered the man's question in his own tongue, and they walked together down the dock. His eyes passed, seemingly without interest, over two men lounging against the pilings. His gaze sharpened as they detached themselves and fell casually into step behind him.

"This way," Jemmy said to the Spaniard, giving him a little push. *"Vaya con Dios."*

Before he'd finished speaking he whirled around and caught the wrist of the man behind him, twisting the dagger from his grasp and kicking it across the rain-slicked planks. As the Spaniard hurried away, Jemmy dropped to a crouch, his own dagger gleaming in the lantern-light as he faced his two assailants, expecting them to run. But they did not.

"Weel, lads," he said pleasantly, his voice unconsciously dropping into the cadence of his youth. "Ye ken this won't be as simple as you'd planned it. And just now you must be wondering where to go from here. Now, my advice is to stop and think this through before you do something we'll all be sorry for. One mistake has a way of leading to another, and I wouldn't want to see that happen here tonight. It's not too late to walk away with none of us the worse for it."

The man who Jemmy had disarmed now pulled another dagger from his back and took a step to the left. The second one spat into the churning water and moved to Jemmy's right. These were no dockside ruffians, Jemmy thought, his dark eyes narrowing, or they'd have taken to their heels the moment he drew.

"Don't rush it, lads," he continued, circling slowly to keep them both in sight. "I'm sure you have no wish to die tonight, no more than I have to kill you. But don't doubt that I'll do it if I have to. And I ask you, what would be the point of it? Instead, why don't you tell me what this is all about, and I'll forget I ever saw you."

For an instant they hesitated, and Jemmy began to hope they would take him at his word. He had spoken nothing but the truth when he said he didn't want to kill them. But in the end, whatever drove such men—a thing Jemmy didn't understand and didn't want to—once again proved stronger than reason. By the time the Spaniard returned with the Watch it was all over and Jemmy was replacing his dagger in its sheath.

A dozen witnesses rushed forward now that it was finished, eager to tell the tale. Two men set upon one, they said, and the one did everything in his power to stop the fight. Irritated with the whole business, Jemmy stopped only to draw the nearest man's cloak from his breast, glancing without surprise at Darnley's crest emblazoned on the blood-soaked tunic.

They were fools, he thought in disgust, flicking the cloak over the man's still face and staring eyes. They could be alive and now they were dead, all for the sake of some ancient fight they didn't even understand.

And now he was part of it again. Which made him, he reflected with sudden weary anger, the biggest fool of all.

"Jemmy!" a voice called, and he looked up sharply, one hand going to his dagger. It fell away as he saw half a dozen men approaching through the mist and recognized their colors.

He had trouble putting names to the faces of the men, but in one or two of them he could see echoes of the boys that they had been twelve years before. But he knew at once the man who stepped forward, throwing the rain-drenched hood back from his face.

When Jemmy had left home, his foster brother Alistair was just seventeen and had already earned himself a reputation as the most promising young warrior in the clan—save perhaps for Ian—and the most enthusiastic wencher—again, with Ian as his only competition. Alistair had looked deceptively angelic in those days with his sil-ver-gilt hair and fine gray eyes, a perfect foil to Ian's dark good looks, and he'd grown from a pretty youth into a striking man.

But now the brilliant eyes were shadowed as they re-garded Jemmy narrowly.

"Alistair," Jemmy began, and then stopped. He had glanced instinctively to Alistair's side, expecting to see Ian, but Ian wasn't there. And for the first time the reality of his brother's death hit Jemmy like a blow. Ian, who had never been still for a moment, was now forever still. Never again would Jemmy see his brother's wicked grin or be drawn into one of his mad adventures. The sense of loss was so keen and sudden that Jemmy was speechless with the pain of it.

Alistair had caught the glance and read its meaning. His gray eyes softened, and even in the midst of his own loss, Jemmy knew that it must be a thousand times worse for his kinsman. For as long as Jemmy could remember it had been the two of them, Alistair and Ian, bound by ties even closer than blood. Theirs was a kinship of mind and heart—even as children each had known exactly what the other thought without the bother of discussing it. There had been jealousy, Jemmy remembered now, on his side and on Alistair's as well. Ian was the link that had drawn them together—and the wedge that had driven them apart.

"Alistair, I'm so sorry," Jemmy said at last.

"Aye, so are we all," Alistair said, so briskly that Jemmy knew he was incapable of discussing Ian's death.

"But now you're back, though ye dinna hurry overmuch that I can tell. Did ye no stop to think we had need o' ye at home?"

"I came as soon as I heard," Jemmy said, feeling instantly defensive without knowing why he should.

"Well, you're here now and not a moment too soon. You're the only one who can stop your poor mad father, and that's what ye must do. Ye must tell him you'll have no part of it. Tell him straight out so there's no mistake."

"Have no part of *what?*" Jemmy asked, annoyed. Alistair hadn't changed a bit. He was just as high–handed as ever, snapping orders right and left without bothering to explain or caring who might be offended by his manner.

"He gone and promised ye—we'll scarce make it back before the wedding."

"Wedding?" Jemmy repeated sharply. "*My* wedding? But—he can't do that!"

"Aye, well, that's what we've all been sayin', isn't it?" Alistair said, and the men around him murmured in agreement. "But he isn't listening. Since Ian—" he stopped and swallowed hard. "Since January, your father's mind has come unhinged."

Jemmy searched the faces of the other men, seeing embarrassment and reluctant acquiescence. Though none would have put it so bluntly, it was clear that they agreed.

"But what does that have to do with any marriage?"

"He's gone and promised ye to Maude Darnley."

"Maude—?" Jemmy blew out an exasperated breath. "God's blood, Alistair, but that's a sorry jest."

"I wish I *was* jesting." Alistair gripped his elbow and led him to a small hut, gesturing the other men away. " 'Tis true enough, Jemmy, and you're the only man to stop it. The Laird is past all reason now."

The rain drummed upon the thin plank roof, and the voices of the other men faded into a distant hum. It seemed there was nothing left of the world but him and Alistair, trapped together in this tiny space.

"Then tell me," Jemmy said. "Tell me all that's happened."

I n the filthy taproom of a squalid little inn, Jemmy drank without tasting the sour ale and listened without hearing to all the news of home. When at last he fell into bed, his mind was reeling.

Though Jemmy had known Ian's death would be a blow to his father, it seemed that matters were far, far worse than he'd imagined. For one thing, Ian's loss had destroyed the Laird's health, bringing on the first of the attacks that Alistair had explained were becoming more frequent and severe. The physicians could say what they liked, but both Alistair and Jemmy agreed that the real cause of the Laird's illness was simple: the old man's heart was broken. But that was the only agreement they could reach.

Alistair believed the Laird was mad as well, while Jemmy knew the opposite was true. Far from unhinging his mind, Ian's death had finally brought the old man to his senses. After a lifetime fighting against his father's warrior code, it was a rather unwelcome shock to find that they had landed squarely on the same side. It gave Jemmy a hollow feeling, a sense of the world having turned upon its head. What made it infinitely worse was Alistair's belief that the only thing that kept the Laird alive was his dream of making peace.

Jemmy could make that dream a reality. It was what he'd always wanted as a child, what he had prayed for during endless nights after days of watching his kinsmen ride out to battle and then be carried home again, wasted deaths in Jemmy's view.

And now there was a hope of stopping the endless, senseless slaughter. *Be careful what you pray for,* his

mother used to say. *Be careful, for one day you may get it.*
Well, this was what he'd prayed for. And now it had come
upon him. All he need do was go home and do his duty to
his clan.

Just the thought of it drenched his body in cold sweat.
Years ago Jemmy had given himself to the sea as other
men gave themselves to women or the church. Now he was
as much her creature as the leaping dolphin or gliding osprey. Like them, he could not survive long out of his ele-
ment. Lately even short visits inland gave him a trapped,
uneasy feeling. He hadn't cared—he could well afford to
hire men to do his business for him, scarcely bothering to
count his profits before setting sail again.

Life at Ravenspur would be no life at all, but death by
slow and painful inches. Likely he'd run mad before the
year was out. And the thought of marriage did not tempt
him in the least. He'd tried that once and it had been dis-
astrous, a mistake he had no desire to repeat.

Surely there was some other way to make the peace. As
the night wore on he turned and twisted on the thin straw
mattress, his thoughts racing like a ship before a gale.

But by the time dawn slipped through the broken shutters, he feared the trap had sprung.

chapter 2

Dawn crept imperceptibly into the tower room at
Aylsford Manor where Alyson Bowden lay listening
to the moaning of the wind, a doleful sound that matched
her mood precisely. She shivered and pulled the heavy
coverlet close, but it did nothing to dispel her chill. Today
she would be married. My wedding day, she thought, a
half-hysterical giggle rising to her lips. No, not mine.
Maude's. But Maude slept soundly in her bed, completely
untroubled by what this day would bring.

The door opened and Dame Becta, Maude's tiring
woman, bustled into the room. Alyson lay feigning sleep
as the servant built up the fire and lit the candles. "Come
along, Mistress," Becta said, coming to the bed and looking down. Her broad face held a trace of sympathy as she
added, "The day's sure to be fine after such a night."

Becta knew, of course. There had been no way to keep
the truth from her. But all the other servants thought that it
was Maude, indeed, who was to be married this morning.

They'd accepted the news with shock and a fair amount of grumbling, for while they might have little fondness for their lady, she was the only one they had. It was shame, they said, to send her to that Scottish swine. During the past weeks they had gone out of their way treat Maude with a sympathy that the lady had mocked behind their backs.

Alyson threw back the covers. No good hiding in bed, she thought stoutly. Never started, never finished. But she could not manage a bite of the food she was given, nor even a swallow of warm ale. At last she stood, bathed and scented, as Becta dressed her. First a soft linen shift beneath a gown of amber, then a sideless surcoat of sapphire blue, richly furred around the hem, clasped about her waist with an enameled girdle in Darnley's blue and gold. Her hair was brushed out and left loose, then the shining auburn waves were covered by a blue veil held in place by a golden circlet.

Maude came to stand beside her half sister at the mirror. Alyson stared at their reflections with the same cold shock she'd experienced near a month before, when they had first stood as they did now. Here were the same blue-green eyes, tip tilted at the edges, the same full mouth and short, straight nose—even the way the hair grew from their foreheads in a small peak was the same.

Oh, there were differences. Maude's hair was gold with a reddish tinge, while Alyson's held all the fire of a winter's sunset. Maude's face was a perfect oval, while the lines of Alyson's jaw and cheeks were more pronounced. One would never be mistaken for the other at close range, and yet for all that they were very much alike. But Alyson's eyes were huge with fear beneath the high-plucked brows, while Maude's were gleaming with amusement.

If only I could get warm, Alyson thought, chafing her icy hands together, then mayhap I could think. Everything was rushing by so quickly that she could not seem to catch and hold a thought for more than a single fleeting moment.

"He'll expect you to be a virgin," Maude said. "I don't suppose you are."

"I am," Alyson answered, her eyes holding Maude's in the mirror.

"You'd better not be lying—he'll be most displeased if he discovers otherwise."

Alyson lifted her chin in perfect imitation of Maude's imperious gesture. "It won't be something I need worry about," she said, mimicking Maude's icy tones. "But what do *you* intend to do on *your* wedding night?"

It took Maude a moment to register the insult, then she slapped Alyson hard across the face, her heavy rings splitting her half sister's lip.

"Here, now, my lady, leave off!" Becta scolded, moving between them and whisking the veil back from Alyson's face. "If ye've stained this I'll never get it clean in time!"

Maude reached past the tiring woman and grasped Alyson's wrist. "Don't dare speak to me like that again," she hissed. "We may have the same father, but never forget the difference between us. *My* mother was a Percy. Your mother was a whore, and you're another."

"Your father made my mother what she was," Alyson cried, her ready temper flaring. "And you make me what I shall be! If I'm to play the whore, you'd best pray I do it well."

"Whisht yer clabber!" Becta scolded. "My lady, go sit down and let me finish here."

Maude subsided with reluctance and flung herself upon the settle, watching through half-closed eyes as Becta dabbed Alyson's lip and rearranged the veil. The tiring woman stood back and examined the girl with a critical eye, then hung a gold and sapphire chain about her neck.

"Don't get too attached to that," Maude said. She leaned back against the cushions of the settle and stretched

languorously as a cat. "I've marked every jewel you're
taking. If even one is missing, you'll hang for it. If you live
long enough for that," she added with a laugh.

Alyson looked at her for a long moment. "What makes
you the way you are?" she said at last. The words held no
anger, just a kind of wonder. For once Maude had no answer. She dropped her eyes to the goblet in her hands as
Becta came forward to fasten the cloak across Alyson's
shoulders and pull the veil over her face.

As last it was done, and Alyson, her heart pounding in
sudden fear, knew the time had come.

"Wait."

Alyson turned in the doorway.

"You can keep the necklace," Maude said with a defiant
lift of her chin.

"Thank you, my lady. But I don't want it."

She waited for a moment but Maude didn't speak again.

When Alyson reached the doorway she found the rain
had stopped, though gray clouds filled the sky and the
wind blew strong and hard. As the grooms led the horses
from the stables, Alyson hung back in the shadow of the
arch, her eyes darting this way and that, hoping against
hope that her brother might be among them. But he was
not. Beside her, Sir Robert Allshouse waited impatiently,
tapping one foot against the stone.

Though he had been her tutor for the past month,
Alyson felt she scarcely knew Lord Darnley's half brother
at all. Indeed, she was more intimidated by him than she
had ever let him see. He was by turns impatient, demanding, and caustically amusing, but never once had he called
Alyson by name or expressed the slightest interest in why
she had agreed to this outrageous deception. He had only
cared to see that she could eat properly, manage a few
chords upon the lute, sit on a horse, and draw a bow—
skills that she had mastered to his grudging satisfaction,
having a strong incentive for success.

Today he was dressed in the new style he had brought from court, a parti-colored surcoat of gold and crimson with matching hose. Beneath a tawny velvet cap with a crimson feather nodding in the breeze, his chestnut hair was curled elaborately about his sharp, clever face.

"Well, lass?" he asked with a grin. "You're looking a bit green about the edges. Not losing your nerve, eh?"

"Sir—oh please," Alyson burst out. "Can you tell me how my brother fares?"

"Brother? What brother?" he said absently, frowning a little as he studied the cloudy sky.

"Robin. He's only seven and so small for his age—please, can you tell me where Lord Darnley is holding him?"

"Holding him?" The knight turned to her, surprise widening his eyes. "Why would he do that?" Then his gaze sharpened and he added, "He said he'd offered you a reward."

"Oh, aye," Alyson answered with a choked laugh. "My brother's life. I thought you knew."

"Christ's wounds," the knight swore softly. "No, I didn't know. But tell me this—would you have agreed if not for your brother?"

"No."

"But surely you understand John's position—and Maude's!"

"He shouldn't have sworn if he didn't mean to do it," Alyson said stubbornly. "It's all a wicked lie."

"But it isn't—well, not exactly, anyway. This marriage was none of John's idea, you know. Kirallen had him by the—the throat," he finished with a little cough. "What else was John to do when Kirallen had young Haddon prisoner? He could hardly let them slaughter his heir!"

Oh, no, he couldn't let his son be hurt, Alyson thought with rising anger, but he wouldn't hesitate to use the same trick on me! Apparently Lord Darnley's tender feelings did not extend to a common boy like Robin.

"John only said his daughter when he swore," Sir Robert hurried on. "I heard him for myself. Strictly speaking, that does apply to you as well as Maude. I thought it quite clever, actually . . ."

He looked away, his face reddening slightly. "Well, it won't be forever," he added heartily. "As soon as John's assembled his men you can come back again."

"Aye," Alyson said quietly. "And then how many are to die because of what I've done?"

"I admit that part's—well, it's not very nice to think about, is it? But it isn't as though they were . . . people. They're Kirallens! Surely you know about them—they're a treacherous lot, bloodthirsty—totally without honor. They've killed more of my kin than I care to think on, and others, too . . ." his words trailed off as he stared ahead, memory darkening his eyes. Then he shook himself and added briskly, "You'll be fine—so long as you remember what I've taught you. Come along now, they're waiting."

Once mounted, Alyson drew a deep, steadying breath and took up the reins. They were blue velvet, as was the caparison of her steed, the same color as the cloak flowing from her shoulders. She adjusted the gauzy veil over her face as they moved slowly forward.

Sit straight, she told herself. Don't talk unless you have to. She practiced lifting her chin and looking down her nose, hoping her haughty expression would discourage anyone from speaking to her. It seemed to frighten everyone when Maude did it, from the meanest servant to Lord Darnley himself. Alyson prayed it would work half as well for her.

chapter 3

Jemmy reined up and stared at Ravenspur across the moor. It was just as he had dreamed of it a thousand times over the past twelve years—stark, imposing, threatening—and home. In his travels he had seen countless castles, every one of them more graceful than this border fortress. But not one of them had ever moved him as the sight of Ravenspur did now.

"Ugly pile of stone, isn't it?" he said to Alistair, speaking past the sudden tightness of his throat.

Alistair didn't answer. His lashes dropped over his eyes, but not before Jemmy had seen the flash of contempt lighting their silver depths. Just like old times, Jemmy thought as he kicked his horse into a gallop and swept across the fields, over the drawbridge, and through the gate. When he dismounted he drew a deep, steadying breath and started for his father's chamber.

The Laird was sitting by the window, the morning light pitilessly revealing the harsh lines scoring his face. For years Jemmy and Ian had referred to the Laird as "the old man," but now Jemmy was deeply shocked to find the giant of his youth dwindled to a shrunken, sickly figure. Ian's death had done this, Jemmy knew.

"Father," he said, taking an uncertain step forward.

The Laird turned with a start, his eyes widening. He leaned forward in his seat and peered closely at his son.

"Jemmy?" he whispered.

"Aye, Father, it's me."

"For a moment I thought ye were—you've changed," he faltered.

"Twelve years will do that."

He held his father's gaze, feeling suddenly fifteen again, all knees and elbows and boyish awkwardness. But it's different now, he told himself. I'm not a boy, and he's asked me to come home.

"Well, sit down. We have to talk."

Jemmy obeyed, giving no sign of his disappointment. While he hadn't really expected that his father would slaughter the fatted calf, a simple welcome might have been nice.

"So what's all this about a wedding?" he asked lightly, helping himself to the wine his father hadn't offered.

"It's Maude Darnley, as I'm sure ye know," Kirallen said.

"I've heard."

Kirallen glanced at his son and then away, as though the very sight of him was painful. "Well?" he asked abruptly. "Will ye do it?"

"I don't know," Jemmy answered honestly. "I have a life in Spain now, my ship, and I've been doing rather well these past few years. I—"

The old man cut him off with an impatient gesture, dismissing all Jemmy's accomplishments, the years of back-breaking labor, the days spent beneath the broiling sun, and the nights shivering on deck, all with a single movement of his hand.

That's when Jemmy knew he hadn't really changed at all, not in the way his father had wanted him to. He hadn't magically transformed into Ian's image. *It's a wonder I never came to hate my brother,* Jemmy thought. *But of course it wasn't Ian's fault he was so damned perfect.*

Now Jemmy slouched in his seat and stretched his legs before him in the way that had always moved his father to fury. He could see the Laird tense and realized they were slipping back into the old familiar pattern. It was so easy to annoy his father, he remembered now. At least for him. As a child he could manage it a hundred times a day without even trying.

He straightened and sipped his wine.

"Come, Father, what's the real plan? How will you get the best of Darnley over this one?"

"I want peace," Kirallen said with unmistakable sincerity. "Ye used to say ye wanted it as well."

"And *you* used to say that you expected your sons to be men, not cowards, and I was a disgrace to the Kirallen name."

He spoke the words calmly enough, but his entire body clenched as he remembered the bitter shame he'd felt when hearing them.

The Laird moved restlessly in his seat. "Aye, well, perhaps I did say that. But things have changed."

There was to be no apology, then. No admission that the Laird might have possibly been wrong.

"Just tell me, Father: why me? Why didn't you make Alistair your heir and let him marry Lady Maude?"

Do you really want me back? he wanted to ask, but he couldn't bring himself to say the words. Instead he kept his face expressionless, though his hands were clenched so tightly around his goblet that his knuckles shone white as he waited for his father's answer.

"You're my only son—Darnley would never have agreed to less."

Jemmy nodded. Poor old bastard, he thought, I'm all he has left. How galling it must be for him! But in time he might come to feel differently. Perhaps it isn't too much to hope that one day he might even be glad that I've come back.

"And I think we can strike a bargain to your liking," Kirallen added deliberately.

"Really?" Jemmy raised one brow. "What might that be?"

"Three hundred marks," Kirallen said. "For three months of your time."

"And what happens at the end of the three months? Do I push Lady Maude down the well?"

The Laird frowned. "At the end of three months ye can return to Spain. By then Alistair will be ready to take over Ian's responsibilities until Malcolm comes of age. We shall provide Lady Maude with a home."

Jemmy rested his elbows on his knees, bending his head as he considered the matter. Of course his father didn't want him back, not permanently, not as his heir. Had he really thought it could be so simple? Nothing Father ever did was simple. There was always some twist to his plans.

So it was to be Malcolm, Ian's son, who would rule here one day, with Alistair to guard his place. Father didn't even trust Jemmy to do that much.

"And am I expected to get Lady Maude with child?" he asked evenly.

"It would be best if ye could. This is to be a real marriage, Jemmy, legal and binding in every way."

"If I succeed in my . . . duties . . . what's to happen to the child?"

Kirallen shrugged. "It will be taken care of, as well."

"But Malcolm is to be your heir?"

"That's right."

Not Jemmy or his child, either, would ever be considered as the future Laird. It would be Ian's son. Of course. Jemmy sat back, tapping one finger against the arm of his chair.

"Alistair doesn't know about this, does he?"

"Not yet."

"But you think he will agree to keep this peace?"

"In time, yes, once the marriage is made and there's no turning back, I am quite certain he will agree. For now, though, I've told him nothing. Nor will you."

Remembering the fanatical light in Alistair's eyes when he spoke of Ian's death, Jemmy wondered if his foster brother would ever give up his hope of vengeance. But then he shrugged. What was it to him if Alistair agreed or not? That was his father's problem, not his.

The Laird was watching him closely, his eyes narrowed. How old he was, how frail! His hands, once so strong and sure, were knotted with blue veins and trembling as he raised his goblet to his mouth. Jemmy realized that finally, for the first time, he had his father at his mercy. He could simply say no, get up, and leave. God knew that's what he wanted to do. The whole plan was disgusting, really, and he no more than a stallion set to service a noble mare. It would be so very simple to walk away from it, go back to Spain, and take up the old familiar task of forgetting he'd ever been born a Kirallen. And there would be no peace with Darnley, not this time, perhaps not ever.

"Aye," he said. "I'll do it."

"You will?" The Laird tried to hide his relief by frowning at his son.

"Why not?" Jemmy said carelessly. "How terrible can it be? And I can always use the money."

chapter 4

After an hour's ride, Lord Darnley's party crested a hill and found the Kirallens waiting beneath their blue-green standard.

"The Laird," Sir Robert said, nodding toward the white-haired man at their head. Beside the nobleman, on a huge gray horse, sat another man. Alyson's mouth went dry.

"Is—is that him?" she whispered, and Robert nodded.

"It must be. He does look rather like a pirate, doesn't he?"

Alyson studied Jemmy Kirallen from beneath her veil, but it was difficult to tell much at this distance. She had a confused impression of dark hair and swarthy skin before he turned back to speak to one of his men.

"*Jemmy,*" Alistair said urgently. "*Stop this now—good God, man, ye canna mean to actually go through with it!*"

Jemmy glanced at Lord Darnley, the hairs on the back of his neck rising. Stronger than any amount of reason was the instinctive response roused by the sight of that hateful blue-gold standard. Darnley. The enemy. He *should* die— he deserved a hundred deaths in payment for the suffering he'd caused.

"My pledge is given," he answered Alistair through tight lips.

"Ye fool!" Alistair cried. "We can take them here and now—give the order, damn ye!"

"No! This is my decision, Alistair, not yours. Keep out of it."

"Christ's blood," Alistair burst out, waving one hand wildly toward the Laird. "You're as daft as he is! Oh; ye want to make the peace, is that it? Ye want us all to live like brothers? What are ye thinkin'?" he cried, his eyes snapping with anger.

"There's been enough bloodshed," Jemmy answered in a furious whisper. "My father is not mad to try to end it."

"This won't end it," Alistair said decisively. "Do ye honestly think Darnley wants this peace? He was forced to it, but he's a canny bastard. If there's a way to break his word, he'll find it."

"He already tried," Jemmy said, remembering the men who met him at the dock. "And failed. I don't see how—"

"God's teeth, he murdered Ian! And now you want to take his daughter to your bed? I always knew you were a sorry brother, but I expected even you would—"

"Why is Ian dead, Alistair?" Jemmy cried. "You were the one he wanted always at his side! Why didn't *you* protect him?"

He stopped, appalled, too late to recall the words he had never meant to speak. Indeed, until he'd spoken them, he had no idea that he held Alistair responsible for Ian's death. It was wrong—wrong to even think it, and even more terrible to say it to one so obviously bereaved.

"I'm sorry," he said quickly. "I never meant to blame you."

"Aye, but ye did. As does your father."

As I do myself. Jemmy heard the words Alistair didn't speak and saw them in the bitter lines etched upon his kinsman's face.

His sympathy, though genuine, vanished when Alistair raised his head and looked him in the eye. "Don't do this, Jemmy," he warned. "You're walking into something ye canna understand. Give the order to attack."

"I will *not,*" Jemmy snapped. "Now get back to your place."

"There's no reasoning with you," Alistair said. "But at least I tried. Just as Ian would have wanted me to."

"And if I go through with it?" Jemmy asked, grasping his kinsman's wrist. "What then? Are we to be enemies?"

"It's not too late," Alistair said, pulling his hand free and jerking his horse's head around. "Think about honor— ye ken the word? Ian's honor. Yours. The clan's. They're all ready," he added, nodding toward the men ranged behind him. "Let's finish the bastard right here and now."

It wasn't until Alistair was gone that Jemmy realized his kinsman hadn't answered his question.

A t a signal from Lord Darnley the company moved forward, at last arriving at the chapel. It was a tiny place, seldom used, that Darnley had suggested, saying he feared his people might disrupt the ceremony. Twenty men dressed in Kirallen's blue and green dismounted; twenty men in Darnley's blue and gold followed suit. They faced each other across the stableyard, hands inching toward their weapons, every one of them tensed to fight.

Darnley shot his men a warning glance as he held out his arm to Alyson. She dismounted, feeling as though her legs would scarcely hold her as they proceeded into the chapel. It was dank and dim inside, early twilight seeping through the narrow windows. The tallow candles smoked and hissed in their sconces, adding to the gloom. No flowers brightened the plain altar.

As they waited for the others to take their places, Alyson was aware of Darnley's fingers gripping her arm with enough strength to leave a mark. Darnley. Her father. Even now she could scarcely believe it was the truth.

Until a month ago, Alyson had no idea that any relationship existed between herself and Lord Darnley than that of maid and master. At first she had refused to accept his assertion that he was her natural father, believing it impossible that her mother had concealed such an important truth until her death.

But once the whole tale was revealed, Alyson understood her mother's silence. Clare McLaran Bowden had sought to protect her daughter from the knowledge of her birth and the terrible circumstances that had led to her own association with Lord Darnley—one that he admitted with no shame.

Alyson swallowed hard against the sickness rising in her throat as she imagined how it had been for Clare, her gentle, fragile mother. At seventeen she had been wrested from her home in the Highlands, torn from her family and all who knew her, carried off as a prize of war, forced into her captor's bed, then given to one of his men in marriage when she was found to be with child.

It was far easier to accept that the man Alyson had believed to be her father was no part of her. Jacob Bowden was a hard man with a hard hand who had never once shown Alyson any sign of affection. She had not been able to mourn his death, nor feel anything but joy that he was gone.

But as bad a father as he'd been, he was still preferable to Lord Darnley. And now she was actually helping this man—this monster—carry out his wicked scheme.

Oh, Mam, help me now, show me some other way, she prayed as Darnley pulled her forward. I canna do this— and yet I must. They'll kill our Robin if I don't. Ye ken I have to do it for his sake—

The journey to the altar was both agonizingly slow and far too quick. The groom did not turn as she walked toward him, knees shaking and head held high. When they reached the altar she shot Darnley one desperate look beneath her veil, knowing all the while there was no hope of mercy from that quarter. He didn't even glance her way as he placed her hand in the other man's and walked away.

The priest began to speak, but Alyson couldn't follow his words. It was all a meaningless gabble. Her hand still rested in the groom's, but it did not even feel a part of her. She stared down at her daintily shod feet upon the flag-stones, then at the man's high boots planted solidly beside her own. They were well worn, splashed with mud, cover-ing worn riding leathers. He certainly hadn't bothered to dress for the occasion!

Her eyes traveled upward, noting the broadsword upon one hip and the Kirallen blue-green tartan wrapped around his waist and fastened at one broad shoulder with a plain silver brooch. Though he stood unmoving, his very immo-bility had a frightening intensity about it, as though he held some strong emotion in tight check. Like a great dark cat, she thought with a shiver, all coiled muscle and deceptive stillness.

At last she looked up, tilting her head far back before she could glimpse his face. She drew a sharp breath and glanced away, but against her will her eyes were drawn to him again. Safe beneath her concealing veil, she studied the planes and angles of his face, forcing herself to con-sider each feature calmly. He had two eyes, a nose, a mouth, the same as any other man. Yet some magical alchemy had combined those parts into a countenance that was darkly handsome and altogether fascinating, as wickedly exotic as the gold ring shining in his ear.

As though aware of her thoughts, he turned to her. Even through her veil she felt his eyes burn into hers, banked fires smoldering within their sable depths. What would it take to ignite the blaze, to shatter his rigid self-control? For the space of a single heartbeat she imagined his arms enfolding her, the touch of his hands, his lips . . .

She tore her gaze from his, heart pounding wildly in her breast. Who *was* this man, this Jemmy Kirallen? What had he just done to her? One slip, the smallest lapse in judgment would mean her death—and Robin's. She could not afford to be distracted from her goal. Yet even now she was aware of him in a way she had never experienced before, with a rush of new and terrifying feelings that coursed through every fiber of her being. Only by the strongest act of will did she stop herself from fleeing down the aisle and out the door. There was nowhere she could run to, no one who could help her now.

The priest coughed lightly. "Say 'I do,' " he prompted.

Alyson darted one wild look about the chapel, seeing the Kirallens on one side, Lord Darnley and Sir Robert on the other, all watching her closely. She could not let this happen. She had to speak right now—but then what? How would she protect her brother when she had no idea where to find him? Oh, Robin, she thought, despairing, I cannot—I *will* not let them hurt you.

When at last she answered, her voice was firm and clear.

"I do."

J emmy scarcely heard the priest's final words. He was stunned by the finality of what had just happened. Bound for life, that's what the priest had said. Why hadn't he considered this before he jumped feet first into his father's plan?

He turned to the woman beside him, grasped her jaw, and turned her face to his. He pushed back the veil and regarded her coolly, careful not to let his expression betray his surprise. Last night he'd been told that Maude Darnley was her father's pampered darling, a harsh, demanding mistress who was heartily disliked among the Aylsford servants. No one had thought to mention that she was beautiful.

Her eyes were just the color of the summer sea, and her hair shone like a pagan bonfire against the gray stone walls of the chapel. He had a sudden impulse to reach out and bury his fingers in the shimmering curls, just to see if they would feel as warm as they looked. When she jerked her chin from his grasp and lifted it proudly, he felt reluctant admiration.

She was so small, so delicate—somehow he'd imagined she would be tall and stout, a formidable lady. She bit her lip, then released it with a little grimace of pain. Of course, he realized, staring at her cut and swollen mouth, they must have beaten her to get her here at all.

His pulse steadied and he felt swift pity for the poor frightened maid who stood before him, trembling from head to foot. This wasn't her fault—even if she was a Darnley.

It seemed Jemmy had always known, as if he had been born with the knowledge, that Darnleys were murdering, heartless things, not really human at all. It had been easy enough to dismiss such tales as nonsense—when he was safe across the sea. Now every instinct warned of danger. Though Jemmy couldn't see what danger this lass could possibly pose to him, he had relied upon his instincts too long to doubt them now.

But danger or no danger, the Darnley wench was now

his wife. When he put his hands on her shoulders and pulled her toward him, she stiffened in sudden fear.

"Calm yourself," he ordered. "I'm not going to hurt you."

She allowed herself to be drawn into his embrace, her slight frame trembling in his arms. She smelled faintly of some light flower scent, very different from the bold musk and ambergris that Spanish ladies favored. Lavender, he thought. That's what it was. In Spain, where the gardens were so highly scented that it made a man dizzy just to walk in them, he had forgotten the sweetly subtle scent of lavender. It brought back a thousand tumbled images of childhood: sunlit days and long cool nights, his mother's smile, Ian's laughter—all of them a part of him he could not escape, no matter how far or fast he traveled. It filled his senses as his arms tightened around her without conscious thought or plan, his fingers twining in her soft, bright hair. Bending to her, he brushed her mouth with his.

It was no kiss at all, just the merest token that courtesy demanded, yet at the first touch of her lips he felt himself stir as eagerly as an untried boy. Surprised and none too pleased at his body's unbidden response, he released her so abruptly that she stumbled. Stopping his instinctive gesture of support, he spun upon his heel, already calling for his horse before he'd reached the door.

chapter 5

Alyson caught herself on the altar rail and pressed one hand to her burning lips as she watched Jemmy stride from the chapel. He was a Kirallen, the enemy—how *could* she have forgotten that? And yet, in the moment when he held her she had felt . . . safe. Protected. Until he all but threw her from him and walked away without a backward glance.

She was too shaken to protest as Lord Darnley caught her against his broad chest and prisoned her with strong and hateful arms. Then he let her go and stumbled toward the door, one hand fumbling at his eyes.

Sir Robert kissed her cheek. "I'll find your brother," he whispered quickly. "Don't worry. I'll see he's safe until it's done. Chin up, now. You'll be home before you know it."

And then Sir Robert was gone as well, and Laird Kirallen was approaching.

"Well, daughter," he said on a sigh.

Poor man, he didn't look well at all. His lined face held
but little color and his lips had a bluish cast that spoke of
failing health. His faded gray eyes regarded Alyson with
sadness. She began to hold out her hand to him but remembered just in time who she was supposed to be.
Instead she raised her chin and gave him Maude's look,
the one she had practiced with such diligence.

"Where are my women?"

She was pleased to hear her voice was steady and it did
sound much like Maude's—cold and proud. And though
she knew she was bound to slip into the familiar pattern of
her homeland, it was no more than Maude did herself.
After a season at court, Maude tried hard to mimic the
strange, clipped accent of the south, but she often lapsed.
Sir Robert had assured Alyson that her own mix of
London speech and border dialect was no less ridiculous
than Maude's.

"Waiting at the manor," Kirallen sighed.

"Then let us go at once," she answered carefully.

She mounted and saw her serving woman, Celia,
helped onto her palfrey by one of Kirallen's men. Of
Celia, Darnley had said, "She'll watch your every move,
my girl. Make one false step, and your brother—" He'd
drawn one finger across his throat in an all-too-eloquent
gesture.

Celia was a pretty young woman who looked as innocent as a spring morning, with yellow hair and wide blue
eyes. But Alyson could see the cold calculation in those
eyes and knew that Darnley had chosen his spy carefully.
There would be no help from Celia.

The rain began again, a sullen drizzle that mingled
with the mist rising from the sodden ground. As they rode
on silently, hour after hour, Alyson's fear receded until she
felt nothing but a dreamlike wonder. This could not be
happening—not now, not to her. Surely she would wake to
find herself back home, Robin snuggled close, the homely

scent of baking bread drifting from the kitchens. And she would rise and dress and go about her work, while Robin ran off to the stables. It was a hard life, to be sure, one entirely devoid of pleasure, but at least she and Robin were alive and still together, just as Alyson had promised her mother.

Promises, she reflected bitterly. How easy they were to make, yet how dreadfully difficult to keep! At thirteen, Alyson had been certain she could get herself and Robin back to the McLarans, her mother's family in the Highlands. Five years later they had made it no farther than Aylsford Manor, not three miles from the place where Clare had died.

Oh, Mam, I'm sorry, Alyson thought. I did my best but it was so hard— She had found work in Lord Darnley's kitchens and a place for Robin, too, but the journey to the Highlands had proved beyond her grasp. It took so long to save, and without gold there was no way the journey could be made. They had no horses and no money to buy them, no way of getting a message to the clan. But just as Alyson had begun to hope that in a year or two it could be done, Lord Darnley had stepped in. Now Robin was a prisoner, and she was setting off to what would surely be her death. It wasn't real, it couldn't be—

The palfrey stumbled and Alyson was jerked into awareness. Lifting her head, she saw they had arrived.

Ravenspur sat on a broad hill, gray stone battlements against a gray and lowering sky. They clattered across the drawbridge and between the watchtowers. Alyson shivered as the portcullis was lowered behind them, the clanking of strong chain ending with a thud as iron spikes hit the dirt. No turning back. She was trapped now, caged behind stout bars. They passed through the bailey and into the courtyard, where a groom waited, standing like a statue in the rain, to help her from her horse.

The rain turned to a downpour, soaking through her

cloak, but still she hesitated before passing through the arch and into the manor itself. I can't do this, I can't, she thought in sudden panic as Lord Kirallen stood aside for her to enter. Then she summoned Robin's image, straightened her back, and went inside.

chapter 6

$\mathcal{L}$❤

The wedding feast passed in the strange, disjointed manner of a nightmare. As soon as Alyson stepped in the door she was whisked upstairs to a chamber filled with women. One snatched the cloak from her shoulders, another pulled the veil from her head and began to comb her hair, while a third knelt and brushed the mud-splashed hem of her gown. All this was accomplished in frenzied haste and total silence.

Though Alyson suspected Maude would have a good deal to say about such treatment, she didn't dare voice a protest. She was cold and tired and so frightened that she feared any attempt to speak would end in tears.

The women finished and a hard-faced matron stepped forward. "This way, my lady," she said curtly, bustling from the room and down the corridor, not bothering to see if Alyson followed her or not. At length she stopped, pointed down the stairway, gave a quick curtsey, and vanished back the way they'd come.

Alyson walked carefully down the narrow stairway. She had expected to be nervous, but not as frightened as she found herself right now. One step, she told herself firmly, and then another. Just take each moment as it comes.

When she reached a landing she stopped and leaned against the wall, staring blankly at two stairways, one leading to the left, the other to the right.

Which one? she wondered. Damn the woman for not telling her the way! Now she would have to go back again and ask. She imagined the women up above, waiting for her to do just that, and started down the right-hand steps.

When she reached the bottom she found a dim, straight corridor that stretched as far as she could see. Listening hard, she heard none of the sounds of a feast in progress. She turned back and climbed the stairs again. Such a petty trick, she thought, anger quickening her steps. So needlessly cruel. You'd think that here, on the very edge of nowhere, people could at least show a bit of charity.

The left-hand stairway ended in a corridor exactly like the first. Alyson walked on, and after a time the scent of food guided her down another passageway and yet another. At the bottom of one short hallway she found herself at the doorway of the kitchens.

Safe in shadow, she watched the familiar rhythm of a manor kitchen at the very pinnacle of activity. Scullions hurried about their tasks while pages and serving girls lingered in the warmth, snatching a bit of meat or bread amid much laughter. Her eyes moving over the busy scene with practiced ease, Alyson noted that the joint over the fire was burning as the spit boy flirted with a serving wench.

Looking more closely, she saw signs of carelessness and waste that appalled her thrifty nature. A split bag of flour had been tossed into a corner and its contents tracked across the flagged floor. Wilting vegetables were heaped on a table along with offal that should have been simmering into a pudding for tomorrow.

But for all its faults, it was a kitchen, bright and warm and blessedly familiar. It was with some effort that Alyson tore herself away and walked back down the passage.

Which way now? she wondered, staring down two equally gloomy expanses of cold stone. How had she come? Which way led back to the stairway?

She chose the left-hand way, thinking that it seemed more brightly lit, but as she traveled on the wall sconces became less frequent, the torches far less bright. When she reached another crossroad she nearly burst into tears.

All right, she told herself, you're lost. But if you're lucky, you might find a way out of here altogether.

The thought restored her, and as she walked quickly in the direction that seemed best to her, she found herself passing a high, deep window. She pressed her face against the small panes, listening to the keening of the wind and the swift patter of rain against the glass. Looking more closely, she saw that the window was hinged.

Think, she ordered herself, pressing her hands against her temples. Where to go from here? Find the stables and steal a horse. Get past the guard—across the moat—and back to Aylsford in the pouring rain, with no moon or stars to guide me. And even if I do succeed in all of that, even if I manage to find Robin, where can we go then? It's hopeless, she admitted to herself.

The light flickered, the torch nearest her but one guttered and winked out. The darkness drew about her, leaving her alone in one small circle of light. For the first time she realized how completely cut off she was from any hope of help. Ravenspur stood alone upon the moor, surrounded by mile upon mile of empty darkness. Anything could happen to her here, anything at all, and no one would ever know. She would simply vanish.

She tensed and peered back along the darkened corridor, every nerve alive. There was something out there in the corridor, a rustle in the shadows, coming closer . . . She seized the rusted window latch and twisted it with frantic haste.

A touch on her shoulder made her scream and whirl sharply. There was an answering cry and a boy jumped back, stumbled over his feet, and sat down hard.

"Christ's wounds, lass!" he cried. "What did ye want to do that for?"

Looking at him sprawled on the flagstones, Alyson began to giggle in helpless reaction to her fear.

"I'm sorry," she gasped. "But you—you shouldn't sneak up on people like that!"

The boy rose, dusted his backside, and grinned. "I didna mean to startle ye. What are ye doing here?"

"I'm lost," she said.

He looked her over curiously. "But who are ye?"

"Al—" she began, then broke off in horror, realizing she'd been about to give him her true name. "Al—as!" she finished feebly.

"Aye, I see you're a lass," he said, looking at her quizzically. "But which one?"

"Alas," she repeated in a doleful tone. "And alack," she added for good measure. "I am lost."

"Aye, I ken that, but—" His eyes widened. "Why, you're the Darnley lady. My uncle's wife."

"Your uncle? Are you Malcolm?" she asked, surprised, and he nodded.

This, then, was Ian's eleven-year-old son, orphaned since his father's death. He was a handsome, sturdy lad with curling brown hair and a winning smile. But now the smile faded from his lips and his bright blue eyes regarded her with a coldness far beyond his years.

"Your father killed my father. I hate him, and I hate ye, too! Why don't ye just go home again?"

"I couldn't even if I wanted to."

"Do ye want to?" he asked shrewdly, glancing from her

to the window in swift appraisal. "Well, ye won't get out that way."

Alyson straightened her back. "I wanted a breath of air, that's all," she said with what dignity she could muster.

The wind gusted against the glass, shaking the small panes in their frame.

"Oh, aye," Malcolm said skeptically. "A breath of air."

"Can you show me to the hall?"

"Aye," he said grudgingly. "This way."

He didn't speak another word as he led her quickly through the maze of passages. Soon they came upon a group of people gathered by the entrance to the hall. As Malcolm slipped away, Laird Kirallen turned to her with another of his sorrowful smiles, beckoning her forward.

After they had stood in silence for some minutes, Alyson began to wonder why they didn't go into the hall. A moment later she understood the delay.

"Where's Jemmy?" someone whispered behind her, and another voice answered, "No one can find him."

"If he's any sense, he's halfway to his ship."

Glancing back, Alyson saw a light-haired man watching her through narrowed eyes, his mouth twisted in a mirthless smile.

There was a burst of nervous laughter, quickly hushed, and Laird Kirallen frowned. "We'll wait no longer," he said, offering Alyson his arm. And so they walked together to the hall.

It seemed a thousand torches blazed in their brackets as the Laird led Alyson to the high table and politely pulled her chair back. Once seated, she looked about the hall and found every eye fastened upon her.

Her face burned and instinctively she bent her head, wishing she could crawl under the table and escape. Chin up, she told herself. You're Lady Maude Darnley, proud as Lucifer and twice as fierce.

With an effort she raised her head and fixed her gaze on

a tapestry hanging on the far wall. It showed a hunt, and Alyson felt immediate sympathy for the poor hind, fleeing for her life with the hounds upon her heels. She knew exactly how the poor beastie must be feeling. It seemed that any moment the dogs must drag her down, and yet, if she could make one mighty leap she might escape their ravening jaws. Yes, Alyson decided, obscurely comforted by the thought. That was how it ended. The hind leaped and the hounds all howled in fury as their prey ran off to freedom.

A squire set a smoking trencher in her place, the scent of roasted mutton making Alyson's empty stomach turn upon itself. She hadn't eaten since . . . she couldn't remember how long it had been. But she feared that if she tried now it would only make her sick. Instead, she lifted her goblet, but her hand shook so that wine splashed over the edge. She looked at the stain upon the linen with horror, glancing about to see if anyone was watching. Her eyes met those of the light-haired man she'd marked before. She set the goblet down upon the stain, trying vainly to conceal it, and put her shaking hands into her lap.

Another course was served and then another. In the lower hall the people had begun to enjoy the feast, and now their eyes were fixed not so much on Alyson as the empty place beside her. The meal was halfway through when Jemmy walked into the hall. His arrival was greeted with cheers and laughter, and he raised a hand, smiling, then dropped into his seat without a word of greeting. He was the only one who didn't look at Alyson; he kept his eyes fixed on the center of the hall where a minstrel played, the music lost in the rising talk and laughter.

Alyson studied him from beneath lowered lashes. He had changed into a tunic of fern green over trews of the Kirallen tartan and a length of the same fabric was fastened at his shoulder by a fine brooch with a blue stone in the center. His hair was loose, caught back at the temples with small braids. From the damp curls rose a spicy scent that conjured images of sunlight and blue water and places so distant she had never heard their names.

When he turned his head Alyson saw the gold ring glistening at his ear and despite the Kirallen colors he wore, she had the feeling that he did not belong here at all. He belonged in some other world entirely, a world of blazing color and adventure.

A pirate, Sir Robert had said. Yes, Alyson could see where one might think that. His long, dark eyes were wary as they went over the crowded hall, and she could see the tension of his form beneath the festive garb. He looked like a man accustomed to danger, formidable and more than a little frightening. The taut line of his mouth seemed incapable of anything as frivolous as laughter.

But Alyson had marked his quick smile when he walked into the hall. It changed everything, that smile. There was no pirate's cruelty about it, but a merry charm that had sent a flush of warmth tingling through her body. The heat still lingered in the pit of her stomach, intensifying the icy knot of fear just below her breastbone. Between the two, she could scarcely catch her breath.

He didn't even seem aware of her. And yet he must be. For all he knew, she was really Lady Maude, his own wedded wife. And tonight, later, when the feast was done, he would lie beside her naked in a bed. Her mouth went dry and she glanced at him again, but his head was turned from her.

As he conversed with his father he idly turned the stem of his goblet between long, brown fingers. Sailor's hands, she thought, strong and capable, the palms criss-crossed with small lines and hard with calluses. Yet for all their strength, they had been very gentle in the chapel when he wound his fingers in her hair, sending bright hot shivers racing down her spine . . .

She felt his gaze upon her and resisted the impulse to look into his eyes. Instead she continued to stare down at his hands, seeing a twisted silver scar running up the back of one wrist, vanishing into the green sleeve of his tunic. She wondered what he'd say if she was to ask him how he'd gotten it, then knew she never would. She'd never have the courage, for one thing, but even if she did, she didn't want to know, not this or anything else about him.

Somehow she had never stopped to think that he would not be simply a Kirallen, but a living, breathing man. A man she was leading to his death. A man who expected— who had every right to expect—to lie with her tonight. She shivered, remembering the rough scrape of his beard against her face, the iron strength of his arms . . . but his lips had been as warm and soft as swans-down.

What if—dear God—what if a child came of this? Never, not once, had she considered that possibility, but it could easily happen. Then what would she do? Whatever could she tell the poor babe about its father? Her stomach clenched and she was certain she would be sick right here and now, but then the moment passed.

Her eye fell on the tapestry again, and now she knew the hind would never make the leap. It was doomed, fated to be dragged down by the hounds, struggling vainly as they tore it limb from limb.

"My lady?"

Her heart leaped in terror at the sound of Jemmy's voice. It was deep and rich with just the slightest sugges- tion of an accent, more a matter of cadence than pronunci- ation. She composed herself and turned to him.

"You should try to eat something," he suggested.

She flicked a glance at the trencher before her, then back to his face. It was one of Maude's favorite tricks to dismiss something—an offered gift, a dish not prepared precisely to her liking—as beneath contempt. From the way Jemmy's polite half-smile vanished, Alyson knew that she had done it well.

"There is nothing here I care for."

"I could send for something else," he offered, coolly courteous, a host doing his duty to a difficult and unwelcome guest.

"No."

The single word hung in the air between them. Alyson clenched her jaw against the almost irresistible desire to add an expression of gratitude. But in the month she had spent in Maude's company, she had never once heard her half sister thank anyone for anything.

Jemmy shrugged and turned back to his father. Alyson sat, spine rigid, face set in a mask of indifference, as the interminable meal dragged on. At last the cloth was drawn, the trestles taken down, and the wild sweet music of the pipes began. Several men stood up to dance, their arms linked as they moved with such speed and grace that Alyson could scarcely follow their steps. For a moment she forgot everything but the beauty of their movements. She caught her breath as they executed one particularly fine leap and twirl, ending with a flourishing bow to her. She wanted to clap her hands and laugh. Instead she yawned delicately.

"I'm weary," she said to no one in particular. "I shall retire now."

When she stood the music screeched to a dissonant halt. Everyone in the hall was staring, and she felt the hot blood rush to her cheeks. What would Maude do now? she wondered frantically, then turned and started for the door.

Jemmy's voice halted her. "So eager for our marriage bed?" he drawled. "I'm afraid you'll have to wait." Wine splashed into his goblet as he refilled it.

Alyson's overstrung nerves gave way with a snap. Rounding on him, she sent the goblet spinning from his hand.

"How dare you speak to me like that?" she demanded.

He rose slowly to his feet and looked down at her. His lips curved in a smile that did not reach his eyes.

"Take care," he said softly. "If I were you, *wife,* I'd take great care, indeed. This isn't your father's hall, you know. It's mine. And these are my men all around you."

She held his gaze while she counted ten, a trick she'd learned at her mother's knee to control her hasty temper. Then she nodded. "I understand," she said carefully. "I still wish to retire. If—if that's acceptable to you."

And because she was very tired and very frightened there was a quaver in her voice on the last words. She hoped he wouldn't hear it, but he must have, for his voice was not quite so hard as he answered, "It is."

Two women hurried forward at his signal. As Alyson followed them from the hall the music broke out again and there was a sudden gust of laughter.

"For pity's sake, will no one dance with the bride-groom?"

Alyson turned to see Jemmy on his feet. A girl stepped forward, crying, "I will, my lord!" and he gave her a flashing smile, his teeth very white against his sun-bronzed skin.

Alyson started up the dim stairway, stumbling a little on the long hem of her gown.

"Ah, that's the worst of luck," the younger of the women breathed, staring with round eyes. "To fall up stairs."

"Be still," the other one said sharply. "Would ye ill-wish the lass on her wedding night? Come along now, my lady," she added kindly. " 'Tisn't far."

What would Maude do? Alyson asked herself again. Make some cutting remark, no doubt, and put the woman in her place. But Alyson couldn't do it. She simply nodded and followed them.

The chamber was not so large as Maude's, nor so well appointed, but to Alyson it seemed very fine indeed. The bed was hung with crimson draperies, and a fire burned brightly on the hearth as the women went about the business of disrobing her. Alyson hardly noticed their silence; she was too busy worrying about what was to happen next. At last they pressed a goblet of spiced wine into her hand and left her there alone.

She sank into a deep chair before the hearth and stared into the flames. There was a step in the hall and she stiffened, then relaxed as it passed by the door. Not him, then. Not yet. But sooner or later he'd appear and then . . .

She finished the wine and poured the goblet full again, draining it without taking it from her lips. Pot valiant, she thought wryly. That's what she was hoping for. Well and why not? It was better than shaking with fright. But she grew no braver, only sleepy. At last she climbed into the bed and lay staring at the canopy. Where was Robin tonight? She wondered if he cried for her and then it was she who was crying, stifling her sobs in the feather pillow.

Never in her life had she felt so dreadfully alone. Even God seemed to have gone over to the side of her enemies. She had appealed to Lord Darnley's manor priest, thinking that he must in good conscience help her. For surely this was sin, this mocking of sacred vows, both Darnley's and the one Alyson had taken in the chapel today.

"Lord Darnley has confessed already," Father Aidan had said sternly. "His soul is in my care, not yours. As for the rest . . . it is sin, true. But to send our lady Maude there would be a far worse sin. Now, as to the groom . . ." he'd considered, then said, "so long as he takes the vow in good conscience, his soul will not be imperiled."

But what about me? a voice cried in Alyson's heart. Do I really matter so little? She knew what Father Aidan would say: God's plan had set Maude far above her; it was her duty to bear anything for her lady's sake. "Bugger God," she whispered. "What's He ever done for me?"

She sat up with a gasp, shocked at her own blasphemy. Why, God had given her Robin, of course. And that alone was worth everything else. She breathed a fervent prayer of contrition, asking that she be given the strength to bear what was to come.

As she hovered on the edge of sleep, it seemed someone sat beside her on the bed and a faint scent of rosemary wafted through the chamber.

"Mam?" she murmured drowsily.

"Hush, now, hinny," a voice whispered, and a soft hand smoothed her hair in a gesture both comforting and familiar. "Dinna greet, I'm here, all will be well . . ."

Alyson struggled to open her eyes, but the effort was too much. With a little sigh she tumbled into sleep.

The fire had burned to embers before Jemmy set his candle on the table and stood beside the bed, watching his sleeping bride. Thick auburn curls lay across her face, but he could see the marks of tears and the dampness of the pillow beneath her cheek. She is Darnley's daughter, he reminded himself sharply, treacherous Darnley, who for years had cut a swath of death through the Kirallen clan. And now, God damn his black soul to Hell, he had killed Ian.

She stirred and murmured something about a robin and burning bread. He leaned down and brushed a shining strand of hair from her face, his fingers gentle on her sleep-flushed cheek and the line of her slender neck. She sighed, a smile curving her full lips.

She looked soft and vulnerable and dangerously enticing, and for a moment he was tempted to climb into bed beside her, bury his face in her bright hair, and forget everything that had happened to him since he came back to this place.

But after a moment his hand dropped to his side. He couldn't do it. Not tonight. She had done well today, all things considered, but her courage had been tested to the breaking point already. What if she fought him? And cried? Or worse, submitted with silent endurance? He'd go so far for the clan, but he drew the line at forcing himself on any woman, wife or not. Let her sleep tonight, and then tomorrow . . . or the next day . . . or the one after that . . .

What's the hurry, after all, he thought with sudden bitterness. I have three months to make the marriage real. And after that, I'll never see her again.

What was that?

Not sound or scent or touch, for those words had no meaning for him now. Yet something had pierced the empty darkness where he dwelt.

He did not live. His body lay forgotten in the crypt, a cast-off shell whose purpose had been served. He did not sleep or dream, for he had neither rest nor imaginings of other times or places. And yet he was not dead. Death lay beyond the door, in the realm of light and music, a place he dared not go. He simply was.

How long he had existed thus he did not know, though if he tried very hard he could catch glimpses of a time when he had borne a name. In the beginning he had clung to those memories, had made the effort to retain the form that defined him as a man, separate from all other men. But little by little he let it go, all but the one memory he must hold, the thing that bound him to this place.

There were others here, yet he was utterly alone. The lost ones were too concerned with their own affairs to give his any notice. And there was nothing he could do to help them. Their time here was measured, by what he did not know, and though he could lead them to the doorway, they could not see it until their time had come to do so. When it did they passed through joyfully, without a backward glance. He used to watch them go, sick with misery and envy, but he never went there now. It only made the darkness darker, the emptiness more empty . . .

For he was not like them. He had bound himself to earth, knowing full well the risk he took. With anguish undreamed of by the living, he had turned his back upon the doorway with its beckoning light and music. He could still find it if he wanted to, but one day—*How long? How long did he have left?*—it would be closed to him. And then he could search for all eternity without finding it again. But even knowing that, he would not leave—not now, not yet, not all alone. And so he waited, each moment an agony of longing, as all that he had been slipped inexorably away.

There it was again. A stirring of the mists, a silken brush of mind on mind, a memory of sunlight and green meadows, laughter, love, belonging . . .

Awake now, his silent cry echoed through the cold stone chamber. *My love, my love, where are you? Come to me—*

He passed up the stairway and into the great hall. It was full tonight and there was a great deal of excitement. Someone had been married. He concentrated hard, plucking the thought from a random mind. Why, it was Jemmy. Jemmy was home? When had that happened? And he had married Darnley's daughter.

What did it mean? What did Jemmy's marriage have to do with him? Why had he woken?

Oh, let it go, he thought wearily. The affairs of the living held no interest for him now. Once he had stood among them, listening to their talk, trying vainly to be part of it again. That was when he had fought the mists with every ounce of will . . .

But the mists were always there; cool, insidious, sapping memory and strength and hope. How hard it was to keep remembering, when memory brought only pain! How much easier to sink back into the mists.

No, no! He must remember . . . something. What had pulled him back? *My love, my love, where are you?* he cried again, but the words held little hope. She wasn't here. Once or twice before he'd thought . . . but this time he'd been so certain. Why had he been certain? He could not remember now, he only knew that he'd been wrong. She was not here, and he was alone, alone forever . . .

His silent wail of anguish ripped through the crowded hall. Two dogs leaped from the rushes, hackles rising. A light-haired man spun on his heel and signed himself uneasily with the cross before resuming his conversation.

The cry faded and he listened to its echo, bewilderment

clouding his thoughts. What had made him cry out like that? Why was he here at all when he never came to the hall? He had to remember. No matter what the pain, he must not slip back again.

She was not here, but she was close. He could feel her presence more strongly than he ever had before. There had to be a reason for it. The hounds backed away, whimpering, as invisible mist swirled through the hall and began to take on shape and form.

Something had changed. It was time for him to wake.

chapter 8

A lyson sat up with a gasp as the curtains were drawn back from the bed.

"Good morning, my lady."

The woman looking down at her smiled, her face crinkling in good-humored lines.

"I'm Maggie," she said, handing Alyson a cup of morning ale. "Did ye rest easy?"

"Aye, thank you," Alyson said automatically, her mind still muddled with sleep. It was morning and she had made it safely through her first night—alone. She gave a great sigh of relief and wondered what the time was, though she knew instinctively it was far past daybreak. She could never remember having slept so far into the morning.

The chamber was dim and very quiet. When Maggie opened the shutters, sunlight streamed into the room to fall across the rich, dark wood of the window seat and brighten the flowers among the rush-strewn floor. Alyson lay back against clean linen and soft pillows, things that no doubt

Maude would take entirely for granted. Maggie was humming softly and the pleasant sound reminded Alyson of her mother, who had often sung or hummed as she went about her work.

Alyson rarely allowed herself the luxury of such memories, for all too often they brought an aching sorrow. But last night she had dreamed of Mother, a wonderful dream that still lingered in her mind.

The door opened and Celia walked into the room. At once Alyson sat up straight.

"What, still abed?" Celia asked, and though the pink lips curved in a smile, the wide blue eyes were hard as agate.

"Och, now, let her rest," Maggie scolded gently.

"I was just getting up." Alyson pushed back the covers and swung her legs over the side of the bed, the peaceful moment shattered.

She allowed the women to dress her, though this was perhaps the hardest lesson she had learned. Maybe someone like Maude needed two or even three women to get her into her clothing, but Alyson thought it ridiculous to allow others to do things she was perfectly capable of doing for herself. She felt foolish sitting helpless as a babe while they brushed out her hair and began the intricate braiding.

Maude had pointed out several times that any lady was accustomed to such service and that Alyson had better seem to be accustomed to it, as well. Alyson thought now as she had then, that surely the servants had better things to do than this! But she gave no sign of her thoughts, for apparently there was something to Maude's advice after all. Alyson's performance last night had been more successful than she'd imagined possible. If the bridegroom disliked her so much on first meeting that he hadn't even come to her bed, she would make it her business to see that he disliked her more every day.

Why, if her luck held she might get out of this without him ever touching her.

They were just settling the gauzy veil over her braids when there was a knock on the door and Jemmy himself came into the room. Alyson's stomach clenched in fear and she got quickly to her feet, though even then she felt at a disadvantage, for her head reached no higher than his chin.

"My lady," he said with a slight bow. "I trust you slept well."

His expression was one of polite interest, but his eyes were dark and cold as a forest pool in wintertime. He knows, she thought, panic seizing her. He sees right through me. She stared at him, too terrified to breathe, and realized that beneath his cool facade was a smoldering flame of anger that sent a welcome rush of heat racing through her veins.

"No, I did not sleep well," she said, biting off each word. "Not well at all."

From the corner of her eye she saw Maggie staring in surprise at her abrupt change of manner as she continued, "The bed was not aired properly. And these rushes are moldy. I want them changed at once."

"Maggie," Jemmy turned to the older woman. "Will you see to it?"

"Aye, Master Jemmy—that is, my lord."

"Thank you."

He glanced at Alyson again, his face impassive. "If there is nothing else . . . ?" Without waiting for an answer he said, "Then good day."

She nodded without speaking, hiding her shaking hands in the folds of her skirt. As he passed by Celia, the girl bobbed a curtsey and said pertly, "And good day to *you,* my lord." He stopped and Celia smiled up at him.

"Who might you be?" he asked, smiling in return, and Alyson was certain she saw a spark of interest in his eyes as he regarded the pretty serving girl.

"Celia, my lord," she answered, giving him a coy look from beneath her lashes. "I came but yesterday with my lady." Her simpering manner made Alyson long to slap her soundly.

"Welcome, Celia. I trust you won't find yourself too homesick."

"Oh, no, my lord. I've no doubt I'll settle in."

Maggie raised her brows, a smile tugging at the corner of her mouth as her eyes went from mistress to maid and then to the door through which Master Jemmy had just passed. That Celia was a saucy little baggage to be flirting with her master before his wife's face. And the lady didn't like it one bit. Then Maggie sighed as she remembered all the work to be done this morning. It was daft, of course, for the rushes had been changed only yesterday, and she had seen to the airing of the bed herself. A lot of work for nothing. Some of the sympathy she'd begun to feel for her new mistress vanished as she bustled from the room.

When Maggie was gone Alyson rounded on Celia. "And what was that?" she demanded.

Celia shrugged. "Ye may be too simple to see the quickest way of learning everything from him, but I am not. And," she smiled slowly, "I daresay I'll enjoy myself right well!"

Alyson stared at her in horror but had no chance to reply, for Maggie returned with two servants who began to sweep the perfectly good rushes into a pile for removal.

"Perhaps you'd like to go into the gardens, lady," Maggie suggested, adding pointedly, "We'll be some time here."

"No," Alyson said. "I think I caught a chill yesterday."

She took up some sewing and went to the window seat, conscious of Celia's smirk of derision. But no matter how she upbraided herself for her cowardice, she could not bring herself to go out the door. Now that she was actually here it seemed impossible that she would not be discovered as the impostor she was. She would betray herself in a thousand small ways, she was certain of it. No, she'd stay here for today and perhaps tomorrow she'd feel differently . . .

But the next day was even worse. Jemmy stayed but a moment on his morning visit, an ordeal Alyson had been dreading. But once he was gone, she perversely wished him back again. At least he spoke to her, no matter how reluctantly! Once he had left, there was nothing to do but wait and worry, pluck a few chords upon her lute, and spoil the sewing she attempted. Alyson chafed at the inactivity, for she'd never spent an idle moment in her life. By the time the women prepared her for the evening meal, her nerves were taut as bowstrings.

What a hideous gown, she thought, staring at the stiff silver folds. And the headdress she had thought so ugly upon Maude looked even worse on her. Bad enough I have to do this, she considered glumly. But do I have to look so silly while I do it? And must I be so damned unpleasant every moment? However does Maude stand being herself?

Didn't Maude find, after she'd insulted everyone in sight, that she was lonely? Perhaps she did. Perhaps that's why she was always so bad tempered. But just now Alyson hadn't time to pity her half sister, for she was too busy praying that she might survive another endless meal.

"What the devil do ye think you're about here?" Kirallen demanded in an angry whisper as Jemmy sat beside him in the hall. "Why have ye no' bedded her yet?"

"I will keep our bargain," Jemmy said. "In my own time."

Kirallen leaned forward. "Is there something I should know about?" he asked smoothly. "Ye are able, are ye no'?"

Jemmy's jaw clenched. "Aye."

"Then get on with it. The sooner she's with child, the better."

"I would prefer the lady to be willing."

"Willing? Christ's blood, man, I trust she knows her duty—which is more than I can say for ye! I won't have it. D'ye hear me, Jemmy? I want it done tonight."

Jemmy rose to his feet as his wife walked into the hall. "I will keep our bargain," he repeated tightly. "That's all you need to know. As for the details, I'll thank you to stay out of it."

Maude was wearing an elaborate gown of silver cloth, a color that did not suit her, with a horned headdress that overshadowed her delicate features. She looks like a child dressed in her mother's clothes, Jemmy thought, stifling a sigh as he offered her his hand. Her small fingers were cold, and he instinctively closed his own around them as she mounted the step of the dais.

Once seated, she withdrew her hand from his and stared into the distance, ignoring him entirely. She was an ice maiden tonight, remote, untouchable, with her wealth of ruddy hair all hidden away in silver-threaded cauls. He had to look very closely to find the softly tempting lass he had watched sleeping. She was still there, but well disguised.

Damn Father and his twisted plans! he thought furiously. But he knew that the larger part of his anger was directed at himself. The Laird's plan would have come to naught if he had not agreed to the deception. But he had agreed. Now he must either take this lass unconsenting, or bring her to his bed with empty words and promises of a future they would never share. No matter how he looked at it, there was no way he could escape with his honor even marginally intact.

He could not break his word. He would not force her. There remained only one course of action.

"That is a lovely gown, my lady," he began, wincing at

the smoothness with which the lie slipped from his mouth. She turned to him, a spark of something—derision? amusement?—flashing in her eyes, only to vanish in an instant.

"It was made in London," she said in a cool, repressive voice. And with that she turned her back to him.

For a moment he was intrigued by the challenge she presented. When was the last time a woman had so completely spurned his advances? If such a thing had ever happened, it was so long ago that he could not remember. In Jemmy's experience, women were the ones to charm and flatter him, setting their pretty silken snares. And it was he who decided whether to be caught, by whom, and for how long.

But Maude was no laughing, light-minded lady. Yet he was not sure exactly what she was. The haughty ice maiden beside him now? The hot-tempered lass who had slapped a goblet full of wine from his hand during their wedding feast? Or the girl who had trembled in his arms before the altar?

He could find out. He had no doubt of that. He could draw her out, set her at her ease, make her smile if he set his mind to it. With time and just a bit of patience he could surely win her trust. And then . . .

All at once he could see her lying naked in his arms, tumbled, rosy, glowing with the aftermath of love. The image was so unexpected, so vivid, so wildly erotic that his body reacted to it instantly. For a moment he forgot everything but the question of how quickly he could get her in his bed.

He pushed the thought away, disgusted with himself. It would all be a lie, a damned foul lie like this whole misbegotten marriage. Once she had learned to trust him, he would abandon her, never to return. And though Jemmy's past was hardly blameless, he had never stooped to lies to lure a woman to his bed. He looked at her averted face, the long, white throat, and clear line of her jaw and felt like the lowest form of life. She was quite right to guard herself from him.

The Laird leaned close. "If ye think ye are doing the lass a kindness, ye are mistaken. She kens what is expected. Best to have it over."

Maude on one side, Father on the other—the devil and the deep blue sea. How blindly he had walked into the trap! Now he was shackled by his duty on the one hand, his honor on the other.

Jemmy could bear cold and hunger, loneliness and disappointment without complaint. The one thing he could not tolerate was the feeling of confinement. Twelve years ago he had fled these walls, abandoning all comfort and security in a desperate bid for freedom. Now the reckless streak that was never far from the surface blazed into full flame. No one held Jemmy Kirallen against his will. And no one gave him orders. God help the man—or woman— who dared try.

Suddenly it didn't matter how or why he had become entangled in this situation. He wanted out. And he would do whatever must be done to make good his escape.

A lyson shed the silver dress with relief and donned a plain chamber robe. Then she paced the floor with restless energy. Two days gone. How many more to follow? And how could she possibly survive them?

She *would* survive, she promised herself fiercely. She would be strong and tough and clever. Nothing—and no one—could be allowed to interfere with that. Certainly not Jemmy Kirallen, with his charming smile and empty compliments. He was not important, not in the least, no matter how giddy and breathless she might turn when he took her hand in his. She would, she *must* get back to Robin, and together they would journey to the Highlands and the McLarans.

"Find where they're most vulnerable," Darnley had ordered. *"I want to know how many men Kirallen has and how prepared they are for battle. Since the older brother died, I've heard they grow lax. Is it true?"*

"Maggie!" Alyson called. "Bring out my sewing. Edina, Mistress Selton—attend me, please."

"It's verra late, my lady," Mistress Selton began.

Alyson quelled her protest with a single glance. At least Maude has taught me one thing of value, she reflected as they settled down and pulled their work into their laps. She would have to remember the trick when she went back to the kitchens.

Mistress Selton bent over her darning, her mouth set in an angry line. She was a formidable dowager, with a stern face and iron-gray hair. Edina Kirallen was more biddable. She was but three or four years more than Alyson, a plump and timid widow with a sweet mouth and a perpetually anxious expression.

"Fine weather today," Maggie remarked, her spindle moving up and down.

The other women nodded, not bothering to answer.

"Let's hope it keeps fine for the gathering," Maggie added.

"What gathering is that?" Alyson asked, and the three women stared at her with identical expressions of surprise.

"A gathering of the clans," Maggie said at last. "Well, not all o' them," she added after a moment. "It's just a small one, ye ken, a time to meet our kin. We'll be leaving in a se'nnight or so."

"Oh. I see."

Alyson bent over her tapestry, frowning as she tried to frame the questions she must ask.

"And what might that be?" Maggie asked, her pleasant

face wrinkling with distaste as she peered at the bloodred stitches Alyson was setting.

"St. George," Alyson said. "This part is the dragon."

"Oh, aye," Maggie said doubtfully. There was an audible snort from Mistress Selton.

Alyson couldn't help but agree that the tapestry was a hideous thing, for the dragon was spouting fountains of gore as St. George regarded it smugly through crossed eyes. Maude had started it some years ago and had given it to Alyson with the air of conferring a great gift. Alyson wondered if Maude had realized that the subject must be offensive to the Kirallens, St. George being the patron saint of England.

She drew her needle through again, then said, "Ravenspur is larger than I had imagined. How many men can the Laird put into the field?"

Mistress Selton shot her an unfriendly glance. "Enough," she said succinctly.

"And better fighting men ye ne'er have seen," Edina cried, startling everyone. Her round face reddened beneath her coif and she added with a burst of spirit, "So long as they're not set upon by treachery."

"Aye," Mistress Selton agreed. "No man, however braw, can stand against a dagger in the back."

"No, I suppose not," Alyson murmured. "But would you say—"

She broke off, astonished, as Edina burst into tears and ran from the chamber. Mistress Selton gathered up her sewing and followed her.

Maggie looked up from her spindle. "Edina's husband was Lord Ian's man," she said.

"Oh," Alyson said blankly. "Was he?"

"Slain last January, ye ken," Maggie went on, looking at her curiously. "By your father, lady," she added bluntly, as Alyson made no response.

"Yes, but—well, it was a battle, wasn't it? And he was a soldier. Of course some men were bound to die."

Maggie snorted. "Oh, a *battle?* Is *that* what ye call it over there? I laid Lord Ian out with my own hands," she continued, her pale blue eyes filling with tears. "Stabbed in the back, he was, plain for anyone to see. He lived long enough to name your father as the man who struck him down from ambush."

"Oh, no!" Alyson exclaimed. "But he said—"

Maggie wound her yarn into a tidy ball. "Aye, lady? What was it your father said?"

Alyson shook her head, not bothering to answer. So much for all the tales of Darnley's glorious victory over Kirallen's heir! The minstrel at Aylsford had even made a song of it, describing each blow in a deadly contest that had lasted half the morning. Every groom and varlet proudly hummed it as he went about his chores. But looking into Maggie's honest face, Alyson knew it for a lie.

"Pray excuse me, lady," Maggie said coolly, dropping the wool into her basket. "If ye've no more need of me, I'd like to get to bed."

In the darkest part of night Alyson woke shaking, her face wet with tears. In her dream she had wandered into the landscape of her tapestry. St. George stood, the crimson cross emblazoned on his snow white surcoat, his gory sword raised high. When he turned, he bore Lord Darnley's face.

"Look!" he cried, "I've slain the dragon! Surely God is on my side."

The blood-soaked form lying in the snow stirred, and Alyson saw with horror that it was Jemmy, his eyes fixed upon her with an expression of mute suffering that was worse than any reproach he might have made.

She fell to her knees and tried desperately to staunch his

wound, but nothing she could do would stop the flow of blood.

"I've slain the dragon!" Lord Darnley repeated, his face exultant. "Come, hear the song my minstrel made of it!"

"He's not a dragon, he's a man," Alyson cried, and Darnley looked down at her, face contorting in rage as he raised his dripping sword above his head—

She started awake with a cry of fear, then fell back among the pillows, pushing the sweat-soaked hair back from her face. It was just a dream, she told herself. Just a dream, no more. It hadn't really happened.

Not yet, at any rate.

chapter 9

The next morning Jemmy came to her door as was his habit. He was dressed for riding, in the same high boots and leathers he'd worn for the wedding.

"Good morning, my lady," he said, stepping into the room. There was a flurry of curtsying from the serving women as Alyson moved toward the window, turning her back to him.

She stared blindly into the courtyard, which at this hour was bustling. The people below called to each other, and though she couldn't make out the words she recognized the brisk laughing tones of people who had no doubt of who they were and what they were about. Once—was it just a month ago?—Alyson had known who she was, too. Now she was no one, not Alyson Bowden, the best cook in Northumberland, and not the Lady Maude.

But no, that wasn't quite true. She was still Robin's sister, the one thing that stood between him and certain death.

"I trust you slept well," Jemmy said, just as he always

did. But this time he sat down on the window seat beside her.

She nodded curtly, not looking at him, though she was very much aware of his presence. Now it was time for her daily complaint, and she found herself at a loss. She was well fed and splendidly clothed. Her chamber was spotless, the bed linen shining, the rushes freshly changed and sprinkled with fragrant flowers. Half a dozen women waited for her lightest word to bring whatever she might desire. Maybe Maude could find some fault with the arrangements, but Alyson could not.

Jemmy leaned back and drew one knee up, clasping his arms about it. "Now let me see," he said. "What will it be today? Would you like me to fetch you the Stone of Scone for a footrest? Shall we pull down the manor and rebuild it bit by bit? Or— I know—perhaps you would like me to hunt you a unicorn this morning!"

She glanced at him and saw he was smiling up at her, his eyes alight with mischief, and for the first time she noted the hint of a dimple beside one corner of his mouth. She looked away quickly.

"What? Don't tell me you are at last content?" He gave a great sigh of mock relief. "Then I see we must look further afield! Today I ride to Dunforth. Why don't you join me? Surely you could suggest some . . . improvements . . . there." He gestured toward the open window. " 'Tis a fine, fresh day."

When Alyson didn't speak he added gently, "You can't stay in this one room forever, Maude. Come out and ride with me."

At his change of tone Alyson felt the breath catch in her throat. She stared out the window, longing to escape. She could almost feel the fresh wind and sunlight as she imagined herself free.

Every day of Alyson's life had been spent in an unending round of work, every moment planned. To ride somewhere she'd never seen simply for the sake of seeing it was something she'd never once experienced. And what would it be like to go on such an adventure with this man beside her? Would he tease her as he'd just done—and, oh, the thought of laughing with him was almost irresistible. Her life had held so little laughter. If only she was Maude and could turn to him and say, "Yes, I'll ride with you." How dangerously easy it would be to do just that!

With a tremendous effort she dragged her gaze back into the shadowy chamber. Lifting her chin, she looked down her nose and said frostily, "I think not."

All the softness vanished from his face as he stood and turned his back to her. As he walked away she nearly cried out for him to wait, that she could be ready in a moment.

Don't be a fool, she ordered herself fiercely. He's only a Kirallen. If he knew the truth he'd show her no mercy, and she could not afford to show him any, either—no matter how winningly he smiled. She had not started this war. It had been raging long before she was born, and no doubt it would continue long after she was dead. It was between the Darnleys and the Kirallens and had naught to do with her. She had no choice, none at all. Robin was depending on her.

Robin. What had she been thinking to even consider her own pleasure when Robin's life was hanging in the balance? Oh, she was a selfish, wicked girl, just as Father Aidan had told her many times.

Jemmy hesitated in the doorway, and Alyson stared down at the floor, terrified that he might speak—or worse, that he might smile at her again. Because if he did that she'd be lost, and before she knew it she'd be riding off to Dunforth with the wind in her hair and the sunlight on her face.

"I'll expect you in the stables in a quarter of an hour," he said evenly, then walked out, slamming the door behind him.

chapter 10

The day was warm and the air was fragrant with the scent of damp earth and pine and heather. Hawks swooped against an achingly blue sky that seemed to stretch forever. The ground was bright with purple pansies and yellow heather as Alyson and Jemmy cantered along the slopes of the triple-crowned Eildon Hills.

Though Alyson was very new to the exercise, riding had been her chiefest pleasure during her ordeal at Aylsford. Horseback was the one place she had been able to escape Sir Robert's demanding, sarcastic tutelage and Lady Maude's petty cruelties. The first time she was mounted had been terrifying, until she realized that horses were no different from people, really. They would take advantage of any weakness—but only if you let them. She had soon come to an understanding with her palfrey, and now the animal obeyed her with no arguments when she slowed it to a walk.

"So, Maude, tell me," Jemmy asked lightly, pulling up beside her. "Have you ever seen a fairy in the hills?"

"You shouldn't speak of them," she answered quickly. "Not here."

"Where better? This is where they are said to dwell."

"You don't believe it, though."

"And you do?" he challenged with a grin.

Alyson began to say that she did indeed believe, but then stopped in some confusion, wondering if the nobility didn't know about the Fair Folk. It wasn't something that had come up in conversation during her time with Maude. She shrugged without answering.

"Look—" Jemmy said, pointing to a tree standing all alone upon the moor. "Just think—this could be the very spot where Thomas the Rhymer met the Queen of Elfland."

"So it could," she said. "Though they say 'twas on the *other* side of the border."

"Two hundred years ago and more—who can say where the border was back then? And what's a border, really, but lines upon a map? Surely the Fair Folk are too wise to care if we call this bit of land a part of Scotland or of England!"

Alyson heard his words with some surprise. The exact location of the border had been a cause of deadly dispute for centuries. Yet he talked as though it didn't really matter.

"Yes," he added, staring at the tree. "I'm sure it was just here. And she carried him away to Elfland for seven years, then returned him to this very spot with the gift of truth upon him."

He lingered a moment longer, then kicked his horse into a walk. "I wonder what a gift that was, really. To be doomed to speak only truth—poor devil. His life must have been a merry hell."

"So you count the telling of lies as the means to happiness?" she asked tartly.

"How like a Kirallen!" he said, finishing the unspoken thought. "Yes, lady, we're all terrible liars. It's what we do best—well, when we're not too busy with murdering and thieving. And on certain evenings of the year we slay new-born babes, as well," he finished, twisting his face into a leer.

She was nearly surprised into a giggle, but just in time turned it to a cough and looked away.

"What? Don't tell me your father left that part out! Surely he told you all about our wicked ways."

"He told me what I need to know," she answered curtly.

"And now you're one of us. Was it very terrible when you learned you were to come here?"

The last question was asked without a touch of mockery. Alyson bit her lip and stared down at the reins between her gloved hands. "My father gave his word."

"Aye, and so he did. But you were never asked. I'm sorry for that, Maude."

Oh, she wished he wouldn't do that, talk to her as if she was his equal, as if anything she might have thought or wanted made the slightest bit of difference. He wouldn't speak that way if he knew who I am, she reminded herself firmly. It's only that he believes I'm noble-born. People like him never stop to think about my kind.

"I trust I'll do my duty," she said stiffly.

"Will you, then?" he asked, and though his tone was light, his glance was very keen.

"Have I any choice?" she answered coolly, pretending that she did not understand his question. But the warm blood rushing to her cheeks said otherwise.

"Do any of us really have a choice?" he asked, his voice suddenly bitter. "We work and plan and then—" he snapped his fingers. "It's gone. Sometimes I wonder if anything we do makes the slightest bit of difference or whether it was all laid out for us before. It's like the horses that turn the mill with a cloth around their eyes, walking round and round in circles, thinking they're actually getting somewhere."

Alyson thought of her mother. Of Robin. Of herself. Of the senseless, violent acts that had destroyed every plan they'd ever made.

"God has given us free will," she argued, troubled at the image. "Or so I've heard it said. But the most important thing is not to lose faith in Him."

"Faith," Jemmy repeated flatly. "Aye, well, faith's a fine thing if you have it, but if you don't . . ." He shrugged.

"You have no faith?"

She was shocked at the casual admission. Prayer, observance of the holy days, regular attendance of mass— these things were as real, as much a part of life as work or sleep. Even Lord Darnley took care to justify his actions as God's will. And though Alyson often disagreed with God and found His ways a mystery, she had never doubted His existence.

"I know the sun will rise in the morning and set at night. Beyond that . . ." He shot her a rueful smile. "Not much, I'm afraid. None of it makes a bit of sense to me. The priests say we have free will, but what does that really mean? Who would choose to be born blind or lame or poor? It seems all the important matters are completely out of our hands."

Alyson had often thought the same thing herself, but it seemed a curious notion for a nobleman to entertain. After all, he was rich and strong and powerful. It was his kind who had the best reason to endorse God's plan.

She had tried to fathom why God's plan would call for her to take part in Lord Darnley's treachery. On the face of it, it didn't seem likely that it could. But Father Aidan had reminded her over and over again that it was not her place to question. God Himself had arranged the world in perfect order. From the lowest villein to the highest of the archangels, every living being had its place. To question the order of her overlord—and her father—was to question God's perfect plan, which Father Aidan had assured her was a greater sin than any other.

. "Of course some people believe differently," Jemmy went on, sitting easily in the saddle. The sunlight fell on his dark hair, lighting the copper highlights in its depths. "They say we live not once, but many times. And our present circumstances are not simply God's will, but the result of what we did in other lives."

"Really?" Alyson said, intrigued by the idea. "If it was true—it would explain so much."

Jemmy smiled. "There's just one problem. It's heresy. Men have burned for less. And really, what difference does it make if we live once or many times? We still have to get through this life as best we might."

"Oh, but it does make a difference," she said earnestly. "If I could just be sure—"

"Then what?"

Then maybe I would know what I'm supposed to do, she thought, but she didn't speak the words. Instead she said, "Well, then I would know. It's always a fine thing to know something for sure. But perhaps we aren't meant to know."

"And yet we're expected to believe? It's a strange God that gives us minds to think and then tells us not to use them! But there, I don't mean to speak against your faith. Are you very pious, Maude?"

His question shocked Alyson into awareness of her own mistake. What had she been saying? Maude had not the slightest interest in religion!

"Oh, it's not something I think about often," she said quickly. "But once or twice—in an idle moment—when the priest spoke of such things . . ." She stifled a yawn behind one hand and kicked her horse into a trot, making toward a small burn falling down the hillside in a shower of glittering spray.

She allowed her palfrey to drink, and Jemmy stopped beside her as his gray bent its neck to the water. A welcome breeze fanned Alyson's hot cheeks and when she realized Jemmy was going to let their conversation drop, the muscles of her shoulders began to soften.

It was very quiet here, very peaceful. Dappled sunlight danced upon the water's surface and the wind soughed among the treetops. As Alyson's uneasiness receded she became aware of Jemmy just beside her, the hard, muscled thigh gripping the horse's withers, the strong, brown hands loose upon the reins. Though she kept her own eyes fixed on the water, she felt his gaze move over her, like a feather brushed against her skin.

What does he see when he looks at me? she wondered. A wife he doesn't want? The woman who will one day bear his children? Whatever he thinks he sees, it isn't me. The water blurred and shimmered before her eyes and suddenly she wished with all her heart that she had never ridden out today.

The palfrey raised her head and blew, stamping a hoof to signal she was finished drinking and it was time to leave.

"Have you traveled much beyond Northumberland?" Jemmy asked as they moved on, obviously making an effort to begin again.

Alyson repressed a sigh. She had known this question would come soon or late. Now it was time to recite the lessons she had learned—all too well, it had seemed during weary weeks at Aylsford.

"Last year I went to London with my uncle," she began, letting her gaze drift up to the white clouds dotting the blue sky. "I was presented to Princess Joan herself and oh, what a lady she is! Not quite as beautiful as she once was, perhaps, but still . . . they say the Black Prince was clay in her hands!"

"I once—" Jemmy began, but she ignored him, just as

Maude ignored anyone foolish enough to try to slide a word in edgewise when she started on her favorite topic.

"At one tournament she had ladies dressed like men ride out to entertain the crowds. Did you ever hear the like?" she demanded with a high, forced laugh. "Oh, it was scandalous, but such fun! They wore tunics that showed their legs up to the thigh and were even armed like men and riding war-horses. Everyone was shocked! They preached sermons about it—said the ladies were not ladies at all—and I agreed. Can you even imagine such a thing?"

Jemmy opened his mouth to reply, but she rushed on, "Every day was something new—jongleurs and minstrels, hunting, feasts, and pageants. . . . And now"—she frowned with a petulant sigh, pleased that she'd remembered exactly where it was supposed to come—"now I'll never know if Alice Perrers is still flaunting her position as the King's paramour—or whether styles have changed. In London the fashion is all for the new Bohemian headdresses," she went on in a breathless rush. "They're so delicate, so airy. I had one made for the last feast I attended. Even Princess Joan noticed it. She said . . ."

Before Alyson finished even half of what she had been forced to hear upon the subject, Jemmy's expression had hardened to bored impatience. And when she launched into a description of the second tournament Maude had seen, he did what she had often longed to do herself—cut off the flow of words with a quick excuse and rode ahead.

She kept her own mount to a decorous walk. But though the sun still shone with full force, much of the brightness had vanished from the day. She could not understand it, nor why she was not more pleased at having convinced him that she was just as vain and stupid as Maude could ever be.

chapter 11

J emmy joined her again before they entered Dunforth, a pretty little village nestled into the enfolding arms of the hills. Clattering over the wooden bridge and past the miller's wheel, Alyson found herself in what could have been the twin of the place where her childhood was spent.

The rhythmic clanging of the blacksmith's hammer was carried on a breeze fragrant with the scent of baking bread. Neat thatched cottages surrounded the village green, where a group of children played the same counting games Alyson had played as a child. They stopped as she and Jemmy rode past, staring curiously.

"God's greetings to ye, m'lord, m'lady," a stout man said as they dismounted before the finest house in the village, a two-storied structure of wood and stone.

"And to you, Master Johnson," Jemmy answered. "Maude, may I present Master Johnson, headman of Dunforth."

Alyson inclined her head as the older man bowed.

"It's been a long time . . ." Jemmy said, glancing about the green with a smile.

"Aye, and that it has," Johnson answered cheerfully. "Ye've grown a bit from the lad who used to chase my prize bull! M'lady," he added, turning to Alyson. "Your husband was a rare one as a boy—no fear in him at all! Said he'd read how the men in Spain would fight the bulls and took the fancy to try it for himself. Such a notion! As if anyone would be so foolish!" Johnson laughed.

"And yet they do," Jemmy answered, a momentary shadow passing across his face. "I've seen it for myself."

"Well, we won't have such outlandish goings-on hereabouts," Johnson said stoutly.

"No, indeed," Jemmy said. "And my father quite agreed with you on that score."

"Och, lad, did he whip ye?" Johnson asked. "Well, 'tis no more than I'd do for me own, and ye seem none the worse for it. 'Tis a pity the same can't be said o' old Angus," he added with a wink to Alyson. "That bull never was the same, I vow! He dinna ken what ye were up to— he'd never read of yon Spanish laddies and their ways! 'Tis a wonder we didn't take your dead body from his pen," he finished, wiping his brow with an exaggerated grimace of horror. "The fright o' my life, ye gave me, but there, it's all over and done with long ago."

"Come inside and meet Mistress Johnson again—she's all in a dither," he said confidentially to Alyson as they walked across the yard. "Been in a rare frenzy o' cleanin' and scrubbin' and what not these past days . . ."

The house smelled deliciously of fresh bread and roasting meat. Alyson was careful to keep herself from showing any of the pleasure she felt as they sat down to the meal.

There was roast capon and lamb and fresh-baked bread, with sweet butter and all the heather honey Alyson could ask for, washed down with mugs of warm, rich ale. She ate with such good appetite that Mistress Johnson's anxiety

about her table was allayed. As the atmosphere grew easier, Alyson listened with interest to the talk of the women
seated near her.

They spoke of comforting, familiar things, of broody
hens and wayward children and the way that linen should
be bleached. Though Alyson did not venture to speak, she
was much on Mistress Johnson's side as that lady argued
in favor of tansy as the most effective deterrent of moths,
agreeing fully that while lavender might be more pleasing
to the senses, it simply would not do the job.

So caught up was she in the discussion that she had almost forgotten about Jemmy, until she chanced to look
across the table. Johnson had unloosed his girdle and was
sitting at his ease, holding forth on the wisdom of putting
sheep in the low pasture, while another man, much older,
shook his head and dourly predicted foot rot as the least of
the evils to be expected from such a daring plan. They both
appealed to Jemmy, who had been turned from them, staring out the window, and he started from his thoughts. His
face was pale, and beads of perspiration stood upon his
brow, though the room was pleasantly cool.

"What? Oh, the sheep," he said distractedly. "Why not
try a few and see how they get on?"

"Aye," Johnson said, shooting him a keen glance. "We
will."

Jemmy stood abruptly. "Excuse me," he said, and
walked out of the room.

When he had gone Master Johnson looked at Alyson
and she smiled with a shrug, wondering if Jemmy had suddenly taken ill. The headman tried first one subject, then
another, but the easy mood was shattered. At last the entire
table sat in silence.

Master Johnson stood. "Will ye come to the green, my
lady?" he asked. "The children would sing and dance for
ye if ye like."

"Yes, thank you," Alyson said quickly, following him

outside. Jemmy stood at the edge of the green, one hand resting against a sturdy oak. When Alyson reached him she saw the color had returned to his cheeks, though his expression was dark and shut as he stared out over the hills.

"Are you ill?" Alyson asked.

"No."

"Oh, good," she said nervously, wondering what had caused this sudden change in temper. "The children are going to sing now."

"Go along. I'll be there presently."

Alyson left him and took the seat Master Johnson offered. Once the singing and dancing began, she dismissed Jemmy's mood with an inward shrug and settled back to enjoy the entertainment. The children were so dear, and one little boy reminded her of Robin. He had golden curls and a sweet mouth, and he sang the songs that she had taught to Robin in a high, pure voice that was very like her brother's.

As the next song began a woman standing at her elbow spoke in a low, rapid voice, meant for her ear alone.

"M'lady," the woman said with a nervous smile, bobbing her head respectfully. "If I could hae a moment of yer time—I dinna mean to keep ye long."

"Of course," Alyson answered graciously.

"It's about Tavis—that's my husband. Oh, lady, could ye but talk to yer lord and ask him to show mercy?"

"Mercy?" Alyson repeated. "What has your husband done, Mistress?"

"It wasna Tavis' fault, lady, not really. 'Tis only that he dotes so on our Bobbie. He's our only child, ye see, since his brother was killed in the fighting two years ago. Bobbie's a good boy, m'lady, and meant no harm at all. He only wanted to see the horse—he loves the animals, ye ken, and wouldna hurt it for all the world. But Sir Calder dinna see it so—"

She stopped to catch her breath. "Slowly," Alyson said. "Take your time. I'm listening."

"Bobbie shouldna have touched the horse. I ken that. But still, there was no cause for Sir Calder to beat him as he did. He's just a bairn. And when Tavis—that's my husband—saw them, he just lost his head. Before God, he never meant to hurt the knight and he didn't, lady, he but clouted him across the face. 'Twas only to make him stop, ye ken. And now—now my Bobbie's still abed and they don't know if he'll be right again—and his father to be hanged for it! I don't know where we'll turn, before God I don't know, and I was hopin', of your mercy, ye might ask your lord—"

"There he is now," Alyson said, putting a hand on the woman's arm as Jemmy took a seat on Master Johnson's other side. "It might be better if you asked him yourself."

"Oh, no, lady, I daren't. But he'll listen to ye," the woman answered, wiping her eyes and trying to smile. "Ye've been wed so short a time—and ye so fair," she added wistfully. "For sure he'll heed ye if ye ask."

She looked over Alyson's shoulder and quickly pulled her shawl close around her face. "God bless ye," she added hastily before melting back into the crowd.

"My lady," Johnson said, half rising from his seat and glaring in the direction the woman had taken. "Has she been troublin' ye?"

"No, no, not at all," Alyson said quickly. "She but told me of her husband."

"Aye." He sat down again and breathed out a gusty sigh. "A bad business, that. Tavis is a good shepherd and a fine man—'twill be a shame to lose him."

"Do you expect to lose him?" Alyson asked.

"He struck a knight," Johnson said shortly. " 'Tis a hangin' offense, m'lady, no matter what the cause. If ye *could* have a word with your lord—but come, let us not dwell on such unchancy matters—look, now, wee Ewan is to sing a song."

Alyson nodded and smiled, but she did not hear a word of Ewan's song. Her thoughts were on the fate of Tavis and his family. Of course the shepherd had defended his son—what more just, more natural? And all the boy had done was to touch the knight's horse!

But the knight had the power to correct the boy in any manner he chose—even if he'd killed him there would be no serious penalty. He might pay something to the family—or then again, he might not, depending on the will of his overlord. But once a commoner dared lift his hand to a knight, his fate was sealed.

She glanced at Jemmy, wondering what he would do. Ever since they had finished supper he'd been in a foul mood, which boded ill for Tavis and his family. Nobles, in Alyson's experience, were far too apt to take their temper out upon their subjects. If the shepherd had struck one of Darnley's knights, he would be swinging from the nearest tree by nightfall.

Wee Ewan finished his song and bowed to scattered applause. Master Johnson stood and stretched.

"Well, then, that's that," he said. "And now to other matters."

Jemmy stood as well. "Yes. Let's get to it. My lady," he added, turning to Alyson. "I'll stay the night here and ride back tomorrow or the next day. Sir Donal will see you home."

"Wait, my lord," she said. "I'd like a word with you first."

"What is it, lady?" Jemmy asked impatiently. "I've much to do this afternoon."

"I wanted to ask you something," Alyson said, glancing about at the crowded green. "Alone."

Jemmy walked with her to the oak tree on the edge of the common. "Well?" he demanded. "What is it?"

This was a bad beginning, Alyson thought. Yet it must be done now or not at all.

"It's about a man named Tavis," she began. "A villager."

"What about him?"

"Apparently he struck one of your father's knights."

"And?" Jemmy asked, lifting one dark brow. "What has that to do with you?"

I have to get this right, Alyson thought. How does Maude manage it so everyone scrambles to do her bidding?

"I want you to spare his life," she ordered firmly.

"Oh, I see," Jemmy said, his eyes glinting with a dangerous amusement. "So you've decided the matter, have you? Well, that's a relief! Here I thought I'd be spending the afternoon holding court, sorting through the villagers' stories, weighing all the facts—but now there's no need for that. Lady Maude has already rendered judgment!"

"I did hear the story," Alyson snapped.

He leaned back against the tree and studied her through narrowed eyes. "Do you think I believe for one moment that you care what happens to a shepherd of Dunforth village? Come, Maude, I'm not a fool. This has nothing to do with him and we both know it. You want to call the tune and watch me dance, but it isn't going to happen. Now go home and let me tend to my affairs."

"This has everything to do with Tavis," she said tightly. "I promised his wife that I would ask—"

"But you didn't, did you? You haven't asked me anything. You simply told me what you wanted done."

"You are being very childish, my lord," Alyson said, fists clenched at her sides. "The way in which I asked you is not the issue here."

"Oh, but it is. It is very much the issue. And do you know *why* it is the issue?"

"No, my lord, I do not know. Nor do I care."

He grasped her wrist and pulled her close. "Because I have *said* it is. Just as *I* will say what becomes of the shepherd."

Alyson's mind raced as she tried to find a way to save the situation. How had she mishandled this so badly? But maybe it wasn't too late to still help Tavis. If she asked Jemmy sweetly, humbly . . .

His eyes held no amusement now. They were bright and hot, shooting sparks of anger. The soft words Alyson had been about to speak were swallowed in an answering flash of rage. How dare he try to frighten her? Especially when he was so completely in the wrong!

"Oh, I understand! All right, then, what was it you *wanted* me to say? Oh, please, my gentle lord, I beg you to give justice? Why *should* I beg for that? Why should any of them beg for what is their right? It is your duty to give them justice!"

"There's no question of begging," he said shortly.

"Oh, isn't there? That's not what Tavis' wife thought. And Master Johnson. Both of them asked me to speak to you—"

"They seem to have made an unfortunate choice."

"Aye, they did," she said, tears of anger and frustration starting to her eyes. "But I hope—I ask—that you don't let anything I might have said—"

"God's blood, what do you take me for? Do you think I'd hang the man on a whim?"

"I don't know," she answered honestly. "If you wanted to there's no one who could stop you."

"Save you," he pointed out, a hint of amusement showing at the corners of his eyes.

"Aye, well, I've made a sorry job of it."

"Oh, I don't know about that," he said slowly. "Considering that you think I'm the kind of man who might hang one of my own subjects for amusement, I'm rather surprised you dared to asked at all."

He glanced down at her hand, still held fast within his grasp, and released it, his fingers trailing over the delicate bones of her wrist. She felt the light touch race through her entire body.

"I'm sorry," he said. "Did I hurt you?"

"No, my lord," she said, suddenly a little breathless. "But we were talking of the shepherd—"

"We were talking about justice," he corrected. "And you were explaining my duty to my people."

She felt herself begin to flush. "I'm sure you are aware of your duty—"

"Are you? You didn't seem at all sure a moment ago. But I'm afraid there's no time now for you to instruct me properly in the subject. So perhaps instead we can strike a bargain."

"What sort of bargain?" she said suspiciously.

"I'll promise to give the shepherd a fair hearing. I can't promise more until I've heard the full tale, but I'll show whatever mercy I can."

"And in return?"

Like summer lightning it flashed across his face, the charming, merry smile that had the power to muddle all her thoughts and set her pulses leaping.

"Do not ever mention the word 'London' to me again. No Princess Joan, no tournaments—and please, for God's sweet sake, no more Bohemian headdresses. Do you think that you can do that?"

She would have to be more careful around him, she thought, biting her lips against the startled laughter struggling to escape. He'd surprised her yet again.

"Yes, my lord," she said. "I can try."

"Then it's a bargain." He put one finger beneath her chin and lifted her face to his. His smile vanished as he stared into her eyes. "But it must be sealed," he said softly.

"I—I—" she began, then stopped. There would be no point in angering him now and losing all she'd gained, she thought, knowing she was lying. It wasn't for Tavis' sake that she swayed forward, one hand moving to touch his cheek.

Jemmy leaned down and brushed her mouth with his. She accepted the kiss shyly, with closed lips and open eyes, and desire slashed though him with a force that took him by surprise. His hand moved gently along her jaw to cup her head, and he slipped the other arm about her waist, bending to her again. Her eyes fell shut and she tipped her face to his.

"My lady, are you ready to go?"

Alyson jumped back at the sound of Sir Donal's voice.

"Yes," she said, her voice shaking. "I'm ready."

Jemmy released her. "Guard her well, Donal."

"Aye, my lord," the young knight answered proudly.

As Alyson mounted she looked back. Jemmy leaned against the oak, his face in shadow. But as she set heels to her horse, she thought she saw his teeth gleam in a smile.

chapter 12

The next afternoon Alyson peered cautiously through the garden gate. Once she was certain there was no one within, she stepped inside and looked about with mingled admiration and dismay. Oh, what a pity that such a lovely place had been let to go to ruin!

Sheltered by the castle buttresses on either side, the garden faced southwest. Heavy bars of golden sunlight fell across the weed-choked beds of flowers and lay bright upon the overgrown expanse of lawn. Someone had obviously planned this place with loving care, but it had been years since it was tended properly. She had passed the kitchen garden on her way, filled with tidy rows of herbs and vegetables—though not so tidy as her own kitchen garden at Aylsford—but this place was made for a lady's leisure hours.

Had Lady Kirallen come here? Had she sat sewing while her two sons played on the soft grass at her side? Alyson almost imagined she could hear the sound of childish laughter and a woman's soft voice bidding them to mind their manners.

But Ravenspur had no lady now. The Laird's wife had died years before and the other lady, Ian's wife, had died as well, in childbed. Oh, Alyson was certain that she could make this bloom again—she cut that thought off immediately. Her stay here would be as short as possible, and she had no business worrying about the gardens or anything else that belonged to the Kirallens. She wandered about, stopping now and then to pluck a blossom and inhale its fragrance.

"What are ye doing here?"

She started guiltily, the flowers falling from her hands.

"You again!" she said, relief sweeping over her as she met the bright blue eyes of Jemmy's nephew, Malcolm. "Do you have naught to do but hide in corners and frighten people half to death?"

"I wasna hiding in a corner," Malcolm answered with an injured air. "These are my gardens."

"Yours, are they? I rather thought they were the Laird's."

"So I shall be—one day. Or should have been," he added, brows drawing together in a scowl that sat ill upon one so young. "Before your father . . . Damn him!" he burst out. "Murdering bastard! I hate him! One day I will kill him."

Alyson regarded him seriously. "I don't blame you for hating my father. Sometimes," she added very low, "I hate him myself."

She could see that she'd surprised him. "Why?" he demanded.

"It was wrong of him to kill your father. It was wicked. I think he's done many wicked things."

"Do ye now?" He considered this seriously. "But ye shouldn't be saying that, should ye? What with ye being his daughter and all."

She shrugged. "Why not? It's the truth. And that," she added sternly, "is just between the two of us. Can I trust you?"

"Of course!" He clasped his hands behind his back and looked her over. "I don't think you're a pawky, stuck-up bitch," he said at last. "That's what they say, ye know."

She ignored the challenge in his words and answered mildly, "Do they? And what do they say of you?"

His eyes gleamed. "They say I'm the devil's own," he answered proudly. "They say they've never seen such a wild boy as me."

Alyson resisted the impulse to laugh. "Oh dear. What exactly is it that makes you so wild?"

"Well," he began confidentially, glancing about the garden. "I'm not. Oh, I did put the frog in Annie's bed and she went all to pieces—but Annie's a bit simple even at the best of times. And I don't like my lessons, that much is the truth, it's no good pretendin' that I do. But Father always said he dinna care much for lessoning himself, and he used to let me ride out with him instead. Now Uncle Jemmy's back, *he* says I have to mind my tutor but I dinna care. *I'm* not afraid o' him."

"Afraid of him? Why should you be?"

"They say," Malcolm said, leaning close and dropping his voice to a whisper, "that he'll be trying to do away with me. Aye," he nodded wisely. " 'Tis true. For he cannot afford to keep me about. My father was the Young Laird, and there's them that think the honor should have gone to me— not to my uncle. I've no doubt he'll murder me soon," he finished with satisfaction.

"Wherever did you get such an idea?" Alyson asked, chilled at this calm discussion of his own death.

"Alistair said so," he answered at once. "Alistair says that Uncle Jemmy's not fit to be the Young Laird, not after he ran off and left us all those years ago. He says that Uncle Jemmy doesn't know anything about us or the way

things ought to be. And he thinks it was a shameful thing
for my uncle to marry ye. Have ye no' met him yet?"

Alyson nodded, remembering the man who'd watched
her during the wedding feast with eyes as hard as granite.

"Well," Malcolm continued, "Alistair was my father's
foster brother. Father used to say that Alistair was even
better than a real brother, because he'd never leave him
like Uncle Jemmy did."

The boy scuffed one toe in the grass. "But ever since
my father died, Grandfather and Alistair are always shouting at each other. I dinna understand it. Alistair is *kin*—but
now Grandfather says he's a dreadful troublemaker. But *I*
still like him. Just as my father did."

"You miss your father, don't you?" Alyson said quietly.

"Ah, well," he said, turning from her. "He died a hero's
death, ye know. And I'm very big now, nearly twelve.
That's far too old to be crying for my father."

"Does Alistair say that, too?" she asked sharply.

"Oh, everyone says that! They all say how brave I've
been."

"I don't think that's brave. I think that you should cry
for him—even the heroes in the old tales wept when one of
their companions fell in battle."

"They did?"

"Of course they did," she said, wondering if it was the
truth. Well, if it wasn't, she reasoned, it should be.
"There's no shame in it, none at all."

He was silent for a long time, then at last sighed and
wiped his hand across his eyes. "Can ye catch a ball?" he
asked suddenly.

"If it's not thrown too hard, I can. But you look as
though you might throw very hard indeed."

"Oh, aye. Harder than any of the others. Do ye want to
try?"

"I really shouldn't—" His face fell and she added
quickly, "For just a short time, then. I have things to do."

They threw the ball back and forth among the flowers and soon Alyson's cheeks were glowing from the exercise.

"You're none so bad—for a lass," Malcolm admitted at last. "But catch this one!"

The ball flew over her head. Alyson searched for it among a thick bank of weeds growing beside the castle walls. She crawled about, then reached a small doorway overhung with flowers. Stepping inside, she found herself in a small room. She ran her hands over the dusty shelf that stretched the length of one wall, looking curiously at the dessicated herbs hanging from the ceiling among a tangle of cobwebs. There were other shelves, as well, some of slatted wood meant for drying herbs, others that held small jars and bottles. A mortar and pestle stood overturned in one shadowed corner.

"This was my grandmother's room."

Malcolm stood beside her.

"Doesn't anyone use it now?"

Malcolm shook his head. "Not since my mother—" he looked down and swallowed hard. "She used to come here sometimes. But no one does now."

"What a shame," Alyson said, picking up a small bottle and pulling the stopper. Whatever it had held was dried now, but the faint scent of chamomile rose from within.

"Do you know about . . . well, herbs and things?" Malcolm asked.

"A little. Not as much as I'd like."

Alyson replaced the bottle and wiped dusty hands on her skirt. "Here," she said, stooping. "I found your ball."

They stepped outside. "It's late," Alyson said with some surprise.

"Aye. I've missed my lesson. Conal will be furious," he said with a satisfied grin. "But now I have to bathe and change before I go to the hall. You, too," he added. "You've got cobwebs in your hair. And dust, just here—" He reached up and touched her cheek, then snatched his hand away, blushing. "I'd best be off," he said gruffly, then turned and ran from the garden.

She followed him more slowly, her spirits falling as she reflected that this had been a mistake. It would be far too easy to grow fond of Malcolm, who was blameless in this whole damnable mess. Poor boy, with no mother and his father so lately dead, what would become of him if he lost both his grandfather and uncle? But at least he'd be alive, she reminded herself grimly. And that's more than Robin would be if she failed.

When she reached the garden gate a man stepped into her path. He was powerfully built, his broad shoulders straining the plain wool tunic he wore beneath the Kirallen tartan.

"My lady," he said with a bow so flourishing she wondered if he was mocking her. "We've met already. Do you remember?"

"You're . . . Sir Alistair?"

"I am." He leaned casually against the wall, blocking her path. "How do ye find Ravenspur? Not what ye are used to?"

"No." She made to walk past him, but he did not move.

"I don't doubt we could all benefit from a . . . lady's touch," he said slowly, smiling in a manner she did not like at all. She was suddenly conscious of the isolation of the garden; the high walls that had seemed so friendly were menacing now, cutting her off from any hope of assistance. When a dove called from among the branches, its plaintive cry accentuated the heavy silence.

"Please excuse me," she said. "I really must be going."

"Oh, not yet. Why, we've hardly had a chance to get acquent."

She stared into his wintry eyes and all at once she was reminded of Sym, a stable lad at Aylsford Manor, who had tried several times to get her alone. She'd been frightened of Sym, as well, back in the beginning. But she'd learned to handle him.

"Get out of my way, Sir Alistair," she said firmly. "Stand back from there and let me pass."

"In a moment," he said, his eyes moving over her with lazy insolence. "There's one or two things I'd like to tell ye first."

"I've no wish to listen to anything you might say—not until you let me by." She brought her foot down hard upon his instep, forgetting she wore a lady's slipper and not the wood-soled shoe she was accustomed to.

His hand shot out and grasped her arm. "Ah, lady, this isn't England. And I'm not your husband to be so easily put off. Ye listen to me an' listen well, for a mistake's been made and I mean to set it right. The Laird is—God help him, he's not the man he was. And as for his son—" he laughed. "Jemmy's no' the man to hold this clan together—not now, not after what he's done to us. He actually thinks that we'il bow our head to a Darnley—"

His eyes went over her again and he smiled mirthlessly, "But then, he's no proper man at all, is he?"

"Let go of me," she said and now she was afraid in truth, for his eyes were blazing with cold anger and his hand was hard as steel upon her arm. Without giving herself time to think, she brought her free hand up and struck him across the face. His grasp loosened and she pushed past him, then forgetting all Lady Maude's careful teachings, she picked up her skirts and ran across the grass.

*O*nce Alyson reached the kitchen garden she stopped, for there was no sound of pursuit. She should go directly to her chamber, she knew, and shut herself inside, but that would be dangerous folly. Celia would be there, and Maggie, and perhaps dour Mistress Selton or poor widowed Edina, and she simply could not face them as she was, shaking, shaken, and all too close to tears. No, she must keep well away from watchful eyes until she had gathered her wits about her once again.

Here there was no one to see her distress save an elderly gardener who knelt among the rows and had not noticed Alyson's approach. She crept to the far side of the low stone wall and sat down in a patch of sunlight.

From here she could see the hills beyond, dotted with white sheep, and could hear the muted bleating of the new spring lambs. Bees droned steadily among the flowering hedges. It was an ordinary spring day upon its surface, as calm as the millpond glinting at the foot of the hills. But like a stone cast into water, Alyson's arrival had shattered life at Ravenspur.

The scent of new-turned earth was sweet beneath the beating sun. As its warmth sank into her skin, her conversation with Sir Alistair began to seem unreal, as though it had happened long ago to someone else. Well, it had happened to someone else, she thought drowsily. To Maude. She wondered what Maude was doing just now—walking in the Aylsford garden, she thought, her eyes falling shut, or hawking by the river . . .

The shadows had grown long when Alyson awoke. The gardener was gone. She sat up and rubbed her eyes, yawning, but her jaw snapped shut when she spotted the figure perched cross-legged on the low stone wall beside her.

Perhaps twenty years old, he was so like Jemmy that she knew at once they must be kin. Curling dark hair fell loose about his face, accentuating the stark pallor of his skin.

"Did ye have a good rest?" he asked, his voice low and soft and rippling with amusement.

She got quickly to her feet.

"Yes," she answered shortly.

"Good. Ye need to gather up your strength. It won't do to let down your guard with Alistair about."

She meant to walk away, but something in his eyes halted her. Dark and luminous, they shone in his pale face with an intensity that drew and held her gaze. Though she did not mean to speak, the words slipped from her lips.

"He frightens me," she said.

"Ye do well to be ware of him. He's no' an evil man, ye ken, but he's a danger to ye just the same. He sees further than most—or did, poor wight. His sight is clouded now," he added with a sad shake of his head. Then he glanced at her and smiled faintly. "But in your place, I wouldna count on that."

"Whatever do you mean?" Alyson asked uneasily, casting a quick look behind her. The door was perhaps ten paces away, set deep into the castle wall. She began to edge toward it, keeping a wary eye upon the stranger.

"Ye bide close to Jemmy. He's keeping his own secrets, but for all that ye can trust him." Her disbelief must have shown upon her face, for he smiled a bit more broadly. And so potent was his charm that against all reason, Alyson smiled in response, even as she moved another step away, her hand reaching behind her to fasten on the latch.

"Ye are a braw lassie," he said approvingly. "Ye will have to be very strong—aye, and very brave. But I think that ye can stay the course. Just remember that things—and people—are not always as they seem. Can ye do that, Alyson?"

"Yes," she answered quickly, turning with relief toward the door. "Thank you."

She had just twisted the latch when the significance of his last word reached her. She turned sharply, but the wall was empty now. Running back, she searched the other side, but he was not there. He could not have vanished into the manor. There had been no time for that. She stood bewildered, turning slowly round. The last sunlight fell upon the garden and the field beyond, without a single rock or tree behind which a man could conceal himself from sight.

But though Alyson stared until her eyes ached, not a living creature could she see.

It was a dream, Alyson decided as she opened the door of her chamber. It must have been. People don't just vanish into nothing! And when she looked at the whole thing calmly, what had he told her that she did not already know? To keep her guard up? To be wary of Sir Alistair? He had done no more than echo her own thoughts and fears. As for his advice to trust Jemmy—well, there was no mystery to that! Wishful thinking, nothing more.

She shut the door and leaned her back against the stout wood with a deep sigh of relief. Maggie, kneeling by the hearth, looked up questioningly.

"Are ye all right, lady? Ye look awfully pale! Did somethin' afright ye?"

Where to begin? Alyson thought, and felt a bubble of laughter—or was it tears?—rising in her throat.

"I—I met Sir Alistair in the garden," she answered, sitting down in the deep chair by the fire. She would not mention that other meeting—not now, not ever. The more she thought of it, the less real it seemed. And she had far more than dreams to worry about now.

"Och, and did ye now? And what's that rapscallion been up to? He dinna hurt ye, did he?" Maggie added, her voice sharpening as she studied Alyson's face.

"No. But he said—I suppose he said what every one of you are thinking."

Maggie sank back on her heels. "What many are thinking," she amended. "Not all."

She brushed her hands together, staring down into her lap. "There's not one of us hasn't been touched by the fighting," she said slowly. "Alistair lost his father when he was just a bairn. He's been fighting since he was old enough to hold a sword. It's all he knows—and it's the same for most o' the men. But then there's others . . . The farmers want it to be over, the shepherds and the drovers, they're weary of seein' their fields trampled, their stock scattered, their sons sent out to fight. War's no' such a glorious venture for the common folk, lady."

Alyson nodded, thinking that Maggie couldn't possibly guess how sincerely she agreed.

"Not that Alistair would be concerned with that," Maggie snorted. "But—but I think Master Jemmy sees how it is for us. There's more than a few of us who are grateful for the sacri—"

She broke off, her round face flushing.

"The sacrifice he's made?" Alyson finished with a wry smile. "Aye. I see."

"No offense meant, my lady," Maggie added quickly. "I'll go heat the water, shall I? There's just time for a bath 'ere supper."

Alyson wandered restlessly about her chamber when Maggie had gone, finally settling on the window seat and plucking at her lute.

This was none of her affair, she reminded herself sharply. She was just one of the common folk Maggie had spoken of, helpless against the orders of her betters. Another fortnight or two and it would all be over.

And then, she thought, staring blindly out the window, the entire clan would know how shamefully Jemmy had been deceived. How Alistair would gloat! *He* would be glad to take up the fight again and see this false peace utterly destroyed, as would the men who followed him.

For the first time Alyson realized how difficult this must be for Jemmy. "He's no proper man at all," Alistair had sneered, but Alistair was wrong. It took courage for Jemmy to stand against them all with no support but that of his ailing father. He acted in the interests of his clan—

even the common people in his care. Which made him, Alyson reflected sadly, the first noble she had met who considered common people worth a thought.

Which was precisely why, if she told him the truth, he'd have no choice but to prepare for battle. Lord Darnley would find out and then Robin . . . She remembered Darnley running one finger across his throat and shuddered. She couldn't do it. No matter how wrong it was, she could not order Robin's death.

Oh, this was all beyond her, she decided wearily, rubbing her throbbing temples. Let the priests and nobles debate the fine points of the issue and God decide the outcome. She only wanted to save her brother's life.

As she did every morning and every night, she dropped to her knees and uttered a fervent prayer for Robin's safety. Then her eyes fell shut and she remembered Jemmy's kiss beneath the oak tree, wondering what would have happened if they had not been interrupted. She imagined his arms tightening around her, the warmth of his breath against her lips, the scrape of roughness against her cheek as his mouth closed over hers.

"What?" she demanded, glaring up at the ceiling. "What is it you want of me, God? Can you not even give me a hint? Is that so much to ask—just a bit of guidance?"

But when she closed her eyes all she saw was Jemmy bending to her and felt again the helpless melting of her bones.

She jumped to her feet.

"Don't think of that," she said aloud. "It doesn't matter, it meant nothing to him. Think of Robin. Please, God, help me remember Robin." She stopped, her throat tightening, as a terrible shaft of doubt shot through her. For a moment she stood on the edge of an abyss, staring into emptiness.

"I do believe," she cried, casting a pleading look toward the ceiling. "I do. Thy will be done." She bent her head

chapter 13

A s always, Alyson approached the high table with her
stomach twisted into a knot of apprehension. Alistair
was seated at the Laird's left hand. In Jemmy's absence,
Alyson took his accustomed seat on the Laird's right.
Malcolm was already in his place beside her empty chair.
The boy nodded as she approached but wouldn't meet her
eye. She guessed that Alistair had had some sharp words
for him after they'd left the garden.

When she was seated, Alistair caught her eye and
smiled slowly, raising his goblet in a mock salute. Lord
Kirallen shot him a suspicious glance, the lines deepening
on either side of his mouth. Alyson raised her own goblet
in acknowledgment of Alistair's gesture, smiling as graciously as if he'd given her a compliment instead of the intended challenge. The Laird relaxed slightly, though he
still frowned in Alistair's direction.

Malcolm had said that since Ian's death, the Laird had
been at odds with Alistair, naming him a troublemaker. But

Alyson knew that wasn't quite the truth. The trouble had been made by Lord Darnley, not Sir Alistair. Every one of the knight's suspicions was well-founded. It was just his bad luck—and her good fortune—that the Laird was not inclined to listen to him.

"We'll be leaving soon," Kirallen said suddenly to Alyson, turning his back to Alistair. The knight stiffened slightly at the insult, and Malcolm looked from his grandfather to his friend, his bright eyes troubled. He doesn't miss a thing, Alyson thought. Children never do.

"And I'll be glad enough to see my kin again," the Laird continued. "We'll have a merry time; the gathering is always such fun for young people. And the journey will do ye good, I'm sure."

He sighed, toying with his meat, then laid his knife down and looked at her directly. "I ken it hasn't been easy for ye, being here among us," he continued in a low voice. "And as for Jemmy . . . ye must understand that it isn't easy for him either, coming back again."

His eyes moved briefly toward Alistair and back to Alyson's face. "Do you know," he added lightly, obviously trying to dispel the tension at the table. "Jemmy was only nine when he said he would go to sea, and I never doubted he would do it. He always did whatever he set his mind to. If it was forbidden he took his punishment without complaint—but then he'd do the same again if he saw a reason for it."

"Did ye whip him, Grandsire?" Malcolm put in curiously.

The Laird smiled at his grandson. "Aye, Malcolm, that I did. Just as I'd whip you if you were to disobey me."

The boy rubbed his backside with a rueful grin. "As ye have before. But," he added to Alyson, "I dinna take it without complaint."

"No, you complained at great length, as I remember,"

the Laird said dryly. "And at great volume. Just as your father used to do."

He added the last in a low voice, his gaze resting with mingled pride and sorrow on his grandson. "Ah, Alistair, he's so like Ian," he said softly.

For that moment all differences were forgotten as Ian's son, his father, and his friend were united in their grief.

At Aylsford Manor they had spoken of Ian Kirallen as one would speak of the devil himself. He was a cold-blooded murderer, a thief, and a coward—or so the stories went. But watching the men's faces, Alyson knew that whatever else Ian Kirallen might have been, he had been greatly loved by those who knew him best.

The Laird spoke into the silence. "Now, Jemmy never even bothered trying to escape a whipping," he said deliberately. "Alistair, do ye remember the time he went after the tinker's lad over that animal—what was it, now? A stray dog?"

The moment of unity was shattered. "Nay, Laird," Alistair said, his expression hardening. "I dinna recall it. Please excuse me."

He stood and looked toward the corner of the hall where Kirallen's knights were seated. The table instantly went still. Alistair jerked his chin toward the door, and most of the men leaped to their feet, abandoning their half-eaten meals as they followed him from the hall.

The few knights who remained looked uneasily at the Laird. He picked up his goblet and sipped slowly, his face revealing nothing of his thoughts.

Malcolm stuffed a piece of bread in his mouth and stood. "I'm done," he said. "May I have your leave to go?"

How much did Malcolm understand of what had just happened? Alyson wondered. Had he recognized Alistair's challenge for what it was? She expected the Laird to order the boy back to his seat, but the old man only sighed.

"Aye, Malcolm," he said. "You have my leave.

"I should forbid it," he said, staring after Malcolm. "Alistair's no good for him the now. But the boy loves him well, as did his father . . . his father . . ."

His shoulders slumped, and he passed a hand across his eyes. " 'Tis all my fault," he murmured through lips gone suddenly pale. "I should have seen it—done something— or did I do too much?"

"My lord," Alyson said, alarmed at his pallor. "You're not well."

"Nay, daughter, I am not. I fear—no, I canna say it. I *willna* say it—"

"Please, my lord," Alyson said, as his words trailed off. "Don't upset yourself this way. Please. You must go and rest."

He levered himself upright, leaning heavily on the table. "Aye. I'll rest. Thank you, daughter. 'Tis kind of you to worry, but no need."

When he was gone Alyson went back to her chamber, where Celia and Maggie waited to help her into bed. Once she was undressed, Maggie went off but Celia stayed behind.

"Well, my lady," the serving girl said with the mocking inflection she always used when giving Alyson the title. "Did ye manage to learn anything useful yet?"

Alyson shook her head without answering. Oh, she'd learned much, but none of it would interest Darnley in the slightest. In fact, he would be enraged if she told him what exactly she *had* learned about his victory over Lord Ian. Lies, lies—was there no end to the lies her father told?

"Well, ye can tell him yourself tomorrow," Celia said.

"Tomorrow?"

"He'll be waiting at the river just after dawn. I had word today."

"Who gave you word, Celia?" Alyson asked, but Celia only shook her head.

"That's nae for ye to know. Just remember," she added darkly. "I'm not the only one watching ye."

The next morning Alyson rose early and dressed for riding. Her women were startled, but she stopped their questions with a single look. One of them said that she supposed she'd have to go along, but when Alyson said that Celia would do quite well, the woman agreed with unflattering alacrity.

Celia led her to the meeting place, a small meadow by the rushing Tweed. They were early but Darnley was there before them. The nobleman wasted no time in greeting her or inquiring how she fared.

"Well?" he demanded. "Do they suspect you?"

"No."

He grunted. "See that they don't. What about Kirallen and his son? Where do they ride and when?"

"I can't say, my lord."

"Damn you, girl, I thought you'd have learned something of their habits!"

"It's very soon," Alyson said. "No one really knows me yet . . ."

"I'll give you another week. I'll meet you here then and by God, you'd better have some news for me or—"

"My lord, I won't be here in a week. There's to be some sort of gathering in the hills."

"Gathering?" he said sharply. "How many are to go?"

"About half the men, I think, and most of the women. My lord," she added hesitantly as he swung himself into his saddle. "Please, how is my brother?"

"I suppose he's well. Robert's looking after him. But it's up to you to see he stays that way. Do you understand me?"

"Yes, my lord. Could I see him next time you come?"

Darnley jerked the reins sharply. "Perhaps. I'll see."

chapter 14

When Alyson returned, she found her ladies busily packing her belongings. Their mood was bright, and despite her own worries Alyson caught a faint echo of the excitement.

It would be easier to lose herself among a crowd than it was here at Ravenspur, she thought. And just the idea of a journey made the blood move more swiftly in her veins. The afternoon passed pleasantly as they decided what to pack for the tenday they'd be gone.

Maggie hung about, obviously waiting to speak, and when they were alone she said frankly, "Are ye thinkin' to take Celia, my lady? For I think she'd do better to bide here."

Alyson knew that Celia was as little liked among the women as she was herself. But none of them could begin to match Alyson's own loathing for her maid. Though a simple dairy maid, Celia had shared Lord Darnley's bed, and that small taste of power had gone straight to her yellow head. Whenever they were alone she would drop all pretense of service, and her condescending manner grated sharply on Alyson's nerves.

"Do you think so?" Alyson murmured, bowing her head to hide the satisfaction in her eyes. "Then by all means, let's leave her behind."

Her pleasure in the small victory vanished, though, as she sat down to supper and Jemmy walked into the hall. Still dusty from the road, he took his seat with only a nod in Alyson's direction, then turned to his father.

"And how did you find Dunforth?" Kirallen asked.

"All's well," Jemmy replied, filling his mug with ale. He drank deeply and set it down before continuing. "There's no foot rot among the sheep, no murrain on the cattle or fever in the swine. The crops are growing. Oh, and there were twins born yesterday," he finished, his lips twisted in a smile. "They say that's a good sign." He pushed his trencher aside and slumped in his seat, reaching to fill his mug again.

What he didn't say was that the villagers were delighted with the peace—and him. From them there was no talk of dishonor, but rising excitement that they might sow a crop and reap it without soldiers trampling their fields. They were glad that Jemmy had come home again, surprised and grateful that he'd held court himself instead of sending one of his knights to do it for him. They actually believed he cared about them and their concerns. He could only imagine what they'd think when he left again, this time for good.

"Jemmy—" Kirallen began unhappily.

"I'm sorry, Father," he said, running one hand through his hair. "I'm tired, that's all. I barely slept last night."

Not last night nor the one before it, either. Even now he felt his stomach tighten and the sweat spring on his brow. He had never liked to be shut up indoors, but in recent years his dislike had grown into something more, until at times he could hardly bear the confinement of four walls.

At Dunforth it had been worse than ever. Sitting in Johnson's small house with all those people crowded round—he had panicked, bolted like a frightened horse to the freedom of the open air.

Now he summoned the image of his ship, white sails against a cloudless sky. Soon, he told himself. Be calm. She's waiting for you. He breathed deeply, in and out, and little by little the urge to run began to fade, leaving him exhausted.

Maude sat quietly beside him. She had abandoned her ridiculous headgear tonight—the Bohemian headdress, he reminded himself with an inward smile—and wore instead simple cauls of golden thread, covered by a veil and golden circlet. It suited her much better, the gauzy folds fell softly around her face, accentuating her luminous blue-green eyes.

She was a bit of a puzzle, this lady who was now his wife. She had certainly surprised him during their ride. One moment she was talking about religion with a lively—and intriguing—curiosity, the next she was boring him senseless with her ridiculous chatter about King Edward's court. And then there was the way she'd defended Tavis. That had been the biggest shock of all, her bursting out with that speech about the rights of his tenants. Where did a sheltered lady get such ideas?

And the damnedest part was, he agreed with every word she said. Under Ian's rule, the knights had been given a free hand, which accounted for at least part of their fanatical loyalty to Jemmy's brother. But . . . but . . . Jemmy's mind hovered on the edge of an incredible idea.

The Kirallen knights did not have the right to behave as Sir Calder had—or at least they *shouldn't* have the right. The knights should never have been given so much power.

Jemmy instinctively tried to push the thought away, but

it returned. Ian had been wrong. Jemmy knew it was the truth, even if no one else at Ravenspur agreed, which they most certainly would not.

Ian had never looked at any side of a question but his own, and that made every decision simple. As nearly every man in the clan was exactly like him, they all thought his single-mindedness a virtue and his decisions the pinnacle of wisdom. His ability to lead men had been born in him— he'd been charming, fearless, effortlessly inspiring loyalty among his knights. He had been, Jemmy reflected wryly, a hero. *And now he is a dead hero, forever beyond reproach. While I have the misfortune to be very much alive and completely unheroic.*

Why, why couldn't he just agree with the things Ian and the others had accepted without question? Why was he so different? Twelve years had gone by but nothing had changed. He was still the outsider here, still alone in the midst of all these people who were his kin.

"My lord," Maude said hesitantly, "I wondered—the shepherd brought to trial—"

And all at once Jemmy was not entirely alone. Something *had* changed. There was one person here who would understand what he had done about the shepherd— and why.

"Oh, yes, Tavis," he said. "Well, it's a long tale—"

"Tavis?" the Laird put in anxiously, his voice rising. "Tavis the shepherd? I knew his father well. He was brought to trial? On what cause?"

"It's finished, Father," Jemmy said. "No need to concern yourself."

A burly, dark-bearded man seated at the corner of the knight's table leaned forward. "Is it Tavis o' Dunforth ye speak of?" he demanded. "I hope he hanged. He near broke my jaw, the insolent lout!"

"The matter has been settled, Sir Calder," Jemmy said.

"Tavis struck you?" the Laird said to Sir Calder. "But why?"

"I but gave a lesson to that brat o' his, Laird," the man said. "The boy was mishandling my horse."

Though the far part of the hall still bustled with talk and laughter, the knight's table fell silent as the men all looked to Alistair.

"What's this about?" Alistair said to Jemmy.

"It's nothing."

"Nothing?" Sir Calder roared. "The churl attacked me. Ye call that *nothing?*"

"One of Kirallen's knights attacked by a peasant?" Alistair said smoothly, leaning back in his seat. "Well, then, the matter seems simple enough."

"Leave it, Alistair," Jemmy ordered. "It's none of your concern."

"I'm sorry to disagree, my lord," Alistair said with biting courtesy. "But Sir Calder is under my command. His welfare is very much my concern."

The knights were very still, their eyes fixed on Jemmy; a few with simple interest, one or two with sympathy, but most with barely concealed hostility. They saw him as the interloper, Kirallen's wastrel son come back again to do poor wee Malcolm—Ian's son, Jemmy reminded himself, one mustn't forget that part for a moment—out of his rights. He told himself he didn't care, that their opinions meant less than nothing to him. And yet he did care.

"The shepherd was flogged and fined," he said curtly. "Sir Calder, I'll speak to you privately of this. Tomorrow."

Sir Calder subsided, muttering, and the others turned back to their food.

"Flogged?" the Laird said. "Tavis? But—"

Jemmy rounded on him. "Do you mean to question every one of my decisions?"

The Laird's eyes flashed. "When there's need for it,

aye, I do. Did you think ye could just walk in here after all these years and take up Ian's place?"

"Aye!" Jemmy answered, his voice tight with fury. "If you want me, then you'll take me as I am and let me do what I must do. Though God knows," he added very low, "nothing I have done has ever pleased you."

"When have ye ever tried to please me, Jemmy?" the Laird shot back. "Or anyone save yourself?"

Alistair was smiling, obviously enjoying the argument, and the knights were listening avidly. Jemmy swallowed his anger and looked pointedly at the knights' table. The Laird followed his gaze, then nodded briefly. "What's done is done," he said stiffly. "We'll say no more about it."

Why bother? Jemmy thought. We both know I'll be gone soon—but not soon enough for me. He couldn't wait to get out of this place and back to his own ship, where any man who dared question his orders never did so a second time. That's where he should be right now, not here in this place where he would always fall short of Ian's shining memory, no matter what he did.

Frowning, he turned to Maude and found her watching him. Her gaze flicked to Alistair and back. She smiled, gave the slightest of shrugs, and looked away.

Jemmy felt as though he'd been dealt a solid blow between the eyes. He had expected her to be furious when she heard what had happened with Tavis, but here she was, taking his part, trying to make him feel better. And he *did* feel better. He would feel better still when he had the chance to tell her what had really happened in Dunforth village.

Oh, Lord, he thought, studying the clear line of her profile. I have to be careful here. She is not mine—not really—or not for long. Once I go, I won't be back again. And here she'll be, just like a widow, but without the freedom to marry again. What a wretched trick this was to play on her! She'll be utterly alone here, just as I once was.

But at least I won't leave her a virgin widow, without even the hope of a child to show she'd ever been a wife at all. Taking her to bed would be the right thing—the *fair* thing to do. That decision had nothing to do with the way she made him feel that day beneath the oak when she had swayed toward him, her full mouth just asking to be kissed. Oh, certainly, he told himself wryly. Nothing to do with that at all.

"We'll be riding out in two days," the Laird said, startling Jemmy from his thoughts. "Have ye ordered the provisions yet?"

"Aye."

Realizing his father was trying to lighten the heavy atmosphere, Jemmy found some suitable comment to make about the journey they'd be taking. But even as he spoke, his thoughts were still on the girl beside him, who had taken his part against them all.

A s the talk turned to the gathering, Alyson reflected that she'd done Tavis no good after all. She had seen men whipped before—in the courtyard at Aylsford stood a post made especially for the purpose. She remembered the sound of the lash against bare skin and the way even the strongest of the men had screamed. When it was done one of the grooms would toss a bucket of water over the cobblestones to wash away the blood.

But brutal as it was, most men survived the lash. It was the fine that was more likely to be fatal. Most peasants had nothing but their bit of land and few animals with which to pay. Once those were gone, starvation was almost certain. But of course that wasn't the sort of thing a nobleman would consider.

Kirallen's voice cut through her reflections. ". . . to the McLarans? What do ye think, Jemmy?"

"Oh, aye," Jemmy said, obviously making an effort to be agreeable. "Emma will be grateful, I'm sure."

"The McLarans?" Alyson repeated, startled into speech.

"That's where the gathering is to be held this year. It's a long ride, to be sure, but a very pleasant one," Kirallen said, obviously pleased at her response. "I must confess I'm looking forward to it myself."

The McLarans. Her mother's people. At last Alyson would meet them and see the place she'd dreamed of for so long. Thank you, God, she thought. I'm so sorry that I ever doubted you. The McLarans would know what to do. And no doubt they could find some way to bring Robin to them. She'd be home, home at last, and she and Robin would be safe.

Jemmy pushed back his chair and stood, grimacing a little as he regarded his dusty riding clothes. "I'm going to have a wash. Good night, Father. My lady—"

Alyson, who had scarcely been listening, nodded her goodnight. But her wandering attention was riveted as he caught her eye. "—I will see *you* later."

And with that terrifying pronouncement he vanished through the door.

chapter 15

Alyson paced before the fire as her women moved quietly about the chamber. Why, why did Jemmy have to choose tonight? In two days they would be gone, and soon after she would be safe among the McLarans. Surely there was some way to put him off for two days more!

But how? The one excuse she could imagine would not serve her now. Every one of her women would know the day her courses started. Nobles had no privacy, she had learned, even in the most intimate of matters. And she least of all, since she was expected to produce the next Kirallen heir.

She glanced at the bed with its soft pillows and thick crimson hangings. It had been her refuge, the one place she felt safe. But now it was the last place she could hide.

Maybe he would change his mind, decide he was too tired after all, she thought, her steps quickening. Maybe he would drown in his bath. Or if she could make him drink too much, he might fall into a stupor. It didn't seem likely, but she asked Maggie to warm some spiced wine anyway.

Maggie put the warming pan over the fire, and soon the scent of cloves and cinnamon rose from the hearth. It reminded Alyson of the first night she had sat here waiting for Jemmy to walk through the door. But he hadn't.

"Some wine, my lady?" Maggie asked. "It's warm now and I've put in a good dollop of honey, just as ye like."

"What? Oh, no, no wine," Alyson said, resuming her pacing.

Maggie pressed her lips together. She thinks I'm being difficult again, Alyson thought. And I suppose I am.

"Then I'll comb out your hair for you," Maggie said.

"No, not now," Alyson said. "Or—yes, all right."

She sat down and pulled the pearl gray chamber robe close around her throat.

"You're shivering," Maggie said. "Here, drink this. It will warm you."

Alyson cradled the goblet between her palms as Maggie unbraided the thick plait. Having her hair combed was one service Alyson actually enjoyed, and she relaxed almost imperceptibly as the minutes slipped past. Jemmy wasn't coming after all, she decided with relief. He must have changed his mind.

At that moment there was a light knock upon the door and it opened.

"Good evening, my lord," Maggie said.

"Maggie," Jemmy answered with a pleasant nod. "You're finished here?"

"Aye."

Alyson jumped to her feet as the women hurried from the room. Jemmy closed the door behind them and leaned against it, arms folded across his chest.

"My lady," he said.

Say something, she ordered herself. Anything. But her throat constricted, making speech impossible. She could only stand and stare, hating her own helplessness. But even Maude would be helpless now, she thought. Not even Maude could refuse to share a bed with her own husband.

Jemmy was clad in a chamber robe of a kind she'd never seen before. It was crimson velvet, hanging to his knees, over a pair of braes made of some silky fabric, cut very full. It was a style she suspected had come from a far greater distance than Sir Robert's London finery. The robe was open down the front, tied loosely at the waist, and when he shifted his arms she could see the dark hair curling on his chest. She had never seen a man's bare chest before, and despite herself she could not seem to look away.

"May I have some wine?"

She glanced up, blushing, knowing he had seen her staring.

"Yes," she managed.

He poured for himself, then picked up her goblet and offered it to her. She took it warily, careful not to touch his hand. Then he clinked the rim of his goblet against hers and drank. She took a small sip without quite knowing that she did.

This was just what she had been afraid of—the strange effect he had upon her thoughts. It was impossible to think properly with him so close, his presence filling the chamber.

He perched on the arm of the chair and looked up at her. The robe fell open farther and now she could see the way the hair on his chest continued over the hard flat line of his belly, vanishing into the shadow of his robe. She resisted the impulse to lean closer and peer into the shadow.

"You're angry, aren't you?"

"Angry?" she repeated blankly. She was many things right now, most of which she didn't understand, but angry wasn't one of them.

"About the shepherd."

She blinked as though coming out of a dream.

"Ten lashes," Jemmy said. "No more. I did it myself."

"Oh, did you?" she asked, wondering if that bit of information was supposed to please her.

"Aye, well, I've had some practice," he said.

"You have?"

"A sea captain disciplines his men," Jemmy shrugged. "It's expected. But I don't mark them. I didn't mark Tavis, either. He's fine."

"Ah. I see. That was—was . . ."

She couldn't say it was kind to lash another man, nor to fine him, either, though it seemed Jemmy expected that she should.

"You heard Sir Calder tonight. I couldn't just let Tavis go."

"Yes, I understand."

And it was true, suddenly she *did* understand that Jemmy had done his best. Sir Calder was well within his rights to demand punishment for the shepherd. Left to Sir Calder's judgment, Tavis would have suffered far more than ten lashes.

"And I gave him money for the fine."

Alyson's head snapped up. "You what?"

He shrugged again and the robe fell open even farther. Her stomach gave a little leap. "You asked for his life, and it is yours."

He sounds as though the shepherd isn't a person at all, Alyson thought. As though Tavis' life is of no more importance than a few coppers lost in a chance wager. And yet, she thought with sudden understanding, that wasn't how he acted. Perhaps all nobles used words like this, to hide what they really thought or felt.

"That was very kind of you," she said. "I thank you."

"No need for thanks. After all, a bargain is a bargain."

And then he did the very thing she had most feared. He looked at her and smiled.

Alyson took a step back.

"Isn't it?" he asked softly, rising to his feet.

"My lord, I'm very tired," she said in a rush. "My head aches and—and I think I caught a chill—" she ended with an unconvincing cough.

"Then we shouldn't keep you standing here," he countered neatly. "Let's go to bed."

Her face burned and she looked away, words deserting her entirely.

"There's no need to be frightened," he said, gentling his voice. "I won't force you, Maude, I promise. No matter what you may have heard, it doesn't have to be unpleasant. In fact—"

He took the goblet from her hand and placed it beside his on the table. She watched him do it, held in her place as though enspelled as he grasped her hand and brought it to his lips. He kissed her palm, then the soft skin of her wrist, and the warmth of his lips raced up her arm in tingling waves.

"—it can be very pleasant, indeed."

"Wait," she stammered. "I—I can't—"

"Of course you can. It's very simple."

And before she knew what he meant to do, he had pulled her close against him. He was warm, so warm, and she wanted nothing more than to bury her face against his chest and let his heat melt the icy fear around her heart.

"No—" she began, her voice a ragged whisper.

"Hush," he ordered softly. "Think of it as a journey to a place you've never been. But it's all right, you can trust me, I know the way."

If only she *could* trust him! It was so tempting to believe she could. He had been kind to Tavis, and surely that meant something. Or did it? Yes, of course it did, but she couldn't puzzle out what exactly it did mean. Not with the hard lines of his body pressed so close to her own and the spicy scent of his skin surrounding her, scattering her wits.

"Wait—" she said again.

"Shh . . ." He put one finger against her lips to stop her words, then traced it gently across her mouth, his eyes never leaving hers.

His kiss was just as she had remembered, a feather-light touch that left her aching with unfulfilled desire. When he bent to her again she rose to meet him, her hands moving of their own accord to encircle his neck and draw him closer.

His lips were very soft and supple against hers. He tasted of cinnamon and honey and something else, something more wonderful than either that belonged only to himself. When he drew away, an involuntary sound of protest escaped her lips. She gazed up at him, dizzy with his kiss, but his eyes were cool and watchful. As though pleased with what he saw, his lips curved in a smile of pure male satisfaction.

He has this all planned out, she realized with a cold shock. Oh, he knows the way of it, all right. No doubt he has made this particular journey a hundred times before. But if he knew who she really was he would not kiss her so sweetly. It was only that he thought her Maude, the bride he hadn't wanted but was bound to nonetheless. He was but doing his duty in the kindest way he knew.

The warmth drained from her limbs, leaving them cold and leaden. Her arms dropped from his neck and when he bent to her again, she moved away.

He gently grasped her jaw and turned her face to his, the question plain in his eyes.

Even if she could have found the words to say what she was feeling, she didn't dare to do it. But he must have read something in her face, for he made the only response she wanted, though she didn't know it until his arms tightened around her again.

A bargain is a bargain, she thought. Even if he didn't understand the bitter truth he'd spoken, his careless words were no less true for that. Once again she had the sense that she was being swept along with no more say than a stray leaf in an autumn wind. She was lost, adrift in a world where everything she had once believed was turned upon its head, and the only solid thing she had to cling to was a man who didn't even know her name.

"Please," she whispered, her lips against his chest, and if she wasn't sure what exactly she meant, he seemed to have no doubt. His hands plunged into her hair, just at the base of her skull, and a long slow shiver racked her body as his lips moved against her neck.

Carefully, Jemmy cautioned himself. Go slowly. He felt her shiver and smiled as her soft hair brushed his cheek, sternly checking his impulse to pick her up and carry her to the bed. There was no need to rush things. She would taste her pleasure to the fullest before he sought his own.

I will be the first, he thought, a little surprised at the rush of tenderness that moved through him at the idea. The first to show her how it can be between a woman and a man, the first to rouse her to desire and hear her cry out in release. The image was almost unbearably exciting but he checked his own need sharply.

He brushed her lips with his again, careful not to startle her. She responded with a sigh and her eyes fell shut. He had never kissed a woman in this way before. There had never been the need for such restraint. He was intrigued by the sensation and eager for another taste. As he deepened the kiss, his ordered thoughts began to unravel like a skein of thread beneath a kitten's paw.

Slowly, he reminded himself with desperate calm. Be patient. He prolonged the moment as long as possible, balancing on the knife's edge of desire and restraint. But when her lips parted beneath his, he was pulled headlong into the rushing tide.

The past and future vanished, instantly and completely. There was nothing but this moment and this woman in his arms, the sweet, entrancing play of tongue on tongue, the wild pounding of her heart against his chest, the silken brush of small hands running up his arms to clasp his neck. A voice spoke in his mind, quietly but very clearly. Journey's end, it said. You've made it home.

Maude *Darnley*? he thought, a ripple of incredulous amusement rippling like a silver stream through the hot tide of his desire. Oh no, it simply couldn't be. Journeys end in *lovers* meeting, or so the old song went. Whatever was he thinking? It was ridiculous, totally absurd. But for all that, it was the truth. He was home at last, where he'd least expected to be, right here in her arms. What difference did her name make now?

He trailed kisses across her face, her neck. She melted against him with a sigh and her lips shyly touched his cheek. The most practiced hands of the most skillful courtesan had never roused Jemmy as did that feather-light touch. He wanted to laugh out loud, to sweep her up and carry her to the bed, and see that glorious blaze of hair spread out across the pillow.

But when he drew back and looked into her face, his laughter faded. Her eyes were shining like blue-green crystals, gazing up at him with an expression he couldn't quite define. It held joy and wonder, but underneath there was something else, a darker hint of sorrow that twisted the heart within his breast.

With gentle hands he traced the sweet curve of her spine and drew her protectively against him. He caressed her shoulders in soft circles, moving slowly downward, every sense attuned to her response. When his hand

brushed her breast, she arched to meet him with a gasp of
startled pleasure.

"Ah, Maude," he sighed. "You are—"

The moment he said her name she stiffened in his arms.

"No! Stop—please, don't—"

"Hush, now, it's what must be."

He wasn't speaking of their duty now, but of what was
happening between them. It was something new to
Jemmy, nothing like the forthright pleasure he'd experienced before when taking a woman to his bed. It was
more like the dizzying joy he felt each time his ship
skimmed out of port and headed for the open sea. And yet
it was utterly different, far more exciting, for this time he
was not alone.

"I know—I understand, I do. But not tonight, I beg
you. Please," she cried desperately, putting both hands
against his chest and pushing him away. "You said you
wouldn't force me."

"There's no need to fear—"

Her struggles grew more frantic until at last he loosed
his grip. She tore free and stood trembling, her head bent.
He put his hand beneath her chin and turned her face to
his. "Whisht, lass, talk to me. Tell me what troubles you."

"I—" her voice shook and she swallowed hard.

He took her hand, relieved when her fingers closed
trustingly over his. It wasn't him, then. It was something
else that brought that look of hunted terror to her eyes.
"You can tell me," he said softly. "Don't be afraid."

He thought that he would do anything she asked, set
right any wrong, if only he could see her smile once again.

Her lips trembled and she drew a shaking breath. His
heartbeat quickened as he waited, barely breathing, for
her words.

And then, before his eyes, she changed. In the space of
a single moment the frightened maiden vanished and another woman stood before him, one whose existence he

had almost forgotten. The pretty softness vanished from her face; her eyes flashed as she raised her chin in the defiant gesture he knew all too well.

"Afraid?" she said, the word light and whipcord sharp with mockery. "Do you really think that I'm afraid of *you*?"

"Of course not," he said calmly, though he didn't believe her for a moment. She *was* afraid, he could sense her fear too well to doubt it. That's why she struck out at him this way. Surely she had not meant to cut him as deeply as she had. "I don't want you to be afraid, Maude. I think—"

"*I* think you should let go of me, you—you Kirallen," she finished, attempting to pull her hand from his. "You said you wouldn't force me—is this all your promises are worth?"

He stared at her in disbelief, every instinct insisting that she lied. She had been about to say something else, something very different—before she had turned into Maude again. But no, what was he thinking? She *was* Maude—and yet she hadn't been—

Or, he thought, his confusion deepening, had it really been that way at all? Had she been just steeling herself to duty, only to find that she could not endure his touch?

He released her and walked to the hearth. This wasn't her fault, not really. He had only himself to blame. She was young and frightened, with no defense but the sharp edge of her tongue. A rather formidable weapon, he considered with bleak humor. With it she had pierced him to the heart and reduced his pride to shreds.

"I did say that, didn't I?" he said, staring into the dying fire, shamed and weary and very much alone.

He sighed and rubbed one hand across his face, starting toward the door. "Get to sleep. We don't have to talk about this now. We'll give it some more time and then . . ."

And then *what*? he asked himself derisively. Nothing

would ever change. What a fool he was to have believed, even for a moment, that she really cared for him, that she would bring anything but cold duty to his bed.

"Good night, my lord," she said quietly.

She had never even said his name. Not once. He made her a sweeping bow, mocking himself and her and the whole sorry jest that was his life.

"And to you, my lady."

Alyson stood, *straight-backed, as Jemmy walked from* the room. But the sound of the closing door broke her resolve. She stumbled forward, half blinded with tears, wanting to cry out to him to wait, to come back, that she hadn't meant it . . .

Stop, she ordered herself firmly, one hand upon the latch. You can't. You mustn't. Just let him go. It isn't you he wants, it's Maude. He isn't yours and never will be—

Then she remembered the happiness that had so briefly lit his eyes when he held her, the terrible bewilderment that replaced it when she denied the truth they had discovered here tonight, a truth that swept everything before it, making mock of birth and rank and all that should divide them. If he hadn't spoken her name—*Maude's* name—she would never have found the strength to stop it when she did. But had she done right?

She didn't know, she couldn't think, and nothing made the slightest bit of sense. She had known from the beginning she would have to bed with him. She hadn't liked it, but she had accepted it as inevitable, the price of the bargain she had made. If she had been prepared to yield herself to a stranger for whom she had no feeling, why did she rebel at the thought of lying with a man she cared for?

Ah, but that's not really the truth, is it? she thought. At least be honest with yourself. You don't just care for him. You love him. You belong to him as you will never belong to any other man. And for that brief moment he had been hers entirely.

How many times, in how many ways, would she be forced to betray him?

"God help me," she whispered. "Please help me."

As the sound of his footsteps faded into silence, she leaned her head against the door and cried.

chapter 16

J emmy shrugged out of the velvet robe and flung it into a
corner, kicking the loose braes after it. He considered
just going to sleep, but then seized a wool jupon from the
wardrobe and pulled it on. Once dressed, he headed for the
hall. This would be the perfect evening to get drunk.
Enough wine in his belly and he wouldn't think about what
had just happened. A little more and he could stop thinking
of what he would say the next time he approached his wife.

His wife. How did this happen? he wondered as he
walked into the hall, listening with half an ear to the
melancholy wailing of the pipes. What am I doing with a
wife? And what in God's name will I do tomorrow and the
next day and all the days after that?

He let his mind wander to a time so distant that
tonight's events would have been forgotten. When would
that be—ten years? Twenty? Where would he be in twenty
years? Not here, that much he knew. He'd be gone without

a trace. Maude would remember him with bitterness—if she thought of him at all.

He'd leave her nothing, not even a child. And though begetting children had been far from his thoughts earlier, suddenly he ached for the little dark-haired, blue-eyed sons and daughters who would never roam the fields and forests of Ravenspur as he'd done so long ago, before the day everything changed forever.

"Why, there's nothing to getting a lass with child."

Jemmy remembered his uncle Stephen saying that, when they'd walked together in the forest, Stephen's hand large and warm around his own. "Any fool can do that much. It's nothing to boast about, Jemmy, if ye dinna mean to do right by her and give the bairn a name. Remember that."

God's blood, how he missed Stephen, even after all these years. Stephen was the one person he could have talked to about what had just happened. Even if Stephen couldn't change things, he would have made Jemmy feel better just by listening in that way he had, as though whatever Jemmy had to say was the most important thing in all the world.

But Stephen wasn't here. Jemmy had been just a child when Stephen went away, but he remembered every detail. And the day Stephen had come back to them was etched forever on his memory. Even now it seemed he could hear his grandmother screaming at the sight of her favorite son, lying dead in the cartbed with the sunlight beating down upon his staring eyes and Darnley's badge laid across the torn flesh of his breast. Oh, Jemmy remembered it all.

That day Jemmy had lost Stephen and the next his mother, who miscarried her babe from the shock and bled to death. Standing between the bodies of the two people he had loved best in all the world, laid out in the chapel, Jemmy scarcely listened to the priest's comforting words. They meant nothing, for though he might speak of peace and forgiveness, it was war and vengeance that would follow.

Jemmy knew then that the priest's words were all lies and the fighting was all useless, all wrong, and he would never, ever be a part of it. He would leave this place one day, just as Stephen had dreamed of doing—as he would have done, if he had not made the deadly mistake of putting one woman at the center of his world.

Not me, Jemmy had vowed as the priest droned on. I'll live alone and make my own way in the world, and I'll never, ever give my heart into any woman's keeping.

Now Jemmy filled his goblet and drained it, then glanced at the only other occupant of the high table. Alistair sat, chin propped in his hand, staring into space. When Jemmy offered the flagon, Alistair held out his goblet, and once it was filled set it down again without speaking. Jemmy rested his elbows on the table, and the two of them sighed deeply at the same moment, then turned to each other with some surprise.

"D'ye ever think on Stephen?" Alistair asked abruptly. Jemmy started.

"I was thinking of him now."

"Hmph." Alistair made a low sound in his throat, looking uneasily over his shoulder. "I was, too. And I dreamed of him last night—" He shuddered slightly and lifted his goblet to his lips.

"What was your dream?" Jemmy asked with some curiosity and a touch of skepticism.

Years ago, when they were children, Alistair had often been troubled by strange dreams. Ian always insisted that Alistair had the Sight, but Jemmy had never been quite sure whether to believe it. But there was no denying that Alistair had made some startlingly accurate predictions in his time.

Now Alistair brushed a strand of white-gold hair back

from his eyes and scowled into his wine. "I dinna remember it too well. I seldom do, these days."

Then he stood and walked away without another word.

Jemmy shrugged and finished his wine, too sunk in his own foul mood to give Alistair any mind. The music changed to a merry tune and soon the floor became a swirl of blue-green laughter. At the high table Jemmy sat alone, his mind straying back to the moment when he'd held Maude in his arms and felt her body mold against his own. At last he tossed back his wine, then rose impatiently and took the hand of the first girl who caught his eye and smiled.

She was a pretty girl, very nimble on her feet. He knew her name but couldn't remember it just now, for the room was spinning a bit more than the dancing would account for. He stumbled slightly on a turn and the girl laughed up at him, grabbing his arm and setting him aright. How much had he had to drink? Far more than was his custom, but what of it? He deserved to have a little fun. Of course he did. He took the next turn easily and laughed with the yellow-haired girl, who really had a most attractive smile.

But what was her name? He should know, he'd seen her often enough in Maude's chamber. Celia. That was it. Celia with the pretty yellow curls and pink cheeks, who, now that she had possession of his arm, seemed determined not to let it go. The dance was over but still she clung to him, and when she offered a fresh cup he took it from her hand. They danced again and drank, and then he lost track of the dances and the wine they drank together, arms linked as they competed to propose the most outrageous toasts.

And somehow—he wasn't sure quite how it came to pass—he and Celia were walking down the passageway together, the silence ringing in Jemmy's ears after the noise of the pipes and the laughter of the crowded hall. Now it was her turn to stumble and his to break her fall and then

there she was, her face turned up to his. So he kissed her.
It seemed the natural thing to do, and as she didn't seem to
mind it in the least, he did it again.

It was nice. Very nice. *She* didn't push him away; *she*
didn't plead an aching head. No, she pressed against him,
clearly asking for more. The wine might be clouding his
mind, but Jemmy's body knew exactly what it wanted. The
feel of her breasts crushed against his chest roused him
with an urgency that would not be denied. And why should
he deny it? Celia was clearly willing, and he bent to her,
his mouth closing over hers. But when her arms went
around his neck, she might just as well have flung cold
water in his face.

Something wasn't right, though for the life of him he
couldn't imagine what it was. Here she was, fair and fresh
and young, wanting nothing but to bed with him tonight.
Which was exactly what he wanted. Wasn't it? Of course
it was; what man wouldn't want her, all pink and gold and
smiling? She had nice teeth, very straight and white, and a
pretty pink tongue that darted out, wetting her full lips.
Yes, here was a woman who knew what she was doing, the
kind of woman Jemmy needed, one who could tease and
please and make him forget everything for one night. So
why wasn't he pleased? Why did he still feel that something wasn't right? She was the wrong shape, somehow, or
she had the wrong scent . . . or no, that made no sense, for
she smelled of gillyflowers, a scent he'd always liked. But
still . . .

She didn't tremble in his arms as Maude had done. She
didn't make that sound—something between a whisper
and a sigh—that Maude had made when he kissed the soft
skin of her neck. No, Celia was quite different from
Maude. Celia was nestling against him, drawing her hand
slowly up his thigh, and he felt nothing but cool distaste,
imagining how many men she'd done this to before. While
Maude . . .

Maude be damned! Why was he thinking of her now? He knotted his fingers in Celia's hair, jerking her head back. And she smiled. She liked it. She wanted more from him. He kissed her hard, and she responded instantly, her hips grinding into his. After a moment he released her and stepped back.

"Too much wine, my girl," he said with a shrug. "I'd be no use to you tonight."

"But my lord—"

"Go on," he said, giving her a gentle push. "Go back to the hall."

He went toward the stairway, puzzled, a little angry, and more than a bit regretful of the opportunity just passed. Had he looked back he would have been very much surprised to see the fury twisting Celia's pretty features and the cold hatred staring from her eyes.

chapter 17

When Jemmy reached his chamber he dismissed the waiting servants. After tending to himself for years it was a constant small annoyance to have these men hovering about, trying to get him in or out of his clothes. God's teeth, he was quite capable of putting himself to bed— even in this state—in half the time it would have taken them to do it. Well, soon he'd have no choice but to accustom himself to their attentions, it was expected of him.

And we all have to do what's expected, he thought, pulling off his boots. Though why was a mystery just now. But it didn't matter. Tomorrow he'd remember why he was supposed to pretend he couldn't do the simplest things himself, but must have others do them for him. Tonight he just wanted to fall into bed and sleep.

Yawning, he unfastened his belt and heard his dagger clatter to the floor. No, that wouldn't do. Have to hang it up. The peg had grown slippery and elusive, but finally, with a muffled "Ha!" of satisfaction, he hooked the leather on the wood, then shivered convulsively.

Good God, but it was cold in here! Had they let the fire die? No, there it was, burning merrily in the hearth, though it gave no heat at all. It was never exactly warm in Ravenspur, but even in January he could not remember such an icy chill as this.

He walked closer to the fire, stretching out his hands, but was within bare inches of the flame before he could feel its warmth. And even when his palms grew hot, he was as cold everywhere else as he'd been before. He touched his warm hand to his icy cheek, then frowned. What strange phenomenon was this? A fire that burned but didn't warm, a cold as deep and endless as the grave . . .

He shivered again, wishing that he hadn't had that thought. The fire was perfectly normal; he was cold because . . . well, because he'd drunk too much. That explanation didn't seem to make much sense, for he'd been drunk before and never experienced anything like this . . .

Shaking his head, he straightened and gave a startled cry when he saw the man beside the hearth.

"What the—?" he began, but could get no further, for his mouth went so dry that for a long moment he was incapable of speech.

At first sight there was nothing about the man to cause such grave alarm. He was young, nineteen or twenty years, and unmistakably a Kirallen. Like Jemmy, he had coarse, dark hair and long, dark eyes and wore the Kirallen plaid across one shoulder. But unlike Jemmy, his skin was white. Very white. Bloodless, in fact, Jemmy thought. As well it might be.

Instinctively Jemmy signed himself with the cross as the other man stood watching. That having no effect, Jemmy blinked hard and rubbed his eyes. When he opened them again the man was still there, still watching, still waiting silently.

Jemmy cleared his throat. "Stephen," he said, pleased at the calmness of his tone. "I was thinking of you tonight."

"Aye, I ken ye were. I always ken when I'm remembered."

"Do you? How interesting."

Jemmy pinched his arm hard but Stephen still stood across the hearth. I am very, very drunk, he thought, and I'm seeing things that aren't there. In fact, I'm talking to someone who isn't here because he can't be, because Stephen has been dead for twenty years.

"Eighteen."

"What?"

"I've been dead for eighteen years, not twenty."

Jemmy blinked. "Aye. And in all that time, I can't believe I'm the only one who's thought of you!"

"You're not."

Stephen looked much younger than Jemmy had remembered him—and yet he looked exactly the same, down to the tiny scar beneath his eye and the one lock of hair that never would lie flat. He looks young because I'm older than he is now, Jemmy thought. The last time we met I was nine and Stephen was alive.

"Well," Jemmy said cautiously. "Have you appeared to all the others?"

Stephen sighed. "They couldna see me."

"They must not have been drunk enough." Jemmy laughed, but Stephen only stared at him with huge dark eyes.

"No, their need wasna as great."

"Need? What need?"

"I canna say all I would, it's not . . . permitted," he finished, frowning a little, as though dissatisfied with the word. "But ye must ken, Jemmy—there's danger all around ye."

Jemmy felt a spurt of irritation. Ghosts always warned

of danger, didn't they? He'd hoped that Stephen might have something more original to say.

"Aye," he said. "And where's this danger coming from?"

"Darnley."

Jemmy sighed. "Your news is stale. I'm married to his daughter—"

"I ken."

"—so you can go haunt someone else. Why don't you visit Alistair? He's the one who's supposed to have the Sight."

"Alistair is in danger, too, perhaps greater than your own. He's blind and deaf to all but his grief—"

"You mean his anger. Stephen, it's been interesting and all, but the night is nearly over and—"

Stephen reached for him, one white hand closing over Jemmy's wrist. The effect was instantaneous. Jemmy jerked upright, suddenly stone sober and very wide awake.

" 'Tisna only for your sake I'm here, but for mine as well."

"Yours? I'm eighteen years too late to help you, Stephen, and I'm sorry for that. Why aren't you in . . . well, in heaven?"

"I should have passed over long ago—but I didna, I couldna, not without— Oh, Jemmy, ye dinna ken how long it's been, so long and all alone. Time is . . . different for me now. Almost I'd forgotten what held me here, forgot all but the wanting—and if that happens, if I truly forget, then I'll never leave this place. But you're here now, and ye can help me, you're the only who can. Please, Jemmy, ye have to help me."

Stephen's voice was so urgent, his face so taut with concentration, that Jemmy merely nodded.

"I'm listening."

Stephen's face worked as he tried to speak, but no

words came from his lips. At last he said, his voice strangled, "Trust your heart."

"Trust my heart? That's what you came from the grave to tell me? Trust my *heart*?"

"Aye! If only ye would *listen*—not to what I'm saying but to what isna being said—"

"God's bones, Stephen, can't you do any better than that?"

"No. I canna. Damn ye, Jemmy, ye didna used to be so hard!"

"Well, a lot has happened since we last met," Jemmy said, sinking down into a chair. "For instance, I—"

But Stephen was gone.

Jemmy sat for a long time, staring at the hearth as the fire warmed his icy limbs. Long after dawn his men found him there, fully dressed and fast asleep.

chapter 18

T*he mountains rose on either side of Alyson, so high
that they took her breath away. The air was crisp and
cool and smelled deliciously of heather. But though she was
on her way to the McLarans at last, she found no pleasure
in the thought that her time at Ravenspur was at an end.

She kept thinking of the gardens, the poor neglected
flower beds. So much beauty and all of it wasted, while the
flowers bloomed unseen and spilled forth their scent into
the empty air. Soon the weeds would choke them and they
would be gone forever.

But one day there might be another lady there, one who
would have time and leisure for a garden. Perhaps it would
be Jemmy's lady. Alyson imagined herself safe among the
McLarans and Jemmy with another wife. If he survived the
coming battle he'd have no choice but to wed again. And
then his bride would stand with him before the fire, would
feel his arms around her. But would she tremble at his touch
as Alyson had done? Would the feel of his lips make her

faint with longing? No, it wasn't possible she could want him half as much as Alyson had done that night.

And it wasn't possible that she would understand him as Alyson did. No doubt his new bride would think, as all the rest of them already did, that he had been mistaken to try and make a peace that was never meant to be. She would never understand that it was strength, not weakness, that made him lead the clan where they did not want to go; that it was wisdom that made him try to stop a war that had destroyed so many lives. She will never truly know him, Alyson thought, blinking back sudden tears. And even if she does, she could never love him as I do.

The Laird rode beside her. After a time Alyson realized he was trying very hard to engage her attention and made some attempt to respond. She watched without interest as a hawk circled the hills, gazed on the gleam of a loch far below, tried to summon a smile for the small yellow flowers the Laird pointed out to her. She had just turned to look at a breathtaking mist-covered mountain rising in the distance when she spotted the band of horsemen approaching at a gallop. Kirallen saw, too, and called for Jemmy, who spurred his horse to his father's side.

In no time at all the horsemen were upon them, aiming straight for the Laird, their drawn swords flashing in the sunlight. Jemmy brought his horse crashing into the leader's, and the man went down, his sharp cry cut short by churning hooves. Then Alistair pulled up and he and Jemmy were fighting side by side, the other men ranged behind them. The battle was short and hot; four of the attackers lay dead upon the ground before the others turned as one and galloped off, the Kirallen men in hot pursuit.

Alyson turned to see Laird Kirallen ashen-skinned and blue-lipped, clutching his horse's mane. She dismounted and helped him from his horse, easing him back against the bracken and taking his hand in her own.

"It's all right, my lord," she said, straining to see what

was happening in the meadow below. "They're gone. Here, now, the men are coming back again, every one of them."

Alistair leaped from his horse and grabbed Alyson by the shoulders, his hands biting painfully into her skin as he pulled her to her feet.

"What d'ye ken about that?" he demanded.

"I—nothing—nothing—" she stammered.

"I dinna believe it!" he cried, shaking her as though to force the truth from her. "Tell me!"

"Alistair, cease—" Laird Kirallen said weakly, struggling to rise.

"What's this?" Jemmy dismounted and seized Alistair by the arm, whirling him around. Alyson stumbled back, dizzy with fear, and sat down hard beside the Laird. "How dare you lay hands on—"

"Those were Darnley's men," Alistair shouted.

"Alistair, no! What are you saying?"

"Who the hell do ye think they were?"

"Reivers. They spotted us and thought—"

"Oh, Christ!" Alistair cried. "Ye dinna ken—ye dinna understand anything that's happening here! Look at her," he pointed to Alyson, who recoiled with a guilty start. "There's some trick here, the whole thing is rotten, and ye canna even see it! Ye dinna ken the first thing about any of this— ye haven't been here, Jemmy, have ye? No, ye weren't here while we were fighting, dying—ye were off doing exactly as ye pleased. It means nothing to ye that Ian lies dead, slain by ambush—"

"Damn you!" Jemmy shouted, now equally enraged. "Do you think I don't mourn my brother? Do you think I've forgotten what they did to our uncle? I was there, Alistair, when they brought him back—I remember it all, and I can hate as well as you. But it has to end sometime."

Alyson heard the ring of bridles as the other men returned. They sat without speaking, watching the two men before them. Then they moved their horses—just a step or two— but enough to show that if sides were to be chosen, it was Alistair they favored. Soon all who remained at Jemmy's back were the twins, Conal and Donal, both of them looking very young and frightened.

"Oh, aye," Alistair spat. "And end it will. It ends when Darnley's dead and we've won, when we've taken all that's his."

"No," Jemmy said flatly. "It ends here and now. It's finished."

"For ye, maybe. But not for me. Never for me."

Shouts of agreements greeted Alistair's words, but he didn't seem to hear them. His eyes were locked with Jemmy's in a battle belonging only to the two of them.

"Alistair, please," Jemmy said. "Listen to me. I've been the world over and 'tis everywhere—the English fight the French, the French fight the Spanish, the Italians fight the Pope! And here—'tis not enough that we fight the English, we're at each other's throats! That's what keeps Scotland down—it isn't them, it's us. Because we can never stop— not for a single moment can we stop the bloody fighting among ourselves. But it doesn't have to be that way."

"Ian is dead—" Jemmy said, and Alistair bent his head, his face wrenched with pain. "'Tis the worst thing that could have happened to the clan, I ken that. But he's dead, and you have to let him go. What difference will it make if you kill Darnley now? It will just start it all up again, the suffering, the dying—and for what? So Malcolm can end the same way? Alistair, we have to pull together, we must, or we'll tear the clan to pieces between us."

"Fine words," Alistair said scornfully. "But that's all they are, just words. I ken ye well, Jemmy, I always have. A man fights for what matters to him most, and ye never fought for anything but yourself."

Alyson watched fearfully, certain they would come to blows. But instead of answering, Jemmy looked away.

"I gave my fealty to Ian," Alistair continued. "Not to ye.

As your brother lay dying, struck down from behind by Darnley himself—aye, by the man who fathered your wife—I swore that I would look after Malcolm as if he were my own. And 'tis for Malcolm's sake I stay. Because when the day comes for the clan to choose another laird, it willna be you, Jemmy. It will be Malcolm. And 'tis I who'll be his regent. That's what Ian wants."

Say something, Alyson silently urged Jemmy. Show him who is in command!

"So 'tis to be Malcolm, is it?" Jemmy said coolly. "You may be right, Alistair. Who can say? But until that day, my father rules here and you take your orders from me. Now get on your horse. We've wasted enough time. Father," he added, turning to the Laird, "can you ride yet? If not I'll wait with you until you're stronger."

"No, I'm well enough." Kirallen stood slowly and drew himself up very straight. He looked from Alistair to Jemmy and then to Alyson. "Daughter," he said distinctly, holding out one arm. "Allow me to assist you."

"Thank you."

When Alyson took his arm she could feel it trembling beneath her hand, though the nobleman gave no other sign of his feelings as he led her to her horse and held the stirrup for her. Mounted, she looked down at Alistair. He stood, arms folded across his chest, and met her gaze with hard, accusing eyes.

After a moment she had to look away.

They made camp for the night in a sheltered hollow of the hills with a broad loch stretched below them. As sunset fell across its waters, splashing them with gold and red and purple, Alyson seated herself on a log by the fire and waited with the others for the food to cook.

The company was subdued tonight. There was no singing and no laughter as they waited for their meal. The two young knights, Donal and Conal, sat on either side of her. At least Jemmy had them, Alyson thought. There might be others who would come to his side—if only he would do something to win them over.

Donal offered her a cup of spirit and she took it, gasping a little as the fiery liquid went down her throat. But after the burning passed she rather enjoyed the warm glow it brought to her empty belly. She took another sip and then another and suddenly the cup was empty.

She accepted her plate of meat and bread, but her appetite vanished when Jemmy came to sit beside her. It was the first time she'd been close to him since that night—but no, she wouldn't think of that. That was all over now and she was going home. And there would be no opportunity for them to be alone during the journey. The women had already spread their blankets on the ground, and the men would stand guard in turn throughout the night.

She should be glad. She *was* glad. Of course she was. Once they reached the McLarans she would be done with the Kirallens forever. She would go to her place and Jemmy back to his, and the two of them would never meet again. It was all quite right and proper. And it would surely break her heart.

Firelight played over his face as he stared into the dancing flames. She traced each contour with her eyes, remembering the joy of running her fingers across the sharp plane of his cheeks, his solid jaw, his lips . . . He had such a lovely mouth. It was set now in a grim line, but she remembered the dazzling wonder of his smile.

She wished that she could see it once again, his smile, with its one merry little dimple. Never, not in her wildest imagination, would she have suspected that dimple. Just now it seemed impossible to believe in it, but she was convinced of its existence. If only she could see it once again, just to be quite sure it was as charming as she remembered . . .

She shook her head and lifted the mug to her lips. Someone had filled it again and she drained it without thinking, then choked a little on the harsh spirit. When she caught her breath she saw Jemmy watching her, but he looked away instantly.

"I'm fine," she declared. When he didn't answer, she dug one elbow into his arm and he turned.

"I'm fine," she repeated. "Just in case ye wondered."

He nodded and turned back to his perusal of the fire.

"Are ye reading the future in the flames?" she asked, then wondered what had happened to her voice. She'd meant the question to come out lightly, but instead she'd sounded belligerent. And unless she was mistaken, there had been a slight slurring of the words. "The future" had sounded suspiciously like, "Th'fushur." Or so she thought. She wasn't really sure.

"I beg your pardon?"

He looked at her, brows raised in question.

"Never mind."

She waved one hand in airy dismissal, mortified when it stuck him on the cheek.

"My lady," he said gravely. "You are weary—"

"Oh, no!" she laughed. "I feel better than I have for—well, for—for a long time!"

"Still, I think it best that you lie down."

"But I'm not tired in the least! D'ye know what I'd like to do?" she asked, struck with the brilliance of her idea. "I'd like to dance! Who's that fellow wi' the pipes? Tell him to play something merry—or no, 'tis no matter, I'll tell him myself—"

"No," Jemmy said, catching her by the arm as she struggled to rise. "Sit down. This is not the time for dancing."

"I don't see why not!" she said indignantly.

His lips twitched as though he was about to laugh. She was affronted, yet at the same time she was intrigued. Perhaps she could win one smile yet before they parted.

"Well, if ye say so," she said grudgingly. "Though I do so love to dance."

"You do?"

"Oh, aye. And so do ye. I kent ye that night—the night of the—oh, *you* ken, the night that we were—"

"Married?" He supplied the missing word with flawless courtesy, but the tantalizing promise of a smile vanished.

"Aye. Standin' up there, callin' out for a woman to partner ye. Oh, I saw it."

"Did you? How interesting. Now I think 'tis time—"

"And that lass—what was her name? I kent her after, the black-haired wench. Bold as brass she was. 'I will, my lord!' I heard her clear enough—"

"Maude, be quiet!" Jemmy ordered, glancing at the people sitting around them.

"But why?" she demanded. "I only speak the truth! And what I meant to say was . . . was . . ."

What *had* she meant to say? Something about their wedding night—or no, Maude's wedding night—something about . . .

"Dancing!" she exclaimed triumphantly. "That's what we were talking about!"

Now he did smile, and if it was a trifle on the wry side, not near enough to make his dimple dance, it was better than nothing.

"Yes. Dancing. It's a pleasant pastime, but perhaps you should finish your supper and we can try a walk instead. The loch is lovely in the moonlight."

She managed to eat the best part of her meal, for once she started she realized she was ravenous. When she set it aside he stood and took her hands, pulling her to her feet.

She picked her way carefully among the people seated near the fire. The ground was far more uneven than she had noticed earlier. But she navigated carefully and soon stepped out of the circle of firelight into cool darkness.

Jemmy walked silently beside her. She couldn't make

out his expression but suspected it was grim. Ah, well, so much for her plan. Even if he was grinning ear to ear, she wouldn't be able to see it. But still, it was nice to be away from the others for a time. As they walked down the hillside, the sounds of the people up above faded into the soft swish of water against the stony shore.

"There is no moon tonight," she pointed out. The loch ahead was invisible, save for the occasional silver flash as a dark wave caught the starlight. "But 'tis still lovely."

She kicked off her shoes and hose, then stepped carefully over the rocks until the water lapped at her bare feet.

"Going for a swim?" Jemmy asked from behind her.

" 'Tis a bit cold for that," she said regretfully. A swim would have been just the thing to clear her head. But the cool water felt pleasant on her feet, and she wiggled her toes, smiling a little. She felt better now, not so dizzy, but still very light. It was a pity that they couldn't dance. Even Maude had admitted that she was rather good at that.

They were quiet then, listening to the endless pull of the loch against the shore. From the hillside came the soft strains of a clarsach, and the sweet harp music was joined by a single voice.

> *My love built me a bonny bower,*
> *And clad it all wi' lily flower*
> *A brawer bower ye ne'er did see*
> *Than my true love he made for me.*
>
> *There came a man by middle day*
> *He spied his sport and went away*
> *And brought his kin that very night,*
> *They brake my bower and slew my knight.*

Such a sad song, Alyson thought, tears welling in her eyes. But then, so many were. At least the songs that were sung on the Borderlands. Sir Robert and Lady Maude had brought other songs from London, merry tunes and pretty little ballads that did not end in heartbreak. But London was another world entirely. In this world, Alyson's world, violent death was commonplace, and those who were left sang of what they knew—tragedy and sorrow, loneliness and loss . . .

She had lost Jemmy already, she knew that, but at least they were still together. When they reached the McLarans she would not have even that. There was so much she didn't know about him, would never know now. So many questions she longed to ask . . .

"You're shivering," Jemmy said, his boots splashing in the shallows. "Come back now and try to sleep."

"Not yet. I'll stay a little longer. You go if you like."

Jemmy heard tears in her voice and wondered at the cause. Whisky, most likely, he decided, stamping down hard on his sympathy. First she wanted to dance, and now she was crying over nothing. No doubt she would turn maudlin next. He sighed, braced for the tears and reproaches she would surely make. But when she spoke, it was not what he expected.

"What was your ship's name?"

"The *Osprey*," he answered, startled both by the question and the wistful tone in which it was put to him.

"Truly? I would have expected a pirate ship to have a different sort of name . . ."

"A pirate ship? Did my father tell you that?"

"Sir—my uncle said . . ."

"Ah. Well, I suppose he could have said worse. I've done a bit of smuggling now and again, but that's the worst of it."

His eyes had adjusted to the darkness now, and he could just make out the outline of her form against the water of the loch.

"Did you have it long? The *Osprey*?"

"Four years. Just long enough to begin to learn about her."

"Her?"

"Aye, well, 'tis custom to call a ship that way."

He was standing just behind her now, close enough to feel the heat of her body against his.

"I wonder why that is," she said casually.

"Oh, I suppose it comes from sailors being too long at sea," he answered, breathing the scent of her hair. "And ships have moods we cannot understand."

One step more and her head would be resting against his shoulder. He decided it would be foolish to take that step and spoil the moment altogether.

"Like women?" she asked, amusement in her voice.

"Aye. Like women."

"But you understand . . . your ship?"

"A bit. At least I like to think I do. She still puzzles me at times, usually when I think I've learned all there is to know. I suppose that's part of her charm."

Her laughter came softly in the darkness. "When you know her through and through, then what? Will you change her for another?"

"Oh, no. I think that if I ever learn her altogether, I couldn't bear to part from her."

The harper ended his plaintive tune and silence fell, while the water pulled back and forth around Jemmy's ankles. A good pair of boots ruined, he thought, and didn't care.

"But you canna be sure of that. Perhaps, when there's no mystery left . . . you willna like what you find."

"That's a chance I'll have to take."

"Is it? Sailors abandon ships, don't they? They do it all the time."

"Not if they're the captain, they don't. Any captain worth his salt will stand and fight."

He stopped abruptly, realizing this conversation was leading somewhere else, a place he didn't mean to go.

"I ken," she said quietly, turning to face him. " 'Tis just like Sir Alistair said before. A man fights for what's important to him." Her fingers lightly brushed his cheek. "It's all a matter of finding that thing, isn't it?"

Against all intention he reached for her, but she slipped past him in the darkness.

Nothing means that much to me, he thought as he splashed back to shore, feet squelching coldly in his sodden boots. *Nothing.* And nothing ever will.

chapter 19

They heard the music first. Pipes and tabors, voices raised in song were the sounds that greeted the Kirallens as they topped the rise of the high moor. Then Alyson saw the people—hundreds, it seemed to her at first, dressed in a confusion of bright colors. Some were dancing, and others stood about talking and laughing together. When the Kirallens were spotted, many of the people hurried over to welcome them.

Alyson stood between Jemmy and his father. The two men were greeted warmly, but Alyson received the slightest bow or curtsey, a murmured "My lady," and no more. She suspected that she wouldn't have received even that much had it not been for the two Kirallens, their very presence demanding she be treated with respect.

At last an older woman approached, wearing a gay plaid of red and gold, her white hair drawn back from her weathered face. She did not curtsey as the others had done, but held out her arms to Laird Kirallen and caught him in a strong embrace.

"Gawyn, I've been thinking of ye every day since we got the news of Ian. He was such a braw lad, I can scarce believe he's gone." They held each other for a moment, then she released him and wiped her eyes, saying briskly, "But I see ye have your Jemmy back, and that must be a comfort. Now let me look at ye," she said, turning to Jemmy. "The last time we met ye were just a bairn."

Her face darkened as though at some painful memory, and Jemmy said softly, "Aye. I remember."

"Ye were gone too long," she said, reaching up to touch his cheek.

"Emma," Laird Kirallen said. "This is Maude, my daughter. Maude, may I present Emma McLaran?"

Alyson nodded slightly.

Emma's expression hardened as she studied Alyson. Then she looked at Kirallen and made a slight movement with one shoulder, almost a shrug. "Ye are welcome."

Alyson could sense the Laird relax beside her, and she realized that she had passed some sort of test.

"And you, Alistair," Emma called, "Oh, I see ye over there. Come and greet me properly! That's better," she said, giving him a quick hug. "Are ye not wed yet? 'Tis a scandal and a wicked waste. I know the perfect lassie—"

Alistair laughed. "And me not here five minutes!"

"You've wasted enough time as it is," Emma said firmly, though she smiled as she spoke and ruffled Alistair's light hair as though he were no more than a boy. "Just let me know and I'll have it done in no time at all."

"Where is Hamish?" Kirallen asked, glancing over her shoulder.

"Abed," Emma sighed. "Poor man, he wanted so to greet ye. Will ye stop and talk wi' him awhile?"

"With pleasure," Kirallen answered. "I hope 'tis nothing serious . . ."

"Och, he's no' so young as he used to be," Emma said.

"Jemmy, Alistair," the Laird said. "Attend me please."

As they moved into the crowd Alyson scanned the people eagerly, her eyes lingering on anyone who wore the McLaran plaid, hoping that she would recognize a likeness to her mother or hear a familiar name. She had been searching her memory for anything Clare might have said that would help her now.

There was frustratingly little to remember. Until her final illness, Clare had never spoken of her past. By the time she realized she would not live to take her children home again, it had been too late.

Alyson did not know the names of her grandparents or any of her kin but had been certain that the Laird of the McLarans would help her there. Now it seemed he was too ill to rise from his bed—yet she still hoped to find a way to see him. Or if not him, then she would have to speak to Emma at the first opportunity.

The children were gathering wood for a bonfire, their laughter ringing through the high meadow. Women came and went, cooking at open fires and talking quickly, catching up on all the news of the past year.

"Hello, Jemmy."

Alyson looked up into the face of what seemed to her a giant, with a broad face surrounded by a flaming beard. He was dressed in the McLaran colors.

"Hugh," Jemmy said, his voice expressionless.

The two men looked at one another warily.

"So this is the Darnley wench?" Hugh McLaran asked, nodding toward Alyson.

"This is Lady Maude, my wife."

"Is it now? You're a braw laddie, aren't ye, bringing her among us? Very brave, Jemmy. Very foolish."

Jemmy tilted his head back and glared into Hugh McLaran's eyes. "Is that a challenge?"

"Och, now, I wouldn't be challenging ye now, would I? Not after the McLaran has forbidden it."

"Then I suggest you shut your mouth," Jemmy said pleasantly, turning to leave.

Hugh put one hand on Jemmy's shoulder. "But I'll see ye at the games."

Jemmy whirled and grasped Hugh's wrist, twisting it until the McLaran grunted with pain.

"Aye, Hugh, I'll see you at the games. Until then, keep your distance from me—and from my lady."

"With pleasure," Hugh said, shaking his injured wrist as he strode back into the crowd.

"I'm sorry for that," Jemmy said, turning to Alyson. "But it shouldn't happen again. Just keep with the women and you'll be fine."

"All right, my lord," she said distractedly, her eyes searching the throng. "I'll be fine, dinna fret. Your father's waiting."

Jemmy left her then and walked to the McLaran keep. He found his father and Alistair waiting for him in the small downstairs chamber with its one narrow window looking out over the hills. The Laird gestured Jemmy to come in and shut the door behind him.

"That was a disgraceful display yesterday," the Laird snapped without preamble, glaring at both the younger men. "Fighting like that before the men—I would have thought you, at least, would have more sense!" he said, turning to Alistair.

Jemmy was amused to see the flush rise to Alistair's cheeks. "How dare ye lay hands upon Lady Maude?" the Laird continued, working himself into a rage. "What kind of example do ye think that sets? The men look to you to lead them—"

"Aye, they do!" Alistair snapped back. "And why is that? Why don't they look to Jemmy? Well, I'll tell ye why—"

"You will *not,*" Kirallen ordered curtly. "I've heard enough from ye. We have made peace with Darnley. 'Tis done, Alistair, a finished matter. Ye hearken to my words, lad, and remember who you're talking to."

Alistair bent his head. "Aye, Laird," he muttered.

"Then that's all. Ye may go. As for ye, Jemmy," the Laird began when they were alone.

"Oh, no," Jemmy interrupted. "Not me. I won't be scolded like a bairn."

"Then stop behaving like one. This arguing with Alistair must cease. 'Tis dividing the knights, and I willna have it."

"I didn't start it," Jemmy said, feeling as though he'd been plunged back into childhood. "This is ridiculous," he added, disgusted. "Don't blame me for Alistair's mistakes."

"Alistair is confused," Kirallen said. "He's grieving. He'll come round."

"I don't see him doing it now," Jemmy pointed out. "I don't see him coming round, Father. He'd lead the men against Darnley in an instant if you weren't there to stop him."

"It will just take a little time. He'll see—"

"He'll never see. He said it himself yesterday. ''Tis not over until Darnley's dead and we've won, until we've taken all that's his,' he said. 'That's what Ian wants,' he said. Not *wanted.* Wants. He talks of him as though he's still alive! Don't you think that's a bit strange, Father? Sometimes I think his wits are turning," Jemmy said, voicing the suspicion that had been growing in him since his return.

"That's ridiculous," Kirallen snapped. "There's nothing wrong with Alistair's wits. He's but misguided—"

"Why do I try?" Jemmy said, throwing up his hands. "What point is there in talking when you don't hear a word I say?"

"Oh, I hear ye, Jemmy. I just dinna happen to agree. But of course ye can't accept that ye just might be wrong. Oh, no. Alistair is mad and I am blind—you're the only one who sees the truth of it. It doesna matter that you've been gone twelve years! Ye think ye can walk right in and know everything it took Ian a lifetime to learn. Every time ye ride out, I can only wait and worry, wondering what ye might do next. I've tried to give ye my trust, Jemmy, but how do ye repay me? Riding roughshod over the villagers' rights, flogging helpless peasants—"

"Father, that wasn't as it seemed—if you'd only let me explain how it happened—"

"What difference does it make?" Kirallen cried, striking his fist upon the mantel. " 'Tis too late now, the deed is done! Ian would never have—"

"No, Ian wouldn't have been there! He would have sent Alistair or Sir Calder himself to do the deed!"

"What do ye know of your brother?" Kirallen demanded, whirling to face him. "Ian was a fine leader and the best son a man could ask for. How could God have taken him and left me—"

He broke off, too late, and the words hung between them in the silence. Jemmy's face stung as if he had been slapped.

"Jemmy, I—I dinna mean—"

"Don't apologize, Father," he answered through numb lips. "I already knew. I've always known."

From the next chamber came the sound of a dry cough.

"There's no point in shouting at each other," Jemmy said wearily. "Though I daresay the McLarans have enjoyed the entertainment. I was a fool to come back here and try to help you when you can't wait to see the back of me."

"Wait," the Laird began, holding out his hand. "Ye were the one who never wanted to stay in Ravenspur—ye said ye wanted to get back to Spain—"

"Did I?" Jemmy said, turning in the doorway. "Did I really? Well, it doesn't matter, does it, who said what. I only wonder that you sent for me at all. I wish to God you hadn't."

The Laird looked away, flushing. "I had no choice—Lady Maude—"

"Ah, yes, Lady Maude. Have you considered what a terrible thing we've done to her? Did you even give it a thought when you came up with your plan?"

"I must do what is best for my people," the Laird said, running a shaking hand across his brow. "All my people, not simply Lady Maude."

"Of course," Jemmy said politely. "But you must forgive me if I can't see it in quite the same light. As far as I can tell neither one of us matters any more to you than pieces on a game board."

"One day, perhaps, you'll understand . . ."

"Perhaps. But will Alistair?"

"Alistair is like a son to me," the Laird whispered, sinking down onto a bench.

"And I am your son. But I warn you that my patience with you—and your plots and plans—is wearing very thin."

chapter 20

Ⅎ

Once Jemmy was gone Alyson wandered through the campsite. She offered to help the women but they refused, and she realized she wasn't wanted among them. Well, what did you think would happen, she scolded herself, that they would take one look at you and welcome you back again? She walked up to the high moor and all at once the ground fell away beneath her feet. The day was bright, and huge white clouds scudding across the sun sent light and shadow chasing each other across the hills and valleys.

"Well, Mam," she said, "I've done it. I'm here. Please help me now. Show me what to do."

She sat down and plucked a bit of grass, tossing it over the edge of the precipice. If only Clare had lived a little longer, even a few hours, Alyson would know far more than she did now. But the day Clare sickened she had been working in Aylsford Manor itself, and by the time she dragged herself the three miles home, she was already raving with the fever. Most of her talk had been nonsense, at least to Alyson's ears. The only sensible thing she'd said was that Alyson must get to the McLarans.

"I canna just tell anyone," Alyson mused. "For what if it turns out to be one of Sir Alistair's friends? There must be dozens of McLarans here from all across the Highlands. Which were your kin?"

A hawk cried out as it circled a small pool far below, then folded its wings and dove. Alyson winced, imagining its sharp beak and razor talons fastening on its prey, then sighed.

"Of course it would be easier to tell Jemmy, but he's not the man he could be. He can hardly solve his own problems, let alone take on mine. I canna trust Robin's life to him," she concluded regretfully. "But I'll find the way. I have to, don't I?"

She stood and squared her shoulders. "I wish you were here to help me, Mam. But that's all right. I'm sure you would be if you could."

For a moment it seemed that Clare stood beside her, a presence so vivid that Alyson's eyes stung with sudden tears when she turned and found herself alone. She waited but there was no answer, no inner certainty. At last she turned away and went back to the campsite. This time, though, she did not bother to ask if she could help. She simply sat down by one of the fires and began to shell a basket of peas. There were six or seven other women present, and they drew back from her a little, whispering among themselves. Alyson felt herself begin to blush but she resolutely continued with her work.

She looked up as Emma McLaran came and sat beside her on the log, reaching into the basket.

"'Tis kind of ye to want to help, lady, but there's no need at all."

"I don't mind," Alyson said.

"Please yourself," Emma said indifferently.

Alyson tried to think of some way to mention Clare, but the other women were listening avidly, and her mind was a frustrating blank.

" 'Tis fine weather," she began tentatively.

Emma nodded without answering.

"And so beautiful here," Alyson continued in a nervous rush. "I had heard it's very pretty, but even so I didn't expect—"

"Och, aye, 'tis pretty enough," Emma said shortly. She threw the peas into the basket and turned to Alyson. "Kirallen thinks he can bring the peace by this marriage, and I'll no' be the one to say him nay. But dinna think that means I approve of what he's done."

Looking into Emma's clear blue eyes, Alyson's bright hopes collapsed. Had she really expected the McLarans would rush to her defense? Likely they wouldn't even want to acknowledge her, though if she appealed to them in Clare's name they might have to do so. But they would not be happy about it. Who was she, after all? Darnley's bastard daughter, that's who she was, an English stranger with no claim to their protection.

And what difference would Robin make to any of them? They didn't know him and he was half English, just as Alyson was herself. They'd never even stop to think of him. What was the life of one child—a common child, a stable boy—when set against this clash of noble houses?

"I was taught that forgiveness is the duty of every Christian," she said quietly, remembering her mother's patient lessons.

"I'd like to know who had your teaching!" Emma answered tartly, rising and brushing the windblown hair back from her brow. "Surely it wasna your father! And I'm afraid ye willna be finding many to agree with ye in these parts. They think 'tis a sign of weakness in Kirallen, him marrying his son to ye. Oh, they'll hold their tongues—or most of them will, anyway. Kirallen has always been a friend to us. But dinna be expecting them to welcome ye or forget that you're a Darnley. I wouldna ask it o' them, for it's more than I can do myself."

When she was gone the other women gathered in a little knot, pointed excluding Alyson, until their work was done and they could join other, livelier groups. Alyson remained by the fire awhile longer, but at last she wandered off in search of her chest. She found it stored in a tiny stone cottage set far from all the others. Though the other buildings were full to bursting, and most of the men to sleep upon the moor, she realized that this place had been reserved for her alone.

Pushing her chest aside, she sat down on the pallet and buried her face in her hands. How many times had she imagined coming to this place, knowing she and Robin would be safe at last? She had invented all kinds of stories about the McLarans and the magical mountains where they lived until it became a nightly ritual with Robin.

"We'll be going soon," Alyson would say. "Going off to the McLarans."

Now she heard Robin's high voice responding, "They live far up in the hills—"

"—so high that ye can touch the sky. And they'll be so surprised to see us—"

"They'll have a feast!"

Robin never left that part out, she remembered now, tears falling between her fingers. He was always hungry. She smuggled him whatever she could from the kitchens, but it wasn't enough. Seven years old and not growing as he should, he needed more than scraps. His face was all bones and eyes beneath his cap of golden curls. Yet his smile had a piercing sweetness and his eyes were merry, fixed on a future that now would never be.

"They'll have meat and oatcakes and all the honey even you could ask for, Ally!" he would say, nudging her with one sharp elbow. "We'll eat until we're bursting—"

"And then they'll play upon the pipes and we'll all dance and sing . . ."

Even now the music of the pipes cut through the gathering darkness and Alyson pressed her hands over her ears, trying to shut it out. It was all that they had dreamed of, but all wrong, all spoiled now forever.

A mighty cheer went up and she walked to the doorway. The bonfire was blazing and dancers were silhouetted against the flame. Dancing and singing and feasting . . .

When Malcolm came to bid her to the feast, she sent him away again, pleading an aching head, and lay down to sleep, trying to blot the music from her ears. But even when she slept she heard it still, in her dreams, where Robin laughed as she danced with a dark-eyed man and was happier than she had ever imagined possible.

When she woke in the gray morning light she lay listening to the rain upon the thatched roof, wondering where she could find the strength to rise and face the day.

chapter 21

The rain stopped and the festivities resumed, though now Alyson made no effort to join the other women at their work. Instead she walked to the high moor and sat alone, her heart heavy with confusion and sorrow. Today the distant mountains were shrouded in mist, only a few jagged peaks rising from the fog. For all their beauty, these mountains were as harsh and unforgiving as the men and women who wrested their living from their slopes.

It was unlikely that she and Robin would have survived the journey, Alyson reflected. Even if they had found this place, she wondered how long her fragile brother would have lasted here. The Highlanders existed in a poverty that was beyond anything she had ever known. Food was scarce and even the simplest comforts were unheard of. Their dwellings were rough cairns of stone, furnished with only the barest of necessities.

Life is very simple here, she thought, propping her chin in her hand. Life and death. Right and wrong. Loyalty to the clan. There was no room or time for ambiguity or shades of gray.

Now she understood how her gentle mother had survived the tragedy that had befallen her. Clare had seemed so delicate, but underneath had run a strength like finespun steel. Never once had she allowed herself to sink into bitterness or self-pity. Her faith had remained as unshakable as the mountains from which she had sprung.

And just as beautiful, Alyson thought, tears starting to her eyes.

"Aunt!" Malcolm cried, arriving breathless at the crest. "Come see! We're to have racing and archery—hurry, now, I don't want to miss the start!"

He grabbed her hand and pulled her down to the meadow. The men were all gone, Alyson noted, off to some meeting at the McLarans' dwelling. It was only the women who gathered to watch the boys compete with bows and arrows and mock swords.

Malcolm had thoughtfully laid a length of plaid upon the ground for her so she felt she had no choice but to remain. The others drew back a little and she sat in a little island among the bright tartans and felt utterly alone. But she did her best to smile when Malcolm ran to bring her the bit of ribbon he'd won in a footrace. When the games were done the women lingered for a time in the afternoon sunlight, and Malcolm plopped down beside her with a grin.

"Did ye see me?" he demanded, laying another ribbon in her lap.

"Aye. You did very well."

"I did, didn't I?" He lay back and crossed his arms beneath his head. "Sean McInnes was good, wasn't he? I never thought I'd beat him. And he's fourteen! But then Alistair says that I'm like my father and he always won everything . . . I think he would have been proud of me," he added on a yawn.

"Oh, he would, Malcolm. I'm sure he would have been very proud. And your grandfather will be proud, too, when he hears how well you did."

"Mmm . . ." Malcolm murmured, his eyes closing. Most of the women were napping, weary from the feasting last night and the preparations for tonight's meal. Alyson blinked sleepily in the sunlight and at last gave into the somnolence of the afternoon. She lay down beside Malcolm and slept.

It was an hour later that Jemmy stared curiously at the two figures curled together on the plaid.

Malcolm had always refused to hear a word against his new aunt, insisting that she was his friend. Jemmy had thought it odd, but then Malcolm was an odd boy who he didn't begin to understand. He had never once imagined that his nephew was telling the truth and Maude returned his affection. She'd never given any sign of doing so. In fact, she'd always been quite sharp with Malcolm when he clamored for her notice.

Now Malcolm's head was nestled trustingly on her shoulder and her sleep-flushed cheek rested on his curls. Why go out of her way to make it seem she didn't care when that obviously wasn't the case? It made no sense, none at all, and Jemmy distrusted things that made no sense. What harm could there be in showing kindness to an orphaned boy who obviously adored her?

It was almost as though there were two people who bore Maude's name, and the one she showed the world seemed determined to make herself disliked. But why would she do something so foolish? How could she hope to survive among the Kirallens, especially after Jemmy was gone?

Malcolm's eyes opened and he sat up. "Uncle Jemmy," he said excitedly. "I won the race and the archery—"

"Did you? That's fine, Malcolm," he said absently, his eyes still on his wife.

He wanted to see her when she first woke, before she

had a chance to put up her guard. Her expression might reveal something—anything—that would help him understand her.

"Look, Uncle Jemmy, I got these—" Malcolm continued, thrusting a bit of grubby ribbon in his face.

"Very nice. Now run along, the games will be starting."

The boy's face fell. "Aye, Uncle," he said, his shoulders drooping as he walked slowly across the moor.

"You could show a bit of interest."

He'd missed the moment of waking. She was already sitting up, her brows drawn together in a frown.

"I've other things to do just now," he said.

"You always have other things to do, don't you?" she retorted, getting to her feet and shaking out the plaid before folding it neatly across her arm. "But *he* doesn't."

Malcolm ran up to a group of men and swung on Alistair's arm, nearly overbalancing him. But Alistair only smiled, and breaking off his conversation, gave the boy his full attention. Jemmy glanced at his wife and saw that she was watching, too, and she shook her head as Alistair put an arm about Malcolm's shoulders and pulled him close.

"Do you *want* him to take your brother's place?" she cried. "With Malcolm, with your knights? Your people need *you*, not him! Why don't you *do* something—anything—to stop him?"

Before Jemmy could answer she turned and ran across the moor. A man fights for what matters, Jemmy thought. Well, there was no denying that. And what mattered—the only thing that mattered—was that he regain his freedom. Let Alistair take it all. That's what the Laird wanted, and that's what would surely be.

So Jemmy told himself, standing all alone on the moor. But for the first time he wondered what *he* wanted—he, himself, not his father's son or Ian's brother. To sail away and be free of all of them?

But why *should* he be the one to go? No matter what

Father thought of him, the fact was that Jemmy was entitled to far more than three hundred marks and his passage back to Spain.

Father believed he was doing the right thing for his clan in sending Jemmy away. But Maude didn't agree. Maude believed that *he* was meant to rule, not just by right of birth, but because of who he was—or who she thought he was. A man who cared for his people. But did he care enough to fight?

Jemmy watched her run gracefully across the moor, bright hair streaming behind her. In that moment he wanted her so badly that nothing seemed impossible, if he could only keep her at his side.

A lyson tried to hide in her cottage, but Malcolm would have none of it. He insisted she go with him to the place where the Kirallens had gathered to cheer lustily for their men. Malcolm didn't seem to notice the dark looks they gave her or the way they drew aside as if fearing any contact. The open hostility of the other clans seemed to have reminded them of the shame they ought to feel at the connection and even the few women who had been cordial before greeted her arrival with stony silence.

Despite herself Alyson was hurt again. As the games began, she watched without much interest. But soon her attention was caught and held by Jemmy, who competed with deadly intensity, as though he would win or die in the attempt.

No man moved more gracefully to toss spear or stone, though in the latter competition one of the McLarans took the prize. When the wrestling began the contestants stripped to the waist, and though she tried not to stare, Alyson could hardly help but notice Jemmy's broad shoulders and slim hips, or that he was all lean muscle beneath his sun-browned skin.

He tied a strip of tartan about his brow to hold the hair back from his face, though it fell behind loose and curling halfway to his waist. He did well, which was no surprise considering his size—he stood taller than nearly all the men. But even when set against Hugh McLaran, the enormous, redheaded man they'd met the day before, Jemmy's agility was so great that he prevailed. The Kirallens clapped and yelled, and at last Jemmy faced off against Alistair.

Alistair was half a head shorter than Jemmy, but he was solid with muscle and moved with a dancer's grace. The match wore on as they came together and broke apart, each taking the other's measure. At last they stood, arms locked and feet planted, each striving to bring the other down.

There was none of the shouted encouragement or good-natured insults that had accompanied the other matches. This had gone beyond an afternoon's diversion and become something else entirely. Alyson's stomach gave a little lurch as she watched Jemmy's muscles knot beneath the glistening skin of his back and arms. And then it was done so quickly that she could not see exactly how Jemmy moved to send his kinsman crashing to the ground.

Without thinking Alyson joined in the applause, laughing. When Jemmy straightened, his eye caught hers and he smiled in return, sending a rush of color to her cheeks. And Alyson was so flustered that she did not even see Alistair rise and spring at Jemmy from behind.

They fell to the ground, Jemmy pinned beneath his kinsman's substantial form. The crowd gave a gasp of surprise at the move, then ten hands at once seized Alistair and pulled him roughly to his feet. Jemmy rose and looked at the other man coolly until Alistair turned, flushing, and stalked off the grounds. Jemmy shrugged, refusing all offers of help.

"I'm well," he said. "It would take more than that one to hurt me."

But Alyson saw that as he bent to retrieve his clothing he winced and when he walked to the sidelines he was moving stiffly. Emma saw as well, for she approached him and laid one hand on his arm, speaking to him earnestly. He began to shake off her hand, then shrugged again and followed her toward the cooking fire. Half a dozen women gathered round him, each offering to help. But Emma said in her clear voice, "Nay, let his lady tend to him."

Then all eyes turned to Alyson. What would Maude do? she asked herself frantically, but this time there was no answer. She could not even imagine Maude in this situation, let alone guess how her half sister might react.

"Belike she doesn't know how," one of the women said, looking at her slyly. And they all began to laugh.

Alyson's back stiffened and she walked toward the fire.

"'Tis nothing," Jemmy said. "There's no need—"

"Let me see," Alyson said, kneeling. "Now sit still, stop fidgeting." She passed one hand lightly over his ribs and he drew in a sharp breath. She looked at him quickly.

"Does that hurt?"

"No."

She felt the heat rise to her face but could not seem to look away. "And that?" she said, trying to sound cool and firm. "Is there pain?"

"No. But don't stop—" he added hastily, and she saw a spark of humor in his eyes, humor and something else she could not name but that made her face flame even more hotly. "I think I might have bruised something after all . . ."

"Where, then?" She asked sternly, though for some reason she could not seem to catch her breath.

"I'm not quite sure. You'd best keep looking. Perhaps it's here—"

He covered her hand with his own and moved it slowly across his warm brown skin. The beat of his heart was strong against her palm. When her fingers brushed his nipple he closed his eyes for a moment and swallowed hard. Alyson felt her own nipples tighten in response, and a cramp of something that was not quite pain rippled downward through her body.

She had forgotten all the others who stood watching. The world narrowed to the two of them facing one another, their eyes locked, the waves of hot and cold chasing each other through Alyson's body, the feel of his hand on hers and his flesh beneath her palm.

And then he jerked away.

"That hurt!" he said, aggrieved.

"Well, of course it did," she answered, suddenly remembering what she was about. "You've bruised a rib—it may be cracked. I'd best bind it for you."

She turned and saw Emma watching them, a long strip of fabric in her hands. "Use this."

"Thank you. Now sit still so I can get this tight."

He raised his arms obligingly as she wound the bandage across his ribs. When she leaned forward to pass it around his back, he pulled away with a yelp of laughter. "Careful, there!"

"What, ticklish?" She couldn't help but smile.

All at once she was conscious of the intimacy of what she was doing. Why, all he'd have to do was lower his arms and they would be embraced. As though he read her mind he made the slightest movement forward, and she snapped, "Stay still, please. I can't get this right unless you do."

"As you will, lady," he answered, sounding suspiciously amused.

"Once more around . . . and then I just have to tie it . . . there, 'tis done," she finished with relief, standing and making a show of brushing at her skirt. "So long as you keep this on it shouldn't hurt. If it does you must tell me at once, especially if you feel pain when breathing or if you begin to cough."

"Aye, if it pleases you. What a fuss about nothing," he said, standing and pulling the tunic over his head. "Thank you," he added over his shoulder and Alyson nodded briskly before turning away.

She imagined she could feel him watching her and reluctantly, almost against her will, she looked back. Their eyes met and held in a long unsmiling glance. Then Emma spoke to him and he turned to answer. The moment he looked away Alyson turned and ran back to her cottage as though the devil himself were on her heels.

chapter 22

No sooner had Alyson gained the safety of her own four walls when she began to regret her hasty departure. Emma McLaran had actually spoken to her, though whether as a peacemaking gesture or an attempt to embarrass her, Alyson couldn't quite decide. Either way Alyson had been a fool to let the opportunity slip away.

She went out the door and back to the fire, but Emma was nowhere to be seen. Though the other women pretended to ignore her, they did answer a direct question, admitting grudgingly that Emma had gone back to her own home to tend her ailing husband. When pressed, they pointed out the way.

Malcolm walked across the moor with her, through a stand of alder trees and to a lovely sheltered glade beside a waterfall where the Laird's dwelling stood. Like all the buildings here, it was stark and simple, a plain tower built of heavy stone. A neat, fenced pasture stretched behind it up the mountain, filled with shaggy cattle. A flock of chickens pecked contentedly outside the door, where four men lounged upon the stoop, resting from the games and drinking from a stone jug.

They barely moved to let her pass, but Alyson ignored their rudeness and knocked briskly upon the door. A young girl opened it peered out, her round eyes widening when she recognized their visitor.

"I'd like to see Lady Emma," Alyson said firmly.

"Oh! Aye, well—a moment, please."

The girl shut the door in Alyson's face. She waited, her heart beating quickly as she tried to imagine what she'd say to Emma. Should she tell her whole truth? Or simply mention Clare's name and see what happened next? She wiped sweating palms upon her skirt, praying that when the time came, she would find the words.

E mma tucked the shawl more firmly about her husband's frail shoulders, then pushed another pillow behind his back, propping him higher on the bed.

"Leave off fussing, woman," he said impatiently. "I'm well enough. Just a bit tired."

"I'm not surprised!" Emma answered tartly. "Ye said ye'd stay no more than half an hour—"

"So I did," Hamish agreed. "But ye know as well as I do that this afternoon wasna the reason—"

"Whisht, now," Emma said uncomfortably, smoothing the coverlet with nervous hands. "If it's rest you're wanting, then—"

"I heard it again last night—and you did, too!" he finished, pointing a gnarled finger at his wife. "Dinna trouble to deny it. Keening fit to break my heart."

"The wind in the trees, no more," Emma said, though she didn't raise her eyes to him. Hamish covered her hand with his.

"Now, Emma, we both know that's pure blether," he

said gently. "Not the wind, nor one of the serving girls, either, as ye told me yestere'en."

Emma looked up at him at last with troubled eyes. "Then what, Hamish?"

"Ye ken, hinny. Ye ken as well as I."

Emma jumped up and began to pace the small chamber, then flung open the shutters and breathed deeply of the summer-scented air. Turning away from the window, she said in a low voice, "If 'tis in truth a—a spirit—and I'm not saying that it is—would it be any wonder? Who'd have thought I'd ever speak words of welcome to a Darnley! Aye, Hamish, I heard it, too, last night and every night since Kirallen brought the Sassenach wench among us—"

She broke off at a timid knock upon the door.

"The lady of Kirallen to see ye," the serving girl said.

Emma gave an exasperated sigh. "What can *she* want here?" Is she a bit thick, d'ye think? Tell her I'm not at home."

Her voice carried clearly through the open window. The men seated on the stoop burst into laughter, and Malcolm's hands clenched into fists. "She shouldna have done that," he said, his voice shaking at the insult.

The door opened and the serving girl looked out again. "Lady Emma's not at home," she said with an impudent grin.

"I see. Come then, Malcolm," Alyson added before the boy could speak. "We've come at a bad time."

"Och, aye, ye came at a bad time," one of the men mimicked, getting to his feet where he stood swaying. "Ye hae no business here at all. Get off wi' ye."

Alyson walked down the path, past the field and back into the trees, taking slow, deep breaths to keep the tears away. It had been foolish for her to try this, but at least the attempt had been made. She had nothing to reproach herself with now.

"I canna believe it!" Malcolm cried, stopping and glaring back. "How *could* she be as rude as that?"

"It doesn't matter," Alyson said through trembling lips.

"Aye, but it does! When my grandsire hears, he'll be—"

"Don't tell him, Malcolm," Alyson said, whirling to face him. "Just let it pass."

"But why?" he demanded, hands fisted on his hips. "She was verra wrong—"

He broke off, looking over Alyson's shoulder.

"You're right, Aunt," he said, tugging on her hand. "Quickly, now, we should be getting back."

Turning, Alyson saw the four men from the keep coming after them. She and Malcolm hurried on their way, down the small path through the stand of alder trees. They reached the other side ahead of the men, but as they stepped out on the high moor, they found three more McLaran men approaching. Her heart sank as she recognized Hugh McLaran's flaming head towering above the others.

"Do not fear, Malcolm," Alyson said, tightening her grip upon his hand. "Just walk by as if they aren't there."

They were just passing the men when their pursuers burst from the trees, calling after them.

"Slow down, my lady," one man cried, his voice thick with drink. "Runnin' awa' an' all—whisht, ye'd think we weren't fit to talk wi' ye."

"Go on, Aunt," Malcolm said, turning back. "I'll hold them here."

Alyson was quite ready to obey him, for she knew Malcolm safe enough. It was her they wanted. But now the other men closed round her, and she realized they, too, had been drinking. Alyson had enough experience with drunken men to know they were at the worst stage—their judgment gone, the claims of hospitality forgotten, but still far from insensibility.

"What is it that you want with me?" she asked clearly.

"What do we want wi' ye?" they repeated, seeming to find the question unanswerable.

"Come, Malcolm, we're expected," she said sharply, taking a few steps across the grass. One man, bolder than the others, grabbed her by the arm.

"What do we want wi' her, lads?" he cried. "What can anyone want wi' a wee Sassenach bitch?"

That set them all to laughing, and the man who'd spoken looked around, pleased with the effect of his words. As soon as he took his eyes from her, Alyson drove her elbow full into his stomach. He released her with a startled "Oof!" and she turned to run, but was stopped by two other men who stepped into her path. Turning again, she found herself surrounded.

"Let her go!" Malcolm struggled to push between the men. "Ye dinna dare hurt her!"

"Och, laddie, we dinna mean to *hurt* her," a dark-haired man said, giving Alyson a leering wink. "Run off now and find yer friends."

"I willna!" Malcolm cried. "Let her go!"

"I said get off wi' ye," the man said more sharply now, backhanding Malcolm across the face. "This is no concern o' yours."

Malcolm staggered, then regained his balance, blood streaming from his nose. Alyson looked in the direction of the camp and jerked her head, signaling for him to run. After just a moment's hesitation he obeyed.

"Come now, sweeting," the man said, grabbing her about the waist. "We'll let ye go for the price o' a kiss."

Hugh McLaran took the jug from his lips and wiped a hand across his mouth. "A kiss for all o' us!" he cried, sweeping her into his arms. She twisted wildly in his grasp and he laughed, bending down to her, his arm so tight about her waist that she feared her spine would snap. His breath was foul with whisky, and she turned her head with a cry of disgust.

"Och, she's got yer measure, Hugh!" a young man with curling nut-brown hair called out. "Give her here, she'll no' be so shy wi' a sweet laddie like meself!"

This jest was greeted with roars of laughter and cries of "Wait yer turn!"

And then a cold voice cut through the laughter. "I'll thank you to take your hands from my wife."

"Ah, Jemmy, don't be like that!" the pretty young man said. "We only wanted to make her welcome."

"Get your hands off her, Hugh. Now."

The redheaded man released her. "Dinna take that tone wi' me, Kirallen," he growled.

"I'll take what tone I like," Jemmy snapped, drawing Alyson to his side. She stared down at the ground, tumbled auburn waves curtaining her face as she tried to still her trembling. Jemmy put an arm about her shoulders, and she leaned against him gratefully.

"Did they hurt you?" he asked.

"No. No, they didn't hurt me."

Jemmy nodded and turned to leave. Alyson realized that he was not alone as young Conal fell into step beside her.

"I said dinna take that tone wi' me, Kirallen!" Hugh McLaran roared. "Come back here and beg my leave before ye go."

Jemmy ignored him and walked on, his arm firm around Alyson's shoulder. The McLarans hesitated for an instant, then ran forward, shouting out their battle cry.

"Get back, Maude," was all Jemmy had time to say before the two Kirallens were engulfed in a swirling mass of red-gold tartan.

"Alistair!" Malcolm cried breathlessly. "Alistair, ye must come at once—"

A dozen men lay at their ease on the grass, a plaid spread between them. Alistair shook a pair of dice in his hand, gesturing toward a pile of coins before him. "Not now, Malcolm," he said. "My luck's in."

"But ye have to come! It's the McLarans—they were botherin' my aunt in the high moor—"

One man started to rise, but Alistair stilled him with a wave of his hand. "They won't hurt her," he said, tossing the dice and smiling at the result.

"But Alistair—there are eight o' them at least—all drunk—and I could only find my uncle Jemmy and Conal—"

"Och, then, what's the trouble?" Alistair asked. "Jemmy's a braw fighter. Sure and he can take eight McLarans by himself. Now stop worryin', it'll all sort itself out." He reached back and took Malcolm's wrist, drawing him forward. "Sit down and throw for me—I'll share the winnings wi' ye, lad, and—"

He sat up, grasping Malcolm's chin and turning the boy's face to his, staring at the blood still dripping from his nose. "Where did ye get that?"

"One o' the McLarans," Malcolm sniffed, wiping one hand across his face. "I tried to stop them but—"

"They laid hands on you?" Alistair leaped to his feet in one fluid motion. "Come on, lads," he cried. "To me! A Kirallen!"

From all corners of the moor the cry was answered. "A Kirallen!" a dozen voices roared back, and a moment later they were running up the slope.

A lyson watched the brawling mass of McLarans with horror, straining to find Jemmy in their midst. Occasionally she would glimpse a bit of blue-green fabric, but inevitably it would disappear before she could see how its owner fared. Finally the melee parted enough for her to see Jemmy on his back, Hamish's huge form towering over him.

Alyson looked about frantically, and seizing a fallen branch, she delivered the McLaran a stunning blow upon the head. He collapsed on top of Jemmy and the two of them lay unmoving. But a moment later Jemmy crawled out from underneath the unconscious form. He shot Alyson a grin, but had no time for more before he was once again engulfed.

How could he smile? Alyson wondered, holding the branch aloft but too afraid to use it lest she wound Jemmy or poor Conal, who was being tossed about like flotsom on the tide. A moment later she skipped back into the shelter of the trees as a band of Kirallens, with Alistair in the lead, roared into the fray.

Just as she thought it must surely be over any moment, the ranks were swelled again as the Frasers joined the fight. After that there was no telling which men fought for whom—it was all a tangled confusion of arms and legs and shouted curses, with the occasional blood-curdling battle cry as a new clan arrived and flung themselves into the roiling mass of bodies. She watched in horror, hands pressed against her mouth, and gave a little scream as someone touched her shoulder.

"Quiet, now," Jemmy panted, putting a finger to his lips. "Let's slip away while we can."

She followed him silently through the trees and down another path that wound past the waterfall outside the McLaran keep. For a moment she was afraid he meant to stop there, but instead he took her hand and they walked together over a path of stepping stones spanning the swift-running stream. At last they reached the campsite, and she gave a long sigh of relief.

It was all but deserted now, and the distant sound of fighting and the cries of the women who had gone to watch echoed down the hillside. Jemmy stopped beside a huge cask of honeyed ale and drew them each a mug. Alyson drained it in thirsty gulps.

"Are you hurt?" she asked when she was done, searching his face. His cheek was scraped, one eyebrow split, but he shook his head and grinned. "Are you certain?" she insisted. "Your ribs don't pain you, do they?"

"No, no, I'm fine. But what of you?"

"I'm well enough," she said, but as the realization of her immediate safety reached her, she began to cry. " 'Tis only—"

"What?" he asked gently, putting his arm around her again. "Did they frighten you?"

"Yes—but—that doesn't matter—" she sobbed against his shoulder. " 'Tis that—they were—*McLarans*."

"Aye," he said, drawing her closer. "They were. I'm sorry, Maude, this is all my fault."

"Yours?" she gulped, leaning into the warmth of his embrace. "Why yours?"

"I should never have left you so much alone. But I never thought anything like that would happen."

She made no answer but relaxed in the circle of his arms, her head against his chest, as his hands smoothed the tumbled hair back from her hot face and pressed against the nape of her neck. What wonderful hands he has, she thought drowsily, so strong and yet so gentle, hands that knew precisely how to soothe. She slid her arms around his waist and sighed, rubbing her cheek against the rough wool of his jerkin, inhaling the mingled odors of woodsmoke and heather and clean male sweat.

"Better?" he asked at last and she nodded, raising her head to look into his face.

"This looks like it hurts," she said, lightly touching the cut above his eye.

"No," he said. "Later, maybe, but not now."

She watched in rapt fascination as he leaned forward, her arms sliding up his chest and round his neck without conscious thought or plan.

He always tastes of honey, she thought dizzily. His

tongue touched her lips and they parted in an unconscious invitation that he accepted instantly, crushing her against him while he explored her mouth with a thoroughness that left her breathless. She clung to him, certain she would fall if not for his supporting arms.

"Uncle Jemmy, ye must come with me to your father," Malcolm yelled, bursting upon them.

"Later," Jemmy answered. "Tell him—"

"Nay, Jemmy, now," he insisted. Alyson saw Malcolm's bright blue eyes were glittering with tears above his filthy, blood-smeared face. "He's taken bad—verra bad—and he's askin' for ye—Lady Emma says ye must come at once—"

"I'm sorry," Jemmy said to Alyson. "I must go to him."

"Of course you must. Send for me if I can help," Alyson called after them and Jemmy acknowledged her offer with a wave as he hurried off.

The fight was finished, the men returning to the campsite with many groans and curses to be tended by their women. Alyson returned to her cottage, smiling a little at the inconstancy of men, who could roar like lions one moment and be reduced to helpless children at the next. But when she remembered the cause of the fight her smile faded, and when she thought more seriously on the afternoon's events, her face grew grave.

She said a prayer for the Laird, hoping that his indisposition would pass off quickly. But even if it did, she knew the signs too well to hope that he would ever be restored to health. His old heart was failing, and there was nothing to be done about it, though with proper care and peace he might still have years to live. Where he was to get those things Alyson did not know, for if he survived this time there would be worse to follow.

When darkness came she shut the door and turned back the coverlet on her pallet. Finally, after only the briefest hesitation, she shot the heavy bolt and drew the shutter.

chapter 23

In a small, snug chamber in the McLaran keep, the Laird of Kirallen lay motionless upon the bed. Jemmy sat beside him, alone now that Emma had gone to tend to her own husband.

"He'll be all right—this time," Emma had said, but Jemmy hadn't known whether or not to believe her. By the light of the single candle, his father looked so gaunt, his skin so pale, his hands so lifeless as they lay folded upon his breast.

When his eyelids fluttered open, Jemmy breathed a sigh of relief. No matter how his father might anger him, God knew he had never wished him dead.

The Laird's unfocused gaze wandered about the bedchamber, then fastened on Jemmy's face.

"I've been lying here thinking of Stephen," he said weakly.

"Stephen?" Jemmy repeated blankly.

"Aye. Such a terrible thing that happened to him. I blamed myself."

"But it wasn't your fault—"

"I never liked him," the Laird whispered, his head moving restlessly upon the pillow. "When he was born there was such a fuss about it and my parents—they favored him. Always."

"Don't think about it now. It was all so long ago," Jemmy said, slipping an arm beneath his father's head and holding the cup Emma had left to his lips.

The laird drank, then fell back with a small sigh.

"When I was younger I used to dream of going off and seeing other places—ye dinna know that, did ye? Oh, aye, I had my dreams, but I always knew they'd come to nothing. I was the heir. Had to bide at home."

"Aye, Father," Jemmy murmured, trying to soothe him back to sleep. But Kirallen kept talking as if he hadn't heard.

"I was married at seventeen—not to your mother, but my first wife, Machara, that was. She was a good woman, I suppose, but hardly a young man's dream. She was older than I, not much to look at, and so grim! Not that I could blame her for that, poor lady. She bore me four children and not one of them lived. God knows what she thought of me—I never did. I was always plain, ye ken, and never had much to say to the lasses. Never had a woman but Machara and she—well, she bore it bravely," he added with a wry twist to his lips.

"And there was Stephen, such a bonny lad, even then the women used to make a fuss over him . . . he was always talking of all the places he meant to see, the adventures he would have . . . He would have done it, too. All the things I wanted came so easy to him.

"Then Machara—God rest her—died, and I wed your mother." Kirallen's eyes lit with the memory. "She was so beautiful—can ye remember how beautiful she was?"

"Aye," Jemmy answered softly. "I remember."

"She was half my age, ye ken, and always so kind, so merry. I was—struck dumb by her. She gave me Ian, and then you, and it was as though all those years when I was so unhappy dinna matter anymore. Ye canna imagine how happy she made me."

"Oh, I think I can," Jemmy said.

"But sometimes—not often, but sometimes—I would see her laughing with Stephen. He was just a bairn when we wed, but as he grew . . . all the lasses used to sit up sharp when he walked into the room."

"Aye, they did," Jemmy said, smiling a little.

"And I would remember how much older I was and try to make allowances—but I dinna like him. I tried to; he was my brother, but . . . He made mock of me and all I had been taught to honor."

Kirallen's eyes fell shut and Jemmy began to think he'd gone to sleep. But when they opened again, they were clear and sharp.

"Ye were always like him."

"I—I knew I favored him."

"When he was dead—and oh, I was sorry for that, the way he went. I wouldna have wished that on anyone, let alone my brother. And your mother went just after him. I'd lie awake at night, wondering what I had done wrong, if I'd somehow made it happen. Mad thoughts, night crows in the darkness. Then I'd wake the next morning and push it all aside. But then ye grew and—well, daft, ye might think, but there were times I'd look at ye and it could have been Stephen all over again, defying me, questioning all I held to be the truth."

"I understand," Jemmy said, covering his father's hand with his.

"How could ye know how it feels to look at your own son and see a stranger? Or no, not a stranger, worse than that, a—a—"

"A ghost," Jemmy said quietly.

"Aye," Kirallen whispered, his hand gripping Jemmy's. "Not your fault. I see that now. Ian was more like me, ye ken, saw things the way I did, but he had your mother's spirit—and her looks. He made everything come right, can ye see that? All the choices I had made, they seemed the right ones . . . while Ian was alive."

"I'm so sorry," Jemmy said helplessly.

The door opened quietly and Alistair looked in.

"You're awake," Alistair said. "Thank God. They were saying—I thought that ye—"

He fell to his knees beside the bed and bent his head.

"I'm not about to die," Kirallen said, reaching out his hand to stroke Alistair's white-gold head. "Whisht, lad, 'tis all right, I'm fine now. Dinna greet."

Jemmy began to rise, but his father gripped his hand hard.

"Don't leave, Jemmy. I want ye both with me."

Alistair raised his head. His eyes were still wet, rimmed with red as they met Jemmy's across the bed.

"We'll stay, Father," Jemmy said, and Alistair nodded. "Go to sleep now."

chapter 24

It was a somber sky that greeted Alyson when she stepped outside her cottage in answer to Jemmy's knock. He looked weary and disheveled, but he smiled when he saw her.

"Forgive me for last night," he said. "My father kept me by his side."

Alyson did not know how to retreat from the new intimacy between them. But surely there was no need to just yet. Plenty of time to be unpleasant later, she decided, giving into the temptation to return his smile.

"He's better then?"

"Aye. For now. But very eager to be home again."

"Surely he can't travel yet!"

"He shouldn't," Jemmy said. "But he says if he's going to die, he wants to do it in his own bed. I think it won't trouble him overmuch if we take it slowly. I said I'd ride back with him—and I imagine you'll be ready to leave here, as well."

"Aye," she said with relief. "How soon do we ride?"

"Will half an hour be enough for you to make ready?"

"I'm ready now," she answered. "My chest can be sent."

"Thank you. Gather what you need and I'll see to the horses."

Before the time appointed she stood beside her horse, but her relief at slipping away without meeting the McLarans again was short-lived. Emma came to see them off, holding Laird Kirallen's arm as he walked slowly toward the small party who had decided to accompany him back to Ravenspur. Alyson bent over her saddlebags as the farewells were made, but lifted her head at a touch upon her arm.

Hugh McLaran stood before her, for all his size looking like nothing so much as an overgrown boy. His fiery head bent, he traced one toe upon the grass and mumbled something that she didn't hear.

"Speak up, Hugh!" Emma scolded, driving her elbow sharply into his ribs.

"I'm verra sorry, m'lady," he muttered. "I was hot wi' drink and sore from my defeat at the wrestlin'—not that that's any excuse," he added quickly, his eyes meeting hers briefly and then darting away. "I'm sore ashamed o' what we did, and ye such a wee—"

"Sassenach bitch?" she finished, so low that no one heard but him.

He flushed to the roots of his red hair. "Och, now, dinna be remindin' me," he groaned, but his mouth twitched in a smile. "I've paid somewhat for those words already, lady. Ye wield a mighty staff."

Alyson smiled in return. "Then we'll call it quits."

"And you, laddie," Hugh added to Malcolm. "I cry your pardon and hope ye won't be holding any grudge against us."

Malcolm gave him a stern look. " 'Tis no way to treat a kinsman, Hugh," he said. "But I'll overlook it this once."

"There's a lad!" Hugh said, clapping him on the back. "Sure and next time ye'll be takin' on the lot o' us yerself, just as yer da would have done. And as yer uncle *did*," he cried, turning to Jemmy and holding out his hand, which Jemmy took.

"I'm sorry, Jemmy," he said. "For all of it."

"Farewell, Hugh," Jemmy said. "Give my regards to the others."

"When they're able to stand again, I will!" Hugh answered with a wink. "But I fear that may be some time yet."

He walked away, his laughter lingering behind him, and Jemmy helped his father to mount. Alyson had just placed her own foot in the stirrup when she was halted again.

"My lady," Emma McLaran said. "A moment, please."

"Aye?" Alyson asked coolly, taking a few steps away from her party.

Emma bit her lip, then said quickly, "That was very prettily done, the way ye spoke to Hugh. I'm grateful. There's been blood spilt for less than happened yesterday."

"It seems blood feuds are cried too easily in these parts," Alyson answered. "God forbid I should be the cause of one."

"I never thought ye meant half o' what ye said to me the day we met," Emma went on quickly. "All yer talk o' forgiveness—I thought it only words—but I see now ye spoke from yer heart. And I know that the real fault yesterday lay wi' me. I never imagined ye would hear me," she admitted, her weathered face reddening. "But I should have kent the open window . . ."

"Don't trouble yourself about it," Alyson said, as coolly courteous as Maude could be herself. She raised her brows and looked pointedly at the Kirallens, who were waiting for her so they might leave.

"Oh, but I am troubled, lady," Emma said. " 'Twas wrong—verra wrong—I spoke out o' the bitterness o' my own heart, but that has naught to do wi' ye. It all happened before you were even born, ye see . . ."

Jemmy approached, leading Alyson's palfrey, but Emma halted Alyson with a hand and called, "Just a moment, Jemmy, if ye please. I'll nae be long here. You see, my lady," she said, "There was a young girl taken from us years ago, Clare was her name. She was promised to Gawyn's brother—the youngest, Stephen. But as we rode to her marriage feast we were attacked." She looked Alyson in the eye and added slowly, "By your father. And Clare was taken."

Alyson's limbs turned to ice-cold stone. Stephen. That was the last word Mam had spoken before she died. Many a time Alyson had puzzled over it, wondering who he might be. All those years and Clare had never forgotten him, had called for him when she lay hot with fever, asking Alyson again and again if he had come. "Not yet," she'd answered, laying cool cloths on Clare's brow. "But he'll be here soon."

"He isna coming," Clare had whispered. "He doesna want me now."

So this was the faithless churl who'd abandoned Clare after her capture! And he was a Kirallen. Alyson wondered that she hadn't met him yet and knew that when she did she would be hard put to hold her tongue. In fact, at that moment she understood more about the desire for vengeance than she had ever wanted to know. Remembering her mother's misery, Alyson burned to put a knife through Stephen Kirallen's heart, though she doubted that pain would be near to that which Clare had borne.

Emma's hair was drawn back in a careless braid upon her neck, and as the wind strengthened, a few wisps escaped to blow about her face. She brushed at them impatiently, and for the first time Alyson noticed her hands.

They were small and pale with long slender fingers, hands that even age and a lifetime of work could not make less beautiful. Alyson held her own hands out before her and stared at them.

"I never had word of her again," Emma said. "It was all a long time ago but I never forgot—you see, my lady, Clare was my *daughter.*"

"Your daughter?" Alyson repeated in a strangled whisper. "She was your daughter?"

"Aye," Emma said.

"Oh, Lady Emma—I didn't know—Clare was my—"

"Half a moment, Alistair!" Emma cried impatiently as the knight came forward, Malcolm at his side, to complain of the delay.

"The morning draws on," Alistair said, giving Alyson a look of annoyance. "We must be gone."

Emma waved a hand at him and turned back to Alyson. "What were ye sayin', lady?" she asked eagerly. "Clare was your—?"

"Not here," Alyson said distractedly. "If we could talk alone—"

"No, go on, Maude," Jemmy said. "This touches all of us."

You don't know how greatly it touches us all, Alyson thought, and God help me when you find out. She hesitated, seeing Alistair and Malcolm were watching her with interest, waiting for her words.

"She was—my—friend," she stammered in confusion. "Though I never—I didn't know—or I would have said something to you before—"

"She *was* your friend?" Emma repeated. "D'ye mean she's dead?"

"Aye," Alyson said. "Five years ago."

Emma drew in a sharp breath and bent her head. "Five years?" she repeated. "All that time—we searched for so long . . . why didna she get word to us somehow? Oh, lady, can ye tell me of her? Anything at all."

"Well, I was just a child then," Alyson managed. "Let me see . . . she was very learned, I remember, and had a lovely voice. She used to sing sometimes to—to the children—"

Emma nodded eagerly, watching her, waiting for her to continue. *She was my mother,* Alyson cried silently, *and I loved her so much. She never knew that you searched for her. If only you had found her, how different everything would be! She never forgot you, never, or stopped longing for her home. But I'm here now, just as I promised her. Look at me, don't you know me? Can't you see?*

But there was no recognition in Emma's eyes, and at last Alyson continued haltingly, "She was married to a sailor. He was a kind man, always laughing and joking. He used to bring her presents from abroad."

"Bairns?"

"Aye." Alyson could barely speak now, her throat felt as though someone had it in an iron grip. "She did have children. A daughter and a son."

"Do ye ken where they are?"

The hope in Emma's face died as Alyson shook her head. "I'm so sorry," she whispered. "I can't say."

"Ah, if I could see them even once. Clare was my only child and verra dear to me . . ." Emma touched Alyson's shoulder. "Thank you," she added, her voice breaking, then turned and walked swiftly across the fields.

Alyson watched her go through eyes blurred with tears. "I'll stay another day or two," she said to Jemmy. "Then ride back with the others."

"You'll meet again," Laird Kirallen said from atop his horse. "And I would feel easier if ye'd come back with us."

"But it would comfort her to speak to me—and I would like to stay a bit, truly."

"You did well to tell her," Jemmy added. "But 'tis

enough. Later she will want to speak more with you, but we must leave as we planned. You can't stay, Maude. Not unless I stay, as well. Get on your horse," he ordered as she hesitated. "We must begone."

Alyson could think of nothing else to say, so she turned and mounted. Jemmy laid one hand over hers on the saddle. "Was it true?" he asked, looking up at her.

"What?" Alyson said, her heart beating wildly in her breast.

"All you said of her husband being such a kind man and all."

"Oh," Alyson said, sagging with relief as she realized what he meant. "Well—no, it wasn't. Her husband was a— a hard man. He could be pleasant enough, but when he drank he was different. She was—frightened of him," she added, remembering Jacob Bowden's terrible rages.

Jemmy squeezed her hand. "It was a kind lie," he said, then released her and swung himself into the saddle. "And now, Alistair, if you're *finally* ready," he said, meeting his kinsman's glare with a bland smile. "We can be on our way."

chapter 25

❦

They arrived back at Ravenspur in the strange half-light of evening. Jemmy dismounted and took his father's arm as they walked across the cobbled yard.

When they reached the doorway he looked back. For all that he had matched his steps to his father's halting pace, Maude was still well behind them.

All during the ride back she had been silent, withdrawn into a place so distant that Jemmy had not been able to break through. He had tried every way he knew to lighten her spirits but had failed to win a single smile.

What had happened to the girl who had kissed him on the moor? She was gone, vanished as completely as if she'd never been. There were names for women who treated men as she was treating Jemmy, whipping him into a fever of desire and then turning a cold shoulder to his advances. But he could not believe she was playing such a game deliberately.

All her moods were real enough, he knew. She wanted

him, but something held her back from giving herself in the way she would have to do to be his wife in truth. He'd heard it said that gently born ladies were sometimes morbidly fearful of the marriage bed. It was a fear that could often be cured with patience—and with time. The one thing he didn't have.

"Good night, Maude," he said, then yawned deliberately. "Sleep well."

A flicker of relief passed across her pale set face. Well, then, at least he knew. And as she herself had told him, it was a fine thing to know something for sure. No matter how much it might hurt.

When the Laird was settled for the night, he looked about his chamber with a contented sigh. The maids had taken advantage of his absence; all the books had been replaced on their freshly dusted shelves and it smelled pleasantly of polish and fresh flowers.

" 'Tis good to be home again."

"Aye," Jemmy agreed, meaning it. "It is."

"In Spain," Kirallen began hesitantly. "Do ye have a home there?"

Jemmy sat down on the edge of the bed. "Not really. I have a place I stop between voyages, in Cadiz. Just a set of rooms that overlooks the sea. Before, though, when I was first there, I lived for a time in a villa. 'Twas—my wife's family home."

"Carmela," Kirallen said, speaking the name that Jemmy couldn't bring himself to say. "We were all sorry for your loss. We had masses said for her."

Jemmy looked away. "I didn't ken that. Thank you."

"What was she like?" Kirallen asked.

"She was very pretty. Very young. We both were." He stood, ending the conversation before it could go any further. "Well, goodnight, Father. You must be tired out. I'll see you in the morning."

Now what had made him mention Carmela, he won-

dered as he walked to his own chamber. It wasn't as if he
thought of her. Not now, at any rate. Or at least not often.

He stood at his window as the last light faded from the
hills. He did not see the stars emerge, though, but green-
blue waves tipped with frothy foam, breaking upon a sun-
splashed shore. He smelled the intoxicating scent of brine
and felt soft sand beneath his bare feet and sunshine warm
upon his head. Yes, it was so clear, even now, the way it
had been so long ago as he strolled along, laughing,
Carmela's hand on his arm.

The first time he'd seen her he'd been struck dumb by
her beauty. Small and plump, with dark hair falling straight
as a waterfall down her back, she'd entered the reception
on her father's arm. Jemmy had watched her all the
evening, and at some point she had become aware of him.
Dark eyes beckoned him from across the room, holding
depth upon depth of mystery and promise. He hung back,
suddenly shy, and she bowed her head, smiling, then
looked up through her lashes with an invitation no man
could mistake. Jemmy moved across the floor as though
entranced. She held out her hand, he took it, and from that
moment he knew that he must have her.

The Velasquezes were a minor branch of an old and
noble family, but years before they had fallen on hard
times. Their villa was lovely but crumbling in the sea air,
weeds growing high between the cracked flagstones of the
courtyard.

They accepted his suit with warmth, obviously believing that the Scottish noble's son must be a wealthy man.
And Jemmy did nothing to correct their mistake. He was
prepared to do anything at all to give Carmela the life she
deserved. She was so delightful when she was happy, so
gay and amorous and charming, so pleased with every gift
he made her.

Her favorite was the pearls. They'd cost far more than
Jemmy could afford, but that meant nothing when set

against the brilliant smile he received when he presented them.

From that day she wore them constantly. On formal occasions she twined them among dark braids dressed high upon her brow. In private she wore them with nothing else at all, and laughed as she wound them about Jemmy's throat and wrists as they lay together in their bed on hot Spanish afternoons, the scent of rose and jasmine carried on a fresh sea breeze through the open window.

His voyages grew longer, and he was involved in activities that were decidedly questionable. The last one nearly resulted in the loss of his ship, and he only just managed to escape the bailiffs, arriving home unexpectedly one night . . .

It was an old, old story, he thought now. If he hadn't been so damned innocent he would have known it was coming. As it was, he was completely stunned to find another man in his bed. Carmela's head was resting on his shoulder, her hair flowing about them like a silken cloak, her hand drooping almost to the floor with the pearls still caught among her fingers.

Eight years later Jemmy could still feel the pain of it, the disbelief, the shattering humiliation and blinding rage. He'd nearly killed the man, though he remembered little of the fight. The one thing he could never forget was the sound of pearls dancing across the marble floor when he ripped the strand to pieces.

Carmela had fallen to her knees in tears, begging for forgiveness. He should have left, of course. He should have walked out as soon as he knew of her betrayal. But he hadn't. Instead he'd listened to her lies, wanting desperately to believe that this had been the first time, that she was frantic with loneliness, that it was really him she loved. He'd wanted to believe it, and he told himself he did believe it.

Until the next time.

Then no self-delusion was possible. He left her but she came to his cabin, pleading, swearing it would never happen again, a scene that was repeated many times over the next two years. And always he'd taken her back, cursing himself for a fool but helpless to resist. When they were together he was in heaven, so violently in love that he could not imagine life without her. But the moment he left he would be tormented by doubts, wanting to believe her promises but certain she was with another man. And all too often this proved to be the case. But then she would cry and she was so muddled and helpless, so genuinely sorry, that he couldn't find it in his heart to turn her away. She simply couldn't bear to be alone, that was the truth of it. And he knew no other way to make his living than to go to sea.

Two years their marriage had lasted, two years of stormy scenes and passionate reconciliations. But in time even the reconciliations lost their charm. He knew that she would never change—indeed, he wondered if she could change even if she wanted to. By the end the only question in his mind was which of them he despised more, himself or her.

And then with a shocking suddenness it was over. He returned from a short run to find that she was dead. It was a summer fever, they said, she'd gone quickly. But seeing the way her father's eyes slid away as he gave him the news, Jemmy wondered if that was the truth or whether one of her many lovers had turned violent. It had happened before. One of the more sordid aspects of the marriage was the constant danger to both of them from the men Carmela took up and cast off as easily as she did her clothing.

But Jemmy didn't press the Velasquez family with unwelcome questions, for he was overwhelmed with relief, quickly followed by shame. At last he did grieve for Carmela, the young girl he'd met and loved, even as he

chapter 26

❤

"My lady."
Celia curtsied, smiling, and took the cloak from Alyson's shoulders.

"No need for any of ye to stay," the serving girl said clearly. "I'll do what's needful."

When they were alone, Celia threw the cloak on the bed and sat down. "Welcome back," she said. "Lord Darnley will be waiting to see ye tomorrow at dawn."

"Tomorrow? But how does he know—"

"He kens all ye do," Celia answered. "Mind that well. Now get your rest and be ready."

The time must be growing closer, Alyson thought as she lay down in the soft bed. How much longer do I have? How long do any of us have now?

It was becoming more difficult for Alyson to slip away unnoticed. On her way to the stables she was stopped first by Maggie, then by Malcolm, who begged earnestly to be allowed to accompany her on her ride. By the time she and Celia turned out of the stable yard, they were far behind their time.

When she reached the clearing she saw Robin standing by Lord Darnley, with Sir Robert still mounted on his steed. With a cry she flung herself from her horse and gathered her brother close, then held him at arm's length and looked at him. He'd put on flesh, she saw at once, the starveling look was gone from his face and his eyes were bright. His hair was neatly brushed, the yellow curls tied back with a bit of ribbon, and he wore the livery of a page.

He explained excitedly that Sir Robert had taken him into his service and already had taught him to ride. ". . . and Ally, just wait until you see! He taught me to handle his hawk and even let me fly her once—" He ran toward the horses and Alyson rose to her feet.

"Well?" Darnley demanded. "Do they suspect?"

"My lord," she said in a low, rapid voice, hands twisting at her skirt. "I cannot do this. I cannot. Please, please let me come home with you. There must be another way, I'm sure Laird Kirallen will listen if you only—"

He gripped her arm so tightly that she cried out. "Oh, no, my girl, we have a bargain. Time is growing short. Then I'll finish them, do you understand?"

"How short, my lord?"

"Never mind that. Just do your part."

"But you don't need me anymore!" Alyson cried. "Let Celia stay—"

"Do you think they'll keep her once you've run off? There can be nothing to arouse their suspicions, not now. You go back and play your part—and by God, you'd better do it well. I'll hear of it if you don't. I'm leaving Robert here. He'll wait for you in this place every morning. If anything goes wrong you or Celia can find him here. I'm taking the boy back myself."

Alyson looked at Robin who was standing, a hooded falcon on his arm, talking with the knight. "Don't think I'll hesitate," Darnley warned. "I'll slit his throat and never think twice about it." He pushed her from him with such force that she stumbled, nearly falling.

Robin ran up then and she examined the bird, pretending great interest as he explained how it had been captured and all about its care. At last it was time to leave and she caught her brother close, holding him for so long that he began to squirm with impatience. "Ally, what's wrong?" he asked, looking into her face. "You're crying!"

"No—well, maybe just a little. I've missed you."

"But you'll be back soon, won't you?"

She nodded and reassured him, then watched him mount and ride off, looking very small beside Lord Darnley's substantial form. When they were gone she ordered Celia back to the manor, saying she would join her shortly.

"Sir Robert," she said hesitantly when they were alone. "If anything should happen to me—"

"It won't," he said at once. "This will all be over soon and you'll come home again."

"Of course," she agreed. Their eyes met and they silently acknowledged the lie. "But just the same, if anything were to happen I'd like to know Robin would be cared for. Would you take him?"

He began to protest again, then stopped. "Yes, I will. He's a good boy, very bright."

"He is. Thank you. I feel much easier now."

"Alyson."

She turned, one foot in the stirrup.

"I tried to send him away, to London. But John found out and stopped it. He was very angry with me. I daren't try it again or he'll send me packing."

"Thank you," she said. "It was good of you to try."

"Wait," he said, coming forward and laying a hand on

her knee. "I wanted to say—I'm sorry I ever went along with this. You had the right of it, John shouldn't have sworn if he didn't intend to keep his word. But it's too late now to stop it. You do what you have to do and get out of that place."

"Yes," she said. "Of course. I'll do what I have to do. Goodbye, Sir Robert."

He stood for a long time after she had gone, trying to ignore the feeling of foreboding that had gripped him in the past days. Had he ever really believed this was a clever trick to play upon the Kirallens? Now it seemed a base and cowardly thing to do, sending a young girl like Alyson to what could easily be her death. No, this wasn't amusing anymore, not at all.

If only he'd stayed in London where he belonged and never come to this wretched place! Once this was over he doubted he'd be back again. Though he and John had never been close, there had always been an offhanded affection between the two of them. Now Robert saw the kind of man John really was, and he realized that he didn't like his brother. In fact, lately he'd come dangerously close to hating him. And Maude, who he'd once thought spirited and rather charming, was no more than a selfish, spoiled child.

What a family, he thought, shaking his head. And I'm no better than either of them. Watching Alyson vanish over the hills he thought, she's the best of us—and look at what we've done to her.

When the whole thing started Robert had never stopped to consider how Alyson might feel, or even if she had feelings at all. If asked then, he would have said she didn't—or certainly not the sensibilities of a nobly born girl. The lower classes were different, everyone knew that! They were hardened to life at an early age, able to bear cold and hunger and discomfort that no noble could possibly endure. Some of them were good people, of course, industrious and worthy. But they were simple people, too, and didn't possess those finer feelings reserved for the nobly born.

That's what Robert had believed. When he'd thought Alyson was tempted by the lure of gold it had all made perfect sense. Greed was a motive he could understand—not approving, but not exactly disapproving, either. It was, after all, the way of the world, and Robert considered himself a worldly man. Then she'd told him about her brother, and for the first time he'd seen her—really seen her as a person, not just a tool to be taken up and used as they saw fit. And what he'd seen made him doubt the wisdom of their plan.

But he hadn't acted. Once he knew the facts he should have found a way to put a stop to it, or at least refused to take any part in something so very wrong. But he hadn't. And he would carry that on his conscience for the rest of his life. He could go back to London and take up his life again, but he would never be the same; he'd always know that had been a part of an enterprise he could only regard as shameful.

Once he'd thought that he would make a ballad of this story, imagining how the Duke of Lancaster's court would laugh at the odd doings of the northern rustics. But now he knew he wouldn't be telling this tale to anyone—save for the priest who would hear his confession. And if what he feared was to happen—well, then, no matter if he purchased pardons from God and all the saints, he would never be able to forgive himself.

chapter 27

❦

The outer bailey was almost deafening. Pigs squealed, cattle lowed, merchants cried their wares. It was rent and market day at Ravenspur, and Jemmy had spent a long, hot morning sitting in the hall, greeting all his tenants and accepting rents as the steward sat beside him, pen scratching furiously as he noted every payment rendered.

By midafternoon Jemmy was relieved to escape the heat and stench—both human and animal—that pervaded the close-packed hall and answer his father's summons.

The Laird was sitting in the solar. When Jemmy's mother was alive, this room had been a merry place. It was always filled with women sewing, talking, laughing, slipping Jemmy bits of candied ginger when he came to visit. Now it was a man's room, with parchments, harnesses, and discarded weapons tumbled on the shelves where bits of ribbon used to lie. Three hounds dozed by the fire where the Laird sat with another man.

Master Johnson, the headman of Dunforth, rose and

bowed. "Good day," he said to Jemmy. "And farewell. Laird, I'll see ye next market day."

As he passed by Jemmy, Johnson said, "Oh, in case ye wondered, Tavis is back wi' his sheep again and right as ever. The boy's coming along. I was just telling the Laird all about it."

"Were you?" Jemmy said, looking to his father.

"Aye. Someone had to," Johnson added beneath his breath, giving Jemmy a wry smile as he left the room.

"It was quite a tale," Kirallen said, reaching down to stroke one of the hounds. "I should have given ye the chance to tell it for yourself."

"Well, you know it now."

"Aye. He had some other things to say, as well."

Jemmy sat down cautiously. "Such as?"

"He told me he had his doubts about ye coming back, but he was pleased to say how wrong he'd been. He thought ye handled the business with Tavis as well as anyone could have done." The Laird glanced up. "And I agreed."

A sudden, not unpleasant heat rose to Jemmy's face. "Tricky situation," he said awkwardly.

"Aye."

"And Maude deserves at least part of the credit. She was quite warm in Tavis's defense."

"Aye, Master Johnson mentioned that as well. Said what a kind lady she was, so pleasant with the children. How surprised they all were, given what they'd heard, to see the two of ye so taken with each other."

"Master Johnson has a busy tongue."

"And a keen eye. Ye said once that I saw ye and Maude as pieces on a game board. I didn't like it—but I know the truth when I hear it spoken. So I'm giving ye the next move, Jemmy. What is it ye want to do?"

Jemmy looked out the window, where an approaching storm had wrapped the hills in mist. He summoned the image of the *Osprey,* sails unfurled beneath a blazingly blue sky, himself standing on her deck. Then he remembered the day on the high moor, Maude resting her head against his shoulder, the scents of sunlight and sweet heather caught among her curls. A muscle leaped in his clenched jaw as he looked at last into his father's face.

"I want to come home."

"For good and aye?"

"Yes."

The Laird leaned back in his seat and regarded Jemmy steadily. "And Malcolm? What becomes of him?"

"Keep him as your heir," Jemmy said. "That matters not to me."

"Perhaps not now, but when ye have bairns of your own, ye might feel differently."

So he still doesn't trust me, Jemmy thought, then realized that his father was not questioning his loyalty, just giving him the chance to think this through.

"I might," he conceded. "But if I give my word, I'll keep it."

"I believe that," Kirallen said. "Though ye may find it harder than ye think. And what of Alistair?"

"What of him? He doesn't like me and he never will, but I think that I can handle Alistair."

"Ye have to work together. He has all the knights with him. Ian may have given them too much leeway, but he ken—as I ken—that ye won't rule long without them. It's a balance, ye ken. Sometimes ye have to give a little."

Never in Jemmy's memory had his father talked to him like this. Like an equal. Like a son.

"I'll find the way," he promised.

Kirallen smiled. "Aye. I think ye will."

chapter 28

❧

Alyson rode for hours, letting the mare wander as she would through the hills. The sky grew dark and a chill wind blew from the north, but Alyson was oblivious to the approaching storm. She considered going back and telling Jemmy everything. Could she trust him? She didn't know. She wanted to—but was that only because of the way he made her feel? He wanted peace, and he must want it very badly to have agreed to this marriage against the will of his clansmen. He was a good man, but was he strong enough to protect her and Robin? Would he even want to?

How would he feel when he learned how completely he'd been deceived? He would—he *must* be angry. But would he turn his anger on her? He might. Even if he didn't—even if he pitied her, which was possible, for he was a kind man—what could he do? Darnley had set the trap, and once Jemmy learned of it, he'd have no choice but to respond.

She couldn't tell him. He'd have to fight Lord Darnley,

that was unavoidable. And the preparations for battle would be seen—and then Lord Darnley would know that she'd told, and Robin would pay the price.

Yet what was the alternative? That she say nothing and stand by, watching them die and knowing it was all her fault.

Despair washed over her and she turned the horse's head into the wind, clapping her heels to its side, galloping over the hills until she reached a high, steep crag. There she dismounted, tying the reins to a bush and beginning the long climb, at last arriving breathless at the top.

She looked down at the river far below, churning white foam over sharp rocks, and shuddered, taking a step back. This was a sin, but it would be a worse sin to go on lying, betraying innocent people to their death.

Robin would be fine without her now. He was happy with Sir Robert, and she knew the knight would honor his promise. Robin would be all right. And when she looked at the situation honestly, there was no way she could ever return to her old life. Even if she managed to survive until the Kirallens were dead, she doubted Darnley would let her go back to the kitchens. She knew too much. And where else could she go? Not to the McLarans, that was certain, not after she had helped plan the slaughter of their friends and kin.

She couldn't go back to Ravenspur. She couldn't go home, for she had no home now. There was nowhere left for her to go, nothing left for her to do. The water rushed by in an endless wave, and slowly, hardly aware of what she did, Alyson moved closer to the edge.

Jemmy galloped his horse over the downs, hoping he'd reach home before the rain began. The approaching storm didn't look like anything to trifle with. He sighed impatiently, thinking that this was a fool's errand if ever he'd seen one. A soaking would be a perfect end to it.

He had waited for Maude to come back again, but his impatience had gotten the best of him in the end. But now he realized how ridiculous it was to think he could find her. She was probably back at Ravenspur already.

So here he was, racing the storm, which bent the long grass to the ground as it approached. Through the keening of the wind he heard another sound, one that made him pull up and sit, listening hard. Yes, there it was, a horse's frightened whinny. He turned toward the sound and found the mare tethered to a bush. It was Maude's horse all right, there was no mistaking the blaze on its nose or the white splash on the withers. But where was Maude?

It was then he saw her standing far above him on the crag, silhouetted against the dark clouds. His first feeling was irritation—silly lass, didn't she know the footing up there wasn't safe? And particularly not in a storm. He made the long climb quickly, for the wind was howling now and the rain only moments away.

When he reached the top he didn't stop to speak but pulled her backward from the edge.

"Sweet Christ, lady, are you mad?"

"Let go of me!" she cried, struggling in his grasp.

"I won't. Not until you tell me what you were doing up there. You could have fallen—"

She put her hands against his chest and pushed with all her strength. He stumbled backward and she wrenched herself from his grasp. The rain began then, falling in a blinding rush as he lunged forward and grasped her about the knees. She hit the ground hard and lay gasping as he made his way up the slope, now a river of mud, until he lay beside her, breathing hard.

"Come on." He grasped her arm and pulled her to her feet, keeping his balance with difficulty. "You're coming with me."

Alyson was too weary to think anymore so she followed him to the place where she had left her horse. The animal was gone, though, no doubt frightened by the storm. Jemmy took her up before him in the saddle and started back.

Where can I go now? What can I do? The words went round and round in Alyson's mind until they lost all meaning. She leaned against Jemmy's shoulder and closed her eyes. He is very strong, she thought drowsily. If only I could trust him how different it would be. But I can't.

Why couldn't she? She didn't remember now, she couldn't think, it was all too much. She should have jumped—she'd meant to—but it seemed her mother's voice halted her on the edge, though when she looked around she was alone. But then she remembered Clare saying that suicide was a terrible sin and despised herself for her own cowardice. If Clare had been able to go on after all that she had suffered, how could she herself do less?

What should I do next? she wondered wearily. Where can I go now? She wished she could go on riding with Jemmy forever, close in the circle of his arms.

But at length they reached the stables. They were deserted, save for the horses munching quietly in the long row of stalls. They dismounted and Alyson stood, her head bent, not moving, as Jemmy unsaddled his stallion and flung a blanket over its steaming back. What was the point of going inside? she wondered dully. What was the point of anything now?

"Maude," he said abruptly. "Are you so unhappy here? We can get an annulment. I'll go to your father and explain—"

"No!" she cried. "Please, my lord, not that!" She put her hands on his shoulders, looking pleadingly into his face. "I'll do anything you ask but please, I beg you, don't say anything of this to my father."

"There's no shame in an annulment. It will be as

though this marriage never happened—it's not too late to set it right."

"No," she shook her head. "Please."

"What were you doing up there on the crag?" he asked sharply. "It looked like you were about to—"

"No, I wasn't, truly. Please, my lord, please believe me. It's just that I needed—wanted to be alone for a time and I didn't notice the storm—"

"Don't lie to me. Not now. I thought you were getting accustomed to us, but if I was wrong, you have to tell me now. Your father won't blame you—I'll tell him that you did your best, it's all my fault—"

She began to shake with cold and the fear of what might happen if he went to Darnley and asked for an annulment. "No!" she whispered. "No annulment. Please."

He put his hands on her shoulders and shook her lightly. "Then what is it you want? How can I help you if you won't tell me? Talk to me, Maude! Make me understand."

She shook her head blindly, trying to force her mind to work. She couldn't tell him the truth. Not now, not like this. But she could think of nothing else to say.

"Is it me?" he asked roughly. "Is that it?"

"No!" she cried. "You've been so kind—"

And then all at once she was in his arms, her face pressed against the sodden wool of his gambeson.

Somewhere a voice whispered that this was wrong, it was foolish and dangerous to forget herself this way. I'll stop it in just a moment, she thought as he bent to her, his mouth coming down hard on hers. She meant to pull away but instead found herself winding her arms around his neck and returning his kiss with desperate need.

His hand brushed her breast, sending such a sharp spear of desire running through her that she gave a startled cry of pleasure. He undid the laces of her gown with hands made clumsy by haste, then pulled the fabric from her shoulder and bent his head, his lips burning against her icy skin,

moving with exquisite delicacy until his tongue touched
the peak of her breast. She wound her hands in his hair and
pulled him closer with a wordless cry.

And then they were lying in a mound of fragrant straw,
and he was helping her pull off her sodden gown, struggling with the clinging fabric. At last she was free of it and
felt no shame, only relief as he pulled her against him
again, his mouth closing over hers. Shyly at first, but with
increasing need, she ran her hands over his body, feeling
the hard muscle of his back, his arms, pulling the leather
tie from his hair and twining her fingers in his damp curls.

With shaking hands she removed his gambeson, shivering with delight at the touch of his bare skin against hers.
There was no fear in this place, no worry over what tomorrow would bring. There was only this moment, the
touch of his hand and the feel of his lips, and an aching
emptiness that she didn't understand and didn't want to,
for her body moved with a knowledge beyond understanding. His hand moved lightly from knee to ankle, then up
again, higher now, and she arched against his palm, the
sweet scent of fresh-mown hay filling her senses as the
rain pounded on the roof.

There was a brief, sharp pain when he entered her and
she cried out, even as she drew him closer—and all at once
they were moving together in a way she'd never imagined
possible. They were one, one body and one flesh, words
that had been meaningless until this moment. As one they
moved inexorably toward something barely glimpsed—
until it broke over her in shimmering waves of ecstasy as
he tensed beneath her hands. She called his name—or was
it he who called to her? She didn't know, it didn't matter,
for in this place they were one.

Alyson gradually became aware of herself again, the
hay tickling her skin, the rapid beating of his heart beneath
her cheek as they lay entwined, their breaths growing

slower. Through her joy she felt an emptiness, a sorrow to be even this much separated from him.

Now that the urgency had passed they explored one another with gentle hands and lingering kisses. His hair smelled of rainwater and wild herbs, and his skin tasted faintly of salt. The feel of him beneath her hands was something to be savored, each contour a new mystery to be explored. At last she lay looking into his eyes, lost in their dark depths, and she was not even aware that she was weeping until he kissed the tears from her cheeks.

"Did I hurt you?" he asked. "I'm sorry, the first time can be painful—but you'll see, it will be better now."

"Better, my lord?" She laughed through her tears. "I can't imagine . . ."

He smiled and her heart twisted in her breast. "You needn't say 'my lord.' Not now."

"Jemmy," she whispered, tracing the dark wings of his brows, the sharp curve of his cheekbone, the roughness of his beard beneath her fingertips. "Jemmy," she repeated softly. Oh, she could say his name a thousand times and never grow tired of the sound of it.

The door opened and a young man walked into the stable. Jemmy pulled a horse blanket from the hook and covered them as Alyson buried her face in his shoulder.

"My lord," the boy said, confused. "I'm sorry to disturb ye. I was just going out to look for ye."

"You've found me."

"Aye. Well, your father sent me. He's worried for your lady, she's still not come back from her ride."

"Tell him not to worry," Jemmy said, tightening his arms about Alyson.

"But, my lord, her horse came back an hour ago and there's been no sign—"

"She's here, Alec."

"Here?"

Alyson raised her head and the boy stepped back a pace,

nearly stumbling over his own feet. "I'm sorry, my lady—my lord—please forgive me—"

He turned and fled.

Jemmy's and Alyson's eyes met, and they both began to laugh. "Well, that will give them something to talk about!" Jemmy said, then sighed, looking toward the door.

"No, sir, you can't go in there now," Alec was saying outside the stable door.

"What do ye mean, I can't go in? Damn you, boy, I need my horse!" replied a familiar voice.

"We'd best get up," Jemmy said, searching through the straw for their clothing.

Alyson dressed silently. She had to tell him, right now, quickly, before she lost her courage. God alone knew what would happen after that, but of one thing she was certain: she would never see him again.

But even as she put a hand on his arm, a voice spoke clearly in her mind. Shouldn't I be allowed one night of happiness? it said. Just one? No, she argued with herself, that would be wicked. It would be a lie. Tell him. Tell him right now.

"What is it?" Jemmy said, looking down at her so tenderly that her throat ached with sudden pain. "What's wrong? Whatever it is, I'll make it right, I swear it."

"I—"

The door burst open and several men walked in, Alistair among them. He stopped and stared, his lip curling in a scornful smile as he took in the crumpled, muddy clothing of the pair before him, the hay covering them both.

"Pardon me," Jemmy said, pushing him aside.

"Of course, my lord. My lady."

Alistair made one of his mocking bows, waving them past, as the men with him broke into derisive laughter.

The rain had stopped, and as they stepped outside the sun burst forth, sparkling on the wet paving stones. "Now,"

Jemmy said, drawing her aside. "What were you going to say?"

Alyson shook her head and tightened her grip on his arm.

"Nothing, Jemmy," she said, leaning her head against his shoulder. "It can wait."

chapter 29

T*hey dined alone that night in Alyson's chamber, served*
only by old Maggie, who beamed with pleasure as she
set the food before them. Later she laughed to herself as
she removed it all untouched, then threw fresh logs upon
the fire and left them there alone. Certain it was that they'd
never even noticed her, for they sat together in a large chair
talking in soft voices and laughing. Thanks be to God,
Maggie thought. It had pained her to see her young master
so unhappy since his return. Perhaps now he'd settle down
and find some pleasure in his new life. She'd had her
doubts about this marriage—well, who hadn't?—but it
seemed Lady Maude had undergone a strange and puzzling
change. Or maybe not so puzzling as all of that, she reflected with a smile, maybe the most natural thing in the
world.

When she backed into the hallway, the tray held carefully before her, she found Celia waiting outside the door.

"They won't be wanting ye tonight," Maggie said.

The girl frowned. "But I have to ready my lady for bed," she said, reaching for the latch.

"I wouldna do that," Maggie said sharply. Celia only tossed her head and opened the door.

Alyson sighed and nestled closer in Jemmy's arms, drifting in a golden haze of pleasure. Right or wrong she would have this night; this one night she wished would never end. That it would end was something she knew all too well, but for as long as she could make it last she would savor every moment.

His chamber robe was soft against her cheek. It was crimson velvet, tied loosely round the waist, and smelled deliciously of Jemmy's own distinctive scent. Sharp with spices, it conjured images of the strange, exotic lands he must have visited in his travels. She touched the gold ring in his ear as she had often longed to do, smoothing the thick dark hair back from his face. She meant to explore every inch of him tonight with a thoroughness that would have to last a lifetime.

Bending, she laid her lips against his chest where the robe fell open, just above his heart, and boldly slipped her hand inside. The hard muscle of his belly contracted beneath her fingertips as he drew a sharp breath of pleasure.

She glanced up beneath her lashes and found him looking down at her with the smile she had hoped to win. This is how she would remember him, just so—his face soft and young and happy, his dark eyes all aglow.

The door opened and Alyson leaned back against him, lost entirely in the feeling of his lips upon her hair, trusting him to send whoever it might be away. But at the first sound of Celia's sharp voice Alyson tensed, reality returning with a rush.

"D'ye have need of me, my lady?" the serving girl asked, bobbing the obligatory curtsey. Alyson didn't want to look into her face and yet she did, finding Celia's eyes, cold as chips of blue ice, fastened on her own. But there was nothing Celia could do, not now, not without giving her own treachery away.

"Not tonight, lass," Jemmy answered easily. "Go along and find your bed."

But Celia didn't leave, nor did she take her eyes from Alyson's. Her glance held warning now, as did her voice when she said, "If you're quite sure, my *lady*."

Alyson knew that Jemmy wouldn't mark the slight emphasis on the last word, but she did, and it chilled her to the heart.

"Quite," she answered, fear sharpening her voice. "You heard my lord, Celia. You may go."

"Very well."

When they were alone again Alyson tried to recapture her feeling of contentment, but it had vanished beyond recall. Whatever was she doing? she wondered in sudden terror. How could she be so wicked as to go on deceiving Jemmy this way, taking what he would never give if he only knew the truth? And yet . . . surely tomorrow would be time enough to tell him. Would one night really matter so very much?

"What is it?" Jemmy asked, catching her change of mood with a perception that warmed and frightened her at the same time. "What troubles you?"

"I don't like her," Alyson said in a low voice, staring at the fire.

"Then we'll send her home again," he said reasonably, broad shoulders moving in a shrug.

"Aye, we will. We'll do just that."

If only it could be so simple! By morning Celia would be gone, running off to Sir Robert with all that she had learned, including what she'd seen tonight. But no, Alyson comforted herself, Celia would never get the chance. Because by morning Jemmy would know the truth and he would stop her. What he would do to Alyson was another matter, but that was for tomorrow. She could still have this one night, and she would, no matter what might come of it. And at the first red streak of dawn she would confess the whole sorry tale.

Oh, but he would be so angry, she reflected, trying to ignore the feeling of his hand upon her shoulder. Best to tell him now before this goes any further. His hand moved gently against her neck, traced the line of her jaw, and finally touched her lips. She opened her mouth to tell him, but instead found herself catching his finger between her teeth and stroking it lightly with her tongue. He made a sound, halfway between laughter and a groan, and stood, lifting her easily and walking toward the bed.

Just one night, Alyson pleaded with her conscience, burying her face against his chest. That wasn't much to ask, not really, not when set against a lifetime spent without him. But, oh, it was so wrong to lie to him like this, the wickedest lie she could imagine. She might be neck deep in deception as it was, but in that she'd had no choice. This lie was different, for she told it of her own accord. Could she really do this? She, who had always prided herself on her honesty?

The bed was so soft, so welcoming, and when Jemmy shrugged off his robe the firelight played upon the sun-browned muscles of his body. If I'm to burn in Hell, so be it, Alyson thought, holding out her arms. Then her thoughts dissolved into a shattering wave of pleasure as he bent over her, his dark hair falling like a curtain round her face.

The night was halfway done when Jemmy woke to find himself alone. Raising himself on one elbow, he saw Maude standing before the window, the shutters flung wide and the moonlight streaming into the room. She was clad only in the mantle of hair rippling halfway to her knees, and between the strands her skin glowed like mar-

ble in the pale light. Jemmy rose and took the blanket from
the bed, moving to stand behind her and enfolding them
both within its warmth.

"You daft lass, you'll catch your death," he scolded,
drawing her against him. "Why aren't you in bed?"

"Oh, I couldn't sleep. Not tonight."

She turned and slid her arms about his waist, leaning
her cheek in the hollow of his shoulder. And there it was
again, that strange feeling of completion. It was like one of
the ornaments he'd seen in Eastern markets years before, a
ring made of separate bands. If one didn't know the trick
they were just two bits of twisted metal, joined yet with no
real connection to each other. But a practiced hand could
fit them neatly as a puzzle, the result far more intricate and
beautiful than either was alone.

He smiled a little, pleased with the image, thinking that
surely he had one somewhere among his chests. Tomorrow
Maude would wear it on her hand. And one quiet day,
when they had been married for years and had nothing better to talk about, he would tell her what it meant.

"Just look," she said softly, drawing him back to the
present. "Isn't it lovely?"

The valley below was touched with mist, all the familiar landmarks softened beyond recognition. Above, the
moon shone silver-bright among countless brilliant stars.
Even as Jemmy watched, one streaked to earth and he
tightened his arms around her.

"There, now. Make a wish, they say, and it will come to
pass for sure."

He laughed as he spoke but she shut her eyes immediately, her brows drawn together in a small frown of concentration.

"Now whatever did you wish for so fiercely?" he asked,
amused.

"No, you first. What would you want if you could have
anything at all?"

"Well . . ." He rested his chin on her head and stared into the night. "Right now I'm thinking if I could have anything . . . I'd take you and go back to sea. This"—he nodded toward the open window—"it *is* lovely, I suppose, but at times it closes in around me until I cannot catch my breath."

He stopped, knowing the futility of trying to describe the sea to someone who'd never seen it, yet needing her to understand. "The smell of the sea is like . . ." he began slowly, groping for the words, "Well, it's not really like a scent at all. It's more like drinking the richest wine you can imagine—and yet far better than any wine could ever be. Instead of making you dull and sleepy it sweeps the cobwebs from your mind—and there's the world before you, all fair and fresh and new."

He closed his eyes and took a deep breath, remembering the taste of salt brine on his lips, feeling the familiar ache of loss. "And the sound of it," he said, his eyes still closed. "The waves against the shore . . . It's always different, and it's always the same as well, a song that gets into your blood until you cannot live without it . . ."

"You'd give all this up for the sea?"

He opened his eyes with a sigh. His first instinct was to give her the pretty lie she no doubt expected, to say that he was well content so long as she was with him. But suddenly it was terribly important that she understand this one thing, perhaps the most important thing about him.

"I've thought about it sometimes—well, every day and every night, if you want to know the truth. Oh, I wish I could show you how it is to stand on deck with the journey just beginning and everything before you . . ."

"And it doesn't matter where you're bound."

"No, not really. It's the—the—"

"The leaving."

"Aye," he said, a little startled at her perception. "That's it exactly."

"I see. But—" she hesitated, then said, "But what is it you run from?"

"It isn't running," he said, though even as he spoke the words he knew he lied. "It's—well, it's the adventure of it, the freedom."

"Aye, well, freedom is a fine thing—or so I've heard. But when you cannot live without it, the leaving, then it isn't really freedom, is it?"

With a sudden change of mood she slanted him a smile. "But still, I would like to try it once myself. Why don't we, Jemmy? We'll go right now, tonight—just leave it all behind and start again."

"Would you?" he asked, smiling down into her upturned face. "Would you come with me if I asked?"

"Aye. I would."

For a moment the longing was so strong that Jemmy felt it almost as a physical pain. "Well, it's a grand dream, isn't it?" he said at last. "But not for us, I fear. I'm afraid the time has come to put that all away. Though, in truth"—he grinned and lightly pinched the soft skin of her hip—"it doesn't seem such a terrible fate right now. And what of you? What was it you wished for?"

She was silent for so long that he thought she wouldn't answer, but at last she raised herself on tiptoe to whisper in his ear.

He laughed, a deep, rich sound of startled pleasure and amusement. Oh, she was a rare woman, more beautiful than any he had ever known. And yet it wasn't her beauty that twisted the heart within his breast. It was her enchanting blend of innocent desire; too shy to say the words aloud, she was still bold enough to ask for what she wanted.

And he wanted her as well, there was no use pretending that he didn't, not with her body pressed so close against his own and his desire plain for both of them to feel. And yet today he'd taken her maidenhead, a process that involved some pain for her, as well as the keenest pleasure he had ever known.

"It would be my honor to oblige," he said gently, setting his lips against her brow. "But we should wait a day or two—"

She wound her arms about his neck and looked into his eyes. "Oh, no, please—let's not wait. I want you now, tonight."

"But there will be tomorrow," he said, kissing her lightly. "And tomorrow. And tomorrow . . ."

"But tonight is . . . special. Different."

"Well, you are different, surely!" he laughed. "What happened to my cool, proud wife who wouldn't even speak to me?"

"That wasn't me," she answered seriously. "It was—well, someone else. *This* is me—here, now, tonight."

"I'm glad of that. For you—here, tonight"—he kissed her once again—"are the woman I love."

He stopped, stunned to hear his own voice saying the words he'd sworn he'd never speak again, even as he recognized their truth. He'd never felt half of what he did now for any woman, not even for Carmela. His love for her had been a boy's love, and later it became a bitter thing, more pain than pleasure. While Maude . . . well, she was like a flame, but with the hot passion there was warmth, as well, a warmth that had revived a part of him long dead. And that was the last thing he'd expected from this marriage.

She was so changeable, such a mystery; he was astonished at the depth of passion she'd revealed, given her behavior since they'd wed. In a single night she'd slipped past every one of his defenses, and though his instinct was to go slowly, cautiously, he feared it was too late already—especially when she looked at him as she was doing now. A surge of protective tenderness swept over him, shocking in its intensity. He wanted to hold her close and never let her go, to shield her from whatever brought that look of sorrow to her eyes.

"And I love you," she said as solemnly as a child. He started to speak, but she laid one hand against his lips. "Can I show you how much?"

And when she smiled he was lost, helpless to do more than follow as she took his hand and led him back to bed.

J emmy had been right, Alyson thought as she lay down on the bed, wincing a little as the woolen coverlet scratched the tender skin of her thighs. On any other night she would have been delighted to simply lie beside him and drift off into sleep. But tonight was not just any other night. It was the only night. And she could not bear for it to end. Even if their union did not bring her the same pleasure it would bring to him, she was determined to have that precious closeness once again. What difference did a little pain make now, so long as they could be together?

As he slipped under the coverlet she pressed against him, expecting him to respond as eagerly as he had done before. But instead of taking her into his arms, he grasped her wrists, pinning her hands beside her head, and smiled down at her with a wicked glint in his eyes. With a touch so light it seemed to burn, he brushed his lips down the length of her arm, across her throat, and back again.

By the time he had completed the journey once, every nerve in Alyson's body was alive and shivering with anticipation. He nibbled each one of her fingers, then kissed her palm, her wrist, and as his tongue lightly traced the soft skin of her inner elbow, she forgot entirely that this was supposed to be for his enjoyment and not her own. When his lips passed over hers, she arched against him, trying to prolong the kiss. But he had other plans.

Hands clasped about her wrists, he explored her inch by inch, an exquisite torment that he drew out to its fullest.

When she realized he sought only to give her pleasure while taking none himself, she tried to capture him, to hold him, but always he eluded her. At last she surrendered to him completely as with endless patience he discovered every secret of her body. There was no reason to fear him, nothing to hold back. She had been made for him and he for her and nothing they did together could be anything but beautiful and right.

Her fingers twined with his, gripped him hard enough to pierce the skin as he brought her to the peak of ecstasy and kept her poised there, a sensation so sharp and brilliant that it was nearly indistinguishable from pain. And at last, when she could not bear another moment, he sent her straight over the edge. And Alyson discovered she could fly.

Only then did he take her in his arms and kiss her with a tenderness more precious than anything that had gone before.

Every muscle of her body was deliciously at ease. He drew her close against him and she sighed, the warm, strong length of his body curled around her back, his arms around her.

As the moments passed, she heard his breathing deepen and felt his arms relax their hold. And then, with a swiftness that took him completely unaware, she turned and wound strong fingers about his wrists, pushing him onto his back.

She regarded him with satisfaction as he gazed up at her with startled eyes. "And what is this, my lord?" she said, turning her head so her hair brushed across his body. "Don't tell you mean to go to sleep?"

"I had thought of it," he admitted, his lips twitching in a smile.

"But that would hardly be justice!"

He drew a sharp breath as she leaned down and trailed the tip of her tongue around his navel. Then she raised her head and smiled sweetly. "Such a fascinating subject, justice. Is it not?"

"Indeed," Jemmy said. His breath grew ragged as she bent to him again. "I find it . . . quite . . . interesting just now."

"I am so pleased to hear you say that!" Alyson said. "For I plan quite a lengthy lecture on the subject, and . . ." she nipped him softly. " . . . I would hate to bore you."

He grinned up at her. "That," he said with absolute conviction, "is the one thing that you could never do."

*Alyson could not escape her awareness of the passage of time. Even as she lay in Jemmy's arms, trembling with the aftermath of their joining, she could feel the moments slipping past, each one gone irrevocably, never to return.

"Sorceress," he said, the words warm and soft against her ear. "I did not mean to do that—"

"Are you sorry?" she asked anxiously.

"Not in the least," he assured her. "So long as you are not."

"Oh, no! I am happy—so happy, Jemmy. Are you? Do I please you?"

He smoothed the tumbled hair back from her brow. "Aye, you please me, love," he whispered. "You please me very well."

*Dawn was an hour away, Alyson thought as the liquid notes of the nightingale pierced the silence of the night. An hour and then it would be done. She tightened the arm flung across Jemmy's chest and buried her face against his shoulder.

He stirred and pulled her closer. "Are you awake?" he

asked and she nodded, so glad to hear his voice that she could have cried with relief.

Before he could fall asleep again, she caught his hand and ran one finger across the raised edge of the scar running halfway up his arm.

"How did you get this?" she said. "I—I wondered when I first saw you, the night of our—of the wedding—"

"Oh, that." He yawned and settled her more comfortably against him. "It happened a long time ago. I was . . . nine, I think. Yes, that was the year—a lot of things happened. But this . . ." He smiled a little, looking into the shadows of the ceiling. "I was walking in the wood and I came upon half a dozen boys. They'd caught a fawn—I don't know how, it was very small, just a few days old, and they had it tied to a tree and were throwing rocks at it. I told them to stop but they weren't about to listen. They were tinker's boys, older than I—proper young louts, too, probably hanged years since—and one had a knife. We fought and—"

His hand clenched, then he opened it again, holding it before his eyes. "I got this. And this, as well." He guided Alyson's hand to a place just beside his eyebrow and she felt the small raised scar. "I was getting the worst of it, as you can imagine, but I did manage to get the knife long enough to free the fawn. And then the tinkers decided that I could take its place. So they tied me to the tree."

"What happened then?" Alyson asked when he stopped.

"Ian and Alistair happened by. What a fight!" He laughed softly. "I can still see them, standing back to back, both of them with daggers drawn. They fought like . . . like they were one. They could have taken twice as many with no trouble at all."

It had been brave of them to fight against so many, Alyson thought. But it had been braver still for Jemmy to face them all alone.

"After the others ran off, Alistair took me to the stream

and washed the blood away. He bound up my hand and I went home again. It was all right for the two of them, but I didn't want anyone to know, because I wasn't supposed to have left the yard. I was being punished for something, I can't remember what, so for the next day or so I kept my hand out of sight and my hair over my face, hoping no one would notice. And they didn't—not at first. But the hand got inflamed and I came down with a fever and soon enough the tale came out."

"Did you get in terrible trouble?" she asked, amused, thinking what she would do to her own young brother for such disobedience.

"No. My mother said I'd done what she would have in my place and that I wasn't to be punished for it. My father knew better than to cross a breeding woman and so he let it pass."

He sighed and moved restlessly beneath her. "I remember it well because she died soon after."

"From the child?" Alyson asked softly.

"In a way. The fighting was very bad that year. My grandfather died and my uncle, Father's youngest brother. When they brought him back—my mother fell down in a faint and the child came that night, three months early. Neither of them lived."

Jemmy was silent then, remembering the day Stephen's body had been returned to them, the shouts and curses and the screaming that went on and on . . .

Alyson felt him shudder and moved closer in his arms. So many dead, she thought, despairing. War was not confined to the battlefield as the songs and stories would have it seem. The evil of pure hatred went on, destroying everything it touched. Just as it would destroy what had happened here tonight. Lies and more lies, deception without end—but this feeling between her and Jemmy was no lie; it was real and true and fine. And yet it must be wrong, for the moment she spoke the truth the fragile bond between them would be irrevocably shattered.

"There, now," Jemmy said gently, stroking the hair back from her face. "I shouldn't have gone on like that. 'Tis all long past and now everything will be different. We'll see to that."

"Oh, Jemmy," Alyson choked. "If only it was so easy."

"I never said it would be easy, but—I think it's what must be. 'Tis strange," he mused, his lips moving softly in her hair, "when I think how hard I tried to fight it. But now I see—I think—that this is where I've always wanted to be, doing what I was born to do. You made me see that."

Alyson felt a guilty pang as she considered that Darnley would have been very pleased at what she'd done. If not for her, Jemmy would be gone—perhaps already—back to the safety of the sea. "But you could be wrong. What you said before—the sea—perhaps that is where you belong—"

"Oh, I still miss the sea, I suppose I always will, but you were right, I've been running for too long. Ian—God rest him—Ian was my brother and I loved him well, but he couldn't do what we will do together. Just think—our children will be Darnley and Kirallen."

He rolled atop her, supporting his weight on his elbows. "You do like children, don't you?"

"Yes. I do."

"I never did much. But now—shall we have a bairn, Maude? Or no, we should have two at least, a daughter and a son. Would you like that, sweeting?"

"Yes," she whispered. "I would. More than anything."

Aye, just the thought of it, the children they might have had together, was more than she could bear.

"Jemmy, I—when I came here—it wasn't—"

"You're trembling!" he said with swift concern, lying down beside her. "I'm sorry, here I have been running on and never thought—you must be exhausted. As I am," he added with a smile that turned into a yawn. "Lie back now and go to sleep. We'll have plenty of time to talk tomorrow."

He yawned again and drew her closer, his hands moving in lazy arcs over her neck and shoulders. She braced herself against his warmth, his touch, clinging desperately to her wavering resolve.

"No, wait—"

"Hush," he ordered firmly, pulling her head down to his shoulder. "Whatever it is will keep until tomorrow."

Tomorrow, Alyson thought. One hour more and tomorrow will be here. One hour to lie here in his arms and listen to the beating of his heart. The moment the sky lightens, she promised herself, at the very first streak of dawn . . . I will wake him up and tell him everything . . .

chapter 30
❧

Maude's chamber was much larger than Alyson had remembered it. Her footsteps echoed as she walked across an endless floor toward the dais. Though the rest of the room was dim, banked candles shed their light on the three figures waiting for her.

Maude was stretched upon the settle. Her father stood beside her, hands clasped behind his back. Sir Robert sat with his legs dangling over the edge of the dais, which was higher than Alyson's head. For some reason the knight was dressed in motley; the bells on his cap jangled harshly in counterpoint to the music coming from his lute. It was a strange air, dissonant and eerie, that reminded Alyson of dried cornstalks clattering together in a gray November field.

Alyson stopped at the edge and curtsied silently.

"You are a very stupid girl," Maude said. "We told you what would happen, but you didn't listen, did you? And now look what you've done."

"Wait," Alyson tried to say, though no sound came from her lips. "Wait, I can explain—"

"Have you nothing to say for yourself?" Darnley demanded, drawing an enormous knife from his belt. "Very well. Bring the boy."

Faceless forms in black laid Robin on the dais, but now it was an altar and Father Aidan stood above the bound figure of the boy.

"You did this," the priest said. "You alone. He is the lamb who will suffer for your sin."

"Ally!" Robin cried, his eyes wide with terror. "Ally, help me!"

Alyson's limbs were leaden, every step impeded, and silent screams ripped from her throat as Darnley raised the knife above his head. With the greatest effort of her life she spurred herself forward and at last found her voice.

"Robin! No, don't! Robin!"

Hands pressed against her shoulders and she struggled to free herself, frantic with terror.

"Shh, now, 'twas a dream, that's all. Just a dream."

She opened her eyes and there was Jemmy leaning over her. With a wordless cry she flung her arms about his neck.

"A dream," she repeated, her voice shaking. "Yes. It was only a dream."

He held her, one hand stroking her hair, murmuring soft words. But there were other voices, too, and Alyson drew back from the shelter of his arms to find the room was filled with men.

"What—?" she began, utterly confused, then saw with a sharp stab of fear that Jemmy was dressed for riding. Oh, she hadn't meant to sleep!

"Why are you up?" she asked weakly. "Is it dawn?"

"Nearly. There's been a raid in Kilghorn and I must go."

"Wait," she said, pushing the hair out of her face and trying to collect her scattered thoughts. "You can't—not yet. Please, my lord, just a moment of your time—"

Celia came forward then, her eyes holding Alyson's as she proffered a cup of morning ale.

Jemmy kissed her hard and quick. "I'm sorry, sweeting. I'll be back as soon as may be—not more than a few days. God keep you."

He touched her hair and smiled. Then he was gone and the rest of the men with him, leaving her alone with Celia.

The serving girl sat down on the bed and sipped the cup of ale. "Well, well," she said, raising her brows. "Did you sleep well, my lady?"

Alyson didn't answer. She sank back among the pillows and closed her eyes. Robin, she thought, tears stinging her lids. My poor Robin. What have I done to you?

B*y the time Alyson was up and dressed, she had convinced* herself that her dream meant nothing. It was not a Sending or a vision of the future, but only a dream brought on by her own fear and shame at what she'd done last night.

She *should* feel shame, she reminded herself sternly. 'Twas sinful to be humming a merry little tune as she went lightly down the stairway. And when she took her seat between Malcolm and the Laird, she found that she was ravenous. She doused her oats with milk and a generous portion of honey.

"Were you caught in the storm?" Malcolm asked. "It was a bad one, wasn't it?"

"It was," she answered. "But I'm fine."

"Did Uncle Jemmy find you, then?"

The Laird's mouth twitched and Alyson realized that he knew—why, everyone must know, just as Jemmy had predicted. The keep seemed so big but it wasn't, really, not when it came to having any privacy at all. And the two of them in the stables together was far too good a story not to get about—

"You're very red," Malcolm said, looking at her curiously. "Are you all right?"

"Aye."

"But—"

"That's enough, Malcolm. Let your aunt eat in peace."

Kirallen was smiling, his eyes filled with gentle laughter. But what would he think when he learned the truth of it?

She pushed the bowl away, her appetite gone.

"Are ye finished?" Malcolm said, jumping up. "Let's go."

"Go? Go where?"

"To the butts! Ye did promise."

"Did I? All right, then."

They took bows and arrows to the archery butts. Alyson stood, her arrow nocked, and faced the target. Sudden anger swept over her and she imagined she had Lord Darnley in her sights.

"That's very good," Malcolm said. "I thought you said you hadn't practiced much."

"A lucky shot," Alyson shrugged, though she was shaken by the hatred she had felt in that moment. "Here, you try."

The boy's arrow hit close to hers. "I'm getting better," he said. "Father used to say—"

"What?"

"Oh, never mind."

"No, tell me. What did your father used to say?"

"You won't like it. He used to say I should pretend it was a Darnley."

Alyson began to laugh and found she couldn't stop. She wrapped her arms about herself, shaking her head wordlessly to Malcolm's questions.

"I'm sorry," she gasped, wiping her eyes. "It's just— they tell them at home to pretend it's a Kirallen. It's all so senseless, don't you see? It's all—just—wicked!"

Malcolm stood, staring, as she burst into tears.

"I'm sorry," he said. "I didna mean to—"

"It isn't you, Malcolm, it's—everyone. Don't you see how wicked it is?"

"But my father said—"

"Your father was wrong! They're all wrong—all of them—"

She sank to the ground and laid her head on her bent knees. After a moment Malcolm knelt beside her and put one arm awkwardly about her shoulders.

"'Tis all right," he said. "I shouldna have told ye. But I willna do it anymore, I promise."

She gripped his hands and her eyes blazed into his. "Will you remember your promise? When you're a man and they say to fight, will you remember? They aren't just Darnleys, they're people, every one of them. Some are good people, too, with families—just like your father. No matter what happens, Malcolm, I want you to remember that."

"I will," he said, his eyes round.

"Aye. I know you will. Go on," she said, looking over his shoulder. "Sir Alistair is waiting for you. It's all right now, Malcolm, just run along."

He left her there, though he wasn't happy about it. She looked so sad siting all alone.

"You're very quiet," Alistair said as they walked together to the practice yard. "What was that woman saying to you?"

"She has a name," Malcolm said sharply. "You should use it. 'Tisn't nice to say 'that woman.'"

"*She* isn't nice. And who d'ye think ye are to be lessoning me in manners? Mind your tongue."

"You mind yours," Malcolm retorted pertly, and Alistair cuffed him—not hard, just enough to remind him of his place. But Malcolm, usually so biddable, was not himself at all today. He just stared at Alistair with his bright eyes gone suddenly cold until the older man hooked an arm around his neck and drew him close.

"Enough of your backchat, laddie," he said. "Take up your sword and show me what you've learned. I'll wager my new knife that ye shan't get past my guard even once."

When Malcolm grinned up at him Alistair was absurdly relieved, as though he'd won back something precious that had nearly been lost.

It was all that woman's fault, he reflected as they began Malcolm's lesson. She was a danger in more ways than one. He didn't like her, and he didn't trust her an inch, though everyone else seemed almost willfully blind to the danger Alistair could feel surrounding them. It was understandable enough, he supposed. The Laird, poor man, had never recovered from the shock of Ian's death. Malcolm was only a boy who couldn't be expected to know any better. As for Jemmy—well, Jemmy was a fool, Alistair had known that for years, besides which he was obviously besotted with his bride.

But he, Alistair, wasn't an old man or a boy or a fool. He was a man—and a Kirallen. Though many had forgotten that Alistair had not been born a Kirallen, he remembered. He could never forget the wretched life he'd had before the Laird had taken him in, given him a home, a family, and a name.

Alistair would not stand by and see the honor of that name destroyed. In his right mind the Laird would never have so shamed them all, going cap in hand to beg peace with Ian's murderer. And he would have known better than to trust Darnley to keep his word.

God be thanked that Alistair was still there to protect the Laird, even from himself. If no one else would act, then he must.

"Here, now, not like that," he said to Malcolm. "You turn your wrist like this—that's it. Now step into it—good, lad, that's the way. Let's try again."

Part of his mind was busy with the lesson, but the other part stood off, thinking as he so often did of that terrible January morning. Ah, Ian, he thought with familiar bitter sorrow, why did ye have to die? Why did ye ride off with only a handful of men? Why, why did ye no' wait for me?

And it was all for those damnable white cows. If Alistair ever got his hands on them again, he'd slaughter every one and burn the carcasses. It was all a game to Ian, those wretched beasts, just one more competition between himself and Darnley. But then Ian had never been serious for five minutes at a stretch.

"Why should I worry?" he'd said once to Alistair. "I have you for that!"

And when he grinned Alistair had to laugh, for it was true and they both knew it. Alistair had always been the practical one, attending to the details Ian tended to ignore, pointing out the dangers Ian never stopped to see.

When Ian had heard about the stolen cows he'd laughed. "Why, that vaunty bastard!" he exclaimed, his dark eyes glowing. "Thinks he can ride in here and take what's ours, does he? Well, we'll just have to show him, won't we lads?"

"What again?" the men cried, groaning.

"Aye, again!" Ian answered. "And again and again— until he understands. We leave at dawn." Then he'd raised his cup and cried, "Crioch Onarach!" and they'd all roared back the toast, draining their mugs to the dregs, with no idea that the good death they wished for was so very close.

It was at that moment Alistair first knew something wasn't right. Ian usually accepted Alistair's flashes of the Sight without question, but that night he had been drinking and had no mind for anyone's ideas but his own.

"You're turning into an old woman," he said, making a wry face. "Don't come if you're afraid."

And that was Ian at his worst—impatient, reckless, determined to have his way at any price. From any other man

those words would have had Alistair's sword leaping from
its scabbard. As it was, he bit back his anger and subsided,
for he knew there was no arguing with his foster brother in
this mood.

The next morning Ian had apparently decided to forget
their quarrel. Alistair wasn't surprised. Ian's fits of temper
never lasted long.

"So ye think this is a bad idea?" he asked, swinging
himself into the saddle.

"Aye, Ian, I do. If ye won't be stopped, then at least let's
take more men."

Ian frowned. "It's too late for that. We'll go carefully."

The morning had been cold, a chill mist clinging to the
hollows and hanging heavy over the moat. They'd barely
reached the other side when Alistair's horse went lame. He
pried the stone loose from the animal's hoof but when it
still limped, he turned back to the stable to fetch another.

Ian sighed, his breath misting the air. "Catch up to us."

"I'll only be a moment."

But Ian, impatient again, just laughed. "We can't waste
the morning waiting about for you! Ye can catch us—and
hurry, man, 'tis late enough already."

The sharp answer Alistair was about to make died on
his lips when he felt the hair stir on the nape of his neck.
His mouth went dry, and though he tried to shout a warning, his words came out as hardly more than a whisper.

"Wait—don't go—"

Ian heeled his horse into a canter and looked back with
a grin. "Try not to miss all the fun!"

"Ian, don't—*wait!*"

But Ian was gone. It hadn't taken Alistair long to find a
fresh mount and then he galloped after them. But even so,
by the time he found them it was done and Darnley's men
no more than distant figures disappearing into the mist.
He'd only been in time to stare, appalled, at the carnage.
Eight bodies lay upon the blood-soaked moor, eight

knights under his command. Or no, he realized. Not eight. Nine. And the ninth was Ian.

He dropped to his knees beside his kinsman. At Alistair's touch Ian opened his eyes and grinned weakly. " 'Twas Darnley—I never expected him to come himself—the bastard! I should have—waited—for you—"

"Christ, Ian, we have to get you home."

But when he tried to lift him, Ian gave a terrible cry of pain and gripped his arm. "Too late—ah, God, Alistair, I'm sorry."

"Quiet," Alistair ordered, swinging the cloak from his own shoulders and laying it over Ian. "Save your strength."

"No—no time," Ian said, stuttering a little with cold and shock. "S-say that it's all right, say that you—"

"I forgive ye, all right? Is that what ye want to hear? Now shut up and let me think a minute."

"Malcolm—watch over him—"

"Like my own son," Alistair promised, tears burning his eyes. "But you'll be there, too. We'll get ye home and—"

Ian coughed bright blood and Alistair was silenced. He could only hold him then, his mind refusing to accept what was happening even after Ian had gone still in his arms.

"It's not supposed to be this way," he shouted to the sky, tears streaming unheeded down his face. "I'm the one—not him—"

He had always known he'd die for Ian. Protecting Ian was his fate, the sacred duty entrusted to him by the Laird when he was just a bairn. God knew Ian needed looking after even then. He went his own way, regardless of the danger, with Alistair a step behind to guard his back. As they grew older, Ian had relied on Alistair not only for the protection he never thought he needed, but to attend to all the tiresome responsibilities of his position.

Not that Alistair had complained. He knew his duty, and he never wavered. And if Ian's demands had been sometimes exhausting, that was a small price to pay for all Alistair had been given. The Laird was a far more devoted father than Alistair's own had ever cared to be. Ian was not only his friend but his brother. Even Jemmy had been a part of it, all those years ago, though he and Alistair had never had much in common. But Ian had always been protective of his little brother.

"Leave him be," he used to say. " 'Tis not Jemmy's fault he's not like us. Just let him be."

It was Alistair, not Jemmy, that Ian had called his other half—joking words with the truth hidden in the jest. They'd ridden their first horses side by side, fought their first battle back to back. They'd shared hardship and victory, jokes and songs and women, too close for any jealousy to come between them. And always, always Alistair had known what his death would be: He would die defending Ian to the last.

"Ye should have waited," he'd said on that terrible morning as he laid Ian back on the earth and gently wiped the blood from his still face. "Why didn't ye wait for me?"

Now, standing in the practice yard Alistair felt the pain tear through him, just as sharp and bitter as it always was. But looking at the boy before him, he was comforted. Maybe there was some purpose to it all, maybe he had survived for a reason. I'll teach him, Ian, he vowed silently. I'll teach him to be what you were.

What had the Darnley bitch been saying to the boy? Alistair didn't know but he could guess—she'd been poisoning his mind, turning him against his kin. Trying to take him away.

At that moment his dislike for her sharpened into hatred.

chapter 31

A lyson threw down her sewing and ran to the window. There were riders approaching . . . but none of them was Jemmy. He'd said a few days, and this was the third. Surely she could expect him any moment. She paced the chamber restlessly, then sat and took up her sewing again. A moment later it had fallen from her hands as she stared blindly ahead, her mind taking up its frantic round.

She could trust Jemmy, she was sure of it. Once he understood he'd help her. But, oh, he would be angry. Angry at Darnley for the deception, angry at her for lying to him. Surely he would see that she had to lie, she'd had no choice. But she could have told him sooner. Would he understand that? Would he understand why she hadn't spoken the truth during that night?

That night . . . when she remembered what they'd done she grew hot and cold in turns. He'd carried her to the bed—this very bed she was looking at right now. The room had been dim; his face was in shadow but the firelight be-

hind him played off his skin as he pulled off his robe and
bent to her. He'd kissed her until she was certain she would
faint—but she hadn't fainted, she'd been very much aware
of what was happening as his hand slid beneath her robe to
cup her breast. She'd arched her back and the robe fell
away until they were naked together in the soft bed, just
where they belonged. He'd shown her a hundred games
that men and women play when they are just discovering
each other . . . Ah, next time, she thought, then her
thoughts stopped with a jerk.

There wouldn't be a next time. She'd had her night, and
that was most definitely the end of that. For a time she'd
hoped she was with child—no matter what happened, she
would welcome the babe who came of that night of joy.
When she'd found that it was not so she'd cried, even
though she knew she should be relieved, for what future
could such a child ever have? No, it was better this way,
for it was only herself she'd be risking when she told him
the truth.

She could trust him. She was sure of it. He'd said he
loved her. But that was when he thought she was Lady
Maude. What would remain of that love when he learned
who she truly was? Would it be enough?

But she had to tell him. She had no choice now, for she
could not betray him to his death. He was her only hope.
Why did he not come? If he didn't come today, she would
have to see Sir Robert and try to discover Darnley's plan.
She couldn't imagine what she'd say to the knight—certainly not the truth! No, she'd invent some tale and pray
that Darnley would hold off for another day or two.

And then she'd tell Jemmy everything. She tried to
imagine the words she'd use but her mind was blank. No
matter, when the time came she'd think of some way to say
it. And then what would he do? He'd be angry, surely . . .
But she had to trust him. Why, why didn't he return?

"He'll be back soon."

Maggie stood before her, her face drawn with concern. "Dinna fash yourself, lady, he'll be back. But he mustn't find you ill. Now eat some of this."

Alyson tried but soon her throat closed and she could not manage to swallow. "I'll have some later," she said, then stiffened, listening. She ran to the window, but the road stretched empty before her eyes.

The day wore into evening and then the evening faded into night. Alyson sat by the window, a blanket pulled about her shoulders, until dawn lightened the sky. Then she rose and dressed for riding, quietly so as not to disturb any of her women. She couldn't put it off any longer, she had to see Sir Robert.

She found him in the clearing, lying against the bank and staring at the sky. "Come and sit," he said with a smile, patting the soft grass. "It's a lovely morning, isn't it? But you don't look well at all. What's happened?"

"Sir Robert," she began, then stopped, biting her lip. She should have thought this out more carefully, she realized now. She was so deadly tired that her mind refused to work.

"There, now," he said, patting her back. "Just rest a moment. You've done well so far, very well indeed. And Robin is fine, so you needn't worry about him. Did I tell you Master Jennet says he has the makings of a falconer? That would be a fine life for him, don't you think?"

His kindness nearly undid her. How could she regard him as her enemy when he had been so kind to Robin, looking after him, making plans for his future? For a moment she was almost sorry that the knight was not more like his brother.

He lay back on his elbows and stared up at the sky. "On a day like this, it seems impossible that men cannot live in peace with one another," he mused. "But in spite of everything, I am glad I came to know you and Robin. Do you

know, Alyson, I wish—I truly wish that you were John's
true-born daughter instead of Maude."

He took her hand and smiled. "Just between the two of
us, you're worth ten of her. She can't even keep to her part
of the bargain and stay indoors. I think that's why John's
in such a fever to wrap this up—he can't control her at all.
Every fine day she's out hawking by the river, and it's only
a matter of time before the secret leaks out. She really is a
most disagreeable girl, you know, and John is even worse.
I regret I ever agreed to help either of them."

He hesitated a moment, studying the sky. "And I'm
done with it," he said abruptly. "It was wrong from the beginning, I should have seen that, but—well, I won't try to
excuse myself. Suffice it to say, I'm finished. And so are
you. Let John fight his own battles. Come with me right
now, Alyson. I'll get Robin out of Aylsford and take you
both to London. What do you say?"

"Thank you. You are so kind . . . If you could take
Robin I would be grateful, but I . . . I cannot leave. Not
now."

"Christ's wounds," he muttered. "I was afraid of that."

"Of what?"

"Celia has been here already." He sighed, giving her a
bright, shrewd glance from his hazel eyes. "She had quite
a tale to tell."

Alyson's cheeks burned as she imagined what Celia had
told the knight. "Then you know why I cannot leave with
you."

"Because you've bedded with Jemmy Kirallen?" he
asked sharply.

"No. Because I love him."

"Love." He stood and paced the grass, the sunlight
glinting off his rings and the jeweled pin in his cap. "My
dear, you don't love him," he said at last. "No, wait, listen
to me. I do understand how you're feeling. I imagine that
whatever happened was quite . . . powerful. But that isn't

love. Oh, in time, perhaps, it would become that. But now—you don't know him, do you? Not really. And, my dear, he certainly doesn't know you. If you were really Maude I would say that you had a good chance of finding happiness with this man. But as it is," he looked at her and his bright eyes were very sad. "When he finds out the truth, Alyson . . ."

"I know. But what else can I do?" she cried, jumping to her feet. "I cannot walk away and let him die! I—Sir Robert, I mean to tell him everything."

"Are you mad?" Robert cried. "Do you think he'll thank you for it? It's far more likely he will hang you."

"No! He would not do that!"

"But you don't know them! I'm telling you that when they find out the truth they won't stop to think at all."

"He won't let them hurt me," Alyson said. "Once I explain everything to him I'm sure he'll let me go."

"It's a mistake. You are not thinking clearly. That's no wonder, given everything that's happened. But Alyson, you must listen to me. These people, they're . . . brutal. It won't matter to them that you're young and a woman, they'll have their vengeance at any price."

She burst into tears and he put his arms around her, drawing her head down to his shoulder. "Poor girl, there isn't much to choose between us, is there? All right. You do it your way. I hope that you are right. I'll wait for you for three more days. If you don't come by then . . . oh, Alyson, I wish you wouldn't do this!"

"Sir Robert, can you tell me Lord Darnley's plan? How long do we have?"

He frowned. "What John has done is wrong. If you want to tell the Kirallens about your part in this deception, I won't stop you. But no matter what he has done, he is my brother. I won't betray him to his enemies."

"I understand."

"You do, don't you?" He hugged her hard against him,

of the survivors had sworn he'd recognized Darnley's men, but that, of course, was impossible. The Englishman would never risk his daughter's safety, not even for the fine sheep and cattle that had been taken from this once prosperous village.

At the thought of his wife Jemmy turned and called impatiently for his horse. He'd missed Maude sorely during this journey. By day his every moment had been full, but at night he hardly slept for wanting her. Every time he closed his eyes she was there, lying on the bed with her hair spread all about her, her eyes darkening with desire at his touch. She was so beautiful, so sweetly innocent, and at the same time so eager to learn how she might please him . . .

"Do I please you?" she had asked, and he'd felt his eyes sting at the wistfulness of the question.

He'd never had a woman who had made him feel as she did, hot and eager as a boy yet tenderly protective, too, ready to kill anyone who brought her the slightest unhappiness. Romantic nonsense, that's what he would have said only a few days ago. He'd had so many women, after all, and every one more skilled in the arts of love than his bride. But when all was said and done they were only women, and what he did with them was something of the flesh, enjoyable but all too soon forgotten. From the moment they'd lain together in the stables, he'd known that there was far more to his feelings for Maude than that. It was something he'd never felt before, as though they'd been truly bound together, not only their bodies but their souls as well, exactly as the priest had said it should be.

He should have brought her. Not only because it would have pleased him to have her with him, but because she could have helped him in this place. He could organize men to clear the wreckage, search for survivors, and bury the dead. The habit of command was strong in him. But when it came to comforting the bereaved . . . He glanced down at young Tam, kneeling beside his wife's grave. Maude would know what to say to him. Jemmy could only imagine how it would feel to lose his own wife and wonder how the man could bear it.

He knew Maude was safe, it was ridiculous to think otherwise, though ever since he'd left her he'd been feeling an uneasiness that defied explanation. He wouldn't be happy until he'd seen her for himself. He pushed his escort as hard as he dared and when they came to a turning in the road he waved them forward and struck out across the fields. The route would take him across Darnley's lands, but that should be safe enough now. He was, after all, the man's son-in-law. That set him wondering if Maude was missing her family, and he was thinking that she might enjoy a visit home, though not too soon, he hoped. He didn't want to be parted from her . . .

He was nearly home when he saw the riders approaching. Four, he counted, and Alistair was at their head. The knight pulled up sharply and said without preamble, "Darnley has assembled a huge force of men. Some of them are quartered at Aylsford, the rest at McInnes'. We have to move—and quickly."

"Hold up, Alistair," Jemmy commanded. "What's this? How did you get this information?"

"I have men at Aylsford who keep me informed. And at McInnes'. The information is certain."

"Let's get home," Jemmy said. "We'll talk about it there."

"No, wait," Alistair exclaimed. "There's more to it than that. Your wife—"

"This is nothing to do with her," Jemmy snapped.

"I'm afraid you're wrong about that," Alistair insisted. "I've had her followed while ye were gone, and just today she was meeting with one of them—"

"You lie," Jemmy growled, his eyes sparking with

anger. "You've always hated her, and now you invent this tale—"

"If you don't believe me," Alistair motioned one of the men forward. "Then ask Conal."

Conal had always been a friend; from the time Jemmy had returned he and his twin brother, Donal, had offered their support. Now the young man ducked his head so he wouldn't have to look Jemmy in the eye.

" 'Tis true," he said reluctantly. "We all saw her. She went down to the border early this morning and there was a man waiting for her. An English knight he was, all dressed in finery. And—and he took her in his arms, Jemmy—she was crying and—"

Jemmy went numb. "Who was this knight?"

"I dinna know—I followed him after and heard his squire call him Sir Robert."

Then Jemmy knew it was the truth. Robert. Robin. The one she had called for in her sleep. "Very well," he said. "Let's get back. Then we'll decide what to do next."

M aggie *was folding linens when the door opened and* her lady burst in, breathless. "Has he been here?" she demanded.

"Who, my lady?" Maggie asked.

"Why, my lord—I saw his horse in the stables. Has he not been up yet?"

The girl's face was flushed, her eyes feverishly bright. "Whisht now, calm yourself. He's not been here today."

"Aye, I will. But Maggie, help me change—"

She was tugging off her riding clothes, letting them fall to the floor. Maggie gathered them up, smiling to herself. Lady Maude was always so neat and tidy, tending her things as carefully as though they were borrowed. Now she was kicking off her skirt without bothering to take off her riding boots first. She whirled and seized a green gown trimmed with gold, pulling it so quickly over her head that she became tangled in the heavy folds. Maggie came to her rescue and soon it was fastened. She'd just begun to brush out her mistress' hair when the girl jumped up.

"Leave it," she said impatiently.

"But my lady, you mustna go out so," Maggie scolded. "At least let me—"

"Oh, I'll do it." And she did, gathering it and braiding it swiftly, if not neatly, so it fell over one shoulder.

"You'll dine here tonight?" Maggie asked.

"Dine?" She stared at Maggie as if she'd never heard the word before. "I don't know—it doesn't matter—"

When she was gone Maggie shivered and pulled her shawl more closely about her old shoulders, then whispered a quick prayer. There was something strange about her lady today, something more than just the excitement of her lord's return.

Something fey.

Jemmy stared blindly from the window as Alistair finished his report. Darnley—the bastard! It was all too easy to believe he'd break his sworn word. But at the risk of his daughter's life? No, he doted on the girl, that was well known. He'd only do it if he thought her safe, if she was somehow involved in the deception. But that simply could not be. Not Maude who had lain in his arms, so warm, so loving. Surely that could not have been a lie!

And yet she'd been seen with the knight. Sir Robert, he thought, and unconsciously his hand strayed to the sword on his hip. He'd find the man and cut him into shreds. Then he remembered all too clearly the men he'd fought for Carmela. Dear God, he'd killed a man for her, and the experience had left him sickened and ashamed. Not again. He would not—he *could* not start the whole wretched business over again. His hand dropped and he felt the hot rage turn to ice. And somewhere, very faintly, a voice asked if it was some lack in him that made this happen.

The thought was not to be borne. He turned and found Alistair was watching him closely, a look of sly triumph on his face. "Well then, Alistair," he said coolly. "From what I gather you have no proof that Darnley is planning to make war upon us."

"No proof? What of the men he's gathering in haste and secrecy? What about your own wife sneaking off to meet—"

"The one may have nothing to do with the other. We don't know. As for my wife—well, you leave her to me. But I want proof of Darnley's intentions before we make a move. It shouldn't be hard to get, now, should it? Not for a man with so many informants. Until I have such proof, this is not to be spoken of and particularly not to my father. I won't have him worried over nothing."

"Aye, Jemmy." Alistair nodded. "I'll bring ye the proof. And then what?"

"Why, then we will attack. But I still cannot believe that Darnley would have risked his daughter's life this way. There must be another explanation."

"Ah, Jemmy," Alistair said, grasping his wrist. "Don't ye ken? They thought she could soften your heart and make ye believe what they want ye to believe—that you'd listen to her instead of your own people. And they were right, weren't they? This talk of peace was just an old man's dream. Darnley thinks he has us at his mercy now that Ian's gone, for there's no one left to fight."

"If that is what he thinks," Jemmy said, and Alistair stepped back a pace before the anger in his eyes, "then Lord Darnley has made a grave mistake. You bring me what I need and then, if you are right—" he laughed harshly. "Then we'll kill them to the last man."

* * *

Alyson ran from Jemmy's chambers to the stables, but he was nowhere to be found. From there she went into the hall, her eyes moving quickly over the people gathered in the long room. At last she glimpsed him briefly within the throng.

"My lord!"

There was no response so she approached, threading her way between the crowd. "My lord!" she called again, and now the voices began to still and heads turn in her direction. In fact, it seemed that everyone had heard her cry. Everyone save Jemmy.

The crowd parted to let her pass and at last she saw him fully. He was half sitting against the trestle, talking to a woman. Alyson stopped, the breath leaving her body in a sickening rush as she saw him smile up at the woman, his hands toying with the fastenings of her cloak.

The silence was absolute now. Everyone had drawn back a little and so she stood alone, Jemmy not ten feet away. Yet he seemed completely unaware of her presence. Even the girl who stood with him turned and Alyson saw with dull shock that it was Celia. She tossed her yellow curls and gave Alyson an insolent smile before turning back to Jemmy.

"My lord," Alyson said again, but her voice had no power now, it came out as no more than a hoarse whisper. But at last he seemed to hear.

"Ah, my lady," he said, "Come to welcome me back? How kind. Now, if you'll excuse me, I'm rather busy."

He stood slowly, turning to say something to Celia. The girl broke into a merry laugh. They left the hall together, his arm draped casually about her shoulders.

Alyson stood rooted to the spot. She couldn't breathe, she couldn't move, she couldn't think at all. It was very quiet and every eye was on her, watching with amusement or pity or simple curiosity to see what she would do next.

Slowly, very slowly, she walked back the way she'd come, her head held high and her back straight. When she reached the turn of the stairway the voices broke out in talk and there was laughter as well, sharp as any dagger. Her courage broke, and she ran the rest of the way to her chamber.

chapter 33

"*What did he say?*"

"He said—" Maggie hesitated, wishing it was anyone but her who had to deliver this message. Then she crossed her fingers behind her and finished in a rush. "He said he is verra sorry, my lady, but he has pressing matters to attend to and canna stop to see ye. But he said he will come to ye as soon as possible."

And may God forgive her for the lie. Jemmy had said nothing of the sort. There had been no apology, no promise that he would find the time to see his wife. All in all, it had been a most uncomfortable and mystifying interview.

Maggie had been kept waiting nearly an hour. When at last she was admitted to Jemmy's chamber, she found him seated behind a long table, head bent as he examined a map spread out before him.

Today, she had vowed, she would add her own opinion of his boorish manners if he dared refuse his lady yet again. No one had the better right to bring him to his senses—and sharply, too. Had she not delivered Jemmy with her own hands? Tended his childish cuts and bruises, sung him to sleep when he was fevered? And been rewarded, aye, with crumpled flowers and kisses and the first carving he had made with his own hands. The crooked boat still stood in its place of honor by her bedside.

But when Jemmy lifted his head, he stared at her with the hard eyes of a stranger.

"My lord, your lady asks that ye sup with her this even," she said, unaccountably nervous beneath that stony gaze. "Or if ye canna spare the time to dine, that ye but speak with her."

Jemmy did not even bother answering. He turned back to the map and waved a hand, thus signaling the interview was over. And Maggie, without another word, had gone away.

"I'm sorry, my lady," Maggie said now. "But he is verra much occupied the now . . . and ye know what they say: 'tis a woman's lot to wait." There being no answer, she added cheerfully, "But I have brought ye the honey cakes ye like. Will ye no have one?"

"No."

"At least let me light some candles, 'tis mournful dark in here."

"No."

Maggie stared at her mistress with concern. Even by the light of the fire she could see how fearfully pale the girl was, her eyes enormous in deep hollows brought on by lack of sleep. She had not wept, or at least not before her women. She'd simply sat in her room for two days now, refusing every bit of food with which Maggie had tried to tempt her.

Looking at the girl, Maggie could not help but feel angry with Master Jemmy. He'd always been a bit wild but kindhearted, too. Now she thought he must have a heart of stone to do such a thing to his bride. All hot and loving

he'd been before he left, and now he could not even find
five minutes to speak with her! While the lass was pining
herself away to a shadow.

"I think I will ride," she said, startling Maggie.

"Oh, aye. That's a grand idea, lady. Here, let me help
ye . . ."

She stood like a statue as Maggie dressed her. When at
last it was finished she looked at her serving woman
gravely.

"You're a good woman, Maggie. Too good for this
place. You should leave."

"Leave?" Maggie laughed a little uncomfortably. "D'ye
want me to leave your service?"

"It's this place. Nothing good can live here, there's too
much hatred. You should get away."

"I've been here all my life," Maggie said. "Wherever
would I go?"

The lady sighed. "I don't know. Never mind, Maggie.
Thank you."

She looked as though she wanted to say something
more, but in the end she just touched the older woman's
hand and left.

Alyson *headed toward the stables. She was leaving,*
now, today. Sir Robert would be waiting in the clearing, and they'd ride to London. As for what would happen
here, she didn't care. Let them destroy each other, there
was nothing she could do to stop it. She had been a fool to
even try. It was none of her affair—she was nothing to any
of these people, and they were nothing to her. Except
Malcolm. She stopped, clutching the wall to keep from
falling as a wave of sickness hit her. There was nothing she
could do to save him now. She would have to trust that
Jemmy would protect him—or if not Jemmy, then Alistair.

They would, she knew, if it was in their power. Just as she would—she must—protect Robin.

It would be hard to live upon Sir Robert's charity, but it must be done. She had considered taking some of Lady Maude's jewels—God knew she'd earned them. But she could not force herself to do it. No, she thought with bitter anger, she'd take nothing from any of them.

Oh, she'd been a fool to believe she meant anything to Jemmy, she knew that now. No doubt he'd had many such experiences before; she was simply one more woman to him. She'd told herself that a hundred times during the last wretched days and she nearly believed it now. But when she remembered the night they'd spent together, her mind and heart rebelled.

He cared for her. She couldn't be mistaken about that— or could she? What did she know of men? Yet he had said he loved her. How could it be possible to share such a night and then simply forget it, as though it had never happened? She didn't know, she didn't understand anything at all. It was all beyond her, the ways of the nobility. She had to go, she had to get away.

She was walking through the courtyard when she saw him. Their eyes met and held; her heart began to beat wildly in her breast. And then he nodded curtly and began to walk past her. Let him go, she told herself. Let him go and be damned to him. It's not my fault if he dies—

"My lord, please, wait," she said, hurrying to keep up with his long steps. When he didn't answer, she seized him by the arm. "Jemmy, for the love of God, *please*."

He gave a small exasperated sigh. "What is it?"

"I must speak to you alone."

He looked into her pleading face, the lovely eyes shining with tears, and for a moment he hesitated. Then deliberately he summoned the memory of Carmela's tears.

"I really haven't the time right now. Perhaps later."

He shook off her hand and began to walk away. "What's happened to you?" she cried. "You said you loved me."

The words hit him like a blow. Oh, yes, he had loved her. God help him, he loved her still.

He turned, one brow raised. "Did I?" he asked coolly. "Well, lady, you can hardly hold a man accountable for what he says at such a time. I thought you would have known that. Now, if you will excuse me . . ."

He left her, walking quickly to the stairway and mounting. When he reached the turn he stopped and laid his head against the cool stone wall, seeing again the way she had recoiled from him, exactly as though he had struck her. A part of him had taken a hurtful satisfaction in seeing his own pain reflected in her face, but now he was ashamed. She'd looked so wild, so desperate—exactly as she had looked when he found her on the crag.

The memory brought sharp fear, and he went back down the stairway, just in time to see Alistair gallop into the courtyard.

"Jemmy!" Alistair cried, leaping from his horse. "Here, ye wanted proof? Then talk to him." He gestured toward the horse beside him, which held a young man with a sullen look and a shock of lank brown hair.

Jemmy looked at his wife and she was staring at the man, horror and recognition on her face. Then her gaze turned to him. "Jemmy—my lord—wait. You must speak with me now. Alone."

"Later," he said. She gripped his arm and turned him to face her.

"No, now. Please."

He looked over his shoulder at Darnley's man, who stood beside Alistair on the cobbles.

"In a moment," he said, shaking off her hand. "First I will hear what this man has to say. You!" he called sharply. "What is your name?"

"Sym," the man said, licking his lips nervously.

Alistair smiled. "Young Sym is not quite satisfied with his place in Lord Darnley's household."

"Aye, that's right," Sym said. "He—" he jerked his head toward Alistair, "said I could be head stable lad here, if I but told ye what I've seen."

"And what have you seen?" Jemmy asked impatiently.

"Men and horses. From my lord Northumberland's demesne. A hundred or more."

"For what purpose have they come to Aylsford?" Jemmy asked and Sym looked at him, surprised and wary.

"Why else, sir? To make war upon ye."

"You know this for a certainty?"

"His lordship never called me into council, if that's what ye are askin'. I doubt his lordship even knows I am alive. But aye, I know it. 'Tis common knowledge he means to do ye in."

Jemmy glanced at Maude and his heart sank. Her head was bent, her face averted, and she had whitened to the lips.

"Well, my lady?" he said, his voice deliberately cold. "Perhaps you can provide an explanation for your father's actions."

She recovered with a swiftness he could not help but admire. "Am I to stand here in the courtyard discussing my father's affairs?" she answered haughtily. "I shall speak to you in private, my lord, or not at all."

And with that she began to walk away.

"Not so fast," Alistair said, stepping into her path. "Ye are not the one giving orders here."

She turned to avoid him and came face to face with Sym. His mouth dropped open in astonishment.

"Here, now, what's this?" he cried.

Maude froze. She opened her mouth to speak, then shut it again without uttering a word.

"Alyson?" Sym said uncertainly. "Is it ye, lass?"

She lifted her chin and gave Sym a look cold enough to freeze him where he stood. "How dare you so address me?"

"It is!" Sym cried. "So this is where ye ran off to! We all wondered what became of ye."

"This man is a troublemaker and a liar," she said clearly. "He always has been. You mustn't credit anything he says."

Jemmy ignored her. "This is Lady Maude," he said to Sym. "Surely you must know her."

"No," Sym said. "She's—"

"My lord, really!" she interrupted. "The man is nothing, just a common stable lad who seeks to better himself by telling lies about—"

"Common, am I?" Sym demanded. "Aye, well, no more than ye, for all the airs ye gave yourself! Lady Maude?" he said, turning to Jemmy with an unpleasant laugh. "Her? Not likely!"

"Then who the devil is she?" Alistair demanded, looking nearly as stunned as Jemmy felt himself.

"Alyson Bowden from the Aylsford kitchens," Sym said positively. "I'd know her anywhere. Haven't I seen her every day these past four years? Right until she up and ran off without a word."

Jemmy watched her face, waiting for her denial. But it never came.

"At least she was Darnley's kitchen maid," Sym added, giving her a puzzled, hostile look. "I can't say what she is now."

She is my lady, Jemmy thought numbly. My wife. The woman who said she loved me. And all of it was lies.

"Nor can I," Alistair said, staring at her with interest. "But ye can be sure we will find out."

"Take her away, Alistair," Jemmy ordered curtly. "Put her in the tower room. And keep that man confined. Say nothing to anyone until we've spoken further."

"Here, now!" Sym cried indignantly. "What d'ye mean, confined? I told ye what I knew, didn't I?"

"Aye, lad, ye did," Alistair answered. "But there's times

a man can know a bit too much for his own good. It won't be for long," he added reassuringly. "Why don't ye come with me while we take your friend here to her chamber?"

"She's no friend o' mine," Sym said spitefully. "Always thought herself too good for the likes of me."

"Her sights were set a wee bit higher," Alistair said dryly.

Why did she not speak? Jemmy wondered. Say something, anything, to defend herself? But she did not seem aware of them at all. She stood, her face as pale and set as marble, completely remote and utterly detached.

"Come along, Mistress," Alistair said, and for the first time Jemmy heard a tinge of respect in the knight's voice as he addressed her.

Perhaps she deserves it, Jemmy thought savagely. It wasn't every kitchen maid who could pass herself off as the daughter of an earl. Even now, she gave no sign of her common origins. Head high, shoulders thrown back proudly, she walked across the courtyard as though she were a queen.

The tower room held only a stool, a table, and a small bed. The fire smoked, and the sullen flame did nothing to warm the chill dankness seeping from the stone walls. Jemmy stood, arms folded across his chest, and stared at the woman before him in disbelief, wondering if he had heard her properly.

"You say you are Lord Darnley's daughter," he repeated.

"Aye. Though I never knew it. He never claimed me, you see, and my mother never said . . ."

"Go on."

"Both he and Lady Maude were very angry at the bargain he'd been forced to make. He never meant to live up to it at all; it only made him more determined to destroy you."

"And yet he took the oath." Jemmy shook his head.

She drew herself up and looked him fully in the eye. It was clear that she had been weeping; her eyes were reddened and her skin had an almost transparent pallor. But she was not crying now. She faced him calmly, with a dignity that would have been admirable enough in one of noble birth, but for a girl of no breeding, no family—well, it was extraordinary. But then, he knew already she was no ordinary girl.

"There was a certain likeness between myself and Lady Maude," she said. "And so they happened on this plan. They sent Celia, as well, and she said that there were others watching—" she shuddered and wrapped her arms tightly about herself.

"But you—whyever did you agree to do such a thing?"

"It was because of Robin, my—"

"I know all about Robin."

"Then you understand," she said, relief warming her voice.

"Oh, aye. I understand." He turned and started for the door.

"Wait, my lord. I know that you are angry, and you have every right to be—"

"Thank you," he said dryly.

"But I ask that your anger would end with me. Do anything you like but please, don't seek vengeance on Robin."

She stepped back a pace, no doubt seeing the anger and disgust on his face. "My lord," she said, holding out her hands in appeal. "You wouldn't. Surely—for pity's sake—"

"This will mean war, d'ye ken that even now? Your—Robin—will have to look to himself. Don't ask me for mercy."

"But you couldn't! None of this was his fault—he's just a—"

"You did it for his sake, didn't you?"

She nodded, saying simply, "I would do anything for Robin."

He left without another word, slamming the door behind him.

Kirallen *sat before the fire, a thick mantle drawn across* his shoulders. As Jemmy finished speaking, he closed his eyes, suddenly too weary to even think of all that must be done. He had failed. There would be no peace, it would all start again now, worse than before.

"Who else knows?"

"Alistair. And the servant, Celia. She's under restraint with Darnley's stable lad. The girl said there were others, as well, though she couldn't name them."

"Ah, yes. The girl. What's to become of her?"

Jemmy looked away. "I have not decided yet."

"Whatever ye say, Jemmy," Kirallen said. "I'll leave it in your hands. For now keep her to the tower—put it about that she is ill. We must think on this carefully and decide what's best to be done. But let no word reach Darnley that we suspect . . . Tomorrow, Jemmy," he said, his shoulders slumping. "We'll decide tomorrow. I'm so weary now . . . it seems all I do goes ill these days, ever since—"

"Since Ian died," Jemmy finished. "Aye, Father, I know." The old man flinched before the bitterness in his son's voice. "It was not that I meant," he said, though neither of them believed it. "I'm sorry for this, Jemmy. I was fond of the lass myself. Even now I can't believe she acted out of malice."

"It doesn't matter what her motives were. The damage has been done."

"Tomorrow," Kirallen whispered. "We'll talk about it then."

chapter 34

I t was midmorning when Jemmy went to fetch her for questioning. When he reached the hallway he saw old Maggie slip from the chamber. She alone had been told the truth and set to guard the girl, though Jemmy doubted she would attempt escape. When Maggie saw him she gave a startled gasp, one hand going to her apron pocket. Jemmy didn't speak; he simply held out his hand. After a moment she removed the square of parchment and handed it to him.

"Who wrote this?"

"She did," Maggie answered.

So, she knows how to write, Jemmy thought. Where had a kitchen maid come by that skill?

Glancing down he saw it was addressed to Sir Robert Allshouse. The name seemed somehow familiar, and he searched his memory, then dismissed the matter. Robert. Robin. That was all that he need know.

"Maggie, how could you?"

Her eyes filled with tears. "I could not refuse her."

"Get out of here," he snapped. "Don't come back until you're summoned."

When he entered the chamber he found Alyson before the window. She was dressed in a plain gown of black wool that emphasized the pallor of her skin and made her hair flame brightly against its darkness. She whirled at his entrance, and he held up the letter.

"I see you're to be trusted no more than your father."

"No, my lord, I suppose not. I would do the same again. Please, can you not see that it's taken to him?"

"You're mad," he said shortly.

"Read it for yourself. There's nothing that can harm you, nothing at all. Please, my lord."

During the long night just passed Jemmy had come to have some pity for the girl. Taken from the kitchens, it was no wonder her head had been turned by the attentions of a knight. But how she could even now care for him was something Jemmy could not understand. The man had used her, sent her here to play the whore—why, he was no better than a panderer! Despicable. And yet still she sought to protect him, even though she must know her own life could well be forfeit. He did not understand it, but after a moment he thrust the letter into his belt.

"I'll think about it."

"Thank you."

She followed him down the stairs, through the hall, and down again, until they reached a chamber few women had ever seen. It stood in the oldest part of the keep, the place that from time immemorial had been used by Kirallen's Laird to take counsel of his most trusted advisors. Torches blazed even on this sunny day, for the thick walls contained only narrow slits, set obliquely to allow air to penetrate, but no light. When this room had been built, windows were considered a superfluous danger.

A table stretched the length of the room. It was burned and hacked, scarred by fire and dagger. At the head sat

Kirallen. To the right of him was Alistair, and about its long surface sat a dozen grim and dour clan elders, with several of Kirallen's chief knights standing behind them. The place opposite Kirallen was empty, waiting for Jemmy's arrival.

Alyson stood before them, a slender figure in black. She bore their questioning well, answering in a clear, steady voice. She hesitated only once, when the Laird asked her why she had agreed.

"I could not refuse my lord and father," she said, glancing quickly at Jemmy. He dropped his eyes to the table before him and did not speak a word.

"All right then," Kirallen said. "Do you have any more to say?"

"Aye, my lord. You were kind to me, and it was never my wish to return your kindness thus. I'm sorry for it. And I pray that you can think of some way to end this without bloodshed."

"You may go," Kirallen said, and she curtsied to him before turning, her head held high.

At a signal one of the men escorted her out of the room and those remaining looked at one another.

"Well, Laird," Alistair said, "I think it's clear enough what happened. The question is, what do we do next?"

Not by word or gesture did he imply that the Laird had been wrong and he'd been right. He didn't have to. Every man there knew it.

But even if Alistair was prepared to move ahead, the rest were not. They went over and over Darnley's treachery, which to them seemed almost monstrous. To have sworn a solemn oath and broken it—that was something so foreign to their sense of honor that they could scarcely credit it. And to send his bastard kitchen slut to wed their Laird's son was not only a deception, it was a deadly insult—one that none of them would soon forget.

Jemmy sat silent, the words ringing in his mind.

Darnley's bastard kitchen slut. His spy. A peasant who had been plucked from the kitchens and sent here to deceive them all. That's what she was—*all* she was—no matter how well she looked in her borrowed finery. He saw her clad in silk and hung with flashing jewels, wearing them as if they were her right. He saw her standing by the open window, her hair streaming down her slender back, then pushed the image away. He was doubly a fool: for falling so easily prey to her deceit and for the wrenching sense of loss he felt even now.

But to the others she had been no more than Darnley's tool, and in herself meant nothing. The knowledge of her birth had destroyed her completely in their eyes. She would die, Sir Calder said, a traitor's death. Jemmy realized that he disliked Sir Calder very much indeed. The knight would go, no matter what Alistair might say about it. And there would be no execution. Not now, not ever.

He nearly gave the order, then saw that Alistair was watching him, waiting for him to speak, waiting to begin the argument. But Jemmy had no intention of arguing this matter. The Kirallen clan would never put a woman to death, whoever she might be or whatever she had done. It simply would not happen. He wanted to make that very clear to them right now, yet he held himself in check. His temper was hanging by a thread already. If Alistair dared defy him by a single word, Jemmy could not answer for what he might do next. And if he and Alistair came to blows—or worse—as seemed all too likely, it was the clan that would suffer. Now, more than ever, he and Alistair must present a united front.

There was no need for it, Jemmy thought, forcing his hands to unclench. No need for any arguments, no need to divide the council. The decision was his, not Alistair's. The council could suggest, but the Laird alone could order. And the Laird had put the matter in Jemmy's hands. Let them say what they liked, he alone would decide what to do about Darnley's daughter. Darnley's *bastard* daughter, who had lied to him with every word she spoke.

"Do I please you?" she had asked so sweetly, lying spent and trembling in his arms. How could she have deceived him so completely? How could he not have seen that it was all a lie?

As the afternoon wore on the talk passed to which of their allies could be trusted to respond with haste and silence. The men looked to Alistair for a decision and Jemmy made no protest, for Alistair was far more familiar with the ever-shifting alliances of clans than he was himself. Alistair returned the courtesy by consulting Jemmy on every decision before it was made final and a message drafted. The men accepted this as natural, and Jemmy realized this is how Alistair and Ian had always worked together in the past, with Alistair attending to the planning while Ian led the men in battle. As Jemmy would do when the time came.

There was a bitter sort of relief in giving up the fight and taking the place that had been Ian's in the clan. Had he really thought he could avoid this? The man who had arrived from Spain was dead, and Jemmy would not mourn his loss. That man had been a fool, with all his childish dreams of escaping the path laid out before him.

Well, he wasn't running anymore. He was Kirallen now. And God help Darnley, for he'd find no mercy at Kirallen's hands.

The torches were guttering in their holders as Alistair finished the last dispatch and handed it to Jemmy. Then he sank back in his seat and rubbed a hand across the stubble of his beard. Despite the weary droop of his shoulders, his heart was light. At last the Laird acknowledged the truth that Alistair had been trying to tell him for so long. There was but one way to deal with Darnley—at swordspoint.

Only now did Alistair realize the full extent of his exhaustion. For months he had been existing on nights of broken sleep, knowing the clan was headed for disaster and helpless to prevent it. But now all would be well. They would go forth in honorable combat, and Alistair would do what he should have done from the beginning: kill Darnley or die in the attempt. And he did not much care which way it ended, either, so long as it was finished and he could have some peace.

"This is the last? Well done," Jemmy said, tossing the parchment on the long table and turning to Alistair with a smile. "Is the messenger ready?"

Alistair nodded and managed to return Jemmy's smile with one equally as false. Now was not the time to show by word or sign his true opinion of his foster brother. This battle could not be won by a clan divided.

"No need for ye to wait for him," he said pleasantly. "I can manage now."

"No, don't bother. I'll finish up here," Jemmy said, stifling a yawn. "You look exhausted."

Alistair felt a flash of resentment. This was his job; it always had been. Ian had trusted him absolutely. But then, Ian had never once suggested completing any task if Alistair was there to do it for him.

For a moment Alistair wondered what it would be like to serve a man who noticed if he was tired or not, someone who would take the responsibilities of ruling seriously. It would be a relief, Alistair thought, to have some of the burden lifted from his shoulders. But they would no doubt argue constantly, both of them wanting to have the final word.

Not that he would ever serve Jemmy. This was a charade, no more, enacted for the benefit of the clan. Jemmy would never rule here. After what he had done today,

Alistair would make it his business to see that Jemmy never had the chance.

"Death to the Darnley wench!" Sir Calder had cried, and no sooner were the words spoken than Alistair knew Sir Calder had to go. Were warriors to seek vengeance on a kitchen maid? It was contemptible. There was no place among Kirallen's knights for a man so totally devoid of honor. That such a thing had even been suggested was a disquieting sign of how far the clan had drifted these past months. But if Calder's words had surprised him, Jemmy's silence had shocked him to the core.

Jemmy should have been the first to shout the knight to silence. Alistair had waited, fully expecting him to do just that, ready to back him to the hilt. But Jemmy had not said a word. And so much for all his pious mouthings about peace and honor! Honor? Today Jemmy had proved beyond all doubt that he had no conception of the word.

The council chamber was nearly empty now. The Laird had retired some time ago, and many of the men had drifted off to find their beds. A few still lingered, and as Jemmy talked with the messenger, Alistair let their conversation flow around him.

"I kent long ago that something was amiss with the lass," one man was saying wisely. "Her hands—did ye never mark them?"

" 'Tis hard to believe a baseborn kitchen slut could have managed it at all," another man put in. "Though right from the start I wondered. D'ye no' remember me saying that there was something a wee bit off about the lass?"

Alistair's lip curved in a smile. Let them say what they like. Only yesterday they had been all taken in by her, himself included. At least he was ready to admit it! But then he knew—who better?—that the baseborn of this world were no different from any other, save that they must use what wits and luck they had been given more cannily than most.

As this lass—no, Mistress Alyson Bowden, he thought,

for he at least would not grudge her a name—had done. She had come among them at her father's order to play the part of Lady Maude, and she had done it well, using all her wiles to bedazzle Lady Maude's intended husband. Bad enough to be humiliated by a woman, but to have it done as publicly as she had done to Jemmy—the very idea of it made Alistair shudder.

Well, he wasn't going to waste any sympathy on Jemmy now. He obviously cared nothing for the lass, though he had seemed very taken with her when Alistair had come upon them in the stables. And there was no doubt at all what they'd been doing there!

A strumpet, and a clever one, that's what she was, and Alistair would wager she set a high price upon her services, as well she should. Even today, knowing she had lost, she had been impressive. Her manner had been truly noble as she answered the Laird's questions with every show of honesty.

Show of honesty? he thought, sitting up in his seat. What had made him think that her honesty had not been real? Wide awake now, every sense alert, he went over what she had told them here today. Aye, she had answered every question, but she had told them almost nothing.

There were others besides her chambermaid involved. She said she could not name them, but she had hesitated before she answered. Or had that come later? He cursed his weary mind that he could not remember, but of one thing he was certain: she was holding something back.

And there was something else that did not ring quite true. Convincing as she might have been when she claimed ignorance of Darnley's plans, how could that be anything but a lie? She and her father must have had some plan to get her out before his men fell upon the keep, which meant she had a good idea of when he was expected. Or was there some other arrangement, a message that the clan could intercept?

The Laird had been too easy on her, he thought. She had faltered at least once during the questioning, he was sure of it, but they had not pressed her for the answers that could mean the difference between life and death for their clansmen.

Sleep must wait another hour, he decided. First he would pay a visit to their prisoner. He sighed and rubbed his eyes, wishing that just for once, someone else would take responsibility for the clan's protection. He was tired, too tired to do this properly, but there was no one else to ask. And it must be done tonight.

She would tell him everything. She must. There were too many lives at stake to flinch from doing anything that must be done to make her talk. One way or another, he vowed, before this night was through, Mistress Alyson Bowden would surrender all her secrets.

chapter 35

By the time Jemmy reached his chamber he was almost too tired to stand, but nonetheless he waved the page away. Once the lad was gone he sank into a chair, though he doubted he would sleep any more tonight than he had done the night before.

There was a knock on the door and he called roughly, "Go away." But the door opened, and Malcolm, trembling from head to foot, moved to stand before his uncle.

"Is it true?"

"What?"

"My aunt. Did the council really say that she will die?"

Jemmy sighed and reached out a hand, but Malcolm twisted from his grasp.

"Is it true?" the boy insisted.

"So the council said."

" 'Tis your fault," Malcolm cried, his face reddening with anger and tears standing in his eyes. "Ye did this—"

"Malcolm, no—she isn't who we thought—"

"I know. But they said she was horrid and she's not, she's kind and good. And now you're going to kill her!"

"She isn't going to die," Jemmy said wearily. "I won't let that happen. They were too angry tonight to listen, but tomorrow I will tell them."

"Then what will happen to her?" Malcolm demanded.

"I don't know," Jemmy ran one hand distractedly through his hair. "I'll decide tomorrow. We'll send her somewhere—a convent, perhaps—and she can live there."

"Forever?"

"Aye. Now go to bed, 'tis late."

"But ye canna do such a thing—how could she live, shut away forever? She couldn't."

Jemmy knew that was the truth. He could scarcely imagine caging such a vital woman behind high walls. But it was better than death.

"No more," he said. "Not tonight. Go on, Malcolm," he added sharply, and the boy turned with a small choked sound and ran from the room.

Jemmy winced as the door slammed, then slowly pulled off his boots. He considered summoning the servants back again, for this was one night he could actually use their help, but the effort seemed too great. Yawning, he stood and fumbled at his sword belt. And it was then he felt the letter tucked behind the leather.

He turned it in his hands, reflecting that to read it would only bring him further pain. He was too weary to be angry anymore. Tomorrow would be, if anything, worse than today. No, there was no need to make it even harder.

He reached to drop the letter on the fire, but stopped, his hand arrested in midair. He blinked and stared. There it was, his own hand, and there was nothing to account for the fact that it simply hung there, motionless and very cold.

That cold. He remembered it from a drunken dream he'd had some time ago. But he wasn't drunk now; in fact, he was far too sober for his own good. The hair on the back of his neck was rising, and almost against his will he whispered, "Stephen?"

His hand was released. In fact, it was flung back at him with such force that the letter fell to the floor. He bent to pick it up, looking cautiously about the room as once again he made to toss it into the flame.

The fire went out. One minute it was burning merrily; the next there were cold ashes in its place.

"God's teeth, Stephen, if you're here, why don't you show yourself?"

Jemmy glanced about the empty room, embarrassed at the sound of his own voice. What was he saying? The shock of the past days had obviously affected him more deeply than he'd realized. Stephen wasn't here, he was dead, and there were no such things as ghosts. But then, there was no such thing as a fire that died in a moment's time without leaving so much as an ember. Or so Jemmy had thought.

"Fine then," he muttered, sinking into his seat. "So be it."

He broke the seal of the parchment and found another letter tucked within, folded small. He put it aside and read the words addressed to Sir Robert Allshouse.

"Dearest Uncle," it began, and he frowned, turning it again to look at the inscription. Allshouse . . . of course, he remembered now where he had heard the name. It was the old Lady Darnley's second husband's. And so Robert must be her son, the present lord's half brother. His eyes went back to the writing.

"I write to you in haste, for it has come, just as you feared it would, and all has been discovered. Please, I beg you to get Robin to safety with all speed. I fear for his life, not only from Lord Darnley's anger, but from the Kirallens as well. I would ask, too, that you keep the truth from him until he is old enough to understand. You will know when that time has come. When it does, please give him the enclosed.

"Sir Robert, I thank you for your many kindnesses to me and mine. I thank you for your counsel, as well, though I chose not to heed it. I was very foolish, just as you said. I wanted to believe that I could trust him, but have found to my sorrow that you were right. Now I am to pay the price for that. I have brought this on myself and do not hold you in any way to blame. Go back to London, Sir Robert, and of your kindness say nothing of this message to your brother. Just as I have brought my fate upon myself, so has he brought his. I fear that there is nothing anyone can do to stop it now.

"Please remember me in your prayers."

Jemmy sank back into his seat, the letter trailing from his hand. Her *uncle*? That was who she had been meeting with? And she'd told him . . . He read the words again. " . . . I wanted to believe that I could trust him."

She must have come straight from her meeting with Sir Robert to him, when he'd sat in the hall with Celia and pretended not to see her. She had come to tell him the truth. Why hadn't she done so before? If only she had spoken none of this would have happened. Ah, but what reason did she have to trust? No doubt the Darnleys had filled her head with all manner of stories of him and his kin. He could imagine what they'd said to her. She must have been frightened half to death to come among them, though he had to admit she'd played her part well. But she hadn't been able to sustain it.

It all made sense now. His instinct had been right; she had wanted him from the first. He remembered the day he'd found her on the crag, when he thought she'd meant

to take her life. What had they done to her? What threat
had they used to bend her to their will? And later, in the
stables . . . she had tried to tell him then, hadn't she? He
remembered everything—every look, every touch, every
word they had spoken. She'd meant to tell him but she
hadn't. And he understood why.

"This is me, here, tonight . . ." she had declared with
a courage he could only now admire. And he'd answered, "You here, tonight, are the woman I love."

Then he heard the echo of his own voice saying
coldly, "A man can't be held accountable for what he
says at such a time," seeing again the way she'd looked
at him, as though he'd stabbed her to the heart. As he
might just as well have done.

She loved him. No matter what she had been forced to
say or do, during that one night she'd spoken only the
truth and had risked her life to prove it. Even now she'd
never tried to turn what had happened between them to
her advantage or asked him once for mercy. No, she'd
asked him only one thing: to spare Robin. And that he
had refused.

Jemmy picked up the smaller letter. He unfolded it
and read.

"My dear Robin. By now you know the full story of
what happened to me, and I fear that you are thinking to
avenge me in some way. That is why I write this to you
now, and I beg you to listen to me.

"Vengeance brings no healing, no peace. It will eat
away at your very soul, a bitter sickness of the spirit,
until everything good in you is destroyed. I have seen
that for myself. The Kirallens are not evil; they are the
same as any other men and women. But they are blighted
by their dreams of vengeance, the hatred they nurture
carefully in their breasts. I would not see that happen to
you, Rob. So I ask you to leave it be, and I pray you will
heed my last request."

Jemmy raised his eyes, staring blindly ahead. A bitter sickness of the spirit. Yes. How well she understood them, both Darnley and Kirallen. They were all sick with fear and hatred, every one of them. Even him. Especially him. He had run from it half his life, but in the end it had caught him just as surely as it caught all the others. He turned back to the letter.

"I would ask as well that you make your way to the McLarans and our grandmother, Emma. She is a good woman who will welcome you with joy. Say nothing to any McLaran of me, lest it cause ill will between them and the Kirallens, who have been allies for many years.

"Rob, you have been the greatest joy of my life. I only wish I could have seen you grow to manhood. I know I would be proud. Your sister, Alyson."

She'd asked her brother to make his way to the McLarans . . . to Emma. Their grandmother. And that could only mean that her mother had been—

"Oh, Stephen," he said softly. "Why didn't you tell me?"

Without waiting for an answer he pulled on his boots and ran from the room, all his weariness forgotten. But when he reached the stairway he stopped, then went out into the night. He needed time to think, to understand what he'd just learned.

He paced through the courtyard, though what he wanted was to go to her and tell her he understood everything now and loved her all the more for what she had done. He'd pick her up and carry her to the great bed, pull the curtains around them, and shut the rest of the world away.

But the world would not go away. Oh, for one night it might be banished, but there would be tomorrow . . . and tomorrow. Soon or late the world would intrude with its laws, both written and unwritten. And one of those laws was that there could be no future for Kirallen's heir and Darnley's baseborn daughter.

He could keep her as his mistress. It was a common enough arrangement. But her position would be impossible—and not only hers, but any children they might have. Certain it was that the Kirallens would never accept her children as their own and no more would the Darnleys. As for the McLarans . . . they would turn their backs on her if she were to so openly flaunt propriety. If anything was to happen to him she'd be friendless, utterly alone. No, he could never ask her to become his mistress. But he had nothing else to offer.

He saw his life stretching before him, an endless span of empty days, all spent alone. It would not matter if he stayed or went, if he married again or not, for he would always be alone now . . .

He sat on the mounting block and looked up at the sky. There was no moon tonight, for the clouds hung low. No shooting stars upon which he might wish things were different. Only the mist that turned to rain and fell upon his upturned face.

Things were as they were. The sooner he accepted that, the better it would be for him and Alyson, as well. But Jemmy did not want to accept it. He was filled with rage against the world; relieved and hurt and longing to hear from Alyson herself that despite all, she loved him still.

He could never ask that of her, though. And he could never tell her all he felt. It would be too cruel. Even so, there were things that must be said between them. He rose to his feet, determined to see her now despite the lateness of the hour. God knew he would lose her soon enough. At least he could be near her for the time that they had left.

He was nearly at the door when he heard it. He stopped, listening hard, but the night was silent once again. Yet there was no question in his mind of what he'd heard, the very faint but unmistakable sound of a woman's scream. And it was coming from the tower room.

chapter 36

Alistair opened the door of the tower room quietly and peered inside. The Darnley lass was sitting on the window seat, playing softly on her lute. So silent was Alistair's entrance that she did not look up, but continued with her song as he stood watching her from the threshold.

She was clad in a simple linen shift, her shining hair loose and falling about her shoulders like a mantle of living flame. Her long, white fingers drew a plaintive little tune from the instrument, a melancholy air that Alistair had never head before, and her expression was one of heavy sorrow. For a moment weariness overwhelmed him and he considered abandoning his errand, then he stepped inside and shut the door behind him.

"I bring you the council's judgment," he said.

She started, the melody lost in a jangle of strings.

"What—what news?"

"Death."

She closed her eyes and swallowed hard, then nodded.

"How?"

"Burning or hanging. It hasn't been decided yet."

Would she scream or faint or make some plea for mercy? He couldn't imagine her doing any of those things, and she did not disappoint him. She raised her chin proudly and said a single word.

"When?"

"Three days, perhaps a week, no more."

He sat beside her on the window seat, and she drew away from him. "Have ye ever seen a burning?" he asked. " 'Tis a most horrible thing. Hanging is better, but not by much. If the neck is not broken on the drop—" he shuddered. "Verra ugly. But I think something might be done for ye—if ye were of a mind to be reasonable."

"What do you mean?" she asked, and though she did not relax her posture, he thought he heard a slight quaver in her voice.

"There's more to your tale than ye have told us. And I mean to have the rest of it."

She held his gaze steadily, but he marked the sudden dilation of her pupil. "I've told you everything."

He took her hand in his. "Now, lass, we both know that's not the truth," he said gently. "There are others besides yourself involved. Who are they? How much do they know of us?"

"I—I dinna ken," she said, pulling her hand from his and rising swiftly to her feet. "Only Celia. She came with me. I wasn't told about the others, just that they were here. Lord Darnley did not want me to know," she added, backing away as Alistair stood as well.

"That sounds well," he said, though of course he did not believe her. There was at least one person whose identity she knew: the knight she had been embracing by the river. "But I think that there is more."

"There's no one else—save for one man, but he is not

quartered here. He gave me Lord Darnley's orders," she went on quickly, taking another step away.

"When? Where?"

"By the river," she said, surprising him. "I met him there. But he is gone now. You cannot find him."

"Who was he?"

"I won't say!" she answered with a sudden burst of spirit. "He was kind to me and sorry for his errand. He would have helped me if he could."

She stopped, her back against the wall. Alistair placed his hands on either side of her head, trapping her between his arms. "Fair enough," he said. "Keep your lover's name if it means that much to ye."

"My *what*?"

She is good, Alistair thought. Very good. The surprise, the confusion in her voice—if he hadn't known better, he would have sworn that they were real.

He shrugged, dismissing the matter. "Whatever he is, he knows of us now. What have ye told him?"

"Nothing," she said. "There was nothing I *could* tell. I had so little time and the ladies never trusted me . . ."

"Perceptive of them," he said wryly.

Her face was but inches from his own, close enough to see a few freckles sprinkling the bridge of her nose. She looked so young and fair, the very picture of innocence, not at all the unscrupulous adventurer who had deceived them so completely. Who, even now, was prepared to go on lying, though whether in the interest of her family or herself he could not say.

Just as I would do, Alistair thought with grudging admiration, if I were in her place.

"So ye told him nothing," he said skeptically. "Is that it?"

"Aye," she whispered, her eyes wide with a sincerity that looked astonishingly genuine. God's teeth, it was no wonder Jemmy had succumbed to her. She could beguile God and all the saints if she set her mind to it.

"But ye ken when the attack will come."

"No. I don't."

"D'ye ken what sort of trouble ye have landed in?" he asked. "It's over, lass, 'tis finished. Your English friends won't lift a finger to save your neck! You're a traitor and a spy and ye have been caught out. There's no help for ye now."

Still she maintained a stubborn silence. Time for a change of tactics, he thought, and traced one finger slowly down the soft skin of her cheek.

"But for all that you're a pretty doxy, and ye seem to know your business well enough. Just tell me when the attack will come and then—well, I think we can come to some arrangement that will please us both. I can see ye safe, and I will, my word upon it. 'Twould be a shame to see a woman like ye wasted on the gallows!"

She turned her head away with a wordless cry.

"Why so coy?" he said. "What I ask is no more than ye have done before."

"You mistake me," she said through trembling lips. "Leave me now."

"You're in no position to be giving orders. And no mistake is possible. Name your price," he ordered in the voice that commanded instant obedience from his knights. "I've had enough of your tricks and games. I want the truth, and I want it now."

"How can I tell you what I do not know?"

And before he realized what she meant to do, she had ducked beneath his arm and was running for the window.

For one terrible moment Alistair thought she meant to cast herself to the cobbles far below, but instead she screamed into the night. A moment later she whirled, eyes flashing with defiance, and bent to seize a stool which she held before her like a shield. No, she would never take the coward's way, he thought. Not this one. She will fight for life with everything she has.

Why, then, had she refused him? She had traded herself at least once before for profit or advancement. And he was prepared to match whatever Darnley had offered, even better it if necessary. Was it loyalty to her father that prevented her from speaking? Affection for the knight she had been meeting by the river? Or was she playing some deeper game, one he had not fathomed yet?

"Scream away," he said with a shrug. "There's no one to hear. And even if there was, who do ye think would help ye? Not Jemmy, if that's what you're hoping. He's finished with ye altogether. Why, he never even spoke against the sentence."

The stool fell from her hands and clattered to the floor.

"Did he not?" she whispered. "Truly?"

Looking at her stricken face, the tears shimmering in her eyes, Alistair felt as though the ground had shifted beneath his feet. God's blood, this was real, it must be. No actress, no matter how clever or determined, could counterfeit so well. His words had truly cut her to the heart.

How *could* such a woman have been so witless as to fall in love with Jemmy? And yet she had. He had only to look at her to see that much. While Jemmy wanted nothing more to do with her.

"Aye," he answered gruffly. " 'Tis true enough. He never said a word. I'm your only help, lass, and your only hope, as well."

She drew a sharp breath and braced herself on the window ledge behind her.

"Then there is no help for me," she said simply. "For I will never give you what you ask. And I cannot tell you what you want to know."

Alistair had seen men face death before, but seldom with such courage. God's blood, he must be more tired than he thought to have so misjudged her. This woman was not for sale, not at any price, and never had been. She would truly rather die than accept the terms of his protection. I am a fate worse than death, he thought, half-amused and half-affronted. But with Jemmy it was a different story altogether!

"Well, you're a fine brave lassie, are ye no'?" he said, annoyance sharpening his tone. "Death before dishonor, is that it? Ye would see Malcolm die—and Jemmy, as well, if your father has his will—and call that honor?"

"No!" she cried. "I wouldn't—but I don't know—he never told me—"

"He never told ye how long ye must be here?" he demanded incredulously. "Oh, surely ye can spin a better tale than that!"

She shook her head. "I was told it might be a month—or more, or less. I was hardly in Lord Darnley's confidence," she added with a bitterness that Alistair knew at once was genuine. "We were never on such terms."

"He couldna have expected ye to be Lady Maude forever! What were ye meant to do when we caught on to your tricks? Ye may as well tell me, for whatever it was, it dinna work."

She bit her lip and stared down at the floor. "We never spoke of it," she said.

"Then how in God's name did he expect ye to get out?"

"I don't imagine he thought about it one way or the other," she answered dispassionately.

Alistair stared at her in shock. Had Darnley really sent her—his own blood, even if she wasn't true-born—among his sworn enemies with nothing but some bits of borrowed finery and her own wits to protect her? It seemed impossible. Had it been anyone but Darnley, he would have said it *was* impossible. But as things were, he knew it was the truth.

Of course her father hadn't told her anything! It had been a gamble on his part, the prize some time in which to send to Northumbeland for men. As for his daughter, there had been no doubt of the outcome. The only question was how many days—or weeks, if her luck held and she was very clever—she could purchase with her life. And as she was no fool, she must have known it from the start.

"Why did ye do it?" he asked curiously. "Not loyalty— what loyalty would ye have for Darnley, when 'tis clear as glass that he has none for ye! What could he have offered that was worth this?"

He was not prepared for the violence of her reaction. She shrank against the wall, the blood draining from her face, her eyes widening in terror.

"I won't tell you that. It has naught to do with you, I swear it!"

Alistair sighed. Coming here tonight had done no good at all. He had been wrong about her from the start, and she knew nothing that could help him. As for why she had agreed, that was her own affair. It would gain him naught to wrest her secret from her, and he had no stomach for the task.

Why is nothing ever simple? he wondered wearily. Good and evil, honor and dishonor—time was he could distinguish one from the other at a glance. Lately they had become so twisted that he could not begin to sort them out. But one thing he knew: she would not die at Kirallen's hands. And she would know it, too.

"Listen," he said abruptly, taking a step forward and laying his hands on her shoulders.

"No!" she cried, twisting wildly in his grasp. "I told you—I will not—"

"Whisht, lass," he said, giving her a little shake. "Stop that! There's no need—"

A cold voice cut through the room. "Take your hands from her. *Now.*"

They both whirled toward the door.

* * *

In the moment of silence that followed Jemmy's entrance, Alyson tore herself free and backed toward the window seat. She threw a shawl over her thin shift, clutching it around her as she tried to still her shaking.

"I wasna going to—" Alistair began.

Jemmy stepped inside and jerked his head toward the door. "Get out. Now."

Alistair's hands fisted at his sides. "I will go when I am ready."

"You will go now. Do it!" Jemmy ordered, one hand moving to his hip.

"Ah, so ye would draw on me?" Alistair said, and Alyson saw that he was smiling as he pulled his weapon from its sheath. "Come to fight for her, have ye?"

"If I must."

Alistair laughed. "Found your tongue at last, eh, Jemmy? Well, don't stop there, man, let's have the truth of it! Ye want to take your pleasure with the lass before ye see her put to death!"

Alyson flinched back against the wall, willing with all her heart for Jemmy to deny it.

"What I am doing here is none of your concern," he answered, and she felt the breath leave her in a sickening rush of disappointment. "As for you—"

"Aye, ye could well ask what I am doing here," Alistair said, stepping back and dropping the point of his sword. "And I could tell ye—"

"Don't bother," Jemmy snapped. "It's clear enough what you were after."

Alistair's jaw tightened. "Ye think so? Or is this just the chance ye have been waiting for? Ye never did much like me, did ye, Jemmy? Even all those years ago. Well, come on then," he said, raising his sword and dropping into a fighting stance. "Let's have at it."

"No!" Alyson cried. "Wait—you cannot do this—"

But neither man seemed to hear her. As Jemmy drew his sword and they faced each other, she gave up the attempt to stop them. Any distraction at this point could prove fatal.

"You are wrong, Alistair," Jemmy said. "I don't want to fight you. I never did. I used to look up to you and Ian."

Alistair feinted and Jemmy parried the blow.

"Oh, aye, ye looked up to Ian. A fine brother ye were to him! Running off the way ye did, leaving him alone. He needed ye, but ye didna care."

"He never needed me," Jemmy said bitterly. "He had you."

"I could not avenge him—not alone. That was for ye to do. But ye would not do it. Now look where ye have led us, Jemmy, straight into Darnley's hands."

There was a flurry of blows, too quick for Alyson to follow. Alistair stepped back and raised his brows.

"You're good," he said, surprised.

Jemmy bowed slightly and held his weapon ready. They engaged again and at last stood, toe to toe, blades locked, for what seemed to Alyson an eternity.

"Think, Alistair," Jemmy said. "Either way you lose."

Alistair pushed hard and Jemmy was forced back a step. Their blades were freed and now the battle was joined in earnest. Neither man spoke a word. Jemmy was retreating step by step, beaten back by the furious blows raining upon his weapon. Even to Alyson's inexperienced eyes it was clear that he sought only to defend himself. But when he could go no farther he turned to the attack.

"Give *over*," Jemmy said. "Damn you, man, put up your sword. I will *not* have your blood on my hands. Dear God," he cried, "What would Ian say if he could see us like this?"

Alistair hesitated for an instant, but that instant was long enough. With a turn of his wrist Jemmy sent the sword spinning from his hand. The knight stood frozen, then made a sudden move for his weapon, stopping only when cold Spanish steel touched his throat. The two men stared at each other for a long moment, then in one fluid motion Jemmy stepped back and sheathed his sword.

"You are a fool," he said coldly. "Now get out."

Alistair retrieved his weapon. He stopped in the doorway, his eyes flicking over Jemmy and then to Alyson.

"God help ye now, lass," he said. "God help us all."

And he was gone.

chapter 37

❦

"**A**re you harmed?" Jemmy asked. "I heard you cry out—"

"I am not hurt," she answered coldly. "Sir Alistair was very angry and I was frightened. I thought—hoped—" Her voice shook and she drew a deep breath before continuing. "But then he told me of the council meeting today."

Oh, Jemmy would just wager that he had. No doubt Alistair had told her exactly what had been said—and what had not. God rot him, he had probably enjoyed it. For a moment Jemmy wished he had run him through when he had the chance.

"He offered to overrule the sentence," she continued in a flat, hard voice he hardly recognized as hers. "I refused. If you have come on the same errand, my lord, your time will be equally wasted."

Jemmy bit back the angry denial springing to his lips. Nothing was going as he had imagined it would. He did not even know this woman who regarded him with such contempt in her eyes. Given all that had happened, could he really blame her for that? But still it hurt.

"I want to ask you something," he said abruptly. "How old is your brother?"

"Robin had his eighth birthday last week."

"And you thought—you actually believed that I would harm him? A child?"

"Lord Darnley will take him to account for my failure," she answered evenly. "Why should you not do the same?"

"Did you really believe I was no better than that?" he demanded, unable to keep the hurt and anger from his voice.

She shrugged slightly. "I fear I know you so little, my lord, that I really cannot say."

"He is in no danger, at least not from me," he said, and she gave a sigh of relief, the tension in her face relaxing slightly. "But as for you—"

"Aye?" she answered, taking a step back and drawing the shawl more tightly around her shoulders.

"Oh, God's blood," he muttered, running a hand through his hair. Was she going to take everything he said amiss?

"You are in no danger, either," he said quietly. "And you never were."

She raised her brows. "Indeed, my lord?"

"Aye. I let the council talk today—they were angry, it would have been pointless to argue about it then. But the decision is mine, Alyson. Mine alone. And I would never have allowed them to carry out such a sentence on any woman—" Let alone you, he almost said, but stopped himself in time.

She searched his face, then nodded. "I believe you."

He leaned back against the mantel, trying to keep his expression from showing the depths of his relief. At least she would not leave this place thinking *that* of him. It was something to be grateful for.

"I can understand why you concealed so much from us," he said. "But what I cannot understand is why you did not tell us that Clare McLaran was your mother."

"What difference does that make?" she asked, obviously bewildered.

"Do you not know? Did she not tell you she was once betrothed to my uncle Stephen?"

"No, she never did," Alyson answered slowly. "She spoke so little of her past . . . but I learned of it later, after I had come here."

"Then she forgot him so easily as that." Jemmy shook his head. "I wouldn't have thought it of her."

"No! She did not forget him. I always knew some sorrow lay heavy on her heart, but she never told me what it was. And then when she lay dying she called his name and wept because he'd never come for her. It was only after that I found out about him. All those years she waited—hoping—oh, it all made sense once I learned what had happened. He didn't come for her because—because of me. Because of what my father did to her."

"She didn't know?"

"She knew well enough that he didn't want her anymore."

"She didn't know," he repeated softly. "Please," he added, "Sit down."

She regarded him warily, every muscle taut, like a deer who scents the hunter.

"I knew your mother, Alyson," he went on gently. "A long, long time ago. She came to stay with us when I was a child. She had been at Kelso Abbey for some time and meant to take vows, but her parents wanted her to wait until she was sure of her vocation. So they sent her to us for a year."

Alyson sat down cautiously, her back very straight.

"Stephen was my father's brother," Jemmy began. "He was born late to my grandparents, and he was so much

younger than the others that he always seemed more like a
brother to me. I adored him—we all did, he had a way
about him, so merry all the time . . . He used to say this
war between us and the Darnleys was a fool's game when
there was so much more to life than dealing death. He
wanted to be away, to make a new life for himself, but his
parents wouldn't hear of it—especially my grandmother.
She couldn't bear the thought of losing him. So he put off
leaving, not wanting to hurt her. And then Clare came."

My mother, Alyson thought. Jemmy had actually
known her as a girl, back in that long-ago time Clare had
never spoken of.

He smiled a little, his eyes distant, remembering. "She
was so lovely, so kind. I think every one of us fell a little
bit in love with her. But Stephen was entirely smitten. The
others used to tease him about it but he paid them no mind.
His heart was set on her, and he cared not who knew it.
And she—well, she was something of a scholar, very shy
and quiet, but Stephen used to make her laugh until she
cried. I can still see them walking hand in hand—they
were always together and both of them so happy . . ."

It was a comfort to think that Mam had once known that
kind of joy, Alyson reflected sadly, even if it hadn't lasted.
At least she'd had that much.

"Both the families were overjoyed," Jemmy continued.
"The McLarans had never been happy to think of their
only child as a nun, and Grandmother had begun to despair
of Stephen ever settling down. So everyone was pleased.
Clare went home again, and he was counting the days until
the wedding, full of plans for the life they'd have together.
The wedding feast was all prepared when word came that
her party had been attacked and Clare was taken.

"Stephen swore he'd get her back again. He took a force
of men and attacked Darnley's manor—but they could not
win through. And so he tried again. And again. My grandfather went with him. Everyone told him to bide at home,

that he was past it—but he loved Clare like his own child and felt responsible for what had happened . . ." Jemmy sighed and rubbed a hand across his face. "He died across the border, and Stephen carried him home again. That was when my father said it had to stop. We'd lost too many men. I've never forgotten that day. When my father said we had to let Clare go, Stephen wept. I was frightened, for I'd never seen a grown man cry before."

So Stephen hadn't given up at once, Alyson thought. At least he had tried. The hard knot of hatred she had felt toward the Laird's young brother dissolved a little.

"Emma McLaran said they'd never had word of her," Alyson said. "At least Stephen didn't know about—about me."

"I don't know what he learned," Jemmy said. "But he knew—they all did—what had most likely happened. I remember one of the men said it was no use going on with it anyway, for it was likely too late for Clare. I thought he meant that she was dead—it wasn't until I was older that I understood what he was saying. Stephen turned and struck him to the floor. Then he walked out. And that was the last time I saw him. He went himself, alone, to try and find her."

He had not abandoned Clare after all. Alyson blinked hard against the sudden tears. Even knowing what had happened, he had still loved her enough to search for her. And she had never known of it. How terrible that seemed, that Clare had never known of it and had died believing herself forgotten . . .

Jemmy rested his elbows on his knees and stared down at his clenched hands. "It was about a fortnight later that a cart came into the yard. I was there with Ian, and we were busy with some game so we didn't pay it any mind. It was just a cart, a plain farm cart driven by one old man. There was something in the back, but we didn't think anything of that until one of the men pulled off the covering . . . and there was Stephen. He was—well, his death hadn't been an easy one. And Darnley's badge had been laid across his breast.

"Then everyone began to shout, and the yard filled with people—they killed the man driving the cart, I remember, just pulled him from the seat and ran him through, though likely he didn't even know what he carried to us. My grandmother came out to see what all the noise was about, and no one even noticed her in the confusion. When she saw him like that—dear God, what a thing for her to see, his own mother, I can still hear her screaming . . ."

He blinked hard and went on in a low voice. "And my mother ran out after her—that was when she lost the child she carried, and her own life, as well . . ."

The room was very quiet then, as the fire hissed and crackled in the hearth. Alyson shivered and pulled the shawl more tightly around her shoulders. She'd known there had been deaths—on both sides. But as long as they had been just names it seemed an easy thing to forgive and let go the past. Now they were not just names but people—her own mother among them. It would never end. How could it? There was too much pain and bitterness on either side.

"The next few years were very bad," Jemmy said. "No one could forget—or wanted to. It was war then and so many were lost, it seemed all the young men I knew were killed. The years went by, things slowly settled down again, and when I was old enough I left. I didn't want to be a part of it, for I knew there could be no end. Nobody wins and everybody loses over and over again, until everything we hold dear is gone."

"But you are a part of it," Alyson said. "We all are."

"Aye, I know that now. But—" He jumped to his feet and began to pace the room. "It's wrong. I saw it then, when I was still a child, but all I could think to do was get as far away from it as I could. The coward's way," he added, very low. "Just cut and run."

"No," Alyson said. "It was the only way. Even if you'd stayed here, what could you have done? Your brother was the only one who could have changed it."

"But Ian didn't want to change it. He saw it as a test of honor, his against your father's."

"My father has no honor," Alyson said flatly.

"Aye, well, we've precious little of it left ourselves. Today I saw how easy it is to be swept up in it all, us against the Darnleys, dying for the glory of the clan. Crioch Onarach," he added wryly. " 'Twas Ian's favorite toast. A good death."

He stood before the fire, hands clasped behind him. Alyson wanted to go to him, slip her arms around his waist, and lean her cheek against his back. But of course she couldn't do that now.

"A good death," she repeated slowly. "It sounds well, my lord, but I think it takes more courage to live a good life. Now it's you who can change things. If you still want to."

"I do. But—" he sighed wearily and turned to face her. "It's all in motion now, and I don't see how it can be stopped. And yet I do know one thing. I can't let any harm come to Clare's children. Stephen would never forgive me for that."

Children? Had he really said— "My lord," Alyson said. "What do you mean?"

"I mean we have to find some way to get you to the McLarans—and your brother with you."

He looked at her, his eyes narrowed. "How closely do you resemble Maude?"

"We do look alike—but we're different, too. At a distance I could pass for her but not at close range."

"Where is she now?"

"She is home," Alyson said, sitting up. "I know she is,

Sir Robert said so. The household thinks she's me—or rather, who I was supposed to be when I was there—a cousin from the Percy side."

"Could you somehow get her alone? If you sent a message and asked that she meet you—if you said you were in trouble—?"

"No, that would never work. She wouldn't care enough to come. But why? Oh! You mean to bring her here, don't you?"

"That was my thought, but I don't see how—"

Alyson smiled. "My lord, Maude is not known for her obedience. Despite her father's command that she stay hidden, she goes hawking by the river every fine day."

"Really?" he said slowly. "Are you sure of that? Then this might just work. Tell me, though, is it true her father dotes on her?"

"He would do anything for her. Why, I cannot say—but it is the truth. He'll make terms if you can get her here. But," she added hesitantly, "but what of Robin?"

"We'll make his safety a condition of the terms."

"No, my lord. I'm sorry but that won't do. He's just a little boy—"

"You think we'll forget him, don't you?"

"No, not now. But I fear Lord Darnley's temper. Robin is nothing to him, don't you see? He's only a stableboy. When Darnley finds that Maude's been taken—and Robin is to hand—I fear that even Sir Robert won't be able to protect him then. And yet I do have an idea . . ."

When she had outlined her plan, Jemmy said, "Absolutely not. That's far too dangerous."

"It is *not*," she said, her brows drawing together in a frown. "I can do it. And I will."

He shot her a glance in which amusement and annoyance were evenly divided. "We can talk about it tomorrow on the way," he said, and she felt a small thrill of victory.

She was to go with him tomorrow. If he had given in this much, she was certain she could convince him of the rest.

"Let us hope the day is fine and Lady Maude goes hawking," he added with a smile.

"She will," Alyson said, her pulse jumping as it always did when he smiled at her in that way. "I am certain of it."

They both rose and stood in awkward silence for a moment. He is just being kind, Alyson thought, that's all, for my mother's sake. And I should be grateful for that. It was no good remembering how he'd held her in his arms and spoken words of love, no good longing for the past and what could never be. No doubt he wanted to forget what had happened between them, and she should forget it, too. But she would not.

She would never forget that night of magic when nothing had existed beyond the two of them. The brush of flesh on flesh. His mouth on hers. His hoarse cry of triumph as he claimed her.

And afterward, the way they had lain together, all passion spent, his head against her shoulder and his breath warm and soft upon her breast, the murmured words and laughter they had shared. Had that really been the same man who stood before her now? It seemed impossible. It *was* impossible, she told herself. That night he had lain with his wife, a woman of his rank and station. Or so he had believed. Alyson Bowden from the Aylsford kitchens could never catch and hold the heart of such a man. Had she not known that all along?

Tears stung her eyes, and she couldn't look at him lest he should see how she still loved him, as ridiculous and unseemly as that was.

She stood before the firelight, head bent, shawl slipping from her shoulders. Through the thin shift Jemmy could make out the swell of her breast and the curve of her slender waist. She is so beautiful, he thought, his body clenching with desire. More lovely than she had ever seemed to him before. But that was because tonight he saw her as she really was. She was not Lady Maude, with her stiff carriage and ridiculous pretensions. Nor was she the calculating spy who had deceived him without feeling. She was Alyson McLaran Bowden, brave and kind and loyal, the strongest person he had ever known.

He imagined reaching out, turning her face up to his. Her eyes would widen and he would draw her close, breathe her sweet scent, watch her surprise melt into pleasure as he wound his fingers in her hair and bent to her, whispering that he loved her, he needed her, that his life was nothing to him without her . . .

But how would he find the words to tell her that in spite of all he felt, they must part?

Let her go, he told himself. To speak now will only make things worse. The break has been made already, and I have to live with that. But at least I shall see her safe. That much I can do and I will do, no matter how high the price.

"Sleep now," Jemmy said. "And don't worry—we'll make it come right."

"Aye, my lord," she answered quietly, her gaze fixed on the floor. "We can try."

chapter 38

❧

The gray light of dawn was just beginning to seep through the window when Jemmy returned. He stopped outside the door and listened to the muffled voices coming from within. When he entered he found Alyson seated, Malcolm kneeling before her with his head in her lap as she stroked his hair. At the sound of his entrance Malcolm looked up and, seeing who it was, jumped to his feet and stood protectively before her.

"Get out," the boy said. "I won't let you hurt her—"

"Malcolm, 'tis all right," Alyson said. "My lord, I'm sorry. I wasn't sure what to say to him—"

Jemmy felt sharp remorse as he saw the tracks of tears on Malcolm's cheeks. What a sorry excuse for an uncle he'd been! He hadn't ever considered Malcolm beyond thinking that the boy was a problem to be dealt with when he had more time, more energy. Stephen would have done far better.

He bent and looked Malcolm in the eye.

"Can you keep a secret?"

"What is it?" Malcolm asked suspiciously.

"I'm taking Mistress Bowden out of here, right now. We're going across the border to find Lady Maude and bring her back."

" 'Tis true?"

Malcolm turned to Alyson, and Jemmy thought it was a sorry thing that his own nephew wouldn't take his word for it.

"Aye," she said. "You mustn't tell anyone, though."

"I'm coming with you."

"You are not!" Alyson cried.

Jemmy shook his head. "I'm sorry, Malcolm—"

"My father would have done it!" Malcolm blazed. "When he was little more than my age, he stole Darnley's favorite horse right out of his stable!"

Jemmy's lips twitched. "I remember. And your grandfather blistered his backside for it."

"Mayhap he did," Malcolm said stubbornly. "But Grandfather is the one who told me the story—and he laughed!" He put his hands on his hips and glared up at Jemmy, defiance blazing in his eyes. "I'll wager Father dinna care that he was whipped. And I willna moan about it, either. Grandfather can cane me all he likes—*after* it is done!"

Jemmy passed a hand across his eyes. "God's blood, 'tis uncanny," he murmured. "That is *exactly* what your father used to say."

"My lord, he is a child—" Alyson began. But nobody was listening to her.

"You must do everything I tell you," Jemmy said, and Malcolm's face lit up.

"I will. I promise."

"And you will listen to Donal and Conal, as well," Jemmy added sternly. "It's a man's work I'm asking you to do. If you cannot follow orders, I'll send you home."

"I can do it."

"Then let's go."

Alyson *was relieved to find the two young red-headed knights* waiting by the gate with saddled horses. Jemmy had chosen well, she thought. Of all Kirallen's knights, the twins were the most outspoken of Jemmy's followers, risking the ire of their Captain with cheerful nonchalance. At Jemmy's order, one of them— Donal, Alyson thought, though she was never sure which was which—fetched Malcolm's pony from the stables. By midmorning they'd reached a stretch of forest outside Aylsford and halted, concealed among the trees.

"Are you sure she'll come this way?" Jemmy asked.

"She always did before."

Before an hour had passed two riders emerged from the Aylsford gate and moved in their direction.

"Can you see?" Alyson asked, peering into the distance.

"Aye," Malcolm said. " 'Tis a woman—she's veiled, though, I can't make out her face."

"That is Maude," Alyson said. "It must be. Who is that with her?"

"A boy—he's got red hair."

Alyson laughed. "I think, my lord, that we're in luck. Unless I miss my guess that's her brother Haddon."

Jemmy whistled softly. "I hope you are right. Come on, then, let's go. Are you ready?"

"Aye," she and Malcolm answered together, turning toward their horses. Donal and Conal nodded and fell in behind them.

They'd picked the place carefully, a turn in the path that was shielded from the manor by tall oaks. When the two riders trotted past, they found themselves surrounded. Jemmy pulled Maude from her saddle and into his, holding her easily as she fought. At the same moment the two knights drew their horses close to Haddon's, blocking his escape.

Jemmy quickly bound Maude's hands and dismounted, lifting her from the saddle and half carrying her into the wood where he tied her securely to a tree. Then he dealt with Haddon in the same manner, so quickly that Alyson could scarce believe it was done.

"Good morning," she said, stepping forward and pushing the veil back from her face.

"You?" Maude shrieked. "What are you doing here?"

"Don't ask any questions—not now. Just tell me where my brother is."

"Your brother? How should I know? Do you think I keep account of every wretched little churl in Aylsford?"

"My brother is no churl. He is Sir Robert's page and your father's hostage. Where is he?"

Jemmy drew his sword and stood next to Alyson. "I suggest you answer her."

"All right! He's in Sir Robert's chambers—at least, that's where he spends most of his time, there or in the mews."

"Good," Alyson said. "Now we'll untie you—long enough for you to get out of your clothes."

"My what? I will not—"

"You do as Mistress Bowden says," Jemmy said.

Maude looked from him to Alyson. "What is this? I will not—"

"You will," Alyson said with deadly intensity. "Just be quiet and change clothes with me."

Malcolm walked over to Haddon and stood looking at him. So this was the boy who'd dared to steal sheep from the Laird's own fold! Malcolm had felt a pang of envy when he heard the tale, imagining that Haddon

Darnley must be twice his size and fierce as the very devil. Now he saw the boy was no bigger than he and didn't look particularly fierce. In fact, he looked extremely frightened. Malcolm took out his dagger and leaned close.

"Not a word out of ye," he said threateningly. "Or you'll be feeling the blade of my knife."

"You wouldn't be so brave if I wasn't tied," Haddon replied with a scornful lift of his chin. "My father says that all of you are cowards."

"Oh, does he? And he's a fine one to be talking! He was so frightened of my father that he set a trap for him—couldn't even fight him like a proper man!"

"He didn't!" Haddon cried. "That's a lie!"

"It's you who lie—you and all your cursed murdering family!"

"Quiet," Jemmy said, stepping forward. "Both of you."

The boys subsided, glaring. Jemmy sighed. So it went on, generation after generation.

He turned to Alyson, who stepped from the trees, wearing Maude's blue velvet riding surcoat with a blue veil pushed back from her face. "I don't like this. It's too dangerous."

"I'll be careful."

"No."

Aylsford rose over the treetops, black against the sky. It looked formidable, threatening—the thought of Alyson vanishing within gave him a sick feeling.

"Please," she said. "Don't say no—not now. We're so close . . . Please."

There had been something bothering him all day, and suddenly he knew what it was. Alyson had changed since the day she was brought to the council chamber. Then she had faced them proudly, her back straight and voice steady. Now she stood humbly before him, her eyes on the ground. Like a servant. Which was exactly what she was.

One day, perhaps, she would be something more. Up in the Highlands the stain of bastardy could be overlooked, so long as Emma McLaran gave the girl her name and the protection of the clan. But even with that, Alyson could never be a fitting mate for any man of noble birth. No, she was destined for some wild Highlander who no doubt would think himself the luckiest of men. And when that happened, Jemmy would keep far away from both of them. Else he would surely kill the man who dared lay hands upon his woman . . .

He muttered a curse, focusing on the present. Alyson was right. They'd come this far successfully; surely she deserved the chance to free her brother.

"All right," he said. "But you have to promise that you'll get out if there is any danger—any at all. We can think of another way."

"I will, I promise. Wait for me an hour—if I'm not back then go without me."

She pulled the veil over her face and mounted Maude's horse, cantering toward the manor. Jemmy watched her out of sight, then went back into the wood. Malcolm gave a great sigh of relief when he saw him.

"Can we go?" he asked. "Where is my aunt?"

"Mistress Bowden," he corrected gently, "has gone to fetch her brother. We shall wait for her."

Maude made an incoherent sound of rage and strained against her bonds. Jemmy took the gag from her mouth.

"If you scream, I'll put it back."

She glared but stayed silent.

He smiled, stepping back and letting his gaze wander from her head to her feet then back again. Feature by feature he could trace her resemblance to Alyson, but the parts added up to a very different sum. The blue-green eyes were like Alyson's in shape and color, but they completely lacked the mysterious quality that made Alyson's every expression so entrancing. And while Maude's hair shone brightly against the tree bark, it did not make him think of sunset after a storm. Oh, there was no doubt that Maude was lovely. Some might think her delicate features even more beautiful than Alyson's. But to Jemmy she looked like a pale copy of her half sister.

"Well, well," he said. "This is an interesting situation. It's about time I saw the woman I married."

"Married?" she cried and he held up the gag. In a lower voice she continued, "We are not married, and we never will be—"

"Now, now, my lady. No need to be coy with me. Why, there were a dozen witnesses—the book was signed by myself, the priest, your father—oh, yes, *wife,*" he added, his voice hard as steel. "It was all done properly."

"I would rather die," she hissed vehemently.

"Such harsh words!" He put his hands over his heart. "Lady, you'll slay me with your cruelty. But don't worry, sweet Maude, you'll soon grow used to the idea."

"You wouldn't dare to touch me—"

"Oh, wouldn't I? I'd be well within my rights."

She deserved to be frightened—it was small enough payment for the damage that she'd done. But when he saw her chin quiver he grew weary of the game. "Don't worry," he said abruptly. "You're safe enough. For now."

"What do you plan to do with me?" she asked, lifting her chin in the arrogant gesture Alyson had caught so well.

"Take you back to Ravenspur. We'll have to see what happens after that."

"Then what are we waiting for? Untie me at once and let's begone."

"Not yet. We'll wait for your sister to return."

"Sister? She's no sister of mine! I always knew she couldn't see it through—I tried to tell my father she'd betray us, the filthy slut—"

He stepped forward, one hand raised. "Keep your mouth shut, or I'll gag you again. You didn't mind sending her to us to do your dirty work, did you? You or your father. You never stopped once to think of what might happen to her."

"To her?" Maude said, genuinely surprised. "What difference does that make? She's just a servant."

Jemmy turned away and stopped by Haddon. "Fear not, lad," he said. "No harm will come to you. You have my word on it."

He walked to the edge of the clearing and stood looking at the manor. For the first time in many years he prayed.

R obin was not in Sir Robert's chamber. Alyson walked down the long expanse of passageway on legs that shook with fear, pulling the veil more closely about her face. The mews. Pray God he was in the mews, for if he wasn't, she had no idea where to look next.

"My lady!"

Alyson quickened her steps, pretending not to hear.

"My lady, wait right there."

God help her, it was Becta, who had known Maude since infancy. Alyson's heart dropped with a thud as the tiring woman approached.

"What is it?" Alyson answered sharply.

"Ye dinna mean to go riding! Your father told ye—"

The woman was within feet of her now. Alyson turned her back and walked away without answering.

"My lady!" Becta called again. "Now dinna be going off like that when your father said ye mustna ride out anymore."

"Father be damned. And you hold your tongue or I'll make you sorry you didn't."

Had she overdone it? No, Becta wasn't following anymore. When Alyson turned the corner she began to run and didn't stop until she reached the bottom of the stairs leading to the stable yard.

There she did stop, for she heard the sound she had been dreading—Lord Darnley's voice. She peered around the corner and saw him vanish into the stables. The mews stood across the cobbled yard, and to reach them she would have to pass in full view of the stable door. She darted across the courtyard and inside the mews, every nerve straining to hear sounds of pursuit.

There were none. The birds were disturbed by her sudden entrance, though, and baited on their perches. She could hear them but she couldn't see them, for it was very dim in here after the brightness of the courtyard.

She closed her eyes and counted ten, then opened them and nearly sobbed with relief. There was Robin, standing with a hawk on one outstretched arm, looking at her disapprovingly.

"My lady, you mustna come in here like that."

"Robin," she said, throwing back the veil. "It's me."

"Ally? Ally, what are you doing back? Wait," he added as she came forward. "You're frightening the birds."

"I'm sorry, but we have to go. Right now. Don't say a word, just follow me."

"I can't," he said. "I have to feed—"

"Robin, put the bird down and come with me. Now."

"Well, all right, but Sir Robert willna be happy . . ." He carefully replaced the falcon on its perch, moving with such deliberate care that Alyson wanted to scream with impatience.

"Listen to me," she said. "I can't tell you everything now, but I've come to take you out of here and we mustn't let anybody see us."

"Is this a game?"

"In a way. But it's a very serious game, Robin, and we mustn't be caught. Just stay with me and no matter what happens, don't say a word."

She looked out the doorway. There was Maude's mare, standing saddled on the far side of the yard. But where was Lord Darnley? Still in the stables? There was no way of knowing, and she couldn't wait to find out.

"Now, Robin," she said, keeping her voice pitched low. "There is my horse, do you see her? We are going to ride out of here together. Ready?"

She put her arm about his shoulders and walked outside. One step, she told herself firmly. One step and then another, and another, and they were halfway across the stable yard. We're doing it, she thought, we're going to make it.

And then she found herself face to face with Sir Robert, who was walking out of the stables.

The knight stopped in his tracks and Alyson realized, too late, that she had forgotten to replace her veil. Sir Robert's eyes moved down to Robin, pressed close to her side, and then back to her face.

"Sir—" Robin called excitedly, and Alyson clamped one hand across his mouth, cutting off his greeting.

Robert glanced at Maude's horse, then back at Alyson, then whirled back toward the stable door. "Wait, John, I've forgotten my best book. I think I left it in my saddlebag—no, you come with me—"

Alyson began to run, one hand fumbling at her veil,

the other pulling Robin by the arm, and it was exactly like her nightmare. How long could Sir Robert delay his brother? When they reached the mare Alyson fairly leaped into the saddle.

"Come *on*," she whispered as Robin's foot slipped from the stirrup. "Hurry."

She hauled him into the saddle and concealed him beneath her cloak just as Darnley walked out the door.

"Maude!" he roared. "Maude, I forbid you to—"

Alyson swept past him at a canter, one hand raised in a casual wave, laughing when she heard him shout for Maude to stop.

chapter 39

It was Malcolm who saw them coming first. "She's back," he cried, then looked about fearfully. "Uncle Jemmy," he said in a loud whisper. "She's coming."

By the time Alyson rode up they were mounted, Maude held securely in the saddle in front of Jemmy, and Haddon tied to his horse. Alyson pulled up and threw back her veil, laughing.

"Any trouble?" Jemmy asked and she laughed again.

"None to speak of. My lord, this is Robin."

The boy sat on the saddle before her, half covered by her cloak. He smiled with a piercing sweetness and nestled closer to his sister.

"Robin, it is a great pleasure to finally meet you. But we'd best be getting back home."

"Oh, aye," Alyson said. "Let's ride."

And with that she was away, galloping over the low hills and into Scotland.

When Malcolm saw his home rising in the distance he

felt a thrill of satisfaction. They'd done it—they'd stolen not only Darnley's daughter but his son and heir as well. This was a story that would be told for years and years. They might even make a song of it! His chest swelled with pride, and he turned to Haddon riding at his side. But the boast died on his lips when he saw how white the boy was, the freckles standing out sharply on his ashen skin.

"Are ye tired?" Malcolm asked. "We're nearly there."

Haddon shook his head, his eyes on the high battlements. "I can't go there."

"Well, ye haven't much choice, have ye?" Malcolm asked practically. "Come on—I'm hungry."

"I can't," Haddon repeated, his voice trembling. "He'll kill me. He said he would if I ever came back."

"Who did?"

"That man—the one with the yellow hair. I think about him all the time," Haddon added in a whisper. "Sometimes I dream about him, too. He said I mustn't ever come on his lands again or next time he'd do it—he'd finish me—"

"Oh. That's Alistair. But he didn't really mean it," Malcolm said, though even to his own ears his voice lacked conviction. "Ye just bide close to me," he added. "And to Uncle Jemmy. You'll be all right."

"You must think me a dreadful coward," Haddon said, flushing.

"After what ye did, coming here to take the sheep from the Laird's own fold? I've never even crossed the border before today," he admitted. "They always said I'm not old enough."

"Me, too. That's why we did it—to show them. But it all went wrong somehow."

"Oh, anyone can take a toss," Malcolm said. "I've had dozens."

The boys looked at each other and smiled suddenly. "Come on," Malcolm said. "I haven't eaten all day."

They rode on together and soon Alyson heard them

laughing. She smiled and pulled up, waiting for Jemmy to catch up before they made the final climb. His horse was weary from its double load, but he still sat straight in the saddle, Maude held fast before him. Looking at the girl's drooping head, Alyson almost pitied her, save for the fact that Maude was exactly where she longed to be herself.

She remembered all too well how it felt to ride with Jemmy, the iron strength of his arms, the broad shoulder against which she had rested her head, the same place where Maude's cheek now lay. Maude—not her. It would always be Maude now, never her, never again . . .

She tightened her arms around Robin. She had him, and that was all that mattered.

"We're going straight to my father," Jemmy said. "Are you ready?"

"Aye."

"Oh, get on with it!" Maude snapped.

"Of course, my lady," Jemmy replied sardonically. "Let's get on with it right now."

They found the courtyard filled with men, not only Kirallens but men from many clans with whom they were allied. Jemmy's face grew dark as he saw how quickly Alistair had moved to rally their forces.

Even as they dismounted Alistair himself hurried forward. "Jemmy! Where have ye been, man? We thought—"

He broke off, his eyes going over the small party standing before him.

"Not now, Alistair," Jemmy said. "Come on—we're going to see Father."

"But who—? Don't tell me this is—" his eyes moved past Maude and settled on Haddon. "Ah, this one I know."

Haddon stepped closer to Malcolm. "You let him be," Malcolm demanded. "I told him he'd be safe here."

"Oh, did ye?" Alistair asked. "And who gave ye the right to—"

"This is not the place for this," Jemmy said, glancing

about the crowded yard. "You can come with us or not, Alistair."

"Oh, aye, I'm coming with ye," Alistair said slowly. "For it's clear that you've gone mad."

K*irallen greeted his son with relief, his eyes lighting* with amusement when he realized what Jemmy had done.

"Well, young Darnley," he said. "We meet again. Don't worry, lad, you'll be fine here. Ye look exhausted—no doubt you're hungry, as well. Go on with Malcolm—but first," he added, suddenly grave. "I want your word you won't run off tonight."

"You have it," Haddon answered.

"Good. Then go along. Sir Conal will escort you."

Conal grinned. "All right, lads, what first? Sleep or food?"

"Food," the boys said together.

"This way, then."

When they were gone, Kirallen beckoned Robin closer. "Go on, Rob," Alyson said. "It's all right."

"Father," Jemmy said. "This is Robin Bowden, Alyson's brother. You knew their mother well."

"Their mother?" Kirallen's eyes sharpened as he studied Robin's face and reached out one gnarled hand to touch the boy's golden curls. Then he looked up at Jemmy.

"Clare McLaran," Jemmy said.

"No!"

Alistair strode forward and knelt to look into Robin's face.

"Aye, Alistair," Jemmy said. "Can you not see it for yourself?"

Kirallen sighed. "He is the image of his mother. I would that we had known of this sooner . . ."

"I'm sorry for that, my lord," Alyson said.

Alistair glanced up at her. "Is it so?" he whispered. "Your mother was truly Clare McLaran?"

Alyson nodded cautiously.

The knight rose unsteadily to his feet. "I—I dinna know—" he said. "Clare was—she was a verra great lady. I—"

He backed away, shaking his head, then turned and walked from the room.

"I'd forgotten how taken he was with Clare," Jemmy murmured. "Stephen used to say it was lucky Alistair was still a bairn, else they'd end with daggers drawn."

"Aye," the Laird agreed. "And I don't think Stephen was entirely jesting." His reminiscent smile faded and he sighed. "I feared for Alistair when she was taken, he grieved so hard. We all grieved," he added, glancing at Alyson. "I'd like to hear the whole tale, Mistress, after you've had a chance to rest. Then we'll see you back to Emma."

He patted her hand. "I can only imagine the joy this will bring to her. We'll speak more of it tomorrow. Jemmy," he added. "Would you see Ralston for me? Have him see Lady Maude to her chamber. Oh, and ask him find a chamber in the west wing for Mistress Bowden and her brother."

Jemmy wondered at the intricacy of his father's mind that even now he would attend to so minor a matter. Then he understood that this had been no chance remark, but a message meant for his ears alone.

The west wing was halfway between the servant's quarters—where Lord Darnley's kitchen wench might sleep—and the place to which Emma McLaran's granddaughter was entitled. Should Alyson visit again with her clan, she'd no doubt be put in the south wing as Emma always was. But for now, with her status still uncertain, the west wing would do.

Kirallen looked at Maude and then at Alyson. They were so alike—yet different as the winter and the spring.

He'd see that the girl went back to Emma at once, before any further damage could be done. But from Jemmy's angry expression, he suspected it was already too late. He half expected some protest but when Jemmy simply nodded, he sighed with relief. It was a hard blow, yes, but apparently Jemmy was made of sterner stuff than he'd imagined. Once the girl was gone he would forget her.

When Ralston had been found and instructed, Alyson turned to Jemmy.

"Thank you, my lord," she said formally, dropping him a curtsey and pulling her small brother forward into a bow.

"You are welcome."

"This way," Ralston said. Alyson and Robin followed the chamberlain down the long corridor. Jemmy suddenly realized that this could well be the last he'd see of her. When she reached the corner she seemed to hesitate, then walked on without looking back.

Jemmy stood a moment staring down the empty passageway. He took one step, then another, without stopping to ask himself what he thought he was doing. He only knew that he could not let her vanish from his life like this. It was too quick, too sudden. If he could only say farewell properly . . .

He strode quickly around the corner and nearly collided with Alyson, who was standing just on the other side of the turn, bending down to lift her brother into her arms.

"My lord!" she said, straightening, wiping a hasty sleeve across her eyes. "What is it? Is something wrong?"

"No."

He looked at her in helpless anguish, seeing the shadows beneath her eyes, the trace of moisture spiking her thick lashes, knowing he had just made things even worse. No words could make this parting any easier. He should have let her go.

"Ally," Robin said, tugging at her skirt. "I'm tired."

"Here, let me take him," Jemmy said gruffly. "He's too heavy for you. Ralston, you may go."

"Very well, my lord," the chamberlain answered. " 'Tis the third door down and to the right."

Alyson did not speak as Jemmy carried the child to the chamber Ralston had indicated. Once he deposited the boy upon the narrow bed, she drew the coverlet over him with a tender smile and smoothed the curls back from his brow. Jemmy watched, telling himself he was a fool to be jealous of her brother. Yet it was impossible not to be.

The boy would be with her every day, would watch her grow and flourish among the McLaran clan. When Jemmy was no more than a distant memory, her brother would be there to share her joys and sorrows. Robin would dance at her wedding.

He pushed that thought aside. There would be time enough later for regrets. Now was the moment to say goodbye, wish her well in the new life beginning for her, one filled with promise and adventure.

At that moment she straightened and turned to him with a smile that stopped the words upon his lips.

"Thank you," she said. When he did not answer she added awkwardly, "We'll be fine now."

"Of course. Well . . ."

He started toward the door, cursing himself with every step. Never in his life had he been so completely at a loss for words.

"If you need anything, just send for Ralston," he said.

"Aye. I will."

He was at the door now, reaching for the latch. Good luck, he thought. That was what he would say. God keep you on your journey. I will remember you each morning when I wake and every night when I lie down to sleep. When I die, it will be with your name upon my lips.

"Good night," he said.

"Goodbye," she answered softly.

The word, so stark, so final, echoed in his mind as he walked back down the silent corridor. It reverberated with all the force of a prison door slammed shut, severing him from life and joy forever.

chapter 40

When Jemmy walked into Maude's chamber the next morning he had a sense of time doubling back on it-self. Maude sat before the fire, just as Alyson had done, while Maggie combed out her hair. As though on cue the girl jumped to her feet.

"Good morning, my lady," he said and the words seemed completely unreal, an echo in his mind. "Did you rest well?"

"No. I did not. What do you mean by putting me in this—this—sty? I have never been so insulted in all my life! The mattress wasn't properly aired and—"

Alyson's performance had been brilliant—she'd caught Maude to perfection. When Jemmy considered how fright-ened she must have been, his admiration went up another notch. Oh, she was a woman in a thousand to have con-vinced them she was anything at all like her half sister.

"—and these rushes are moldy! I want them changed at once! I don't see what's so amusing about that!" Maude added indignantly, looking from Jemmy to Maggie as they burst out laughing.

Maggie wiped her eyes. "Ah, she's a braw wee lassie, isn't she?" Jemmy knew the serving woman wasn't speaking of Maude.

"Aye, she is," he agreed. "Don't you worry for her, she'll be fine now."

"Whatever are you talking about?" Maude demanded, stamping one foot. "You haven't heard a word I've said!"

"On the contrary, my lady. But I'm afraid you'll have to bear the discomforts of Ravenspur—for the present."

"When will my father be here?"

"This afternoon. Until then Maggie will look after you." He began to walk from the room, then hesitated and turned back. "It must be a strange thing to find yourself here, after all the trouble you've taken to avoid it."

Maude sniffed, sitting down on the window seat and pulling the tapestry frame close.

"Does it make you wonder, lady, if some things are meant to happen, whether we will them to or not?"

He wasn't sure why he had even asked the question, but now that it was spoken he somehow felt that her answer was terribly important.

"What?" she said impatiently, glancing up from the gory picture stretched on the frame before her. "Whatever are ye blethering about?"

"I'm talking about the doctrine of free will as opposed to that of predestination," he went on, a little amused at the relief washing over him. Had he really doubted that Alyson's reflections on the subject had been her own?

Maude raised her chin. "Naught happens to me but that I will it."

Jemmy looked at the pure oval of her face and the unquestioning arrogance in her eyes and felt a touch of pity. Though her age was near to Alyson's, Maude was still a child in ways that her half sister had never been. He feared she had some difficult lessons before her on the way to womanhood.

The trouble was, he didn't want to be the one to teach them.

"Until this afternoon, my lady," he said courteously, not at all surprised when she didn't deign to answer.

chapter 41

Alyson put the last of her and Robin's belongings into a bundle and tied it securely while Robin, perched on the bed, talked happily about the journey they would be taking tomorrow. Alyson tried to share his excitement but could not. She had not seen Jemmy again since their return. *Nor should I expect to,* she reminded herself sternly. He was gone from her completely now, and this very day would be wed to Lady Maude.

It had all worked out perfectly. Lord Darnley would have no choice but to sanction the marriage now, as they had both Maude and Haddon. So the peace would be made. Alyson and Robin were to go at last to the McLarans, just as they had dreamed of for so long.

She put the bundle by the door, then looked about for something else to occupy her time. She wished that they could leave today, but since Laird Kirallen had kindly arranged for an escort and given them two mountain ponies for the journey, she could hardly complain of the arrangements. But she did wish that they were far from this place already.

She laid out bread and cheese and ale, then sat and watched as Robin ate. He looked so well—surely he had grown in the past weeks. His cheeks held bright color as he told her everything that Sir Robert had taught him.

"I don't suppose we'll be seeing him again," he said wistfully.

"Oh, I don't know. Maybe one day we'll go to London and visit. But not any time soon. We'll be too busy, Rob. There will be so many people to meet and so many new things to learn. It's very beautiful up in the Highlands."

"Can you really touch the sky?"

"Well, almost." She laughed, ruffling his hair. He ducked his head from her hand and she realized with a pang that he wasn't a baby anymore. The weeks he had spent apart from her had changed him in some way not easily defined. It went beyond the growth she was convinced that he had made—he had gained a new confidence and maturity. That was for the good, she knew, for Robin had always seemed younger than his age and had depended on her completely. But she felt very much alone as he jumped up from the table.

"I'm going to take these crusts to the pony," he said. "I think I'll call him Sam."

"A good name," she agreed. "But mind you keep out of the way. Some of those horses are very big and—"

"Oh, Ally!" he said, rolling his eyes. "I know."

When he was gone she sat, staring out the window. There was a knock on the door and she said, not turning, "It isn't locked. What did you forget?"

"Why, nothing that I know of."

She jumped to her feet and saw Jemmy in the doorway. He was dressed in the same clothing he had worn to their wedding feast, a fern green tunic that accentuated his dark hair and eyes, richly furred as befitted his rank. She rubbed her palms nervously over the skirt of her woolen kirtle. It was very plain, of course, nothing like the gown she had worn to that feast. The king's law forbade commoners to have any fur about their clothing.

"I've come to say farewell," he said. "May I come in?"

"Of course, my lord," she said, dropping a quick curtsey.

"And I wanted to give you this."

He held out a parcel and Alyson took it, opening the wrapping to find a length of the McLaran tartan, woven in the clan's distinctive red and gold design. She held the fabric close. "Thank you. How kind."

"It will not suit you as well as ours," he said and she smiled, though she did not raise her eyes to him.

"Oh, I think that it will suit me well enough," she said, laying it carefully aside. There was an awkward silence and Alyson stared down at the table, waiting for him to leave, wanting him to stay. But as the silence lengthened she began to wish he *would* go, for she could not breathe properly with him in the room and her heart was pounding in quick, jerky beats.

But he did not leave. He sat down on the bench. "Come, sit a moment," he said, touching the wood beside him. When she was seated there was another silence and Alyson cast about frantically for some remark that would not be completely foolish.

"Did you know," he said at last, "that you talk in your sleep?"

"In my—? I beg your pardon?" she said, certain that she had not heard him correctly.

"You do," he said gravely. "Twice I heard you for myself. Once was the night of our—of the wedding. I went to our chamber and you said the name 'Robin' and something about . . . let me see, I think it was burning bread."

Why was he speaking of this now? It was all done and

there was nothing to do but try to forget. To keep remembering would only break her heart afresh.

"And the other time——"

"I remember," she said hastily. That had been the morning she dreamed of Robin's death and woke calling for him. The morning after the night . . . Now her face was scalding and she blinked back tears of humiliation.

"My lord, please——"

"Shh . . ." he said, taking her hand in his. "Listen. Do you remember the morning I returned from Kilghorn?" She nodded miserably. "I'd been thinking of you all the time we were parted, missing you——"

"No," she said, trying to remove her hand from his. "You said——"

"I know what I said." He tightened his grip on her fingers. "Just hear me out. It was the same morning you met Sir Robert. But I don't think you realized you'd been followed."

She looked at him for the first time, her eyes wide.

"It was Alistair, of course. He and several of his men. They met me coming home with quite a tale—how you'd been seen with an English knight, weeping as he held you in his arms. They told me his name was Sir Robert and I thought—I assumed . . ."

"You thought that I—that he—? But why did you not say something?"

He sighed. "Because I am a fool."

"No," she said slowly. "I think you sensed that I wasn't being honest with you. And for that I am sorry. I should have told you that day in the stables——"

"You should," he said, then gave her his rare, flashing smile. "But just think what we would have missed!"

Despite herself she laughed.

"There is another reason that I did not speak," he said, growing serious again. "I never told you, did I, that I had been married very young? Indeed, I've never told anyone about her. Her name was Carmela Velasquez and . . ."

As he spoke Alyson could see him as he'd been then, young and foolish and so terribly unhappy. She understood how hurt he must have been when he thought he had been betrayed again, even his desire to strike out at her. And she could even pity Carmela, who had not been able to appreciate her wonderful good fortune at being married to such a man.

When he finished she said gently, "You must have loved her very much."

"No." In an achingly familiar gesture he put his finger beneath her chin and raised her face to his. "I thought that once but I know better now. I've only loved one woman, and I fear I'll never love another."

She no longer cared that he was to be wed that very day. Nothing mattered but the joy of hearing his words, and when he bent to kiss her she closed her eyes and held him close. He slipped his arms beneath her knees and carried her to the narrow bed. But after a moment she pulled away, saying breathlessly, "No. Even now they're waiting for you."

"Damn them all," he said roughly. "I care nothing for any of them—"

"No," she repeated, though her voice wavered as his lips moved against her neck. "We cannot."

He pulled her against him so suddenly that she cried out in surprise.

"Stay with me. Please. I swore I wouldn't ask this but I will, I must, I can't just let you go—"

"How can I stay?" she cried. "As what? Aye, I know I'm not fit to be your lady, but I will not be your whore."

He flinched and drew back a little at the harshness of her tone.

"Oh, I know what you're thinking. I came to your bed

before—and you're right, I did, but—oh, I knew it was all a lie, but I believed—I wanted to believe—"

"That it was real," he finished softly. "And it was. That's why you must stay here—"

"No, 'tis all different now. You'd be married to her—my half sister—and I would be your leman for everyone to see. How long do you think we could be happy like that?"

"Forever," he whispered, brushing the tears from her face. "I swear it, there would never be another—"

"Save for your wife," she said flatly, turning her face away. "There would be her. No, Jemmy, I won't. Please don't ask it of me." She spoke firmly but was a little frightened by the expression in his eyes as he rose swiftly to his feet.

"So this is farewell?" he said. "You go to your kin and I to Maude? That is what you want?"

"It isn't what I want, you know that. But think of your people, Jemmy. Think of Malcolm. You don't want him to end like his father, do you? Like Stephen? This is the chance—the one chance you'll have to make terms with Darnley and end it all forever."

He looked at her sharply, then his teeth flashed in a smile that chilled her to the heart. "That's what it's been about, hasn't it? Me making terms with Darnley. Well, perhaps it's time that Darnley began to worry about making terms with *me*."

"What are you going to do?" she asked anxiously as she followed him to the door.

He grasped her wrist and pulled her through the doorway. "Why don't you come see for yourself?"

chapter 42

By midafternoon *Sir Robert was so exasperated he could easily have shaken his niece* until those lovely teeth rattled in her head. He'd explained to her a dozen times why this marriage must be made. Patiently—and then not so patiently—he'd recounted the long list of the dead, including many of her relatives and the families who had served at Aylsford for generations. He'd appealed to her in the name of duty, of pity, of justice—and always she had made the same reply. "But I want to go to London. I will go, too. I won't stay here."

"Lord Jemmy might take you to London—if you ask him properly," Robert said, looking at Laird Kirallen with appeal.

"That might be arranged," the nobleman said with distant courtesy.

"There, you see? He's a good man, Maude, widely traveled—he'll treat you well enough if you—"

"Good? He's a monster, carrying me off like he did—

bringing me to this dreadful place—I won't do it, I won't!"

She wept, she screamed, she stamped her foot like the spoiled child she was.

Darnley was no help at all. He acted as though his beloved Maude was going to the grave, not simply fulfilling the vow he himself had sworn. His behavior alternated between blinding rage and abject apologies to his daughter. If only he'd held firm, Robert thought, she would have been brought to some realization of her duty. As it was, Robert was ashamed for both of them.

Kirallen sat straight in his chair, hands lightly resting on the arms, and stared into the distance. Haddon huddled in a corner and beside him was Kirallen's grandson, Malcolm, who was muffling his laugher behind one hand. The boy broke off at a sharp look from his grandfather, though his bright blue eyes continued to sparkle with amusement as he watched the Darnley family make utter fools of themselves.

And on top of everything else there was a light-haired man standing by Kirallen's chair, one hand laid protectively on the hilt of his sword, his face taut with anger and distaste.

"The devil take them!" he burst out at last. "For Christ's sweet sake, Laird, let me slit their throats and be done with this!"

"Peace, Alistair," Laird Kirallen said, but Robert thought the old man looked tempted by the offer—and who could blame him? Robert was half tempted himself. Anything to stop this arguing! His temples were pounding and he greeted Jemmy's arrival with profound relief which quickly changed to pity when he saw Alyson slip into the room behind him and join Malcolm by the window.

Poor man, Robert thought as Jemmy stared about, frowning at the noise. What a dance he'd been led—married, unmarried, now to be wed again. Robert understood that he was trying his best to make peace, but there was no denying that his position was more than a bit ridiculous. He looked grim as he perched on the corner of a table, staring thoughtfully at Maude as her fury rose to a high-pitched shriek.

"Will no one shut her up?" Sir Alistair cried.

Darnley rose and started toward the knight, his fists clenched. Robert sighed and prayed for strength but just then his mind took a little sideways skip and he realized how ridiculous this situation was, better than any comedy he could invent. He had the most absurd desire to burst out laughing—

His eyes met Jemmy's and he managed to compose himself, but the Scotsman must have seen, for he grinned suddenly in return and lifting one hand, he brought his palm down sharply upon the table.

Everything stopped. All eyes turned toward Jemmy as he rose to his full considerable height. What a sensation he would make at court! Robert thought. With that height and those dark good looks, he'd rival even the Duke of Lancaster himself.

"Enough," Jemmy said. "This has gone far enough. Alistair, stand back. Lord Darnley, sit down. I said *sit down*," he repeated when Darnley didn't obey at once. Then he walked over to Maude and stood looking down at her. "Be quiet," he said simply and Maude shut her mouth with a snap.

"Now, my lord," he continued, turning back to Darnley. "I suggest you give some serious thought to your situation. You are entitled to precisely nothing at our hands. I could kill you here and now in payment for my brother's murder and give your daughter the same treatment you gave to Clare McLaran. Don't think I haven't thought of it. Believe me, there is nothing I'd like better than to run a dirk into your heart."

"Jemmy—" the Laird cried.

"Let me finish," Jemmy said evenly. "I'm not going to kill you, Darnley. I could, but I won't. Because this has to end somewhere. If you were a reasonable man, instead of the backstabbing, murdering bastard that you are, we could work this out between us. But you can't be trusted."

"Why, you young—" Darnley snarled, half rising.

"I suppose I could simply toss you into the dungeon and keep you there," Jemmy continued as if Darnley hadn't spoken. "But would it be enough? No, we would have to keep your children—and certainly Sir Robert. And that would be . . . tiresome for us all."

"Quite," Robert said with feeling, though he was fairly sure that Jemmy didn't mean to keep him at Ravenspur. What exactly he did intend to do, Robert didn't know, but he suspected that Jemmy had some plan that he would divulge when he was good and ready.

"As for you, my lady," Jemmy said to Maude. "You've made your feelings about this marriage very clear. Very well, then, perhaps another husband would suit you better. Sir Alistair, my nearest kinsman, would be the likely choice. After all," he added, turning to Alistair, "you always had such interesting notions on how Lady Maude's husband should behave."

"How dare you?" Maude cried angrily, though for the first time she looked genuinely frightened as she stared at the light-haired knight.

"Are ye mad?" Alistair snapped. "Do ye think that I would ever—"

"Well, perhaps not," Jemmy said. "Although the idea does have certain merits."

Robert bit back his laughter as Jemmy caught his eye. The man was thoroughly enjoying himself here, and Robert didn't grudge him a single moment of his pleasure. As for what he meant to do next, Robert could not

quite decide. Perhaps he merely meant to frighten Maude
into some understanding of the helplessness of her position. But Robert thought there was some other motive behind his words.

"Well, if Maude won't have me—and I won't have
Lord Darnley—then where does that leave us?"

His eyes flicked to Haddon and then to Sir Robert.
And all at once Robert felt as if he was performing in a
masque and had been given his cue to speak.

"There is one way," he said and all eyes turned to him.
"My lords," he bowed slightly toward Laird Kirallen and
then turned to Darnley. "If Haddon was to stay here for a
time, I'm sure Laird Kirallen would train him for a
knight."

Fine words for what amounted to the boy being held
hostage for his father's good behavior. But still better
than if Jemmy had suggested it himself.

"Why, Sir Robert, I believe you've hit upon the perfect plan!" Jemmy said quickly, before anyone else could
speak. "We would be pleased to foster Haddon. And, of
course, to pledge his safety."

What *is* the man up to? Robert wondered again. Why
go to all this trouble when it would be so much simpler
to marry Maude as planned?

"Never!" Darnley cried, just as Robert had expected
that he would.

"Shut up," Robert ordered. "Would you rather end
your days in the dungeon?"

"He wouldn't do it."

The words had scarcely left Darnley's lips when he
stumbled back, almost falling over his chair, the point of
Jemmy's sword against his throat.

"Would you care to try me, my lord?"

Before Darnley could answer, Malcolm stepped forward, neatly taking up his part.

"Grandfather?" the boy said. "I think *everyone* would feel better if we took an oath on Haddon's safety."

Malcolm glanced meaningfully at Haddon, who was standing very small in a corner of the room.

"You first, Uncle Jemmy," Malcolm said.

"I give my solemn word," Jemmy said, sheathing his sword, his eyes never leaving Darnley's face. "Before God and all the saints, I'll guard Haddon Darnley like my own kin."

"Now you, Alistair," Malcolm prompted.

Alistair turned away. "I will *not*. I don't make war on children, but nor will I pledge protection to a Darnley."

"But Alistair, you have to," Malcolm insisted. "Else the other knights willna do it, either. You know they willna."

Alistair shrugged without answering and Robert saw the ruin of Jemmy's plan in the knight's steel-gray eyes. But then Jemmy spoke again.

"Do it, Alistair," he said in a voice all the more threatening for its quiet tone.

Alistair folded his arms across his chest. "Or what?" he asked with studied insolence. "Will ye draw on me again? I thought ye dinna want my blood upon your hands."

"I don't. But you're the one who told me that a man fights for what matters. This is it, Alistair. You're my foster brother, so I'll warn you one more time: don't get in my way, or before God, I'll cut you down."

Malcolm came forward and put one hand on Alistair's arm. "Go on, for my sake," the boy said. "Please, please do it."

Robert was astonished at the effect these words had upon the knight. His face wrenched with sorrow as he looked down at the boy.

"I canna," he said. "Not even for you, Malcolm."

"You will!" Kirallen thundered and everyone jumped

a little. "Kneel. And swear to guard young Haddon's life."

"No."

"Get back, Jemmy," Kirallen snapped. "Put up your sword. Now, Alistair," he said quietly. "I call upon the oath ye took and command ye as your Laird."

"Nay, Laird," Alistair replied formally. "Not even for that."

"Do ye ken who ye are talking to? Kneel and do your duty!"

"I canna do it," Alistair said, hands clenched at his sides. "I took another oath, if ye remember. To Ian. There is a debt of honor here," he said, gesturing toward Darnley. "He bears a blood curse and he must pay it, at my hands if not at yours. I will *not* so shamefully dishonor Ian's memory."

Darnley jumped to his feet, his eyes gleaming. Robert forced him back into his seat. "Wait," he whispered. "Let the Laird speak."

"I will not argue it with you," Kirallen said. "Not again."

Alistair inclined his golden head with distant courtesy. "Nor will I ask it. Do what ye must, Laird, and I will do the same."

"No!" Malcolm cried, tugging at Alistair's sleeve. "Please—"

"I'm sorry, lad," Alistair said. "But this is what must be. We will bear it as best we can."

"Then let me come with you!"

For a moment Robert thought the man's eyes misted, but his voice was firm when he spoke. "Nay, Malcolm. Your place is here wi' your grandfather and your uncle." He gave the boy a quick hug and released him. Then he turned and faced his Laird, his shoulders thrown back proudly.

"I canna simply let ye go," Kirallen said. "Ye understand that?"

"Aye."

The Laird drew a deep breath. "Alistair Kirallen, ye are a banished man."

Malcolm buried his face in his hands with a stifled sob.

"Ye have until dawn tomorrow to quit my lands. No man or woman on my demesne may give ye help or shelter, and all man's hands will be against ye. If slain, no blood guilt will be claimed or gold due your kin."

Alistair nodded, silently accepting the sentence.

"Then take what is yours and go."

The knight bowed slightly, then turned with a swirl of his cloak. When he reached the door, the Laird burst out, "D'ye have need of anything, Alistair?"

The knight looked back and a trace of the iron pride in his face dissolved. "Nay, Laird, I've all I need. Farewell."

Then his eyes moved to Darnley and he smiled. "Watch your back, my lord," he said softly. "Watch it well. One day I'll be there."

When he was gone the room was silent, save for the soft sound of Malcolm keening. Jemmy put a hand on the boy's shoulder and pulled him close. Malcolm drew a shaking breath and wiped one sleeve across his eyes.

"Let it end here," Robert said. "Maude," he turned to his niece. "You come with me to London for a time. John, I think you should join us. We'll get Maude married properly and give everyone a chance to settle down. What do you say?"

"Yes, Father," Maude said, tugging on his arm. "Let's go. Please."

"I don't know," Darnley said.

"I think that my son and your brother have the right of it," Kirallen said. "Haddon will be fine here."

"Haddon?" Darnley said. "What say you to this?"

. "I'd like to stay," Haddon said. He looked at the door-way through which Alistair had passed. "Now that they've sworn—"

Darnley sighed. "All right," he said abruptly. "It's done."

Robert drew a deep breath of relief and was about to suggest that they leave immediately, when Jemmy spoke again.

"Not quite," he said.

chapter 43

"What d'ye mean?" Darnley asked, his face tightening with suspicion.

"Well, you all came here expecting a wedding, and I'd hate to disappoint you."

He held out his hand to Alyson, who accepted it. So this was it, Sir Robert thought. It was for this that Jemmy had enacted the entire charade here today, nearly wrecked the peace, and seen his kinsman banished. For Alyson. Kirallen realized it at the same moment, and his face flushed with rage.

"Jemmy," Alyson said, her voice shaking. "Ye cannot mean to do this."

"Why not?" he answered lightly. "I believe that our marriage was real. Somewhere I got the impression that you felt the same. Am I mistaken?"

Alyson blushed to the roots of her hair. "I—well, I—"

"Ye canna do this!" Kirallen cried. "I forbid it."

"Father, don't upset yourself," Jemmy said. "You have

what you want from me, don't you? I'll stay here and maintain the peace. But I will not do it without my lady at my side."

"Don't be a fool! We've made a beginning here today, and I don't doubt that ye can see it through. But this—it's asking too much of the clan to expect them to accept Mistress Bowden as their lady. You'll lose all ye have gained."

"Alyson is my wife. In time the clan will accept her. I'll see to it. But just so there's no question after, we'll say the vows again."

Was she his wife? Robert wondered. It was Maude's name on the legal documents, after all. Alyson had but stood proxy for her half sister at the ceremony. Under English law, Maude was the one Jemmy had wed that day in the chapel.

Yet it was to Alyson that Jemmy had said the vows, and it was she who had answered. And the two of them had consummated the union. By the laws of Scotland, Robert seemed to remember, that was enough to make a marriage. Either way, the vows they were about to take meant nothing in a legal sense.

But they meant a great deal to the two people most closely concerned. No, Robert decided, he would not speak out and spoil their moment. If the clan was prepared to accept the marriage as binding, then who was he to question? Perhaps he would mention the matter to Darnley later, just in case the question came up when Maude was wed. Or perhaps not. Why stir up a hornet's nest when no one would ever know or care what had been done in some isolated little chapel on the Borderlands?

As Alyson and Jemmy took their places before the priest, Robert felt a stab of apprehension. Legality aside, this marriage was a chancy business. Today had been the first of many battles that lay ahead of Jemmy, and he had no doubt that Jemmy knew it, too. Yet for Alyson's sake he was prepared fight them all. Oh, she had been right to trust him, he thought. He must love her desperately to risk so much.

"Now," Jemmy said, turning to the priest. "If you will . . ."

Robert sat, a little dizzied at the speed with which matters had moved. "You mean it this time, don't you, John?" he asked in a low voice.

"Yes," Darnley answered. "This one's nothing like his brother."

Robert realized then that John was sorry that the older brother was gone, though he'd hated him for years and in the end had killed the man himself. Oh, I have to get back to London, he thought. For I don't understand anything in this place.

Alyson and Jemmy stood hand-fasted before the priest as he began to read the words that would join them forever. Robert's eye was caught by a flash of movement, and for the first time he noticed a man and woman standing by the door. They must have slipped in during the excitement, for he was certain they hadn't been here earlier.

The man was obviously a Kirallen, for he wore the clan's tartan and bore a strong resemblance to the groom, but the woman's red-gold plaid was unfamiliar. They made a striking pair. His darkness offset her golden beauty to perfection. When he leaned down and spoke into her ear she hushed him sharply, though the effect was rather spoiled by the fact that she was giggling helplessly at whatever he was saying.

Really, thought Robert disapprovingly, they should have a little more decorum. Then his eyes went again to the bride and groom, for now the priest had paused in the midst of the ceremony.

Jemmy reached up, bending his head to twist at something in his hair. A moment later he held out his hand, a bit of gold shining in his palm.

Alyson looked from it to him and smiled brilliantly.

Then the priest was done and Jemmy turned to his wife with a smile that lit him like a flame. Catching her in his arms, he lifted her from her feet and kissed her soundly, then set her down, though he still kept her hand firmly in his own.

In the rather strained silence Robert moved forward.

"Let me be the first to congratulate you," he said, kissing Alyson's cheek. "My lady," he added with a bow. "And you, my lord."

"Thank you, Sir Robert," she said, blushing.

And then Robert was astonished to find Maude at his side.

"Here," she said, holding out something that glittered in her hand. "I gave it to you before but you wouldn't take it. Will you now?"

"Aye. And thank you."

Alyson put the chain about her neck, the blue stones bright against the plain stuff of her kirtle, and the half sisters smiled at one another. Wonder of wonders, Robert thought, maybe there is hope for Maude after all. And then the boy Malcolm was there, as well.

"Now you are my aunt," he said. "I always said you were."

Robert glanced about for the two he'd seen earlier, wondering why they didn't come and greet the bride and groom. But they must have slipped away while he wasn't looking, for they were nowhere to be seen.

He forgot the matter a moment later as Kirallen stood and strode from the room without a word to anyone.

The time had come to leave—and quickly, before anything else happened. Robert knelt and bade Haddon farewell. "Are you sure you want to stay here?" he asked, rather belatedly realizing the boy had been given but little say in the matter.

"Oh, yes," Haddon said. "Malcolm's going to show me

how to make my own bow—and then there's a gathering up in the hills and he's promised to take me—"

"Did he?"

Robert looked at the Kirallen boy, who was standing close to Alyson, smiling. So much depended on this young man, on him and Haddon both. He felt a little shiver of apprehension run down his back when he considered that the future of both houses rested on their shoulders.

But maybe—just maybe—it was possible this peace would last.

Jemmy and Alyson walked with them to the courtyard and waited while they mounted. Robert stopped his horse at the edge of the yard and looked back with a wave. But neither bride nor groom saw anything but each other. With a grin the knight turned his face toward home. Before they'd gone a mile he was wondering if his ballad—leaving out the names, of course—might be salvaged after all.

chapter 44

"**W**ell, my lady," *Jemmy said when the others were gone,* turning to her with his brows raised.

"It is true?" She laughed a little shakily. "Did all that really happen or was I dreaming?"

"No, 'twas no dream—as I'm afraid you'll find soon enough."

Tomorrow would be hard, he thought, forcing himself to smile reassuringly. Once the clan learned what had happened this afternoon, there would be the very devil to pay. He sighed, wondering how the knights would take the news of Alistair's banishment. Not well, he suspected. Not well at all. And that would only be the start of it . . .

Alyson looked up at him with shining eyes and he felt a pang of remorse. For all the clan's complaining about Lady Maude as their mistress, there were many who would like this marriage even less. And they would find a thousand ways to make Alyson suffer for it.

But there was no need to spoil her happiness today.

Soon enough she'd see the hardships of the path they had chosen. Then he looked more deeply into her crystal gaze and realized she had no illusions. She saw it all, perhaps more clearly than he did himself.

" 'Twill be all right," she said. "You'll see."

"Aye, it will," he answered, the words catching in his throat. "I swear it will."

"Come on, then, husband," she added, with a delightful teasing note in her voice that he had never heard before. "Let's go find Robin and tell him all the news."

"Oh, I think Robin can wait an hour," he answered, tipping her face up to his and laughing at the blush rising to her cheeks.

"As you will, my lord," she said, casting her eyes down demurely.

"No, as *you* will, my sweet lady," he answered, catching her against him and kissing her, feeling the heat rise in his body as he remembered the silken brush of her skin against his own.

"Oh, then we'll see Robin," she said and he drew back, a little disappointed that even now she would put her brother first.

She glanced up through her lashes and smiled, raising herself on tiptoe to whisper in his ear. "For an hour won't be near enough, you know."

"How true," Jemmy said, smiling down into her upturned face. "You're wise as well as bonny, lady."

Her laughter was the most delightful sound Jemmy had ever heard. She would laugh often, he promised himself fiercely. No matter what might happen, he would make sure of that.

"Of course," she answered airily. " 'Tis why you wed me, is it not?"

He kissed the tip of her nose. "Your wisdom. Aye. That and a thousand other reasons, every one of which I mean to tell you . . . as soon as we've seen Robin. Where is he?"

"I think he's in the stable."

He arched a brow. "The stable, eh? Oh, by all means, then, let's go at once."

As they walked across the courtyard he thought of his ship, still docked in Spain, and knew that he would sell it now without regret. That's because I'm home, he realized suddenly. *I'm home. I finally made it.*

He glanced down at the bright head leaning against his shoulder. *Journeys end in lovers meeting.* It was true, at least for him. *She* was his home, and if not for her, he would have wandered lost forever. He wanted to tell her that, to thank her, but his heart was too full for speech. Later, then. There was time. He was home for good, his journey ended.

Then Alyson looked up at him and smiled and his pulse leaped as it always did at the start of an adventure. Oh, no, he thought, tightening his arm around her. It isn't ended. It's our journey now, our adventure.

And it's only just beginning.

chapter 45

Alistair halted his horse upon the hilltop. *Hands* clenched upon the reins, he watched Alyson and Jemmy walk through the courtyard, arm-in-arm. His gaze moved past them to the small party vanishing toward the border.

Was that really Darnley—the man who had murdered Stephen and Ian and countless others, despoiled Clare McLaran, sent his own daughter off to almost certain death—riding merrily homeward under the Laird's own protection? Oh, the world had gone completely mad—or else *his* wits were lost. How else could he explain the fact that he, the Laird's beloved foster son and Captain of his knights, now had no home, no name, no past he wanted to remember, and a future too bleak to contemplate?

He sat as the sun moved slowly westward, staring down at Ravenspur below. There, at the corner of the oasthouse, he had kissed his first lass. And there was the orchard where he and Ian used to lie, eating apples and imagining the adventures they would have when they were grown.

He sat until the harsh cawing of a corby startled him into awareness that the shadows had grown long. It was time he was away. But where? The McLarans were his only kin, but that road was closed to him now. Emma would not forgive the man who had threatened Clare's daughter with death. All hands were truly set against him, just as the Laird had said.

"What a balls up! Well, the only thing to do is get drunk and go to sleep. Tomorrow it will all look better."

Alistair started. The voice had seemed so real, so close. Then he remembered Ian saying those very words—not once, but many times—when one of his wild plans had gone awry. But what would Ian say about this situation?

The answer came, swift and very clear. "God's blood, Alistair, will ye never leave off brooding? So it all went wrong! So what? Life's too short to spend in grieving for the past. Come on, let's ride ahead and see what happens next!"

There being nothing else to do, Alistair turned his horse's head and passed, a solitary shadow, into the darker shadow of the trees.

Turn the page for a preview of Elizabeth English's

Laird of the Mist,

Alistair Kirallen's Story,

the next book in the Highland Fling series.
Coming in January from Jove!

D eidre leaned closer to the pool, hardly daring to breathe, as a waiting stillness descended on the clearing. It was about to happen, she could feel it . . . the entire world seemed to stop in hushed expectancy.

And there was nothing. The surface of the pond was blank. Tears started to her eyes, and she clenched her fists, summoning every bit of energy she had.

"Show me," she cried aloud, half-plea and half-command. "Show me my true love."

T here—a faint glimmer of light at the end of the passageway. Alistair made for it, stumbling with weariness, driven on by the certainty that it would vanish any moment. As he drew closer he perceived the dim outline of a doorway. The door was closing, closing—he flung himself outside. Cool wind fanned his face and he gulped in air fragrant with damp earth, the scent of life itself. He did not see the two shadows that slipped from the passageway as the door slammed shut behind him.

As his breathing steadied he looked about. Moonlight streamed through twisted branches to light a path ahead. With a little shrug he followed it, expecting to come out at the waterfall. Instead he stepped into a small bright clearing.

A woman sat on the edge of a dark pool. She was sobbing, hands covering her face, midnight hair streaming like a shining cloak across her shoulders.

"Why do ye weep, lady?" Alistair asked.

She lifted her head and he drew a sharp breath, staring dumbly into the sapphire depths of her eyes, bright with tears and framed by thick, dark lashes. Ah, but she was radiant—too beautiful for any mortal. Surely she was a fairy sent to guide him.

"What—" she began, and then stopped, her eyes wide. "How did you come here?"

"I hardly know. There was a waterfall—and a passageway—I couldna find my way. I thought ye must have called me forth," he finished in confusion. "Are you no' one of the Sidhe?"

She laughed softly and the sound was tinged with bitterness. "No, I am but a mortal woman."

Her voice was low and musical, its rhythm falling softly on his ear. He would have been content to listen to her talk forever.

He sat down beside her and looked into the pool, where her reflection shone dimly in the moonlit depths. But though Alistair leaned close to the water, he could not see his own image. Of course, he thought with a ripple of amusement, my body is back behind the waterfall. And this is nothing but a dream.

Deidre glanced at the man beside her, wondering that she felt no fear. The moment he walked out of the darkness of the forest her heart had leaped in joyful welcome, though she was certain they had never met before. This was a man she could never have forgotten.

He was powerfully built, with the arms and shoulders of a warrior, and yet for all his size, he moved with a dancer's silent grace. Though the clearing was dim, she could see him quite clearly, down to the twisted pattern of the brooch at one broad shoulder and the small green gems winking in the dagger at his belt. A lock of fine fair hair fell over his brow as he stared into the pool. When he turned to her his smile was bright as quicksilver and hot as living flame. She looked away, dazzled and a little frightened by the strength of her response.

"Why were ye crying?" he asked again.

She weighed her instinct for concealment against the almost irresistible impulse to confide in him. Why should she trust him with her secrets? But then, why had she trusted him at all? Why had she not run screaming at the first sight of him?

Then she understood. Of course, it all made sense! The way he walked out of the forest without a rustle of leaf or crack of twig to herald his approach, the unearthly glow of him, even her own calm acceptance of his presence was nothing to be wondered at. Worn out with longing and worry, she must have fallen into sleep. And for all her failure to summon an image, Deirdre knew enough of magic to understand that a dream so vivid was bound to have some deeper meaning.

"I came looking for my own true love tonight," she said, gesturing toward the pool. "But he isn't here."

"Is he a silkie then, that ye seek him in the water?" The question was asked without a trace of laughter, confirming her belief. Why not a silkie? Anything was possible in a dream.

"Nay, I sought his image, not himself."

"Why? Is he in Ireland?" he asked, giving her a bright, shrewd glance.

She shrugged. "Perhaps. But it does not matter, for I am here in Scotland, wed these four years past."

"Four years wed and still ye pine for a man ye left behind in Ireland? Why, then, is your own husband such a fool that he canna make ye love him?"

"Ours was not a love match," she answered sadly. "Or, at least—sure and I don't know what it was on his part, desire maybe. But even that—" She made a pretty, helpless gesture with her hands. "Whatever it was he wanted, I did not give it to him. Nor have I given him a son. I think he hates me now."

"A fool indeed," he said, his voice deep and soft.

A long slow shiver wound down Deirdre's spine as she looked into the stranger's cool gray eyes. But of course he was no stranger. It was him, the one she had waited for, the one she had despaired of ever finding. Hadn't she always been certain that she would know him?

Too late, she thought bitterly. *Where were you four years ago when I accepted Brodie?* But of course he was not real at all. Such things only happened in dreams. *Still,* she thought with a sigh, *it was a lovely dream, the finest she had ever known. If only it could go on forever . . .*

But then, without quite knowing how she knew, Deirdre was certain it was about to end—or in the manner of dreams, to change into something very different.

"What is it you came to say to me?" she asked, standing and looking warily about the clearing. "Why have you disturbed my dream?"

"Nay, lady." He smiled with a flash of even teeth. "This is my dream, not yours. And a verra pleasant one it's turning out to be."

He rose in a single graceful movement to stand before her. He is perfect, she thought, tall and strong but not so ungainly large as Brodie. She imagined how snugly she would fit against his shoulder, then smiled wryly. Of course he would be perfect! He was her invention, after all!

She was a bit surprised that her imagination had fashioned such a man, when she had always thought dark slenderness the very model of male beauty. But now she saw how wrong she had been. The man before her seemed spun from moonlight, with his silver-gilt hair and cool gray eyes, yet he was strong and solid as the earth. Exactly as she had dreamed of him so long ago, when she was still a child.

But, she realized suddenly, she was no child now. She was a woman grown. What would it be like to walk into his embrace, feel those strong arms close around her? For all his strength, his touch would be gentle, Deirdre thought, and a tingle started somewhere in the region of her heart, moving slowly downward. It was a strange feeling, not unpleasant, but unfamiliar and a little frightening.

Four years of marriage had taught Deirdre many lessons, but none of them prepared her for the dizziness she felt when she looked into his eyes. And he knew— he understood without a word between them—for the same dazed wonder was etched upon his face.

This is a dream, she thought, staring wide-eyed as he extended his hand to her. *I can do anything tonight and it won't matter.*

Yet even as she moved forward, she stopped, knowing she had been wrong. This *did* matter. It mattered very much. Dream or no dream, he was more real to her than anyone she had ever known. And whatever was to happen between them now would change her for all time. She hesitated for the space of a single breath, so short a time that he could not have noticed it. But still, it was too long. She watched in horror as his outline shimmered and began to fade.

"Wait," she said desperately. "Oh, don't go—please—"

She reached to grasp his outstretched hand, then cried aloud in wordless disappointment as her fingers met only air.

But Alistair felt the warmth of her touch. It streaked through him like a burning brand. Quickly, before she could vanish altogether, he leaned close and kissed her full soft lips. At that moment a flame leaped between them, searing him to his soul, so sharp and sudden that he could not tell if what he felt was pain or pleasure.

She drew a quick breath and stared up at him, one hand pressed against her mouth. She had felt it too, then, had been burned by the same fire that had marked him for all time. Oh, he did not want to wake. Not now. Whatever she was, wherever she had come from, he would stay with her and gladly, even if he could never have more of her than this.

Her sapphire eyes were large and wondering, shimmering with sudden tears. He moved to draw her into his arms, knowing from the start that it was hopeless, yet powerless to stop his instinctive gesture of comfort. She swayed toward him, then froze with a small gasp of fear, her gaze moving over his shoulder. Turning, he saw nothing but the forest and heard naught but a bird's harsh cry.

"Two ravens," she whispered. "There, just behind you. What does it mean?"

"Ravens?" he repeated. She began to waver before him, as though he viewed her through a veil of water. "Ah, corbies. Two corbies," he said and was seized with an unreasoning terror, as though he had pronounced his own doom.

"Ah, no—farewell!" Her voice was small and distant, and as his sight faded, he tried once more to reach her.

"Wait!" he cried. "Who are ye? What is your name?"

Whatever answer she might have made was lost in the rushing of the waterfall. Alistair pulled the stiffened hide around himself and stared into its depths as dawn slowly lit the sky beyond.

DO YOU BELIEVE IN MAGIC?

MAGICAL LOVE

The enchanting series from Jove will make you a believer!

With a sprinkling of faerie dust and the wave of a wand, magical things can happen—but nothing is more magical than the power of love.

❑ *SEA SPELL* by Tess Farraday   0-515-12289-0/$5.99

A mysterious man from the sea haunts a woman's dreams—and desires...

❑ *ONCE UPON A KISS* by Claire Cross
0-515-12300-5/$5.99

A businessman learns there's only one way to awaken a slumbering beauty...

❑ *A FAERIE TALE* by Ginny Reyes   0-515-12338-2/$5.99

A faerie and a leprechaun play matchmaker—to a mismatched pair of mortals...

❑ *ONE WISH* by C.J. Card   0-515-12354-4/$5.99

For years a beautiful bottle lay concealed in a forgotten trunk—holding a powerful spirit, waiting for someone to come along and make one wish...

VISIT PENGUIN PUTNAM ONLINE ON THE INTERNET:
http://www.penguinputnam.com

Prices slightly higher in Canada

Payable by Visa, MC or AMEX only ($10.00 min.), No cash, checks or COD. Shipping & handling: US/Can. $2.75 for one book, $1.00 for each add'l book; Int'l $5.00 for one book, $1.00 for each add'l. Call (800) 788-6262 or (201) 933-9292, fax (201) 896-8569 or mail your orders to:

Penguin Putnam Inc.
P.O. Box 12289, Dept. B
Newark, NJ 07101-5289
Please allow 4-6 weeks for delivery.
Foreign and Canadian delivery 6-8 weeks.

Bill my: ❑ Visa ❑ MasterCard ❑ Amex _____ (expires)

Card# _____

Signature _____

Bill to:

Name _____

Address _____ City _____

State/ZIP _____ Daytime Phone # _____

Ship to:

Name _____ Book Total $ _____

Address _____ Applicable Sales Tax $ _____

City _____ Postage & Handling $ _____

State/ZIP _____ Total Amount Due $ _____

This offer subject to change without notice.   Ad # 789 (3/00)